I0760460

Stars & Promise

Sentinel Rising · Book 3

Crystal Frost

Praise For Crystal Frost

"In the conclusion to the Sentinel Rising trilogy, Crystal Frost skillfully ties all of the events and characters together, brings every emotion to the reader, and answers your questions! As you read you will discover the power of family - whether of blood or of choice, see strength in togetherness, and truly understand the hope of redemption and the beauty of second chances! You will also be surprised by a twist or two! Frost brilliantly closes this story on the same field where these events all began! I am left with warmth and sadness, sadness that it is over and am also deeply touched by the life lessons shared through the story. I am not ready to say goodbye to the Sentinels! I eagerly await whatever Crystal Frost creates next!"

Angel C. - Stars & Promise

"Sentinel Rising is a trilogy you can see on the screen as you read it. With vivid imagery, heartbreak, triumph, twists, cookies, and characters, even bad ones, with depth, I was sucked into the world of wolven from the start. Crystal Frost delivers another nonstop page turner that will keep you reading all night. I can't wait to read more from Frost either in the wolven world or beyond!"

Melanie S. - Stars & Promise

"There is action, there is romance, there are rivalries, sleepovers, and cookies.An absolute page-turner!"

Janesa Watson - Sun & Blood

"Very engaging. I couldn't put it down and cannot wait for book no. 2! It transported me to another world. Very descriptive!"

Juli M. - Sun & Blood

"I literally could not put the book down and was hooked from page one right till the end. I felt like I was transported into the Sentinel Clan world and was so sad when it ended. My exact thoughts were, okay where is book three."

Anel G. - Moon & Ruin

"Frost had so many twists and turns that I could hardly put Moon & Ruin down. The writing was absolutely captivating! This exciting book included lots of adventure, and even slow moving and clean romance! It was truly a pleasure to read."

- Debbie Barry, NASM Master Trainer - Moon & Ruin

"Sun & Blood is a book that will entangle you in the intertwining webs of its story, and will leave you with a burning desire to know what happens next. The adventure I did not expect became an adventure worth experience again and again."

OhMyMuffins (Mikey) - Sun & Blood

"I laughed. I cried. I cheered. I wanted to grab my boxing gloves. I was yanked into this world and fell in love with the characters from the first chapter. I'm excited to see what comes next."

Erin K., Amazon Reviewer - Sun & Blood

Also by Crystal Frost

<u>Sentinel Rising Trilogy</u>

Sun & Blood

Moon & Ruin

Sentinel Rising · Book 3

Crystal Frost

Stars & Promise

Printed in the United States of America.

Summary: ***Sentinel Clan is in tatters after the last attack from Blood Moon. Jax strives to lead the clan into battle while Violet leaves to find the lycans, hoping to turn the tides of war.***

For information contact :

http://frostcrystal.com

Cover and Interior by Crystal Frost

Hardcover ISBN: 978-1-957051-07-9

Softcover ISBN: 978-1-957051-08-6

Ebook ISBN: 978-1-957051-06-2

First Edition: April 2024

10 9 8 7 6 5 4 3 2 1

To the loved ones left behind:
they live on through us.

Chapter 1

Cas

Copper scented the air *of the Blood Moon clan house, and dark red blood* splattered the length of the floor. Buer's body had been dragged away, but Cas couldn't erase the image of his death from his mind. The speed at which the poison had spread through Buer's system was concerning. What was even more concerning was that it did so without an open wound, seeping through his skin and into his bloodstream.

Cas sank further into the old leather couch in the corner and rested his head back. When was the last time he had slept through the night? His gaze darted around before drifting shut. The scrape of a boot lurched his eyelids open and sent his heart racing. No one had moved. Red-eyed men and women still lined the walls, the closest person to him was nearly twenty feet away, and the dark throne remained occupied by a woman with a head of white dreadlocks.

He ran a hand down his face, then laid his arm across the back of the couch, feigning ease. Showing weakness amongst these wolven was not an option. Neither was sleeping, unless you knew how to sleep with your eyes open. He was going to need to find a safe place to rest soon.

"He's waking up, again." The sickeningly sweet voice of the Blood Moon clan leader poured through Cas' veins like ice water.

Clenching his jaw, Cas rolled his head to the side and gazed at Patrick's limp form dangling from the chains Cas had snapped around his wrists days ago. Someone had taken Patrick's chair away, leaving him to hang by his arms. He had plenty of slack to stand, but the drugs they continued to pump through his veins kept him weak, ensuring he stayed under their control.

Cas narrowed his eyes when Patrick's fingers twitched. Groaning, he pushed off the couch and made his way toward the man standing to the right of the throne. "Allow me." He held out his hand for the syringe he knew the man was holding onto. "It was my plan to have him here in the first place."

"No." A lithe hand lifted into the air, stopping Cas in his tracks as Ivy turned on the throne. Her legs fell off the arm and her feet landed with a thud against the floor before she targeted him with her large, doll-like sea-green eyes. "Topher will handle it." She nodded to the man in front of Cas. Topher dipped his chin before stepping around Cas and making his way toward Patrick.

Fury boiled low in Cas' stomach. "You may be the leader of this motley crew, but don't forget you would still be wandering aimlessly through California without my plan."

Crimson filled Ivy's gaze and she slowly made her way to her feet, her movements predatory as she stepped toward him. "Don't forget. Your plan would be nothing without us."

The growl tipping her voice toward her animal side warned him to stand down. He didn't see any poison on her, but that didn't mean she was empty-handed, and he needed to live. At least a little longer. At least to see his plan succeed. They were close.

"We need each other." Cas lowered his chin a fraction, ignoring the furious shouts of his wolf in the back of his head. "Why don't you let me take care of Patrick so you can focus on the next steps. Topher is an asset. He knows more about Sentinel Clan than anyone else in this room, even me. He needs to be in the field."

"Do not tell me how to run my clan!" Ivy snapped her teeth and stepped closer to him. It took everything in him not to launch away from her, but that's what she wanted. She wanted to intimidate. To force him to submit. He wouldn't do it. "Inside these walls, *my* word stands over all others. Not yours."

Cas quirked a brow as a sudden realization hit him. She was feeling threatened. Slowly, he ducked his chin a little lower, keeping his eyes trained on her. "Of course."

Seething through her clenched teeth, Ivy pointed past Cas. "Topher is administering the toxin because I don't have to worry about him overdosing our prize."

He couldn't stop the snort from leaving him or his next words from skipping gleefully across his lips. "Overdosing Patrick wouldn't serve my plan. He's no good to me dead. He can't suffer when he's dead."

Ivy's palms slapped against his chest, pushing him back a couple of feet, and her fingernails scratched against his shirt. "Get out of my face before I permanently make your plan my own." She flicked her lithe fingers toward the door. "Go relieve Frank. You can take a turn babysitting, and use that time to think about the proper way to address your leader."

Nodding, Cas slowly backed away from her, not turning his back until he was nearly halfway across the room. Too many pairs of blood-red eyes followed his movements. He was losing his position here. If they turned on him, he was as good as dead. He couldn't fend off an entire clan by himself. The moon still clung to the sky, and the crisp night air was a shock to his system, startlingly different from the stagnant warmth of the clan house. It was a welcome change, and the pressure on his shoulders eased a little.

Blood Moon typically overran the area at night, but with the raid on Sentinel Clan, most were making their way back or patrolling the borders. They had all grumbled about doing so since securing Stanislaus's territory. They weren't used to staying in one place and having to defend it.

But, that also meant fewer eyes on Cas, which he was grateful for as he stepped around the side of the building and pressed his back against the wall. One quick glance to both sides told him he was alone. He closed his eyes and leaned his head back, breathing in deep breaths to settle his nerves. He was playing a dangerous game here. After another breath, he looked down at his chest and felt around. Thankfully his shirt was intact and his skin appeared normal. Ivy hadn't poisoned him... this time.

"You're playing with the devil," spoke the wolf in his head. The one being who couldn't desert Cas. No matter how much Abel wished he could.

"I've told you before, it's necessary."

Abel sighed and Cas imagined his wolf half shaking his head. *"Vengeance is never necessary."*

"If you don't like it, then why pay any attention?"

"I loved her too, Cas," Abel's words startled Cas into gasping. They'd made a deal never to talk about her. Abel was breaking that deal. *"This isn't what she would have wanted."*

Cas growled. *"Shut up."*

Frustration pulsed through Cas' mind. *"No. You need to hear this. It's been three and a half years. You need to move on."*

"This is how I move on!" Cas yelled inside his mind, clenching his fists at his side. It was infuriating arguing with someone no one else could see. An argument in

your own mind.

Sorrow pressed heavily on Cas' thoughts. *"No, Caspian. This is how you stay lost."*

Abel slipped back into the recesses of Cas' mind.

Old anger and pain seeped through Cas, making his hands tremble as he marched two buildings over. He restrained himself from kicking the door in, but it still banged off the wall with the force he used to throw it open. Frank launched to his feet, startled and snarling.

"Get out!" Cas snapped, and Frank eagerly darted for the door. "Return to Ivy and tell her I'm watching over your post."

Frank didn't give him any indication that he would follow through with that order, or that he had even heard Cas, but he was heading in the right direction at least.

Cas grabbed the door and closed it, eyeing the hinges and locks for any damage. He hadn't even thought about the locks that should have been in place when he'd barged through. "Idiot didn't even lock the door," he muttered to himself. His fingers quickly secured the five locks that traveled the length of the door adding a touch of reinforcement to the fairly fragile blockade.

With all of the locks engaged, a sigh of relief sagged Cas' shoulders and the exhaustion from the last few days sank deep into his limbs. Maybe playing guard for the night wouldn't be so bad. He would know if anyone tried to enter, giving him a chance to get some sleep. Restless as it may be, it was better than nothing.

A guttural cry shattered the silence and Cas clamped his hands over his ears as he spun around. His heart hammered while he stared down the hallway. A softer cry followed, then a whimper. The crack of bone made him flinch. Then another... and another.

Hesitantly, Cas made his way toward the gut-twisting sounds. The building was almost set up like a doctor's office, but bars lined the walls and replaced doors. Stanislaus had not been as well off as Sentinel was, which was why Blood Moon had targeted them. As Cas wandered down the barred hall, he couldn't help but compare Sentinel's Lockup to this jail.

Low snarls mingled with whimpers met his ears as he approached the farthest cell. The stench of human hit his nose, but it was twisted with some kind of musk. A shock of white-blond hair caught his eye, cascading from a bent-over form. The last glimpse of fur disappeared beneath her porcelain skin. Lengthy arms and legs trembled beneath tattered clothing, and shaky breaths left her in bursts.

"Lexie," Cas breathed her name and guilt dug into his chest. She was never supposed to get caught up in this.

Violet's best friend shook uncontrollably on her hands and knees in a barred cell of an enemy clan. She was lucky to be alive.

Lexie sniffed loudly. Then sniffed again. A low, menacing growl rumbled through her and she slowly lifted her head.

Drawing in a slow, steady breath, Cas clenched his jaw. Bright red eyes, nearly luminescent in the dim lighting, glared at him. But he'd been surrounded by crimson eyes for months. What bothered him was that the red was not contained to her iris; it discolored her entire eye. No white or black could be seen.

Maybe *lucky* wasn't the right word.

She snarled, exposing wolf canines. She shook her head when her ears lengthened, then whimpered when they inched upward on her head. Panting replaced her shaky breaths and a pained groan left her as she curled in on herself.

"Do you remember who you are?" Cas asked, daring a step closer to the bars. "Or has the monster taken over?"

An ear-ringing shriek that was a mix of human and animal ripped from her throat. She launched herself at the bars, but was snatched back at the last moment by a thick, metal collar.

Cas flinched as her body jerked back, then landed heavily in a heap. A sob wracked her body, and she curled into the smallest ball she could manage.

The twist of guilt in his chest shifted to his heart. His face pinched as he watched her.

"You did this to her." Abel accused him, pressing forward in his mind. *"She would be safe in her human home tonight if you had listened to me. If you hadn't gone down this path of revenge."*

"Stop it." Cas growled at his wolf, but it was more of a plea than he wanted. The only person he wanted to suffer was Patrick... and in the process, his mate. But it was always the plan to kill his mate quickly. Cas hadn't meant to become Violet's friend. To care about her. Now Blood Moon had other plans for her. Patrick would suffer... but now, so would Violet.

The snap of bone, and a cry of agony, pulled Cas from his thoughts. His brows pulled together as he watched Lexie writhe in pain. She pushed up onto her hands and reached for the bars. Another crack sounded, somewhere in her torso, and she collapsed.

Cas clenched his jaw against his betraying emotions.

Lexie lifted her face toward him once again, tears streaming down her cheeks, and stared at him with *very* human eyes. Bright, blue, beautiful human eyes.

"Help."

The sob was a knife to his heart. Barely audible beneath the cry that stole the word from her when another bone snapped and her body began to shift again. Her fingers shortened while her nails curled and turned dark. Gray fur sprouted from every pore in her skin. Red consumed the gentle blue in her eyes. Finally, a gray wolf thrashed against the collar holding her back, gnashing her teeth and attempting to reach him with her large clawed paws. Lexie was a wolf. Not a giant one like what he and other wolven turned into, but a large timber wolf. The biggest wolf breed that was known to humans.

Another crack and a loud, high-pitched cry filled the room. Wolf Lexie backed off and cowered against the floor.

She was shifting again? Already? Cas looked out the barred window and stared at the sinking full moon. How many times would she shift? And... would she live through it?

Cas flinched when she convulsed through another bone breaking. "I'm sorry," he said, turning away to leave.

"No!" Abel snarled at Cas and his body froze in place. *"You don't get to leave her alone like this. You made this happen. You are staying."*

"I can't help her!" Cas yelled into his mind. His body shook with effort as he strained to leave the room, but Abel wasn't relinquishing his hold. *"There is nothing I can do to stop her from shifting."*

"Maybe not. But you can be with her through this nightmare." Abel's voice softened when Lexie's cries turned more human. *"It's the least you can do for her."*

Cas clenched his teeth. After a moment, he nodded. "I'm here, Lexie. I don't know if you'll remember any of this when it's over, but I am sorry you were dragged into this."

Trembling, Lexie turned her mostly human face toward him. Her snout slowly shortened to her normal lips and high cheekbones. It was impossible to decipher any emotion in her eyes other than pain and fear, but he was sure she blamed him. He blamed himself.

"I'm not asking you to forgive me, but I am sorry. And I'm sorry I can't help you get through this." He ground his teeth together as anger and loathing for himself pulsed through his body. This was not supposed to happen. All the stories he'd ever heard of a human being turned into a wolven never ended well. Their frail human bodies couldn't withstand the shift, and their minds were not strong enough to fight off the madness. The harsh reality of her future made Cas' heart hurt. With unsteady fingers, he gripped one of the bars before lifting his gaze to meet hers again.

The tears streaming from her eyes were a punch to his gut.

"You're not alone," Cas said firmly, clenching the bar until his knuckles turned white. "Do you hear me?"

There was no indication if she understood him or not, but she held his gaze until her body started ripping itself apart for another round.

Chapter 2

Violet

Sorrow blanketed Sentinel Clan *and wails of agony rent the night sky. The* tormenting sounds eased as dawn approached, but the sun only revealed the amount of precious blood spilled. Bodies lined the dirt road, covered with white sheets. Too many bodies. Too many lives.

Violet stared at the blazing pier where they had laid her mother earlier that morning. She could still feel the heat of the flames caressing her skin and scalding any tear that dared to fall. Evalyn Draven was a wonderful luna. A mother to all. A welcoming home to those who needed it.

A liar.

Guilt stabbed at Violet and she pinched her eyes shut. No. Her mother was not a liar. She just sacrificed her life for Violet's and never told her. Never told her that Evalyn's death would give life to Violet's wolf. Violet curled her hands into fists that shook at her sides. A set of twins, unheard of in the wolven community. One destined to be the future alpha. The other, a miracle child, destined to kill the luna.

The sound of the knives driving into Evalyn's body lanced through Violet's mind, making her flinch. No, Violet hadn't killed her mother... but Evalyn Draven was dead because of her.

Eventually, Jax led her home and sat her on the couch. Unsettling quiet had fallen over Alpha House. Everything was untouched as if the night's events hadn't happened. If she closed her eyes, Violet could almost imagine her mom sitting at her desk with a sparkle in her eye and headphones in her ears. That's how the night should have gone. A peaceful night at home, with her mom. They would have talked and drank hot chocolate, and Evalyn would have told Violet everything. It would have been shocking, but at least she would have known and could plan the rest of her life accordingly. Jax would have returned in the morning, radiating confidence from his newly united bond with his wolf, Dalim. Waffles, bacon, sausage, and eggs would have been prepared for a celebratory breakfast, and Patrick and Lexie would have been there. Alpha House would have been filled with riotous laughter, teasing jokes, and celebration.

But life rarely gives those perfect moments.

And life was far from perfect.

Violet's eyes stung from all the tears she'd shed and the new ones threatening to fall. She opened them, allowing a couple of trapped drops to fall before she wiped them away. Metallic vanilla made her jerk back before touching her face. The smell churned her stomach. Blood stained her claw-tipped fingers. Her mother's blood. A violent wave of nausea made Violet rush to the kitchen sink. Her body heaved, but there was nothing to give. She stood and stared at her foreign hands, then with a shaky breath she threw the sink handle so the nozzle would spew hot water. It was slow to heat, but Violet used the time to slather soap over her skin and dug under her claws. Steam filled the sink and rose into the air. She shoved her hands under the burning water and sucked a breath through her clenched teeth. Her skin cried out under the extreme heat, but she continued to scrub. Red-tinged water ran down the drain, but it wouldn't come off. Why wouldn't it come off?

Soft footsteps descended the stairs. "Violet?" Jax's voice carried gently through the room. "Violet!" A moment later he was at her side, smashing the handle to cold water. "Are you crazy?" He held her arms still so she wouldn't pull her hands from the icy temperature. "What were you doing?"

"I needed to get the blood off," Violet answered in a deadened tone.

Jax's wide, alarmed gaze softened and sorrow drew his face taut. A heavy sigh left him. "Burning your hands in the process is not how you do that."

"Sorry," she mumbled.

He grabbed the towel from the oven door, then turned off the water and wrapped her tender, pink hands in the soft cloth.

One of her claws caught when he tried to pull it away, and she flinched. "Wait. I'm stuck."

Taking extra care, Jax lifted inch by inch of the towel until it fell away from her weaponized hands. "You know..." He placed the towel on the counter. "I think you can change back to your normal nails now."

Violet shook her head. "I don't know how."

"Have you tried?" Jax softly asked.

Her shoulders sank as she nodded.

Jax made his way toward the couch, running a hand through his damp hair. He must have left to take a shower. Why didn't Violet remember him leaving?

"I grabbed this after my shower. I thought you might want it." He returned to her side with a familiar mass of dark-green material and held it out for her to take.

Violet froze halfway to grabbing it and stared at her hands. She hadn't even noticed, but her tender, raw, pink flesh had already healed to her normal tanned tone.

"Glad to see your healing works," Jax commented, then moved the bundle an inch closer to her. "Here."

She took the fabric from him, letting it unravel in the process, then stared at Patrick's shirt. It felt like a lifetime ago when he'd let her borrow it after Blood Moon's first attack on Sentinel Clan. Chocolate peppermint filled her nose and she drew in a deep breath. Her heart longed for him, but he couldn't return. Alpha Draven had banished him... er... the former alpha had.

Her amethyst eyes rounded and she looked at Jax. "Holy crap, you're alpha."

Jax snorted. "Yeah. That's not the only thing that's changed." He nodded toward her, and a mirthless hint of a smile tilted a corner of Violet's mouth. "I tried to call him, by the way." Jax crossed his arms over his chest. "He still won't answer."

Violet placed the shirt back on the countertop. "He needs to know what happened."

"I know." He nodded. "I'll keep trying. When he does answer, I'll invite him to come home."

A dark hollow opened inside Violet, threatening to consume her. "What if he doesn't?"

"If he doesn't, it's only because he thinks it will protect us."

Fatigue settled deep within her. The idea of Patrick refusing to return was too much for her to think about and she didn't want to cry again. She was so sick of crying. Of fighting. A bone-weary sigh left her. She was so very tired.

Jax pushed away from the counter and reached for the cupboard Violet and their mom used. Her breath caught when her twin pulled the teapot out.

"You like hot chocolate when you're upset, right?" Jax asked, setting the teapot gently on the stovetop. "I've never made it with a teapot, but I can learn."

Tears were back, threatening to stream from Violet's eyes. So, she left. She walked out of the kitchen, taking Patrick's shirt with her.

"Violet?" Jax followed her, leaving the teapot behind.

When she collapsed onto the couch, Jax sat sideways beside her so he could see her. One of her claws snagged Patrick's shirt when she tried to smooth it across her lap. A thread tugged away from the others, creating a small loop. She sucked in a quick breath and frantically tried to fix it, but her claws snagged another section.

"No, no, no," she pleaded, trying once again to smooth the fabric, but the more she tried, the more damage she caused. "I need to fix it. I have to..."

A large hand settled gently over hers, stilling her movements. "Violet."

Ragged breaths caused her chest to rise and fall in rapid succession as she lifted her watery gaze to her brother's. "I'm so sorry. For everything. I'm sorry about Aiden. I'm sorry I lost Lexie. I'm sorry Patrick had to leave. I'm sorry about Mom... I'm so sorry I couldn't save her."

Jax's jaw clenched. His eyes swirled molten gold, then slowly returned to purple-a mirror image of her own. "Do not blame yourself for Mom's death."

Violet shook her head. "You don't understand."

His brows slammed down. "Vikter killed Mom, Violet. Not you."

"But I made the choice that killed her!"

Confusion spread across his expression. "What are you talking about?" He tried to catch her gaze, but she looked away. "You told me you didn't have a vision."

"I didn't." Violet clenched Jax's hands. "I don't know what she did, but Mom was dying because of me. She... somehow she made it so that when I shifted for the first time I would get her wolf, Aurora. That's why my wolf eyes look like hers and I'm guessing Aurora is the wolf that saved me when Zander tried to kill me."

Jax's fingers tightened around hers, but he stayed quiet.

"I decided not to fight back." Her voice broke and a sob rattled her chest. "I was going to sacrifice myself so Mom would live. I was going to let Vikter kill me." Hot moisture lined her lashes and she shook her head. "But our warriors were dying. Our clanmates. I couldn't let them die." Another sob left her. "If Vikter hadn't killed her, my choice to fight back would have."

Violet's tears splattered against their intertwined hands. He was going to hate her for this.

Jax let out a long breath and it fluttered through the hairs along the side of her face. "If you died, do you really think Vikter would have stopped?" His question made her breath catch, but he wasn't done. "Do you honestly believe he would have just walked away? He would have kept going until every single warrior was gone and then probably moved on to the houses. Mom has been growing weaker for months. She wouldn't have been able to stop him."

"But I was the reason she was weak!" She wrenched her hands from his and glared at him.

"That decision was never yours to make!" Jax's voice rose before he shut down. His hands curled into fists against his knees and his eyes closed. A few deep breaths through his nose made his chest rise and fall. She'd never seen him exercise such restraint. When he opened his eyes again, the last remnants of gold were vanishing. "That was her choice, Violet. She chose to give you her life because she loved you."

A heart-wrenching sob pulled Violet's shoulders inward and she dropped her head into her hands.

"And I'm glad she did." His voice cracked and his hand settled against her back, rubbing softly. "Because my life would be incomplete without you. You are my twin, Violet. We are two sides of the same coin, and I can't imagine living without you." The hand that was intertwined with hers wiggled free and gently lifted her head until they were staring at one another. Agony mirrored in each other's amethyst eyes. "Don't ever try to die without me again."

Violet sob-laughed and she managed a small nod. A smile that didn't reach his eyes lifted the corners of his mouth. He tugged her against him and wrapped his long arms around her. There was so much pain between them. A new life they had to learn to navigate. But, as they sat alone together in a silent house, Violet knew they would get through it together.

Her breathing settled, and her pulse slowed. Tingling spread through her fingers and she leaned away from him to stare at her hands as the bone claws slipped back to regular human fingernails.

"That's going to take some getting used to," Jax admitted.

"Try being the one it's happening to," she turned her hands over in awe. "I don't know how to be a lycan. I've always been the super weak daughter of the alpha. Now I'm supposedly this powerful royal?" She shook her head.

Jax's chest deflated with a sigh. "We'll figure it out, but for now, you shou—wait. You're lycan."

Violet lifted a brow and blink. "I think we've covered that."

"But you have Aurora?"

Violet shook her head again and shrugged. "I don't know. I haven't felt her presence, but I don't even know what that's supposed to feel like. I don't know how I can have her and be lycan too."

"We'll figure it out," Jax repeated. He lifted a hand and grabbed the tip of her ear. "I do like the points though."

Violet batted his hand away. "Are they still pointed?" she asked as she self-consciously felt her ears. Sure enough, the tops of her ears were angled instead of round.

An amused smirk lit his face, but when he opened his mouth to comment, his eyes glazed over. "We're needed in the parking lot."

"What?" Violet asked as Jax jumped up from the couch and headed for the front door. "I thought Dr. Penmann was handling things so we could process for a day?"

"She is." Jax shoved his feet into a pair of sneakers, then raised his brows when he realized she hadn't moved. "And she said we need to get to the parking lot. Both of us."

Groaning, Violet pushed off the couch and followed him as he ran out the door.

Only a few warriors were out along the dirt roads as they ran toward the parking lot. Most only tossed them a curious glance, but a few stopped in their tracks and watched them for a moment. Everyone was on high alert, but they knew Jax would have sounded an alarm if another attack was happening.

They rounded the seven-foot hedges that offered a privacy shield for the clan against any unwelcome visitors and Violet skidded to a stop. Jax slowed to a stop a few steps later and looked back at her. Her breathing hitched and her heart pounded against her ribs. There, at the far end of the parking lot, sat an achingly familiar old red truck.

Multiple warriors, and a few wolves, circled Patrick's truck.

"You said you hadn't been able to reach him," Violet breathed the words as she started walking again.

"I haven't."

Panic shook her hands. She would know, right? If what Jax had said about her being Patrick's mate and not Zander's was true... she would've known if something happened to him. Right? No bond had been sealed, so she didn't know for sure. Why didn't he tell them he was coming?

Dr. Penmann walked a handful of steps to meet them. "I'm sorry, Jax. I wanted to give you both time to grieve, but you need to see this." She directed them toward the truck and they followed.

"Where's Patrick?" Violet asked.

The older woman sighed and her usually soothing raspy voice hit Violet like a brick wall. "We don't know."

Violet's brows pinched together.

"No one saw who left Patrick's truck here; it must have been dropped off during the attack," the doctor explained, "but they left a note." She stopped at the tail of the truck bed and pointed at its contents.

Violet turned to stare at the contents of the bed. A knot built in her throat and she swallowed it down as she stared at a pale body laced with black veins. Lifeless blue eyes gazed at the bright, morning sky and despair for a friendship that once was weighed down Violet's shoulders.

"Zander." Violet's gaze trailed over his clothes.

He was dressed the same tux he'd been wearing the night he'd tried to strangle her, but the sleeves were torn, revealing his black vein-riddled arms. Dried blood marred his white shirt, surrounding a dagger that had been buried hilt deep in his chest, pinning a folded piece of paper in place.

"There are injection points along both of his arms and his neck," Dr. Penmann's raspy voice explained. "Whoever did this to him wanted to make sure he wouldn't survive."

"Has anyone read the note?" Jax asked, his voice even and level.

"No. We were waiting for you."

Jax jumped into the truck bed, then turned and offered Violet a helping hand. She placed her hand in his and he easily lifted her up. Together, they carefully stepped around Zander's body to get a closer look at the paper. Violet scrunched her nose as an acrid smell hit her nose and throat, making her cough.

Jax reached for the dagger and she seized his arm. "Stop," she coughed as the smell turned sour like a bucket of vinegar had been poured into the truck bed. "I think it's poisoned."

He quirked a brow. "We already know their blades are poisoned, Violet."

"Not the blade. I think the entire dagger is—including the handle."

A warrior standing close to the truck bed stepped back and Violet sneered at him. It's not like the weapon was going to leap out of Zander's chest and fly toward the warrior.

Jax tipped his head to the side. "Okay. No dagger." He yanked the paper off Zander's chest and unfolded it.

Dr. Penmann eyed the note from her position on the ground, her gaze slightly narrowed. "The lack of blood on the note, and in the truck bed, tells me Zander didn't die in here and that this dagger was added postmortem, as well."

Violet's face scrunched and her heart hurt. "You mean he was stabbed, but then stabbed again after he was dead just to attach the note?"

The doc nodded. "It's very possible."

"That's horrible."

“Violet,” Jax called, pulling her attention. He extended his arm to her, the note clutched in his hand. "It's... it's for you."

"What?" She hesitantly reached for the paper and when he placed it into her hand the familiar scent of coffee and almonds washed over her. "It can't be."

With shaky fingers, she unfolded the note, which read;

A PRESENT FOR THE NEW WHITE WOLF.

VIKTER LET PARANOIA AND REVENGE BLIND HIM.

ZANDER HAD HIS CHANCE AND WASTED IT.

IT'S FINALLY MY TURN.

-C

“Who’s C?” Jax asked.

“Cas.” Violet lifted her gaze and stared at her twin as fury and disbelief warred within her. Claws grew from her nails as she clutched the note in her hand. "Cas is behind this. He used me."

Jax's eyes swirled molten gold. "And he'll pay for it."

Chapter 3

Jax

***Sorrow shrouded every act** Jax made in place of his father, the former alpha* of the Sentinel Clan. Every choice he made weighed heavily on his shoulders. The pain of losing his mother combined with the agony he felt from his clan members, who were mourning their own losses, often overrode his ability to think clearly. He'd never been more grateful for Dalim's presence. His wolf half slipped into control when Jax started losing his. The reprieve was needed, and their desires were in line with each other's so Jax never had to worry about his wolf deciding something he didn't agree with. Jax couldn't have asked for a more perfect guide into the intense world of an alpha.

Gravel crunched beneath his shoes as he and two warriors made their way to Lockup. They were silent and remained that way most of the time. If Patrick was there Jax would've demanded they leave him alone, but with Blood Moon's attacks growing more and more aggressive, the warriors demanded he had protection.

The clan couldn't lose another alpha.

Stone walls peeked from behind large boulders and trees, and soon the entirety of Lockup was within his sight. The guards on duty, both human and wolf alike, bowed their heads respectfully as he and his protectors passed. A lot of decisions had been made in the last two days. One of which was to have more guards on duty at all times inside of Lockup in case of another breakout attempt. Another was to have Noah Draven under guard and heavy sedation.

Jax led his two protectors up to the top floor, ignoring the meager amount of

Blood Moon wolven they held captive on the first two floors. He would check on them later. Right now his mind was set on one person.

Dalim's comforting presence pressed against his mind. *"Remember to approach this gently. It didn't go well last time."*

"I know. But I can't do everything alone. I need help."

"That's what our mate is for."

"Yeah well..." Heart-splintering yearning crashed through Jax's chest. *"That's not an option right now, is it?"*

Sorrow and loneliness that echoed his own filled Dalim's next words, *"We'll find her."*

Someday. Once all of this Blood Moon chaos was behind them. They would find her. He'd never realized how big of a support his mother had been for his father. How could he have? It's not something one would understand without experiencing it. He knew Evalyn had helped with a few things, but now he wondered just how much she had handled on a day-to-day basis.

The scent of salty tears permeated the air of the third floor. Soft cries pulled his thoughts back to the present and he turned his head to gaze at a middle-aged woman hugging her rounded stomach, rocking back and forth on her mattress while humming a lullaby. Her mate had been killed during Blood Moon's full moon ambush two nights ago. Doc had been worried because she had refused to eat, but the two empty food trays told him that was no longer the case. She hadn't needed sedatives, but Doc had administered an IV and wanted to keep a closer watch on her due to her pregnancy. Her big brown eyes turned to him and she offered a soft, sad smile.

Relief coursed through Jax. She would be alright.

Two rooms down an older man lay on his side, his silver hair glistened in the overhead lights as he slept with his back to the plexiglass wall. His pain weighed heavily on Jax. He'd been in Lockup almost as long as Mya and he'd made no improvement. Doc suspected he wouldn't survive much longer if things didn't start to turn around. He'd given up.

Another two rooms and Jax's feet froze to the floor. A low growl emitted from behind the plexiglass, a sound he knew all too well. The deep timbre echoed in many of his memories of growing up.

"You should look at him," Dalim softly told him.

"How am I supposed to look him in the eye knowing his only desire is to kill Violet?"

"Because you're his son."

After a deep inhale, Jax turned his head to gaze at the man he called father. Former alpha Draven swayed back and forth on the foot of his bed, his unfocused glazed eyes permanently fixed in a dull golden color. Most of the room's contents had been emptied because he'd broken through the plexiglass of another cell using the desk chair on his first night. Misplaced revenge was the only thing driving Noah Draven. His hatred scorched Jax's thoughts if he focused on them too much.

"There is nothing of the man I once knew in there," Jax said sadly to his wolf half.

"Perhaps," Dalim agreed. *"But one day, when he comes out of this, you'll be able to tell him you were here, waiting for him."*

"You mean if. If he comes out of this."

Doc had been very clear that she'd never seen such a severe case of revenge in a widowed wolven. The amount of sedative she'd had to keep him on was insane. Violet was not allowed anywhere near Lockup for fear that he would hear her and go on a rampage.

An older woman with silver just beginning to highlight her dark hair walked out of a far cell, dabbing at her eyes with a handkerchief. Tucker's blond head of hair appeared after her and he stopped to lock the door behind them.

"Good morning, Alpha Draven."

Her greeting was soft, but Jax flinched. "Please, just Jax."

The woman's attention flitted to Noah when she approached and she nodded. "I understand this is still very new for you, but try not to disregard the respect that comes from your new title." Her blue eyes were an echo of Tucker's who Jax nodded to when he came to stand behind the woman.

"I'll try," Jax answered honestly. "May I ask what you're doing here, Mrs. Mack?"

"I come to talk to those who, like me, have lost their mates. Elliot and I were not as cosmically connected as they were. We lived a happy life and found joy in one another. I couldn't have asked for a better companion." Tears gathered in her eyes, then she shook her head. "But, we were not Moon Fated. I try to sit with those who want company and offer words of love and encouragement to them."

Mya's coiled brown hair poked out of her room, two cells down, and she shuffled into the hallway.

Mrs. Mack turned to smile at the young woman who offered a small wave in return before wrapping her arms around her middle as she waited.

"Mya and I have especially enjoyed our visits. It's been good for both of us."

A small nod from Violet's friend confirmed what the older woman was saying.

"How long have you been doing this?" Jax wondered, and why hadn't he been informed?

Mrs. Mack shrugged. "Since I lost my mate during the attack on solstice. Once I realized others were in much worse shape than I, I decided to dive into the service of my fellow clan mates."

Warmth and love spread through Jax's chest, and he closed his eyes, relishing in the emotions he was feeling from her. His shoulders eased, lowering a fraction. A soft exhale left him and when he opened his eyes again, Mrs. Mack was gazing at him with a warm smile.

"If you ever need me," she paused, and tipped her head to the side as if she were contemplating her next words. "I would never dare try to replace your mother. I don't think anyone could carry the immense weight she carried. But if you ever need a motherly presence, or guide, or listening ear..." she looked over her shoulder, then reached up and rested her palm against Tucker's cheek. The silent guard closed his eyes and leaned into his mother's touch for a short moment. "I've had some practice."

Pain lanced through Jax, but he nodded. "I appreciate the offer."

The woman bowed her head respectfully, and then made her way around Jax's protectors.

Tucker cleared his throat. "We'll be serving breakfast soon. Things have been quiet here since the chair incident." He nodded his head toward Noah Draven, who continued to softly growl. "Most of our clan members on this floor are recovering well, but all at their own pace. I'll see my mom out and return to my duties."

He went to leave, but Jax rested a hand on his shoulder. "Thank you for everything you do here. I don't know how you're handling all of this, but I know your father would be proud of you. I am honored to work beside you."

A strange mixture of pride and guilt washed over Tucker's face. "Thank you. I'm doing my best."

"That's all I can ask for." Jax nodded to him. "So many things are uncertain right now. Sentinel Clan is going through some large changes."

Tucker released a large sigh. "Let's hope there's still a Sentinel Clan when this is all over."

Jax squeezed his shoulder lightly, then dismissed him. Only a couple of months ago he had punched Tucker in the face for participating in a bet to see how far he could get with Violet. Now, Jax was finding a friend in the young man who had shown incredible maturity with recent events.

But Tucker was another oddity—prone to random shifts into his wolf form. Blood Moon's attack during solstice resulted in Lockup being emptied and Tucker's father being killed. He wouldn't turn eighteen for a few more months, but the only explanation Doc had for Tucker's sudden ability to change form was emotional distress and the threat to his life. Because of the early timing, the young man didn't have the same control as other wolven did. They watched him closely, fearful that he would lose his mind like Zander had, but Tucker was as sure and steady as ever. Perhaps even more so.

"You said you had something you wanted to talk to me about?" Mya's gentle voice called Jax out of his thoughts.

"Oh, yes." He shook his head, and stepped toward her, ignoring his father's ever-present growling. "Good morning."

A small quirk of one corner of her mouth was all she gave. Her eyes were still full of sorrow, but the debilitating pain she'd felt when Aiden died had subsided to a lower ache.

"From what the doc and my sister have told me, you're not ready to leave Lockup."

Panic widened her eyes and she hunched her shoulders forward. "I can't. I know Aiden and I weren't together for very long, but we were Moon Fated, and our connection was strong." Mya shook her head. "I... don't want to be surrounded by all the things that remind me of him. Here, I only have my own memories. He was never here."

Jax took a moment, drew in a deep breath, and let it out before responding. "That's fine. We don't want to rush you. However, we could really use your help." He looked over his shoulder where Mrs. Mack and Tucker had disappeared then returned his gaze to her. "You could continue staying here, but you would also have a job to do. It would be very similar to what Tucker's mom is already doing. We need someone who has spent time here to make this place more comfortable for our clan mates who are recovering from their wounds—whether that be external or internal."

Mya shifted her weight uncomfortably. "I don't know."

The sound of a door opening behind him made Jax's ear twitch. A sweet aroma of maple syrup filled the hall, announcing the arrival of breakfast. Moments later, the door closed again and a cart rolled toward him, its slightly squeaky wheels stopping a few feet later at the next door.

Jax offered Mya a gentle gaze. "I know this isn't the first time a job offer has come to you. We've tried to bring it up a few times, in fact."

"Jax—"

"Mya, I need help," he admitted, his firm words exposing the truth of his statement.

She froze with her lips parted. Her brows pinched together.

Another door opened behind him.

"I'm..." He let out a long breath and Dalim encouraged him to continue. "I feel like I'm suffocating. I can't do everything. My mother is dead, my dad has lost his mind, my beta is gone, and my sister is..."

Mya's large brown eyes softened. "I'm sorry," she said quietly.

The door closest to him, his father's door, opened.

"How is Violet doing?"

An ear-splitting roar filled Lockup and Mya clamped her hands over her ears while Noah Draven shouted, "VIOLET!"

Jax turned as the former alpha threw the warrior who'd been delivering the meals into the plexiglass wall. The young man hit, then slid down the clear barrier into an unconscious heap on the floor while Noah sluggishly stomped toward the open door.

Jax jumped in front of his dad, but the man had already taken two steps out of his room. "You have to go back to your cell."

"Get out of my way."

"I can't do that."

Noah took another thundering step. "I must find her."

"You're not going anywhere, Dad." Jax gripped the older man's shoulders and leaned his weight against him. "You're not thinking straight."

Under Jax's weight, Noah staggered back a step. A low growl vibrated through the room and a chill swept down Jax's spine. In a surprisingly swift movement, Noah seized Jax's throat.

"How can you defend her? She killed your mother!"

Jax latched a hand around his father's wrist, pinning it in place, then slammed his other hand into the back of Noah's elbow joint, driving the man down. His knees smacked against the floor. Rage and pain burst from Noah and the raw power behind the emotions felt like a punch in Jax's stomach. He scrunched his face while he fought off the onslaught of emotions, and forced his father's elbow to bend so Jax could pin Noah's hand behind his back. Noah growled when Jax hauled him off the ground, but was otherwise helpless.

"She killed your mother!" Noah shouted, pressing back against Jax to slow his walk back into his room.

Sorrow swept through Jax and clung to his words. "No. Vikter killed Mom."

Noah twisted out of Jax's hold, then swung a punch toward Jax's face. The breeze generated from the speed of the former alpha's attack brushed against Jax's cheek, but he was able to lean away, avoiding the hit. Noah pulled his elbow back for another strike. Instead, his eyes glazed over and his arm hesitated in the air before slowly sinking to his side. He stumbled a step toward Jax, then collapsed into his arms.

"Dad?" Jax staggered under the weight of his father's mountainous body.

Mya stood a few feet behind Noah, her chest rising and falling rapidly as she clutched an empty syringe in her raised fist. Her brown eyes were as wide as saucers while she stared at Noah.

Jax looked down at the limp man in his arms, then back at her. "What did you do?"

"Um," Mya swallowed hard. She shrugged and held out the syringe. "I uh... it's a sedative. Fast acting. Doc gave it to me in case someone tried to break into my cell again. I thought now was an appropriate time."

Grunting in agreement, Jax repositioned his father so he could drag him back to his bed. "How long does it last?"

"I'm not sure. I haven't had to use it." She followed him into Noah's cell, then hurried around them toward the bed in the corner. "I'm sure she would have made it strong enough to last a little while. That way I'd be safe until someone arrived for help."

Her small hands swept the blankets back and fluffed the pillow before Jax dragged Noah to the bed.

Jax tried to set his father on the bed gently, but even with his strength, the guy was massive and heavy. He practically dropped Noah's upper half onto the mattress before bending to grab his feet. "She didn't tell you how long?"

"Oh, I'm sure she did, but I was a little freaked about the possibility of tranking someone."

A small laugh escaped Jax while he pushed his father into a more comfortable position. He stood and rolled his shoulders back. Mya was across the room, kneeling down in front of the young warrior as he came to, shaking his head.

"Easy," she softly ordered, pressing a hand against the young man's shoulder. "You were thrown pretty hard."

"The headache I have told me that," the guy groaned.

Jax approached and offered a hand to the warrior, who took it with a sheepish look on his face. "You okay?"

The warrior nodded once he was on his feet. "I'm sure I'll be fine. Wounded ego more than anything else."

"From now on, have two people deliver to the former alpha and always close the door." Jax gave the warrior a pointed look.

"Will do," he nodded again before returning to the meal cart for a fresh tray. After setting the food down beside the bed, he disappeared down the hall to continue his rounds.

"I'll do it," Mya's soft voice filled the quiet.

Jax turned to find her wringing a brown coil around her finger. "Are you sure?"

She shrugged and followed Jax out of Noah's cell. "You need help and I'm already here." She closed the cell door behind her and the locks automatically latched into place. Her warm chocolate eyes watched the former alpha for a moment before she spoke again. "I know who is here, and why, and what could make their stay more comfortable. And I can give reports to you and the doc."

A relieved sigh left Jax, sinking his shoulders a fraction. "That would help a ton." He shot a quick glance at his father. "It might be good to avoid saying my sister's name while in earshot of him for the time being."

Mya nodded. "Agreed. How is she, by the way?"

Shaking his head, Jax leaned against the wall. "I don't know. I'm sure she could use a friend right now. A lot has changed. *She* has changed."

"It's true then?"

Jax lifted a brow.

Mya tilted her head to the side. "I might be staying here, but I hear the warriors talk." She threaded the coil back into the rest of her hair. "They said an explosion of magic left her when she shifted and that when she shifted back, it was like nothing they had ever seen. More magical than any transformation they'd ever witnessed."

"It was like she just morphed into a new form. Clothes and all." Jax reminisced. "It was incredible. Although she is struggling to control the smaller changes like having claws, fangs, and pointed ears."

Surprise lit her face, raising her brows and widening her eyes. "So, she really is lycan?"

"It seems that way." Jax shook his head. "We just don't know how."

Mya looked down the hall when the young warrior returned with a now empty cart. "Well, let me know if there is something I can do. I'm sure having her come here isn't an option." She eyed Noah's cell again. "Maybe... maybe we could meet outside sometime. In front of Lockup."

Warmth spread through Jax's limbs and he smiled. "I'll tell her you said so. I'm sure she would love to see you." He stepped away, heading for the exit. "I'll be in touch and I'll let Tucker know about your new position. He should be able to give you everything you need."

Unease fluttered through Jax and he turned to see Mya with her arms around her middle. Without allowing himself to think too much, he took three large steps and closed the distance between them. Mya's body tensed when he wrapped his arms around her shoulders and squeezed her into a hug.

He waited until she relaxed and let out a long breath before he stepped away again. "Thank you. I know you'll be amazing at this."

A soft smile lifted the corners of her mouth and slightly creased her eyes. It was the most genuine smile he'd seen from her in a long time. "I'll do my best."

Chapter 4

Patrick

Liquid fire seared Patrick's *veins, consuming his thoughts and weakening* his body. Alistair sluggishly clawed through his mind, unable to form complete sentences. No demands, retorts, or annoyed sounds sounded in his thoughts.

There was no reprieve. He tried to stay quiet when he regained consciousness. He tried to act as if he were still out of it. But they knew. Somehow, they always knew. The crazy lady with the white dreadlocks had his dosage down perfectly. Each time the burning started to ebb, more poison was forced into his system, never allowing the pain to ease beyond a fraction. Never allowing him to heal. Never allowing him to regain his strength.

At this point, he wasn't sure if he ever would. Each of the last six syringes of the wolfsbane concoction felt like a tug toward death. His body didn't have anything left to fight with.

His limbs twitched when the itching began. The tiny lacerations the white-haired woman inflicted had only grown about three inches the first few days he'd been held captive. Now, they were stretching farther with every passing hour. He looked down at his bare chest and mentally cursed. The tips of the inky black veins had disappeared from his sight. How close was it to his throat now? How much longer did he have?

The doors to his right flew open, making the men and women lining the room jerk, and then stand a little straighter. A stark white head of dreadlocks appeared followed by rich brown hair and a face that'd been haunting Patrick for weeks. Someone he knew from somewhere. Someone he knew shouldn't have been trusted. Someone who'd betrayed Sentinel Clan.

Cas smashed the doors closed behind him, blocking a few red-eyed wolven that had been following him and the woman. "Ivy, listen to me..."

"No! You listen!" Ivy spun to face him and pointed a long finger at his chest. "We've been following your plans for months, but this isn't your clan. It's mine." She turned her finger on herself and jabbed her sternum. "They follow *my* order!"

He raised his hands and softened his tone. "I know." After a tentative step toward her, Cas continued, "Sometimes plans have to change. If my record has proven anything, it's that I know what I'm doing."

Ivy snorted, then crossed her arms over her chest. "What's so wrong with the original plan?" She turned her head and caught Patrick watching them. Her sea-green eyes narrowed before churning blood-red. "He killed your mate. The plan was to kill *his*."

"No," Patrick grunted, drawing Cas' attention. Short, panicked breaths left him as he shook his head and stared Cas down. "No."

Cas eyed him up and down. Pain and fury sharpened his features and he closed the distance between them. With each step Cas took, silver claimed the green in his eyes. He stopped a couple of feet away. Patrick wanted to lunge at him. To take him down before he could cause Violet or anyone else he cared about more harm. But even the thought of tugging against the chains that held him captive was exhausting.

He watched as Cas came to the same conclusion. It was clear as day. His silver gaze darted from Patrick's head to his bare chest, down to his feet, and then back up before he glanced at the chains. The silver faded from his gaze and a smirk rose to his lips. Confidence and condescension oozed from him when he leaned toward Patrick.

"Don't worry," Cas chuckled darkly. "We realized she's far too valuable."

Alistair reared his weary head, a weak snarl whispering in Patrick's head, and he tugged against the chains. The ones attached to the wall rattled... a little. But his limbs shook from the effort, and a huff of air left him before his legs gave out. His shoulders groaned in agony as his body sagged, suspended by the chains attached to the ceiling.

"Not anymore," snapped Ivy.

Drawing both male's attention once more.

Cas' pleased expression turned cold and he twisted to glare at the woman. "What do you mean?"

"Violet *was* valuable. Before we found out she's a freaking lycan!" Ivy snapped.

She pointed at Topher who'd just entered the room and was making his way toward Patrick with another vial of poison clenched in his fist. "The only reason Dev is on our side is because he turned years ago."

"We can persuade her," Cas argued.

"Absolutely not. Do you have any idea how hard it is to take down a lycan?"

Cas snorted. "It's not my fault you waited too long to grab her. She would have been a lot easier before she turned."

Ivy's voice pitched. "You didn't bring her in when Zander had her!"

"How exactly was I supposed to do that?" Cas growled and stepped toward her as Topher blocked Patrick's line of sight. "I had both Zander and Patrick already. There was no way I was going to be able to handle all three of them."

The pop of a cap caught Patrick's attention. He tried to pull away when Topher reached for him, but the fully healthy lycan easily snatched his arm and held it still. The needle slipped into Patrick's arm, making his nose scrunch. It burned and the liquid fire that remained in his veins reignited. He clenched his teeth, growling as it flooded his senses, making his thoughts cloudy.

There was no fighting this. Patrick lowered his head, succumbing to the pain that would envelop him in a matter of seconds. But Topher abruptly released his arm. Patrick started to lift his head, but a large hand kept it down... Anger pulsed through Patrick until his eyes focused on the syringe in Topher's other hand. Milky white liquid still filled half the vial. His brows creased, but the fury drained from his body. Slowly, he attempted to raise his head again. This time, Topher allowed him to. When their gazes locked, the older lycan put a finger to his lips.

Confusion pinched Patrick's brows together as Topher walked away. Half a dose. Why would he do that? What would it do at this point?

"Your plans have failed," Ivy accused.

Patrick's attention snapped back to her, but his mind was starting to slip away. This was important. A divide was happening. He needed to stay conscious.

"No," Cas defended. "They've just changed."

"Maybe you knew all along she was lycan."

"No one knew she was lycan!" Cas nearly shouted. "She was born to two wolven!"

"Then perhaps your feelings are getting in the way." Ivy's lullaby voice smoothed out, making her threatening tone all the more creepy. "Maybe you want her for yourself. It wouldn't be the first time you came to me over a supposed mate."

A low snarl rolled through the room before Cas said, "I had a mate. I'm not looking for another."

Patrick's hearing grew warbled. He only caught bits and pieces of the next thing that was said.

"You can't... choice... kill him... or her."

Panic settled in his mind as his vision blurred. He tried to reach through the small void in his mind that connected him to Violet. He tried to picture her smile and smell her Christmas cookie scent... but the bond was silent. His chin dropped to his chest as the sedative won and the fire consumed him.

Chapter 5

Violet

"Geeze, you hit hard!" *Jax seethed, taking a couple of steps back and shaking* out his padded hand.

A ribbon of glee spiraled through Violet. "Sorry," she muttered and tried to hide the growing smirk tugging at the corner of her lips.

"Pfft, no you're not." He rolled his shoulders and threw the pads on the ground, uncovering his fists. If it weren't for the hint of a smile tugging at his mouth, she would have thought her twin was mad at her. "You're gloating."

He lunged for her, but she ducked away. "Am not."

"Are too." Jax swung again, and she batted his hand away like it was a fly. A fly that had a really good cross jab. "You're fast too, ya know."

Violet nodded after delivering a flat-palmed strike to his chest. "Yeah, I've noticed my speed has increased, too."

Jax's face pinched and he rubbed his chest. He let out a shallow grunt, then nodded his head.

Worry pulled Violet out of her fight stance. "Are you okay?"

She'd never had to be worried about hurting anyone before, but these abilities were brand new. They hadn't had time to test her limits yet, and she had no idea how to control them or hold herself back. She'd nearly ripped her bedroom door off its hinges that morning.

A mocking expression fell over her brother's face. "Really? I train with Patrick, too, sis."

"Yes, but Patrick knows how to hold back." Violet wrung her hands in front of her. "And... I'm apparently a lycan now."

Jax's brows pulled together in confusion, but he stayed quiet. One of his hands raised and beckoned her forward. "Again."

They threw a few more punches and Jax let out a tense breath when her knuckles grazed his cheek.

"I think you're faster than Patrick."

She groaned. 'Cause she really needed one more thing to make her weird. Being stronger and faster than the guy you liked was definitely up there. "And again, *lycan*." She indicated to herself.

Jax paused and his readied stance eased a fraction. "Am I missing something?"

Sudden anger burned through her, and she delivered two hits to his stomach before smacking him over the head. Bam. Bam. Thwap! He staggered a step, then shook his head out and released a huff of a laugh.

"I don't know, Jax," Violet bit. "You mean other than your ability to block?"

Rubbing the spot on his head where she'd smacked him, Jax said, "Take it easy, okay? I've always had to restrain myself whenever we sparred. It's an adjustment." His arm lowered to his side again. "Keep hitting me like that though and I'm gonna snap out of it real quick."

"Good," Violet snapped.

Her next series of attacks were mostly dodged, but there were a few that grazed against her brother. A brush against his shoulder here, a glance across his ribs there, and he blocked her so solidly well on a couple of attacks that she was sure her bones would have broken a week ago.

Slightly labored breathing left Jax when he stepped away. "Better." After another breath, he nodded and she moved into step with him again. "You know about Patrick's past, right?"

"I know why Alistair is the way he is," she danced around the answer in case there was anyone listening who didn't know.

That line returned between Jax's eyebrows. She'd seen that line grow deeper since Vikter had led his final attack against the Sentinel Clan. Since her twin had become alpha.

"What?" She asked, tossing her arms to the side when he continued to stare at her.

He attacked first this time and she barely missed a kick to her ribs. His foot breezed through the loose fabric around her waist. Her momentary surprise was rewarded with a flat-palmed attack to her chest—a mirror of her earlier strike. Whatever she might have been, it didn't stop the sting or keep her on her feet.

Her butt hit the matt ungracefully while she struggled to breathe.

"Ow." She wheezed, slowly making her way to her feet. "Guessing you weren't holding back on that one?"

Jax's lips tipped up in a smile. "Yeah, it's getting easier."

"Good for you," she grunted.

"Do you know how Alistair appeared?" Jax threw a few punches for her to block.

She did. Then bounced on her toes a bit while contemplating his question. "What do you mean? Like how old he was?"

"Nooo." Jax attacked again. "That he's lycan."

Violet froze and his left hook slammed into her face. Her vision went black and she dropped to one knee. He swore under his breath and strong hands were on her shoulders a moment later as her vision cleared.

She held up a hand to stop him when he opened his mouth. "I'm okay."

His gaze narrowed. "Really?"

"Yeah." She tipped her head back and forth, but other than the blinding pain for a second, she didn't feel any lingering effects. "Really. I'm fine."

"You really didn't know?"

"Why would I have known that?"

"With everything you've seen. With everything you've been through with him. With everything he has shared with you?"

"He didn't share that!"

"I'm gonna kill him."

"No. You're not." She sighed and held a hand out to him. He hauled her to her feet and stared at her, fury churning the gold in his eyes. "Maybe he thought I already knew. Or had figured it out. I..." She remembered how her father's say didn't have much of a hold on Patrick. How he was stronger and faster than every member of the clan. His control over Alistair... but... he *had* Alistair. Lycan's didn't have a wolf spirit. She shook her head. "He can't be. Alistair—"

"We don't know how that happened, either, but he is definitely lycan." Jax interrupted and then watched her cautiously. "Are you okay?"

"Okay?" She let out a rough laugh and put her hands on her head as her chest constricted. "How could any of us be okay, right now?"

Tension settled over him. "That's not what I meant."

She held out a hand when he stepped closer to her. "I know. I just..." Tears lined her eyes. "If he's lycan then where is he?"

"Violet..."

"No! He would have been able to resist Dad, so why did he leave? Why hasn't he answered his phone? Where is he when everything is falling apart?" Her voice grew louder and louder with each word, combating the rising din of voices in the training center. Finally, she clamped her hands over her ears. "Will everyone just be quiet!"

She seethed through her teeth when they grew louder—more insistent. Angry, and ready to pick a fight, she snapped her gaze around the room. Many clan members had stopped sparring to stare at her, but none of them were talking. Her head began to throb. The anger faded away as more and more voices filled the room... no. Not the room. Her mind. She fell to her knees, clutching her head.

"Violet!" Jax rushed toward her, crashing to his knees in front of her, but he sounded so far away. Like trying to communicate with cans tied together by string.

So many voices. Too many voices.

Warriors on patrol reported to their superiors while they followed the clan boundary. Other warriors at Lockup were having a snarky conversation while they stood outside the doors. Someone was complaining to their friend about a bad hair day. And a ferocious blush burned her cheeks when a rather private conversation between mates and plans for the evening flitted quickly through her mind. But the worst were the thoughts of those in the training center with her. Watching her. Judging her.

Strong. Angry. Loud.

"What's wrong with her?"

"She should be in Lockup."

"I can't believe Jax allows her around everyone like this."

"VIOLET!" Jax's voice cut through the pain like a knife through butter. The sheer volume chased away a few of the quieter voices. Their twin-link came together like two puzzle pieces being snapped into place. She clung to his half as if it were her lifeline and tugged, pulling his voice closer.

"Jax. What do I do?" She wasn't sure if she was speaking out loud or through their link, but it didn't matter as long as he could hear her. "So many voices... it hurts."

His fingers tightened against her shoulders. *"How many?" he asked.*

"So many." She shook her head. *"Too many."*

She thought he may have sworn out loud, but it was too hard to hear over the voices thundering in her head. It could have just been another wolven cursing in their mind.

"Focus on my voice," Jax instructed her. *"Tune out the rest like you tuned out Dad whenever he was mad at us."*

She snorted. *"You mean when he was mad at me."*

"Focus, Violet."

Even focusing on his voice alone was helping, but she tried to ignore the others like he said. It helped, but not as much as she would have liked. Finally, she had drowned out enough that the throbbing receded. She lowered her hands to her lap and her shoulders sagged under the weight of her sigh. "Thank you."

"Any time." Jax dropped one of his hands, but rubbed the other along her shoulders. "You okay?"

"I feel like someone threw an anvil at my head, but yeah. I'll be okay." She pinched her eyes shut and flinched when someone angrily screamed into the link. "I can still hear them."

When she opened her eyes again, Jax was staring at her with pinched eyebrows. "You're saying that like you can hear other people's conversations."

"I think I am," she shook her head, then caught the angered expression of a nearby clan member. Lowering her voice, she leaned toward Jax. "I think it might be the entire clan. Everyone who is speaking through the link."

"I..." Jax blinked, then let the hand that remained on her shoulders fall to his side. "I don't know what to say to that. I've only ever been able to hear who I'm directly talking to. Even when I make a clan-wide announcement, I can feel them, but I don't hear them."

She groaned. "Great. One more ability I don't know how to control."

"Patrick would know how to help you."

"But he isn't here."

"No..." Jax sighed. "He's not." He pulled out his phone and opened a note-taking app. There were a few things listed there already.

- transforms into white wolf – magically?
- Faster
- Stronger
- Better reflexes – tested by throwing a fake knife at her

Her knuckles collided with his shoulder and he fell to his butt in surprise. "That knife was fake?"

"Ow." He rubbed the spot she'd hit and then smirked at her. "You thought I threw a real knife at you? What if you hadn't dodged?"

"Then I'd probably be dead!"

He snorted and shook his head before his thumbs flew across the screen to add...

- Can hear the clan link—all of it?

"I'm sorry I can't help you more." He made his way to his feet, then pocketed his phone before offering a helping hand to her. "I keep the list to try and research what I can. You might not know this, but Dad kept some books in his office on lycan lore. I think he was researching Patrick."

A ripple of anger rolled up her spine. She tried to shake it off. Her father was mentally checked out and they had no idea what was going on with Patrick. It would do no good to hold on to such destructive emotions, but they clung to her and she anxiously shifted her weight while Jax snatched their bags from the mat.

"From what I've seen, they're mostly bogus, but I'm hoping that I'll find something useful soon."

"I need a lycan teacher, Jax." The bite in her tone made him turn a shocked expression her way and if she wasn't mistaken, there was an edge of hurt there as well. She tried to soften her voice and push down the anger still lingering inside of her before speaking again. "I appreciate everything you're doing, I really do, but I need help. I need Patrick. *We* need Patrick. Has there been any news?"

Jax's shoulders sank under the weight of his next breath. "No. His phone is still going straight to voicemail. None of my contacts outside the clan have seen him or have any clue as to his whereabouts. I even reached out to the Kings and Queens, but of course, they haven't responded."

"He left with his truck. He wouldn't dump it. He wouldn't give it to someone else to care for while he was gone. Someone else got a hold of it and drove it here. The question is, who and how did they get the keys to drive it? And where is he now?"

Her brother opted for silence while her mind spun out of control and she had to ignore the devil on her shoulder telling her to scream at him for not offering solutions.

"Jax, what if something happened to him? Would we even know? Would anyone know? Would..." The words lodged themselves in her throat and she swallowed hard to clear them. "Would I?"

Understanding softened Jax's features and he stepped into her space to wrap her into a hug. "We will find him, I promise."

Violet buried her face against her brother's shoulder, then added, "You know, we could use more lycans in this fight against Blood Moon, too."

A humorless laugh left Jax and he mussed her hair when he turned away to grab their bags. “How do you suppose we go about doing that?” He hoisted the shoulder straps of their bags over one shoulder and held his arm out toward the door. "It's not like they roll out the welcome wagon to any wolven passing by."

Violet led the way to the doors, pushing frustration and hurt down alongside the anger as she tried to ignore the uncomfortable stares of every clan member they passed. Her jaw clenched from the effort to ignore them. She was pretty sure that wasn't the definition of ignoring them, but it was the best she had... other than the ideas floating through her mind, and then she snapped her fingers. "Do you know where the lycan's are?"

He quirked a brow. "Only a general area, why?"

"That's better than nothing." She seized her bag from Jax' shoulder, then grinned. "I'm going to find them and bring them here."

"What? Violet, that's a horrible idea. By the time you find them, this battle with Blood Moon could be over, besides, I already told you they don't associate with wolven."

She nodded. "Yeah. But, I'm not wolven."

Chapter 6

Cas

***Anguish filled Cas' heart** as he stared at Lexie's unconscious form. She'd* fitfully fallen asleep about an hour ago, and only minutes had passed since she had slipped into a deep sleep. Her hair was matted from sweat and tears, but still managed to lay splayed about her head. Cas made a mental note to see if he could find a hairbrush for her... and a new set of clothes since hers had been reduced to tatters from shifting to and from wolf form for days.

"Think she is done shifting?" Cas' wolf spirit softly asked within his mind.

Cas' face pinched with concern.

He'd never witnessed what she was going through. Honestly, he was shocked she was still alive with the amount of times her body had ripped itself apart and pieced itself back together in a different form.

And every time he watched from the other side of the bars, his chest ached.

This wasn't what he had wanted.

And yet, he found himself sitting beside Lexie's cell more and more as Blood Moon planned and prepared their next attack. The power dynamic had shifted. Ivy wasn't interested in his plans anymore. Things were getting out of control, and he needed to find a way to fix it.

"How do we fix this, Abel?" Cas asked his wolf, but his inner beast only sighed.

Cas pulled his feet closer to his body so he could rest his arms over his knees. Someone had taken the chair that he'd put in there, leaving him to sit on the floor with his back against the wall. It wasn't the most uncomfortable position, but it did make it harder to stay awake. Falling off a chair was a much bigger motivator than slumping sideways.

When was the last time he'd slept?

He grumbled quietly to himself because he wasn't sure. If it weren't for his wolf half, he'd be passed out somewhere for sure.

Sleep didn't come easy in the Blood Moon boundaries, but returning to his apartment was out of the question. Ivy was dangerously suspicious of his feelings toward Violet and was convinced he was going to betray them. There was a target on his back and he would be lucky to make it out of this alive. But he'd known that when he first set out to recruit the Blood Moon pack in his plan for revenge.

There was a saying he was very familiar with... "He who seeks revenge digs two graves."

He had no idea who said it, but Cas was prepared to lose his life for his cause.

Lexie whimpered in her sleep and his brows pinched together.

"We have to find a way to get her out of this, Cas." Abel's voice was firm and held a note of conviction Cas hadn't heard in some time. He felt it, too. And maybe Cas wasn't as prepared to dig that second grave as he once was.

Chapter 7

Violet

Violet's feet stumbled over *a rock in the dirt path. She righted herself and* nodded to Jax when he asked if she was okay. Satisfied, her twin turned back to Dr. Penmann who was walking with them. The doctor eyed Violet briefly before brushing a hair out of her face and continuing her conversation with Jax.

The voices hadn't receded from Violet's mind and while the doctor was keeping a close eye on her, there wasn't much she could do for Violet. But focusing was growing increasingly difficult. Violet's lack of sleep didn't help either. It was hard to rest when she was hearing everyone's conversations. Didn't people sleep anymore? It took her a while to realize that while the majority of the clan was sleeping, there were still the warriors and guards who were on duty. They were plenty talkative.

It'd been two days. Two days of nonstop talking. Two days of a constant headache that often peaked into a migraine. Two days of hearing things she really didn't want to hear. Two days of...

"I don't think I can take another one today." Mya's sweet voice chased away all the other conversations and Violet froze in the middle of the path. *"Can you cover them?"*

Was Mya talking to her? She couldn't be. She didn't know Violet was unwillingly listening in on everyone. She hadn't told anyone besides Jax and the doc. She also hadn't tried speaking back to anyone because she felt like she was intruding even though it wasn't her choice to do so. People already thought she was enough of a freak; she didn't need them knowing she could hear their private conversations.

"Don't worry about it, honey," answered a gentle, mothering voice. *"I can finish up."*

Nope. Mya definitely wasn't talking to Violet. That motherly voice must have been Tucker's mom. Violet had been so excited when Jax had told her that Mya accepted the job, but sometimes her friend became overwhelmed and there were a couple of the clan members Mya couldn't bring herself to work with. They couldn't push her too hard without risking a relapse, so Tucker's mom had been asked to be a backup for Mya. The two of them together were exactly what the healing members needed. Between the two of them, they'd been able to help a few clan members return to their homes. The occupancy of Lockup was still high, but they were making progress.

Violet groaned when the cacophony of conversations seeped back into her thoughts and she started after Jax and Doc. They'd stopped and were watching her again. Always watching. Always waiting. Waiting for something to happen. She tucked some hair behind her ear, but stopped when the tips of her fingers slid up its tapered top.

Right, that's why she'd left her hair down today.

She quickly flattened her hair over her ear again. At least it was just the ears. Yesterday she had woken up with fangs, and getting her new lycan features to go away was a lot harder than she thought it should be. Thankfully her claws had not reappeared since her first transformation.

A conversation pitched louder, making Violet flinch when her head began to throb. She triple-checked that her mental walls were up, but they didn't help much. The best she'd done was muffle the constant hum as if they had a blanket thrown over them. Focusing in on one conversation like Jax and Doc had suggested didn't work because the conversations were typically short and ended quickly. The ones that were longer were the ones she was uncomfortable listening to, but even they ended eventually.

Violet mashed the heel of her hand against her forehead and rubbed.

The clan's former beta, Paul, had suggested that Jax confine her to her room or place her in Lockup. He accused her of being unstable and that she shouldn't be left unattended, especially around their brand new alpha. Jax had quickly reminded him that Paul was no longer the beta and that Violet was his sister. As the new alpha, Jax picked his own beta, but without Patrick around, Paul seemed to think the position was still his.

It didn't help that Jax was treating her like *she* was his beta... which was absurd.

Besides, the more Violet thought about what Paul had said, the more she believed him. She was as unstable as a ticking time bomb.

"Violet?"

Fingers wrapped around her arm and she seized the person's wrist before Jax grabbed her hand with his free one. "Easy."

She let out a rough breath as she released his wrist. "Sorry."

He rubbed his wrist and said, "It's okay."

She had stopped walking again. Disappointment dragged her shoulders down. "Sorry," she mumbled again.

An easy smile, that didn't reach Jax's eyes, stretched across his face. He rubbed the top of her head, scattering a few hairs into her face, before resting his elbow on her shoulder like he had years ago when he'd first made contact with Dalim and started growing like a weed. He'd grown a foot so rapidly that his bones had ached. While at the same time, Violet had stopped growing. Every day had felt like she was having to tip her head farther and farther back. The familiarity behind the gesture was odd now, especially with how distant he had been in the last year, but it still held some familial comfort.

"Stop apologizing," he told her. "You have a lot of new things you're dealing with."

"Ya, but at this rate it's going to take us an hour to get to Lockup." Violet tipped her head to the side to rest against her brother's arm. "I was really looking forward to seeing Mya today."

Dr. Penmann eyed the two of them and pinched her lips together. Finally, the older woman's gaze landed on Violet and she asked in her raspy voice, "No progress in blocking the other conversations?"

Disappointment flicked through Violet. She shook her head.

"Any ideas, Doc?" Jax asked, and the mischievous tone he used made Violet cast a side-eyed glare at him. That tone held the promise of a choke hold and a nasty noogie that would make knots in her already messed-up hair. He was just waiting for an invitation.

But the doc's sigh chased away Jax's playful antics and he froze beside Violet. "I'm sorry," she answered softly and absently rubbed at the edge of the scars striping her throat. "I wish I could be more helpful, but I don't know much about lycans. They make sure to keep it that way. I only know as much as I do because of working with Patrick, but he is a unique case. Lycan abilities present differently than ours. And even more unfortunate is that you are a unique case, too, Violet. Just as unique as Patrick, if not more. He is a lycan with a wolf spirit, which as far as I know, is unheard of—while you are a lycan born of two wolven. On top of that, you've only had your abilities for the better part of a week." Another sigh left her and she tucked her tablet under her arm. "Even with the knowledge I've learned... it isn't helpful in this instance."

"What isn't helpful?" a familiar male voice asked. The three of them turned to find former beta Paul trudging up the path toward them. Sunlight streaked across the silver hairs at his temples when he turned to gaze at each of them. "And why wasn't I invited to this little pow-wow?"

Jax turned to square his shoulders off with Paul, his arm falling away from Violet. "You weren't invited because there was nothing to invite you to. The doc is just updating me on the progress of the Clan House." He lifted an arm to gesture at the newly reframed building beside them. "But anyone can watch the progress from day to day."

Unease settled in the pit of Violet's stomach when Paul's eyes narrowed. "Of course. I'm only trying to help in whatever capacity I can."

"Of course." Jax's face remained void of emotion and Violet wondered when he had gained so much control.

A tense moment of silence passed between the four of them before Paul cleared his throat. "That being said, I would like to remind you of my previous advisement."

Jax's head dipped to the side. "What advice was that?"

Paul's gaze darted to Violet, then back to Jax. "About the company you keep during official meetings."

Tension rippled through the twin-link and Violet shifted her weight back and forth. Outwardly, Jax looked almost bored with the conversation, but if his emotions were leaking through their link, he had progressed more than she'd realized in his self-control.

"I'll say it again," Jax hesitated, his voice sounding a touch more restricted than before. When he spoke again, his tone had returned to being conversational. "You are no longer beta."

"You remind me of that fact often."

"Then why do you keep forgetting?"

"I'm only offering my help while you choose my... *replacement.*" The word held an undertone of resentment that Violet wondered if Paul had meant to share.

Jax clasped his hands behind his back and Violet watched as his knuckles blanched. "Patrick is my beta, Paul. You've known that for years."

"But he isn't even here," Paul scoffed.

"And I am working to fix that." Jax's voice rose a fraction, but the intensity behind his words made Paul take a step back and lower his gaze. "In the meantime, I will ask for your advice when it is needed. My sister and her whereabouts are not your concern."

Paul's hands curled into fists at his sides. "If she is a danger to the clan, she absolutely is my concern."

"Enough," Dr. Penmann snapped in her raspy, slightly airy tone. "Do you honestly believe I would be so careless with such a diagnosis? Do you think that if I believed Violet to be a threat of any kind, that I wouldn't advise Jax? Honestly, Paul." She shook her head and her gaze was saddened. "You've allowed poisonous talk to cloud your judgment. All you know about Violet is what Noah spewed in your direction, and I can guarantee you have the wrong girl if you're looking to peg that description on someone."

Violet's sudden anger at Paul's declaration had nowhere to go and she didn't know what to do with it. It built in her chest, burning her from the inside out. She closed her eyes and pinched her brows together while she attempted to will the powerful emotion away. A shoe scuffed on the ground and her eyes snapped open.

The world was in hyper-focus. Silver bled into the edges of Paul's weathered, hard brown eyes while a vein began to bulge along his forehead that was dotted with tiny beads of sweat and the rancid salty stench wafted up Violet's nostrils. Her gaze dropped to Paul's throat when he swallowed. She heard it; the moist sound of saliva being forced down a dry throat. Unfortunately, Violet was not nearly as practiced at hiding her emotions as Jax and her face twisted into a disgusted mask before she could stop it.

"I see." Paul finally spoke, allowing Violet the chance to pull herself together. Her eyesight returned to normal while he added, "Thank you for your candor, Doc." He turned as if he were about to leave, but then looked at Jax again. "Just remember, *young* alpha, your father would never have let her be privy to clan business."

Jax nodded. "As the doctor just said, when it comes to Violet, you only know what my father told you." He closed the distance between them and Dalim's growl came through his next words, "For your sake, it's a good thing I am not my father. He would not have tolerated your actions as well as I have."

Paul's olive complexion paled, and he softly said, "I am not the only one who's questioning your choices. Be wary of that."

No one said another word until Paul was a good distance down the road. You couldn't be too careful with how heightened wolven hearing was.

"Why did you tell him I was giving you an update on the Clan House?" Dr. Penmann asked, sounding tired. She rubbed at her temple and briefly closed her eyes. "We were discussing the gate."

Jax ruffled the top of Violet's hair when he was within reach, then looked at the doctor. "That's what we *were* discussing. Now you're going to update me on the Clan House."

"Hmm." Doc narrowed her eyes momentarily then lightly snorted and flicked through something on her tablet. "You should be more careful with Paul. He has a lot of knowledge on how the clan was run. He could be a huge asset to you."

"I know, but he has to learn that I am not my father and treating Violet that way will not be tolerated."

"You're pushing for a lot of change really quickly, Jax."

"I know, but until..."

Their words grew fuzzy and the overwhelming urge to go to bed hit Violet like a truck. She hadn't been sleeping well, but this was something else. Dryness coated her mouth and her limbs ached. The burning in her chest from before turned to throbbing pain in pinpointed spots across her torso. Violet rubbed her wrists feeling phantom pains from when Zander had kidnapped her and her skin had been rubbed raw from the ties he'd kept her in. The tips of her fingers went numb and then her knees gave out.

"Violet!" Jax caught her before she hit the ground. "Are you okay? What's going on? Is it the voices?"

She clutched his arms, steadying herself while her senses slowly returned to her and all that was left was a sharp pain in her skull. "It's okay. I'm okay." She patted his shoulder. "Also, when you say 'the voices' like that, it makes me sound like a crazy person."

"Wolven only hear voices when they connect to the clan-link on purpose. You don't do any of that on purpose, so maybe you are crazy," he teased.

Violet smacked his shoulder, but the effort was halved and he gave her a look that said, "Really?"

"I think I'm just tired."

Nodding, Jax wrapped an arm around her waist. "I'll walk you."

"No. I can do it." Violet tried to push out of her brother's hold, but she felt like she was back to being a suped-up human because he didn't budge.

Dr. Penmann was watching them closely, her gaze narrowed as her faded gray eyes darted over Violet's body. What she was looking for, Violet had no idea. She wasn't any different than before.

"Violet, you almost collapsed in the middle of the road and we weren't even moving." Jax argued. "I'm walking you home."

"I'll have one of my nurses meet you there with a light sedative." Dr. Penmann informed her. When Violet opened her mouth to protest, the doc held up a hand to stop her. "I insist. You need rest and I'm assuming your new abilities have made that difficult."

Violet allowed a small smile to lift the corners of her mouth. It was nice to have people on her side. "Okay, but only a small sedative."

The doc smiled, too. "Of course."

Jax turned them toward Alpha House and Violet wriggled in his hold. "I can walk on my own."

"Can you stand on your own?"

"Jaaax."

Purple eyes identical to her own glared down at her. "Why didn't you tell me it was this bad?"

She tugged at his fingers clenching her waist. "It hasn't been. I've just been tired and having a hard time focusing. I don't know what that was. It was like..." Unsure how to describe it, Violet shook her head.

"Like what?"

"I-I..." She grumbled and shook her head. "I don't know! Like my body was remembering what it was like to be held captive by Zander, but I don't remember having pain across my torso like I'd been stabbed."

Jax gave her that 'really' look again and added a raised brow to it. "You don't know what being stabbed feels like."

"So having Patrick's claw dig into my back didn't count?"

Jax's features relaxed and his eyes darted back and forth as if he were reading something or putting the puzzle pieces of a clue together. "Violet, what if you weren't feeling *you*?"

"Huh?" Violet's face scrunched in confusion while she pried Jax's fingers off her waist. "You lost me."

"No, he's right." Dr. Penmann came to stand beside them again. "I'm sorry to butt in, but we are going the same direction so..." She waved a dismissive hand. "That's beside the point. Violet, it is possible for mates to sometimes feel what the other is feeling. It's usually brought on by a heightened state or emotion. If we are to assume you are Patrick's mate..."

Violet's breathing hitched. "But that would mean..."

"No wonder we haven't found any trace of him." Jax muttered a curse under his breath and Dr. Penmann sent him a disapproving look. "It was weird when he didn't come back after finding you. Even more weird when his truck showed up with Zander's body and a note from Cas. I have been hoping this whole time that Patrick was off somewhere, living away from all of this, but I was fooling myself. Cas has Patrick."

"No." Violet wrapped her arms around her waist as if she could hold all of her new heightened emotions and feelings inside herself, but they were leaking through her arms and between her fingers. She was about to combust. "Blood Moon has Patrick. Cas is working with Blood Moon."

"But how did they get to him?"

"Patrick is a hard person to take down." Doc shook her head. "I don't think Cas could have done that on his own."

"Unless he played dirty. He fooled us all into thinking he cared about this clan... about Violet."

Violet closed her eyes and tried to shut out their conversation. Even hearing the rest of the clan's conversations would be better than what was happening right in front of her. Sound swirled around itself like it was being sucked through a tube until there was none left. Violet doubled over and her knees hit the ground. Fingers curled around her shoulders.

"Help." A raspy, quiet cough filled her ears, drowning her senses.

Violet's head bobbed when someone shook her.

"Someone. Help," cried that same soft, child-like voice. A wave of coughs followed.

Violet turned her gaze up the hill. There. Just outside the tree line, but almost out of sight from Clan House, where they had deposited the remaining rubble of the old building. She shoved against the person holding her shoulders and sprinted up the hill.

"Help."

"I'm coming!" Violet called, but it sounded weird in her ears. Like they were plugged and needed to pop. "I'm coming!"

She reached the pile of rubble faster than she thought possible and started looking into the heap from the outskirts.

Jax appeared in the corner of her eye, panting. "Violet, what's going on?"

She watched her brother for a moment. Did he really not hear the cry? "Someone is trapped in here. They need our help. I think it's a child."

"Violet, I don't hear anything." Jax held out a hand like he was trying to calm a dangerous animal. "Come on. Let's go home. Doc will help you sleep and you'll feel better when you wake up."

"I'm not crazy, Jax!"

He shook his head, but the fear in his eyes betrayed his next words. "I didn't say you were."

Hot tears burned her eyes and blurred her vision as she peered back into the rubble. "Hello?" She called, desperate for a voice to answer her. "I'm here!"

She and Jax froze. The longer they waited, the more tears fell down her cheeks. "I'm not crazy," she whispered. "I'm not."

"Violet..." Jax wrapped a long arm around her shoulders and pulled her into a hug. "Let's get you home."

She allowed Jax to turn her back toward Alpha House and lifted her feet to follow. It was just lack of sleep, she kept telling herself. She just needed a little more sleep.

"Hello?" Called a small voice and both Violet and Jax spun around. "Are you still there?"

Jax looked from the rubble to Violet and back again, "I-uh-yes! We're here!"

"Where are you?" Violet called, her voice warbled with the wave of tears that now ran down her face from relief. Jax heard it too.

"I'm stuck."

Violet's gaze snapped to a spot in the rubble. "Keep talking. We'll find you."

"It's hard to talk."

"You gotta try," Jax encouraged. "What's your name?"

"Bailey," whimpered the girl and Violet followed the sound like someone pulling her in with rope. "We were just playing."

"I know, Bailey." Jax mirrored Violet's movements on the opposite side of the rubble. "You're not in trouble, but can you tell me how you got in there?"

"My friends..." the girl's voice broke. "I fell and they left me here."

"Those don't sound like very good friends."

"Jax!" Violet hissed and he raised his arms up like he didn't know what he'd done wrong.

He sighed. "Or maybe they are and they were just scared. Maybe they ran for help." He looked up at the sky and Violet followed his gaze. The sun was setting. It was getting dark.

"They left a long time ago."

Violet paused when she saw something unusual in the rubble. "Okay, Bailey, I need you to look up for me."

The unusual mound shifted and Violet's vision cleared. It was a head of hair, and one arm was trapped above her. Slowly, the girl managed to tip her head back and Violet smiled when she saw the girl's precious, big round brown eyes. "I found you."

An ear-splitting scream made Violet clamp her hands over her head.

"Bailey!" Jax appeared at Violet's side and he held his hands toward the little girl. "It's okay! You're safe!"

"A-alpha Jax?"

A soft smile lit Jax's face. "Yeah. It's me. This is my sister, Violet."

"Why are her eyes like that?"

Violet's gaze darted to Jax who grinned up at her before he chuckled. "She's special. She was using her abilities to find you. Her eyes glow like that sometimes when she's trying really hard."

"Glow?" Violet asked, but Jax ignored her.

"Okay, Bailey. We're gonna get you out of there, now."

It took a few minutes and Jax called in some other wolven, along with the girl's parents and Dr. Penmann, but Bailey was free in a matter of minutes once everyone was there and ready. Dr. Penmann checked over the girl who Violet guessed couldn't have been more than six, and she overheard the doctor's conversation with the parents.

"She has some bruised ribs and minor cuts and scrapes, but those will heal quickly. She's a lucky girl."

Violet paced back and forth waiting for Jax to be done with his alpha duties. When he approached her, she glared at him. "You thought I had lost it."

He shook his head.

"Don't lie to me."

Jax sighed. "I don't know how all of this is affecting you. You don't talk about it unless I press the issue and you happen to be in a talkative mood. For all I know, you could be slowly slipping away, just like Zander did."

"Zander didn't slip away. He left and came back a different person."

"Violet—"

"No!" She crossed her arms in a huff. "I am scared enough as it is. I don't know what's happening to me. I can't control any of it. I have one pointy ear today. Just one! I need someone to believe in me. Someone who won't look at me like I'm a ticking time bomb even though that's exactly what I am."

Sorrow dragged Jax's mouth into a frown. "You're not a ticking time bomb."

"I am. If I don't figure out how to control all of this. Or how to tame these overwhelming emotions and urges... I don't know what will happen."

Jax looked at the ground and put his thumbs in his pockets. "I'm sorry I don't know how to help you."

"But maybe a lycan can."

His gaze snapped to hers once again. "We don't exactly have those in spades around here, Violet."

She nibbled on her lower lip then stepped toward him. "Then I'll go find them."

Surprised, Jax jerked his head back. "What? Violet, that's not..."

"We know about where they are. I can go start looking for them. You can keep me updated on how things are going here. I need answers and we need help against Blood Moon. We can't go up against them by ourselves."

"We won't be." Jax started pacing between two trees. "I was going to tell you when we got home, but I've been in contact with the other local alphas. We're going to pool our resources and numbers together. Sentinel Clan is about to become a base of operations while we prepare for our final fight against Blood Moon."

"See! Then we definitely need the lycans!"

"And what if you don't find them? We need you here, too!"

"I'll be back before the first strike. You'll make sure of it in your updates to me. You can tell me how things are progressing. I'll have plenty of time to make it back."

"Violet..."

"Jax!" She shouted, drawing his full attention again. "Let me do this. I'm asking you, my brother, not my alpha. Let me go get us some more help. Let me find a way to tip the odds in our favor."

Tension edged every aspect of her twin while he ran her words through his head. Finally, his fists eased and he shook his head while a resigned sigh left him. "Looks like we have a road trip to prepare you for." Violet darted across the space between them and threw her arms around his neck. He laughed as he stumbled back a couple of steps, then patted her back. "*After* you get a full night's rest. You can pack in the morning and leave after nightfall tomorrow." He mussed her hair and she pulled away to fix it.

"Think Patrick will mind if I take his truck?" Violet asked.

Jax smiled. "Not at all."

Chapter 8

Patrick

The ache in Patrick's *shoulders pulled him from a foggy slumber. He needed* to get his feet under him. He needed to relieve the pressure on his shoulders. With a herculean effort, he managed to lift his head, but it lolled to the side and then his chin hit his chest once more.

Two more times and he was awake enough to realize he was sitting down. Someone had returned his chair. He was grateful for the generosity amongst those who clearly had none, but that also meant he was probably due for more torture under Ivy's hands. His chest had been riddled with three more marks than the last time he woke up, at least awake enough to remember anyway.

Seconds passed in drugged confusion before he looked at the chains keeping him captive. Whoever had designed them, knew what they were doing. The chains from the ceiling made it difficult to use any momentum or leverage to break them and the ones around his ankles attached to the walls at his sides... almost. He was tucked into a corner so it wasn't exactly at his sides, but it made it so he couldn't get a running start or back up enough to kick. Not that he had the energy to kick.

Actually—he did have more energy than he normally did when he came to. Curiosity called his gaze to look around the room. The *empty* room. He hadn't seen the room be empty even for a moment since they'd dragged him in there. His vision was a little hazy, but nothing like before.

Before...

Why would it be different this time?

Before...

Half a syringe.

Topher.

Or as Blood Moon liked to call him, *Dev*. The older lycan had only given Patrick half a dose last time. Did Topher really keep it a secret? If so... Blood Moon wasn't expecting Patrick to be waking up right now. He tipped his head back and looked at the chains above him. If only he could get enough leverage... but would he be strong enough?

A familiar presence pressed against his thoughts.

"Alistair?" Patrick called to his stronger half.

"Did you just question our strength?"

Surprising relief nearly brought tears to Patrick's eyes. He hadn't heard his darker half in days. Or had it been weeks? Without windows he had no reference of how much time had passed.

"Aw, shucks. I didn't know you cared so much." Alistair mocked.

"I don't."

"Your thoughts are my thoughts, Boy Scout. You can't hide from me."

"Whatever," Patrick grumbled. *"Are you ready to get out of here?"*

"Stand up and give me the reins." Alistair's growl was full of menace. It promised death to any who got in their way. *"I'll show you how ready I am."*

Patrick hesitated. He wasn't strong enough to take control back if Alistair refused to relinquish it.

"Boy Scout, I'm not strong enough to hold onto it, either." Alistair's voice was a mirror of Patrick's own, if his voice were permanently marred by a growl, but Alistair sounded weary. They'd both been suffering. *"We can get back to fighting each other if we get out of here."*

"Don't you mean when *we get out of this?"*

"No. I meant if."

The final note in Alistair's tone made Patrick uneasy. His darker half was always confident. It was unnerving to hear him be unsure.

An annoyed growl filled Patrick's mind. *"We're wasting time."*

Drawing in a deep breath, Patrick leaned forward and pressed his feet into the floor. If he thought lifting his head earlier was a herculean task, that was nothing compared to this. Tremors took hold of his entire body and his breathing rapidly increased from the effort to stand. But, the added height allowed his arms to bend and Patrick grinned.

"Leverage." He and Alistair said together, then Alistair added, *"Look."*

Patrick forced his eyes to focus on the shackle bound around his right wrist. In the first link, only noticeable if you were looking for it, was a chip in the metal. It looked like it was made recently and a thin, hairline crack zigzagged after it.

"Looks like someone started our escape for us," Alistair observed as he made his way to the forefront of Patrick's mind and Patrick imagined himself taking a step back.

His arms raised high above his head, shoulders protesting against the movement. His weight shifted as he rose up on his toes. Alistair extended his body as far as it could go before dropping back into his heels, bending his knees, and curling his body inward. Blinding white pain tore through his wrists. He clenched his jaw so he wouldn't cry out loud—or maybe Alistair had.

Either way, it burned. It ached. And when Patrick was able to see again, he found blood dripping from under the cuffs where they had sliced into his flesh. He held his trembling hands in front of him, staring at the tips of his numb fingers.

"I wouldn't move those," Alistair advised. *"I felt bones break in your wrists. Give it a minute. We'll heal."*

"You don't know that! Broken bones? Geez, Alistair!"

"We're free aren't we?" The wolf snapped.

Patrick blinked and realized he was indeed staring at his hands that were now low in front of him. Not hanging above his head. The shackles remained, but the chains had been broken. He looked up to find the long chains swinging aimlessly, no longer attached to his body.

"Alistair... that drug..."

"I know!" He snapped, just as aware as Patrick was that it would hinder their healing ability.

And yet... His pointer finger twitched. That didn't hurt. He tested each finger, groaning deeply when he found the ones that hurt. One. Two. Four. Six. Six of his fingers hurt to move. Hurt, but it was still possible.

Patrick's gaze drifted down to his ankles. Breaking the chains that were holding his arms had been worse because there was one arm for each. Using both hands on one chain... His head dipped to the side as he thought about it. Yeah, that would be very doable.

"Not yet." Alistair pulled on the controls, holding Patrick's body still. *"We need to heal."*

"We don't know how long that'll take," Patrick argued. *"We don't know how long we have until someone comes in here."*

When Alistair didn't chime in again and he felt the hold on his body relax, Patrick bent down to grab the chain, but his hand hovered over the forged metal. There, in the fourth link away from his foot was another chunk missing. The pad of his finger snagged a little when he brushed over it. Someone definitely wanted him to escape.

Warning bells went off in his head and he launched himself up. His hazel eyes darted around the room, landing on the doors, and froze. *"This is a trap. It has to be."*

"Trap or not, it's our best chance of getting out of here. We are smarter than they are, or at least I am"

Patrick snorted.

"*We can get out of this."*

With a heavy sigh, Patrick lowered himself again and grabbed the chain. It took more time than either he or Alistair would have liked. They were already weakened and the pain in Patrick's hands and wrists was pure agony. When the second chain finally broke he fell onto his back and drew in long deep breaths.

"We have to move, Boy Scout."

Patrick nodded, took two more breaths, then rolled to his feet—much less gracefully than he was used to. He got stuck halfway up and had to roll to his knees to finish standing.

"That was beautiful," mocked Alistair.

"Shut up," Patrick griped out loud as he made his way away from the door.

"Um, where are you going?"

"There has to be another way out of here," he explained.

"Hey genius, I'm pretty sure they picked this room because there is only one way in and out."

Patrick ignored him and continued to the darkest corner of the room. The heavy copper scent of pennies made his nose scrunch. He turned his head and stared. Instead of pennies, bodies were piled in the corner of the room. Bloodied, broken bodies. He recognized a couple of the faces. They were the wolven who had lined the room every time he woke up. That couldn't be all of them, but some. One person couldn't have taken them all down.

"What about a lycan?" Alistair suggested.

"You think Topher would have done that?"

"I don't know, but someone helped us. Either to lure us into a trap to kill us or to help us escape. Either way, I think the same person who killed them cut our chains."

Patrick agreed. It made sense, while at the same time, none of this made sense.

Why would Topher help him? Why would anyone in Blood Moon help him? They had to know he killed one of their daughters. Ivy's face materialized in his mind. She looked similar to one of the girls who'd been in the car with him.

Alistair snarled. *"We don't have time for this! Move, Patrick!"*

Heeding his orders, Patrick returned his attention to the dark corner he'd been limping toward. In the far corner, out of eyesight from where he'd been chained, there was another door. "Told you."

He seized the handle, grimacing when his bones complained, and pushed. It didn't budge. He shoved again and it opened a little, but was met with a moan of pain. Alistair flooded his senses and they both asked in a growly voice, "Who's in there?"

A wet cough answered him, followed by shallow breathing. Red-stained fingers curled around the base of the door and Patrick released it so the person on the other side could open it. Blood splattered the scarred face of Topher, who slouched against the wall on the floor.

"Glad you got..." He released another wet cough. "... my message."

Patrick shoved the door open the rest of the way, then knelt beside the older man. His eyes tracked the blood across Topher's face, before getting hung up on the black veins peeking over his collar.

"Shouldn't be long now." Topher struggled for another breath. He coughed again and his hand clenched his side where blood was seeping through his fingers.

"You're dying," Patrick stated, not sure how he should feel for the man before him. The man who he'd known years ago. The man who had betrayed his kind and joined Blood Moon.

"Ah." Topher winced. "So, the prince noticed."

Patrick shook his head. He'd always hated being called that. A quick look around told him they were in some kind of office. It was small, dark, and his vision still wasn't the greatest, but he could make out the shape of a desk with a chair seated behind it and a couple of bookshelves. "Where's the antidote?"

"There's no antidote here." Topher sucked in a sharp breath. "Ivy never intended there to be an antidote."

"Then we'll get you one when we get out of here."

"What?" Alistair chimed in while Topher tried to shake his head.

"I'll be dead soon. Go while you still can. It took you longer to wake up than I was hoping."

"So it was you."

A weak smile stretched across the unmarred cheek. He pointed toward the desk. "There's a tunnel behind that bookshelf. Ivy never let us use it, but kept the entrance on the other side guarded. They won't be expecting you."

Patrick liked the sound of that. He didn't know how many he could take on in his condition. "How many?"

Topher huffed a laugh, but ended up wheezing. "If they followed orders. Three. Armed with poison-tipped daggers."

"Where does this tunnel let out?"

"Close to the Northwest border." Topher waved a hand in that general direction. "Keep going West. You'll hit a road."

Patrick nodded, but instead of moving to leave, he watched Topher a little longer. "Why? Why are you helping me? Why now?"

"Tell the clan I'm sorry." Moisture lined Topher's eyes. "I was so angry. They abandoned me when I needed them most. He was my best friend." Emotion clogged his throat, choking off his words. It took a few breaths before he continued. "It-it was an accident. They didn't listen. All they saw was red eyes. They threw me out."

Old pain lanced through Patrick's chest. He knew exactly how that felt, but he'd been young enough that his father had tried to find someone to take him in. Someone who was willing to watch him and give him a chance. But he'd still been banished. They never gave him a chance to see if he could handle the side effects or not.

Topher snagged Patrick's arm, making him jump. "Show them. Show them they were wrong. And then... tell them. Tell them I never stopped fighting. Tell them, I wanted to come home." Tears rolled down Topher's cheeks. His words were growing softer and more airy. "Then, make sure this doesn't happen to anyone else." He struggled for another breath, removing his hand from Patrick's arm to wrap lightly around the base of his own throat. The black veins were nearly to his jaw now, but he managed one last word. "Go."

Blood oozed from Topher's side when he moved his trembling hand to reach into his pocket. His face was tense as he pulled something from the fabric and slapped it into Patrick's hand. He gave a final squeeze of his hand, then aggressively pointed to the bookshelf.

Patrick nodded, pocketed the item, and moved. He shoved against the side of the bookshelf and thanked the goddess that the pain in his hands and wrists was minimal now. He hesitated when the tunnel opening gaped before him and stood with his palms planted on either side. Topher was struggling for another breath.

"Go, Boy Scout." Alistair's voice was surprisingly gentle. *"He wants you to go.*

There's nothing we can do for him now."

But there was.

Patrick shoved away from the tunnel and hurried over to Topher who looked at him with wild, panicked, ruby eyes. Even as he struggled to breathe, he pointed to the tunnel.

"No," Patrick told him, then grabbed the sides of the man's face. Topher seized Patrick's wrists in a vice-like grip, but Patrick held firm. He tried to soften his expression as much as possible, and keep the emotion from his voice, while he said, "Let me do this for you."

Topher's eyebrows pinched together before understanding dawned and his features softened. The red faded from his eyes. He took in one last pitiful breath, released Patrick's wrists, and nodded.

It was over with one sharp twist.

And silence fell.

Patrick gently laid Topher's body on the floor and then brushed a hand over the man's eyes to close them.

Slowly, sound returned to Patrick's ears. *"Thank you, Alistair."*

The wolf grunted, but his words were softer than usual when he spoke, *"I couldn't let you be the only noble one."*

"Still. Thank you for saving me from hearing that sound for the rest of my life."

"It's not gonna be much of a life if you don't get moving!" Alistair snapped and flooded Patrick's body with his power, propelling him toward the tunnel. *"Move!"*

Patrick hurried into the cooler temperature of the dark tunnel and descended a flight of stairs. Once the ground leveled out, he pulled the item Topher had given him from his pocket as he hurried down the tunnel and almost laughed when he saw the bloody flip phone in his palm. He flicked his thumb under the top piece and it popped open, lighting the screen. The battery was low, but it would survive one phone call. He punched in the number with his thumbs while he kept moving. If Topher's intel was correct and this tunnel really did let out close to the border, he was going to be walking for a while.

The screen flashed when he hit the call button.

No signal.

Patrick groaned. He'd have to call once he made it out of the tunnel.

"Then let's move." Alistair urged him to go faster, lending Patrick his abilities.

The sound of conversation met Patrick's ears some time later. *"We must be getting close."*

"I hope you're ready for a fight, Boy Scout."

Patrick released a breathy snort. *"Me too."*

Chapter 9
Jax

***Jax hated the alpha** office. Everywhere he looked he saw his father. From the* dark red walls to the mahogany desk and gaudy throne-like chair. He still hadn't sat in that thing. It didn't feel right. Instead, when he needed the room he stood awkwardly, paced the room, or perched on the edge of the desk like he was now.

"You need to choose a different beta," his father's beta, Paul, snapped while he paced from wall to wall.

Ignoring the older man, Jax continued to study the room... there were tons of books; tomes upon tomes of ancient lycan lore—most of which painted their kin in a horrible light. There were texts about blood witches, as well, and manic scribbles over page margins that Jax couldn't make sense of. Like the book he currently held in his hands. Scribbles were written along lines of underlined text about how lycan mates, once they'd found one another, could supposedly sense each other.

"Patrick isn't here." Paul abruptly stopped his pacing and Jax lifted his gaze from the psychotic writing in his hands to find the older man glaring at him. "You don't know where he is or if he's ever coming back and on top of that—he is lycan!"

Jax furrowed his brow. "What does him being lycan have to do with it?"

Paul must not have anticipated Jax asking that question because his mouth gaped like a fish and he stuttered over his first word. "I-It has everything to do with it."

"Why?" Jax set the book down on the desk beside him with a loud thump, and then crossed his arms. "Explain that to me, because I'd think having a lycan help lead the clan would be a great thing."

A loud scoff left the older man and he took a disturbed step back. "Until the day he decides to stab you in the back and take the title of alpha right out from under you. As a lycan he has the right to rule the clan." Paul stomped forward and slammed his hands onto the desk. He turned to glare at Jax who simply stared at him in return. "We can't be led by a lycan," he spat the word as if it were poison. "They have different rules. There is a reason we keep ourselves separate from them."

"Patrick's told me multiple times that he has no desire to lead."

Paul snorted and shoved off the desk.

Jax eyed him uneasily as he continued, "He agreed to being beta as a service to me, not because he wanted the position."

"I can't believe you trust him."

Fury scorched Jax's insides, but Dalim helped temper the flames so he could appear calm and collected on the outside. He clenched his jaw one time before speaking again and was shocked at how level his voice was. "I trust Patrick with my life and the life of my sister."

Paul pointed a finger at Jax. "Don't get me started on your *sister*."

Jax's fingers curled until he was clutching his own arms.

"Calm down," Dalim said in a soothing tone. *"He's baiting you. Don't fall for it."*

"Is he?" Jax wondered while he watched the older man begin pacing again. His mouth was still moving, but Jax didn't hear his words. *"Or does he really believe what he's saying?"*

"Does it matter?" Dalim asked. *"He spent years at your father's side listening to his lies. You can't let him affect you."*

"That's much easier said than done."

"Jax!" Paul shouted, drawing Jax out of his private conversation. "Are you listening to me? Picking a beta—"

"Is *my* decision," Jax interrupted him. Paul's face pinched when Jax stood and unleashed a wave of his alpha abilities. Slowly, his father's beta bowed his head to Jax in a sign of submission. Forced submission was not how Jax wanted to lead the clan. He wanted to earn their respect and trust, but he knew there would be times when this action was needed. "I have told you what my decision is. I know I need a beta to help me. There's too much for one person to do. I am delegating."

Paul snorted, but kept his chin lowered. "You've delegated to three children who are all unstable."

"Enough!" Jax snapped and Paul bent a little lower. "I am not my father. I will not do things the same way he did. There is corruption in our clan and I intend to destroy it. It doesn't matter who the person is, what they are, or how old they may be—if I know a way they can serve their clan, then I'll ask them to do so. Violet is highly intelligent and her abilities are growing by the day. Mya is suffering from losing her moon-fated mate, but she is recovering and has a way with people that is vital in Lockup at this time. Tucker has grown and matured faster than anyone thought possible and has taken on every duty of his father's without being asked. If those are the three you have problems with, then you have a problem with me and I assure you—" Jax stepped into Paul's space when the older man looked up. "—I don't back down easily."

Paul swallowed hard, and then cleared his throat. "You need help," he said softly. "Help from those who have been in this position before."

Shaking his head, Jax huffed a laugh. "Not if those people expect me to be like my father. Not if they have a problem with people younger than them leading."

Silver leaked into Paul's eyes, but it disappeared as quickly as it came.

"I didn't ask to be alpha this soon," Jax reminded him. "I was content to let my father continue for a few more years even though he knew I was stronger. He lost his mind when my mother was killed. That is not my fault, but I am here. I am fulfilling my duties the way that I believe they should be done and I am doing the best I can. A little support from you would go a long way."

Tension rippled between the two males. Jax could see the wheels turning in Paul's head. His gaze darted all over Jax, probably sizing him up. Paul had made it quite clear that he wasn't happy about this situation, but maybe Jax could get him to understand and see there was a better way.

Paul opened his mouth to speak, but was interrupted by a loud buzzing. Both men turned toward the desk where Jax had left his cell phone. It skittered across the wood with each vibration until Jax's fingers wrapped around it. He didn't recognize the number, but sometimes the government called from strange numbers. He'd had a lot of experience with those over the last few days. For the most part, the United States government left the wolven territories to their own devices, but they liked to be kept in the loop, especially when shifts in power happened.

After releasing a long sigh, Jax accepted the call and placed the phone to his ear. "This is Jaxon Draven speaking, may I ask who's calling?"

Unease splintered his professional demeanor when labored breathing sounded on the other end of the call. Goosebumps fled down his arms and a chill raced up his spine. "Finally," came a breathy, pained reply.

"Hello?" Jax tried to keep his voice calm and his fingers from crushing the fragile device in his hands, but a knot had begun to coil in his stomach. "Who is this?"

A static *shhh-shhh* filled the line, like the sound generated by dragging your feet through the underbrush or pushing past a particularly dense section of trees. "I was getting worried that I'd forgotten your number."

Jax's eyes widened as a note of familiarity flicked through him. He turned to stare at Paul who had pinched his eyebrows together. Jax's mouth had gone dry and he wet his lips before daring to ask, "Patrick?"

Paul's brows turned down, contorting his face into one of rage as his arms crossed over his chest.

"Not exactly," answered a growly, winded voice. "Boy Scout's struggling." A loud grunt made Jax flinch. "We both are."

Terror made Jax's blood run cold. If Patrick's crazy wolf half was admitting he was having a hard time, things were very bad. "Alistair, where are you?"

A barely audible curse whispered on the other side. Patrick's labored breathing gained speed.

Jax threw open his link to Violet. *"I have Patrick on the phone, where are you?"*

"Where is he? Is he coming back?" came her immediate reply. *"I'm at his truck. I was getting ready to head out."*

"Good. I'll meet you there."

Jax moved for the door, but Paul stepped in front of him. "Where are you going?"

"Get out of my way, Paul." Jax felt his purple eyes shift to molten gold and a low growl underlined his words.

Unwillingly, Paul stepped aside, but kept on Jax's heels as he hurried out of the office toward the front door of Alpha House. "You can't leave!"

"Patrick, where are you?" Jax asked into the phone, ignoring the man chasing him down.

"I don't..." A wet cough cut off Patrick's words and Jax's worry spiked. "Northwest area of Stanislaus territory." A long labored breath followed. "I don't know exactly where."

Jax swallowed the lump in his throat before asking, "How bad is it?"

Patrick released a shallow huff of laughter, but it was Alistair who answered in his wolfish tone, "Bad. We've been poisoned." He groaned and a thump echoed through the line. "And we're bleeding."

Jax felt his pockets and found the syringe he'd been carrying around for days. A single antidote for wolfsbane. "I'll bring the antidote. You'll heal quickly after that. You always do."

"I'm trying," Alistair's breathy voice faded away.

"Patrick?" Jax called, but when no reply came he tried again, "Alistair!"

There was no response, but the call hadn't ended. Jax yanked open the front door and jogged down the steps.

"Jax, you can't leave!" Paul yelled from behind. "You're the alpha! You have to stay here." The older man seized Jax's shoulder and spun him around. "You lead from here. That's how your father did it. He rarely left the base."

Rage coursed through Jax's veins. He knocked Paul's grip off and snarled. "Maybe if my dad had left from time to time, and showed that he cared for the clan instead of just ruling over them, we would be in a better position than we are today! I'm going to find my beta."

Paul didn't try to stop him when Jax turned and sprinted toward the clan parking lot. Opening his mind, he found the link that connected him to Dr. Penmann and gave a mental tug.

"Doc, I need you to listen and follow these instructions before you come after Violet and I."

"Come after you?" came her immediate response. *"Where are you going?"*

"I'll explain everything, but first..."

Their conversation ended moments before he took the last turn too sharply and his tennis shoes skidded through the gravel of the parking lot. If Dalim hadn't been lending his abilities, Jax was positive he would have fallen on his face. Thankfully, his wolf half had impressive skills when it came to agility, and Jax found himself skidding into a controlled slide before taking off toward the red truck at the other end of the lot.

Violet was wringing her hands together when he approached, but immediately launched into questions. "What did he say? Is he okay? Where are we going?"

"Get in," Jax ordered, running around to the driver's side.

She did so and then handed the keys to him when he slid behind the wheel. The truck was filled with tense anticipation and worry as Jax maneuvered the vehicle through the security gates.

Once they were on the road, Violet turned toward him. "Jax, you need to tell me something. I'm freaking out. My heart is beating weird and I'm having trouble breathing." She looked out the front window again and rubbed her arms which, with a quick glance, Jax noted were covered in goosebumps. "My skin doesn't feel right."

"Violet," Jax answered slowly. "I think you're feeling Patrick."

Her gaze snapped back to his. "What?"

"He's not doing well and I will explain everything, but I need you to try and find him." Jax dared a glance at her before looking back at the road and gripping the steering wheel until his knuckles turned white. "I only have a vague location of where he is."

"How the heck am I supposed to do that?"

Jax shook his head. "I don't know, but I've read some interesting stuff in all the books I've been going through in Dad's office. Earlier today I read that lycan mates have the ability to find one another across long distances."

"What?"

"It's not the first time I've seen something like that mentioned." Jax dared a quick glance at her and saw she was staring at him with her mouth partially hanging open.

He returned his gaze to the road, but saw her head shake from the corner of his eye.

"Jax, if you're right, and I really am Patrick's mate then that's amazing, but the bond wasn't ever solidified—"

"Lycan bonds are different than wolven. I'm not entirely sure how, but they are." Frustration rippled through him. He wished he knew more. He wished he knew how to help her. Violet quietly said his name, clearly at a loss, and he sighed. "Look, you *are* his mate. You always have been. I think that's why he ended up in our clan. I don't think he knew it at the time, and you definitely didn't, but I think he was led here by your connection. Just...." He waved a hand through the air before returning it to the wheel. "Reach out into the same void that you do when you are speaking through our twin link. Start there. It's the best idea I have right now."

Violet was silent for a long time before she softly said, "I'll try."

"By the way," Jax said softly, breaking the quiet when it started to drag on. "I told the doc to follow us with some warriors. We might need backup."

"That's great," she sighed. "But if you want me to do this, you're gonna have to be quiet so I can concentrate."

He apologized, and refocused his attention on the road, taking them closer to Stanislaus' territory with every passing minute. Well... what was left of it, anyway. Blood Moon had ambushed the peaceful clan when Patrick and he had gone there for business. The alpha was old and passed the title to Talon, someone who Jax had started to think could make a great ally—but in the end—Talon hadn't made it out of the territory alive. He'd sacrificed his life so other families could get away. In his short time as alpha, Talon had done more for his clan than Jax had ever seen his father do. Noah did his duty, but he would have never put his life on the line for his clan.

Jax wanted to be a better alpha than his father. The leather on the steering wheel moaned as his grip tightened. He *would* be a better alpha than Noah was.

It took a lot longer than he would have liked to make their way to the Northwestern territory line of what was now Blood Moon territory, and Violet was lost in concentration for the majority of it. That's why when she loudly blurted, "Turn right!"

Jax jumped. "Right?" He looked out her dark window and stared at trees. "Violet, I'm not crashing Patrick's truck into a bunch of trees."

"Jax, turn right!"

He eyed her like she'd lost her mind.

"Now!"

If he hadn't been looking for a break in the trees, Jax would have missed the narrow path and what looked to be a very forgotten dirt road. He yanked on the steering wheel, sending them careening off the road. Both of them jostled in their seats while the tires followed the uneven path and Violet planted her hand on the roof. Her breathing had rapidly increased and her eyes were as wide as saucers.

"Violet," Jax called to her gently. "Talk to me."

"He's up ahead. I know it."

"This is a dirt road that hasn't been taken care of in ages. We don't even know if there is an outlet at the end of this and I don't think I'm skilled enough to back us out of here."

"Jax, just..." Her wide amethyst eyes were pleading. "Trust me."

His gaze darted between his sister and the haphazard road they were bumbling down. "I do, Violet. I trust you." Something screeched along the side of the truck and Jax groaned. "Patrick is gonna kill me if I scratch his truck."

"I think he'll forgive you," Violet breathed, and then pointed straight ahead. "Look. This lets out onto a road. Turn right up there."

Jax followed her orders and was very thankful when they turned onto a paved road. It was an old, thin, two-way road that hadn't seen a maintenance crew in who knew how long, but it was paved. They passed a small outlet where cars could pull off to the side when needed and Jax glanced at Violet. "Now what?"

She shook her head. Her fingers splayed against her window. "I don't... I can't."

She sucked in a sharp breath. "Patrick!"

The passenger door flew open and Jax barely had a chance to slam on the brakes before Violet was out of the truck. He yelled after her as she took off down the side of the road. Muttering curses to himself, he followed her in the truck until she dipped down the embankment into the trees. He opened his mouth to yell for her, but his jaw clamped shut.

"Don't," Dalim warned. *"You don't know what's out there. Park the truck and go after our sister."*

Jax nodded to himself, threw the truck into park, and hurried out the door. He followed the sound of her labored breathing and soft cries.

"Patrick. Patrick, come on, wake up."

His feet gained speed until he saw Patrick's body in the underbrush and Violet slowly rolling him onto his back. Jax's knees hit the ground beside his best friend while he fished the antidote out of his pocket.

Violet sobbed. "Patrick, open your eyes."

The cap to the syringe came off with a soft pop, but then Jax froze. He stared at Patrick's torso, bare, bloodied, and riddled with black veins. The dark lines emerged from five different cuts across his chest and abdomen. Jax's gaze traveled over the length of his friend. Patrick's eyes were closed and circles of dark skin made the eye sockets look like they were sunken in. A dark bruise had formed along his jaw and his lip was split.

Violet's trembling hand slipped off Patrick's other side. She sniffled and pressed her hand against his side again. "He's been stabbed. It's bad."

Jax swallowed the lump in his throat. This was bad.

Blood oozed from under the metal cuffs at Patrick's wrists and ankles. His feet were bare and bleeding, as well. How far had he run?

"Jax, snap out of it and give him the antidote." Dalim's presence surged through him and his hand that was clenched around the syringe moved over Patrick's chest. *"There are too many points of infection."*

"Then we'll just have to do our best." Jax drove the needle through Patrick's skin, just below his ribcage, and injected the antidote.

"It's not working," Violet whispered when the black veins remained after a few moments. She looked up at him. "Jax, it's not work—" Her words cut off and her gaze snapped to Patrick, then down at his chest. Her breathing stuttered. "No, no, no. Patrick, stay with me."

Jax dropped the syringe and placed a couple of fingers over the large vein in Patrick's neck, feeling for a pulse while his other hand rested on his friend's torso.

His heartbeat was slow... painfully slow and growing slower by the second.

Thump thump... thump thump... thump

Thump... thump thump...

"Patrick," Violet called to him, lightly shaking his shoulder while tears dribbled off her chin and splashed into the blood at his side.

Thump thump...

"Patrick!" Violet's shuddering hand clutched her chest as she doubled over. Agony ripped through the twin bond Jax shared with her and he ground his teeth.

There was no flutter, no familiar pulse under the tip of Jax's fingers.

Violet's face tipped toward the sky as a suppressed scream tore through her lips and her brokenhearted cry rent the night.

They were too late.

Jax stared as his twin lowered her trembling hands to rest helplessly against Patrick's cooling skin.

This wasn't right.

This wasn't fair.

Patrick deserved so much better. And Violet...

Warmth surged through him when Violet's opalescent eyes landed on him. Tears cascaded down her face. She clutched her stomach and sobbed.

How much could one heart take? Hadn't she been through enough?

He had to fix this. Heat pooled in his palms, growing hot against Patrick's skin.

Violet leaned over Patrick and rested her forehead against his, pleading to the goddess to bring him back.

Fear tied a knot in Jax's stomach as he thought of his mother, his father, and Mya. He watched as his twin shattered before him and knew he couldn't lose her, too. Jax had only started to repair the damage he'd done to their relationship, he wasn't about to let her lose her mate.

"This isn't how it ends," Jax growled.

"I'll lend you whatever power I can," Dalim offered from the recesses of his mind.

"Jax, stop." Her head lifted until their gazes collided. The knot in his stomach tightened at the vacancy in her eyes. She was shutting down. "He's gone."

"No."

"Please," she pleaded, then sniffled as she sat back on her heels. Her hands lifted toward her face only for her to jerk back. Another sob rattled from her when her gaze fell to her blood soaked palms. Patrick's blood. "We should... we should take him home."

She moved to lift Patrick's shoulders, but Jax pressed down on his friend's chest.

"Jax," she scolded. "He's gone! There's nothing we can do. Please," her voice broke. "Let's go home."

Her pleading only solidified his resolve and he shook his head. "No."

His eyelids were heavy. He was getting tired. So very tired. He slumped a little to the side and jerked upright. Pain lanced across Jax's torso and he released a low growl that evolved into a muted yell.

Violet's small hands seized his shoulders and she shook him. "Jax!" Terror made her voice shrill.

Thump.

Jax's eyes shot open. He looked down at his best friend. The black veins that marred his skin were disappearing, shrinking back to their origins. The bruise that had been nearly black along his jaw had softened to a light yellow, then disappeared entirely a moment later.

Thump thump.

"What are you doing?" Violet whispered, as her fingers curled into Jax's sleeve.

Jax's body began to tremble while the dark circles around Patrick's eyes lightened and color returned to his cheeks.

Violet looked back and forth between him and Patrick, her eyes wild with confusion and fear. "Whatever you're doing, it's hurting you!"

Patrick's chest rose with a deep breath, startling Violet into releasing Jax's sleeve.

Jax collapsed. His shoulder hit the ground before his head and he thought he heard Violet calling his name.

"I've got you," Dalim told him as all the pain and sound disappeared. *"Rest."*

Violet rolled Jax onto his back and he stared up through the tree canopies with unblinking eyes at the stars in the sky. They were so bright.

People surrounded them and Jax worried for Violet's safety until Dr. Penmann appeared beside his sister.

Oh good, he thought. Violet was safe. She would be okay.

The older woman's mouth moved quickly, but the words didn't reach him as he sank into a blissful quiet.

"It was an honor to be with you," Dalim spoke gently in his mind. A final farewell before they both surrendered to sweet oblivion. *"Goodbye, brother."*

He'd fixed it. Violet wouldn't lose Patrick. They would be okay. Everything would be okay.

Chapter 10

Violet

A different kind of *pain blossomed in Violet's chest. This was a deep rooted* anguish. She hurried around her twin and rolled him onto his back. His pale amethyst eyes stared blankly at the sky. "Jax, look at me. Say something."

Her ear twitched at the sound of movement coming from the direction of Patrick's truck. Dr. Penmann's voice cut through the trees, ordering people to follow her.

"Here!" Violet cried, desperate to get their attention. "Over here!"

A handful of Sentinel warriors charged around her in a protective circle while Dr. Penmann fell to her knees beside Violet.

"What happened?" Dr. Penmann asked as she briefly glanced at Patrick before taking in Jax's condition.

Violet shook her head. "I don't know. Patrick's heart..." She choked on the word and tried again, "Patrick's heart stopped. I said we should go, but Jax... He wouldn't let go of Patrick. He started bleeding and Patrick started healing. I don't know what happened."

"I've heard of alpha's healing their clan members before, but nothing on this level." Dr. Penmann spoke quickly, her raspy voice coming out in a rush, as she tore Jax shirt open to assess his wounds. "You heard Patrick's heart stop?"

Violet nodded. "Felt it."

Dr. Penmann froze for the briefest of seconds, then seized a handful of thick bandages from the bag she'd dropped on her other side. "Hold this to his side. He's loosing a lot of blood."

Tears fell from Violet's eyes as she did was she was told. "Is he going to be alright?"

"Patrick?" Dr. Penmann asked, her voice sounding a little distracted as she laid smaller bandages over the other slices across Jax chest.

"No. I know he'll be fine. His heart is getting stronger by the second. What about Jax?"

The look Dr. Penmann shot her dumped a bucket of ice water into her veins. Violet clenched her teeth and her hand slapped over her chest as a deep-rooted pain twisted her core.

Dr. Penmann's head snapped in her direction, then her wide eyes focused on Jax's chest. By the time the heel of her hand drove against his chest, her other had already wrapped around it. Keeping her arms straight, she shoved downward. Two pulses later the crack of bone made Violet flinch.

The doc called for something, but Violet's ears were ringing. A warrior placed a small box beside Jax's head before pulling pads and wire out.

"Violet, we need you to move so Kellen can help me."

Violet dragged her gaze away from the odd box that read AED to look at the doc, but her attention was captured by the rhythmic pulse of the older woman's hands. Jax's head rocked with each compression, but his gaze remained glassy. Pale amethyst eyes that were a mirror image of her own stared vacantly at the stars above them. Witnesses to her twin's death.

Violet's chest caved under the weight of the word.

Death.

Tears lined her eyes before cascading down her cheeks.

Her twin...

Death had laid claim over the Sentinel Clan. How many more would die before Blood Moon was stopped?

Hands shoved under her arms.

Jax lurched and drew in a deep, strangled breath, making Violet and the doc jump. The hands under Violet's arms disappeared, and the person let out a startled scream.

Violet grabbed her brother's shoulders, "Jax?"

Dr. Penmann snagged one of his wrists and placed two fingers on the inside while Jax continued to drag shallow, ragged breaths into his lungs. "His pulse is steady. A little slow, but steady." She turned her attention back to Jax. "Jax, can you hear me?"

He shook off her hand and lifted a thumb. "Loud and clear, Doc."

A cry of relief left Violet. She threw her arms around her twin's shoulders as soon as he was sitting and squeezed, making him whine.

"Ow. Ribs."

"Sorry," she eased her hold, but didn't release him. Instead, she buried her face against him. "I thought you were dead."

He patted her back. "I think I was."

Violet leaned back onto her heels. "But, you're okay now?"

Color slowly returned to his cheeks while he lightly patted himself down. A small wince twisted his face when his hands tapped over his ribs, but he nodded. "I don't feel the greatest, but yeah, I think I'm okay."

Her breathing came in short bursts and she smacked his shoulder before she could stop herself. "Jerk."

"Hey!" Jax rubbed the spot she'd hit. "I just came back from the dead and I think I have a broken rib!"

She shoved a finger at him, ignoring his loud complaint. "Don't you ever do that to me again!"

Jax's eyes narrowed. His mouth opened like he was about to reply, but a warrior stepped beside Violet, clearing his throat. "Sorry to interrupt, but we're technically on enemy territory. If it's alright with Dr. Penmann, we need to get moving."

The doc stared at Jax another second even after he told her he was good to go. A sigh left her when she slowly looked away from him to focus on Patrick. She shook her head and shrugged. "Alpha Jax seems to be alright. Patrick appears to be stable." She threw up her hands while making her way to her feet. "You're all enigma's to me. Let's get everyone home."

"I'll drive," Jax announced.

Violet scoffed, then snatched the keys to Patrick's truck from his hands after he'd removed them from his pocket. "Absolutely not. You just had a near-death experience. I'll drive."

"I would like Patrick to stay with me," Dr. Penmann told the group as a couple of people came to lift his unconscious form from the ground. She turned toward Violet. "If that's alright with you?"

Violet nodded. "I know next to nothing about medical stuff and there isn't room for him to comfortably rest in the truck. I'll leave him in your very capable hands, Doc."

The older woman glanced at Jax who was looking a little pale after making his way to his feet. "Do I need to order you to come with me?"

"No. I'm going with Violet. I'm fine, just a little tired."

With final farewells, they all climbed into their respective vehicles. Violet stood with the driver's door open, watching as a few warriors gently positioned Patrick into the back of one of the SUV's before the doc climbed in after him.

"Violet, get in," Jax ordered, drawing her attention back to the truck. "He's in the best hands right now."

She drew in a deep breath and looked at the stars above. "Thank you," she whispered, quietly offering her gratitude to the moon goddess. "I don't know if you can hear me or if you had anything to do with what just happened, but thank you. Thank you for bringing them back to me." Violet cleared her throat and wiped away the tears that threatened to escape before she climbed into the cab of the truck. She started the vehicle feeling lighter than she had in days and pulled onto the road to lead the way home.

Chapter 11

Cas

***"You've got to be** kidding me!" Cas yelled as he snatched what had been* Patrick's chair and threw it at the wall. The flimsy wooden frame shattered, sending a wooden hail storm to the floor. He spun on his heel to glare at the few Blood Moon wolves who were snatching the bodies from the corner. "Who let this happen?"

One of them scoffed. "We didn't *let* anything happen. We were given orders to patrol while most of the pack went with Ivy to attack the Whisky Clan. He was under heavy drugs. He shouldn't have been able to escape."

Cas' nose wrinkled when he snarled at them, "But he did!"

Another wolven stepped toward him, this one was tall and built like a linebacker. "We don't take orders from you." His eyes glowed like rubies in the light of the cabin. "Ivy told us the only orders we take from now on are from her."

"Then who told you to leave our captive unattended?" Ivy's cool, scathing tone brought all movement to a screeching halt.

Everyone turned to look at the white-haired woman dominating the doorway with a bloodied dagger in hand and red splattering her face. A second woman with dark, stringy hair stood slightly behind Ivy to the right. Cas felt a chill go up his spine and he immediately turned to square his shoulders to the two women.

He hadn't seen the blood witch since Vikter used the woman's abilities to slaughter two of Patrick's neighbors. She had no problems creating chaos and breaking the laws of nature to do so. Her appearance was proof of that. A stern set fit her mouth and a hard edge lined her light-colored eyes. Cas knew she was about forty years old, but he assumed she used her abilities to remain young because she looked like she could have been his same age. No age lines marred her porcelain skin, but the fine cut of her jaw sliced a bit too sharply, making her appear slightly underweight. Redish-black lines fell from her eyes as if she had cried blood and it had mixed with old mascara before permanently drying there. Her fingertips were tinged black and there was a tiny skull of some poor animal protruding from her chest just below her clavicle.

The woman dragged her attention off the back of Ivy's skull before landing on him, and wicked humor tilted one corner of her mouth skyward. She broke away from Ivy and sauntered toward Cas while one of the other wolven stammered over an explanation.

"De-Dev gave the order. He said he w-was directly relaying the message fro-from you and that he would personally keep an eye on the... on the prisoner."

"And where is Dev now, huh?" Ivy snarked.

"I don't... I'm not sure."

The woman was uncomfortably close to Cas now and though every inch of him told him to run, he held his ground while Abel paced back and forth in the recesses of his mind.

"Imbeciles—the lot of them," she whispered, drawing her chin over his shoulder as she circled him. "But you... you have the tangy scent of revenge."

"What are you talking about?" Cas grumbled and clenched his jaw when he felt a finger glide across his back.

She chuckled. "I'm a blood witch. Do you know what that means?"

"That you defy the laws of nature to do whatever you want to do no matter the consequences."

She groaned. "You sound like my sister. She was always telling me that I needed to be mindful of the cost of this kind of magic." She reappeared in front of him. "I think she was just afraid of the power."

Cas angled his chin lower so he could look her in the eye. Bright red flecks floated in her light blue irises. "And you're not?"

A dark laugh rang from her delicate throat. "Absolutely not." She launched toward him, covering the last few inches between them and brought her nose close to his jaw. "I relish in it." He jerked away from her when he heard her draw in a deep breath and she chuckled. "I could do so much with that blood of yours."

"You mean, with *me*, right?" Cas clarified.

"No, just your blood."

Warning sounds went off in his head and Abel was losing it behind the mental wall Cas had thrown into place. He tried to play it off like he didn't care what she said, like it didn't affect him, like he didn't want to run for the hills with his tail tucked between his legs. "And what would my blood do for you?"

She clicked her tongue a few times. "More than you know. With blood tainted by vengeance there are so many wonderfully dark and powerful spells I could perform. Ivy's just barely cracked what I could accomplish with your blood. Not many have allowed revenge to seep into their every pore. It's a unique and difficult ingredient to come by. I could sell it on the dark witch markets, but why not keep it all to myself?"

Cas took a step away from her when she tried to lace her fingers through his and she cackled. "Wouldn't I be more useful to you alive then? Your own personal blood bank?"

The blood witch shook her head. "Sadly it doesn't work that way. The moment I hold you captive, your revenge would begin to fade, replaced by the driving need to escape. It's better that I just drain you before that can happen." Her eyes widened and she blinked a few times. "Oh don't worry, I have a preservation spell that I can use to keep it fresh." She sucked her lower lip between her teeth, then clicked her tongue once more. "Ivy won't let me do that, of course. Not yet, anyway."

"Check the back office," Ivy ordered, saving Cas from responding to the crazy lady in front of him.

The blood witch turned and meandered toward their white-haired leader, supposedly finished with Cas. Not that he was complaining.

"Good!" Abel snapped at him. *"If you were complaining, I was about to make a vow to find a way to take over and force you to leave."*

"You can't do that."

"Watch me," Abel growled, and Cas felt a splatter of nerves mar his insides. *"We need to leave. That witch thinks you're a blood donor and Ivy has made it very clear that she's done with you. We can free Lexie and leave."*

Cas mentally rolled his eyes at his wolf half. *"How do you suggest we do that? You don't think we'll be noticed trying to leave with their last remaining game piece?"*

"We can't leave her here, Cas."

"We can't leave at all! We started this. We're seeing it through to the end. We'll just have to figure out another way to help Lexie."

"What the—" The guinea pig wolven that was sent to check the office shoved against the door when it got stuck, then rammed his shoulder into it. It moved another couple of inches and he stuck his head through. "Dev's body is blocking the door. He's dead. The bookcase has been moved. Looks like he died trying to stop the prisoner."

Ivy growled and her red eyes began to glow as she stomped toward the office. "I didn't give Dev any orders which means that blasted lycan was playing us." She pushed her way into the office and a couple of seconds passed before an unhinged growl rolled through the cabin. It turned into a roar of rage and she reappeared clenching something in her fist.

Abel's power flooded Cas when Ivy made a beeline for him, but Cas tried to appear mildly curious instead of defensive.

"Do you know what this is?" She badgered, thrusting her fist toward him. Her fingers unclenched to reveal a half-empty syringe.

Anger boiled Cas' blood, but it was tempered when the blood witch took a couple of steps toward him and inhaled deeply.

"It looks like a half-used dose of Patrick's serum," he observed in a bland tone. "Dev did this?"

"I'm not sure." Ivy spun the needle of the syringe toward him and pointed it at his throat. "Maybe it was you and you're just trying to cover your tracks."

"Or maybe you overestimated the loyalty your pack has for you."

"We are a clan!" Ivy shrieked and a vein in her forehead began to bulge. "We have the territory!"

"By force! How many wolven died in the process of gaining this because *you* didn't want to live like a vagabond anymore?" He looked around the room and found a couple of wolven shifting their weight uncomfortably. "By my count, it was about half of what we started with!"

Ivy released an outcry of rage. "Everyone knew what we were getting into. It was worth it for the chance to have a home."

Cas daringly took a step toward her and to his surprise, she backed up. He had the upper hand. "And what did that chance cost you? Do you really think the clans are going to allow you to stay here? Do you think the kings and queens are going to overlook what you've done here?" He pointed at the other wolven in the room. "Maybe Dev, or what was his real name... Topher? Maybe *Topher* didn't like seeing a fellow lycan being tortured! You ordered him to do that, not me!"

Barely leashed rage flickered across Ivy's features along with a hint of uncertainty.

"Are there any other lycans in Blood Moon that we should be concerned about?"

Ivy jutted her jaw to the side, then let out a heavy breath through her nose.

"There are a few."

"Do you think we have a problem with them?"

She was quiet for a moment.

"Do you?" Cas pressed the matter.

Her eyes narrowed to slits. "They have defied orders in the past."

Cas snorted. "Might I suggest you worry about those under your rule, Ivy, instead of the man who came to you seeking revenge?" He nodded his head toward the witch. "Your blood witch will attest that I have not wavered."

Ivy turned her head to look at the dark-haired woman who was gleefully smirking. "Oh no. He smells as delicious as ever."

There wasn't enough time to stop the shudder that rolled up his spine. His reaction to her words only made the witch's grin widen.

He nodded when Ivy returned her attention to him. "Instead of throwing ridiculous accusations, why don't we deal with the foxes in your own henhouse?"

"Then what?" Ivy asked, throwing the syringe at the floor. It shattered and sprayed the contents a few inches in every direction.

She was turning to him for advice again and triumph spread through Cas. He allowed a disturbed smile to widen his mouth before answering, "Then the real fun begins."

Chapter 12

Violet

Hours had passed since *Violet and Jax had found Patrick. They'd returned* home to a crowd of people, mostly warriors, ready to start a fight. Violet couldn't blame them—not after everything they had been through—but the sting of betrayal sliced through her already delicate heart.

Word had apparently spread since Patrick left to find Violet when Zander had kidnapped her. The whole clan knew about his red eyes and rumors were circling about the possibility that he was lycan. A multitude of warriors insisted on following Jax while he remained in Patrick's company. They weren't willing to risk losing another alpha and were furious at him for leaving without taking a few of them with him.

The doc had secluded one of her rooms at the clinic for Patrick, and had ordered that the only people allowed inside were herself, Jax, and Violet. That was when the crowd of warriors had started their ruckus in the waiting room. Dr. Penmann stood her ground in the doorway of the exam room, knowing they wouldn't dare push past her, but that hadn't stopped them from talking at Jax.

"I'm fine!" He shouted, interrupting a warrior who was pointing out everything that could have gone wrong.

Violet flinched against the volume, but was grateful that her twin's outburst had quieted the masses.

While Jax stepped out of the room to reassure his clan, Violet sat beside Patrick and wiped a cool cloth across his brow. He hadn't woken, but his eyes twitched about beneath his lids like he was dreaming, his temperature had risen, and a light sweat had started a couple of minutes ago.

"I understand your concern and I appreciate it. I have a lot to learn about being your alpha. Running off on my own is something I need to work on, but I will never put my life above one of your own. *Every* life is important. There were things that could have gone wrong tonight, but thankfully they didn't. There are concerns about Patrick's mental state; I understand rumors have been running rampant. So, let me put those rumors to rest."

Jax paused and the silence weighed heavily on Violet. Her hand had paused over the bowl beside her, waiting to dip the cloth in the cool water again. When Jax sighed, her anxiety spiked, making her feel antsy. She dunked the cloth in the water, but as she pulled it out again, she saw claws had replaced her fingernails.

"Patrick's wolf eyes have been red from the day he arrived here," Jax announced.

Violet whipped her head around and stared wide-eyed at the door frame where the doc shifted her weight uneasily.

The room was silent, but the voices in Violet's mind began to build. They'd been surprisingly quiet since she'd arrived, but perhaps that was because everyone was loudly speaking their minds. Now the crescendo was so great that she dropped the cloth, closed her eyes, and mashed her palms to the sides of her head as if she were attempting to keep her brain from exploding.

"What did he say?"

"That can't be right."

"We would have noticed!" "Is he lying?"

"Alpha Draven wouldn't have kept that from us!" "Are you sure?"

"We've learned he did a lot of things we didn't know about." "This isn't right!"

"WHY is he HERE?" "A LYCAN SHOULDN'T BE HERE!" "WE SHOULD HAVE LEFT HIM WITH BLOODMOON!"

Violet whimpered as the voices and words blurred together. Growing and growing and growing—

"Violet." A calm, warm familiar feminine voice cut through the cacophony of noise, calling to her. *"Listen to my voice. Mine alone."*

As this mysterious voice spoke, the throbbing in Violet's head ebbed and the other voices began to fade to a dull ache in the background.

"Who are you?"

A soft chuckle danced through her mind. *"We've met before, but only once. I told you to rest then. Now I need you to focus, young one."* Memories of a wispy wolf with translucent fur and crystallin claws surfaced as the female spoke. *"Let me tell you a story about a young girl who was locked away because of her differences. Once upon a time..."*

It was a familiar story, one her mother had told her many times; a half-blood girl who had been cast out of her clan, but ultimately found true love in a mate who also had mixed blood. And, the longer the voice went on, the quieter Violet's mind became.

"I know you." Violet softly interrupted, and the voice in her mind waited for her to continue. *"You're the wolf that stopped Zander. Aren't you?"*

"I am." The words lingered in Violet's thoughts, like the way a beautiful note hangs in the air of a room with good acoustics.

Violet sucked in a breath as excitement washed through her. She hadn't seen or heard anything about that wolf since that day. *"How did that happen? Who are you? Why are you here now? Are you my wolf? Wait, I'm lycan. I shouldn't have a wolf."*

"You are many things, young one," the she-wolf stated. *"I will answer your questions in time, but your attention is needed elsewhere."*

Violet was about to ask what she meant when cold fingers wrapped around her wrists, and the strangely comforting, raspy tone of Dr. Penmann reached her ears.

"Violet, are you alright?" She gently pried Violet's hands off her head, then sucked in a quick breath when Violet opened her eyes to look at her. "I don't know that I will ever get used to those eyes of yours."

Pulling her eyebrows together, Violet said, "My eyes have been purple as long as you've known me."

Dr. Penmann softly laughed, sliding her hands down Violet's arms before giving her fingers a light squeeze. She let go as she said, "Yes, but they haven't been able to change for very long."

"Oh." Violet blinked a few times, unsure how to make her eyes return to their amethyst hue, or if they had already.

"Are you okay?" the doc repeated.

Violet grabbed the cloth she'd dropped off the floor. "Yeah. The voices aren't so loud anymore."

"Good." The doc looked at Patrick and pinched her lips together.

"What about you?" Violet asked, then moved to drop the cloth in the sink set in one of the countertops.

"I don't understand why he hasn't woken up yet. He looks completely healed. His heart and lungs are clear and strong."

Violet snatched a clean cloth from a cupboard and turned to find Dr. Penmann shaking her head.

"There's nothing more I can do for him."

A sigh left Violet as she returned to her seat beside Patrick. Taking her time to soak the cloth in the cool water, she said, "It's okay, Doc. You've done so much for Patrick, Jax, and I. For everyone really. Do you..." She stopped and nibbled on her lower lip for a moment.

Dr. Penmann watched her curiously with her arms crossed over her chest.

"Do you think it's his mind?"

"I honestly don't know. He's lycan. Maybe this is how they heal from grave injuries. I just don't know."

They fell quiet while Patrick breathed softly beside Violet, lightly tickling the underside of her wrist with each breath while she dapped at his forehead some more.

Jax was still talking with the warriors, but the conversation had settled and was much quieter now.

"I was trained to treat wolven," the doc's tone was almost reminiscent as she continued, "which traditionally doesn't require much. Wolven heal quickly and hardly ever get sick, and even when they do it's nothing serious though everyone around here treats seasonal allergies like it will be the death of them."

A huff of laughter left Violet and the corner of her mouth tilted into a half-smile.

"The occasional setting of bones and cleaning wounds," Dr. Penmann continued, "Some prenatal, delivery, and postnatal care, but over the last few years I've been required to do so much more." She backed up, drawing Violet's attention. Once she bumped into the counters, she leaned heavily against them, grabbing the edges beside her hips. Her gray eyes were sad. "Wolven medicine isn't like human or lycan medicine. With you, I had to learn more about the human body than I've ever had to learn before. You weren't quite human, but you weren't quite wolven either. With Patrick, I was thrown into lycan medicine with no guide or helping hand. The lycan's wouldn't talk to me so I was left to research what I could on my own, and believe me there isn't much made readily available. And the only reason we have an antidote for wolfsbane is because my instructor insisted I learn it, but it's not something I'd ever had to worry about before. The clans were at peace." She shook her head. "There is so much I don't know that I wish I did."

Violet rested the cloth over Patrick's brow and drew in a deep breath. "Maybe now that there are two lycan in the clan you'll be able to have more access to that side of the medicine."

Dr. Penmann nodded thoughtfully. "Maybe. I would like that."

Jax stomped into the room, shaking his head and muttering under his breath. "They're fine. For now. They'll keep watch outside instead of crowding your waiting room."

"You can't blame them for being worried," Violet told him.

He crashed into the chair a few feet in front of Violet and slumped low in the seat. "I don't. I blame them for being narrow minded and needing someone to hold their hand as they are walked through the years of proof that Patrick is trustworthy."

"Some of that is your father's doing." Dr. Penmann reminded him. "That's going to take more time to correct than a few days. And their emotions are heightened right now due to recent events."

"Doc, I'm fine." Jax gave her a pointed glare.

"But you weren't!" The older woman snapped, startling Violet. "Your heart stopped too, Jaxon!"

Violet hadn't heard anyone call her brother by his full name since they were very little. "She has a point."

"Guys, I'm fine." He ran a hand down his face and stared at Patrick. "I could have saved Mom."

Confusion rolled through Violet, making her pinch her eyebrows together. "What?"

"If I could do that for Patrick, I could have saved Mom."

"No," Dr. Penmann said firmly. "Patrick had been dead for moments and your heart still stopped. Your mother had been gone for much longer by the time you arrived. That *would have* killed you."

Violet stared at the floor. "She gave her life for me, Jax. How do you think she would have felt if you died to save her?" When he didn't answer, she lifted her gaze to watch him. Their identical purple eyes clashed and she could tell he was mulling over what she'd said. "You would have been replacing her life with yours and she would have died again as soon as I shifted. That wouldn't have been helpful for anyone."

"But I could have tried," Jax's voice broke and his jaw pulsed. Moisture lined his eyes as he held Violet's gaze.

Mirrored anguish and suffering rippled through their twin bond—a feeling Violet knew all too well. They were both hurting, deeply, but hadn't been given a moment to truly grieve or process it yet. She reached a hand out for her twin, which he stared at before leaning forward to take it. It was a tight squeeze of fingers, something she wouldn't have dared do even a month ago, but Jax was acting more and more like the brother she once knew a long time ago. It felt right. Comforting each other. Being friends again.

It'd taken time, but Violet had finally realized that although she was unique and may have been a sort of outcast, she wasn't alone. She'd felt that way for so long, even knowing she had Lexie and Mya's friendship. So much had changed in the last four months. She had a tribe of people who loved her and always would and she knew that with unflinching certainty.

"From what I understand of Luna's situation," Dr. Penmann gently spoke, breaking Violet's thoughts. "Her death was a condition of magic. No amount of healing was going to stop whatever deal she had made to ensure *both* her children survived."

Jax nodded, squeezed Violet's fingers one last time, then let go and leaned back in his chair. "I know. That doesn't make it hurt any less."

"No. It doesn't. But Jax," the older woman moved toward him then rested a hand on his shoulder. "You need to explore this new ability of yours with extreme caution. We don't know how you have it, or why, or what you can do with it. Have you healed anyone before?"

"No."

"Hmm." The doc tapped her chin and narrowed her eyes. "So, it's a new ability. I wonder..."

Her voice trailed off as Violet thought back, wondering if Jax *had* healed someone without realizing it. Of all the people that had been hurt or killed recently, there was only one that snagged her curiosity. A dark forest filled Violet's mind, one she had stumbled blindly through before falling into the same dried up ravine as her best friend, but Lexie hadn't gotten so lucky in her fall.

"What about Lexie?" she blurted, but when she looked at them, Violet realized she had interrupted some sort of discussion. "Sorry."

Jax sighed and the amount of sorrow that crossed his features made him look so much older than his eighteen years. "We don't know where she is. I've had people looking for her, but whatever trail there was dried up a long time ago."

Violet shook her head. "Not that. I know you've been looking for her, and so have the human police." An ache punched through her chest and she rubbed the spot as she continued. "I know you won't give up, but I wasn't talking about that. Do you remember when we thought Lexie had broken her ankle?"

His face scrunched. "Yeah. That was the night Blood Moon attacked the tourney."

Nodding, Violet leaned forward. "You and Patrick were positive she'd broken her ankle. Why?"

"She couldn't move it," Jax started, his voice sounding far away. "At first when I touched it she was in so much pain, so I moved up to her knee and started to feel my way down her leg to find where the pain began. By the time I made it back down her to ankle, I was trying to massage her muscles because they were really tight and she..." He trailed off and stared at Violet.

"She said it felt a lot better and that what you had been doing had helped," Violet finished for him. "Jax, I think Lexie was the first person you healed."

Jax looked down at his hands resting in his lap. They rolled over so his palms faced the ceiling. "My hands grew really warm when I was healing Patrick. Lexie said her leg felt warm. It was warm, but I thought it was just because I was massaging it."

"But you weren't eighteen yet," Dr. Penmann said.

"My abilities started coming through before I was eighteen," Violet reminded them. "We didn't know they were lycan abilities, but I still had some extra strength sometimes or a burst of speed."

Jax leaned forward and rested his elbows on his knees. His fingers pushed into his hair. "I wish she was here."

"Me too," Violet agreed, then looked back at Patrick. "We got one of them back. We'll find her, Jax." She smiled softly. "Who knows. With any luck, Patrick will wake up and tell us he knows something."

Her twin mumbled something about hoping so too and the conversation in the room fell silent. Violet returned to dabbing Patrick's forehead, and after a few minutes, Dr. Penmann excused herself to go do some research.

Over the next hour, Patrick's temperature cooled to a normal level for wolven and lycan, which would have registered as a fever for any human thermometer. Jax had fallen asleep with his head tipped back against the wall, and Dr. Penmann was still in her office, so Violet celebrated the small victory alone.

She ran her fingertips through the ends of Patrick's curly hair and whispered, "You need to wake up, Patrick. There is so much to do and so many people who need you." Flattening her palm against his cheek, she said, "Come back to me."

"Violet?" Jax's sleepy voice called to her. "Everything okay?"

Something tugged at her, keeping her attention. She shifted her hand so her fingertips pressed gently against Patrick's temples and had a strange urge to do so with the other hand.

"Violet?" Jax repeated, but he sounded much more awake now and slightly alarmed.

Rising panic charged through Violet's mind, warring against the unwavering calm in her heart. Patrick's eyes moved rapidly beneath his lids and he sucked in a sharp breath as a chill ran up her spine. Whatever hold was on her must have been affecting him, as well. She tried to break it—tried to pry her hands away from his head—but nothing she did worked.

Her body began to tremble like she'd been out in the cold too long. Jax was at her side a second later, grasping one of her arms and calling for Dr. Penmann. He pulled against her arm and a light green translucent aura pulsed from her body, knocking his hands away.

He called her name again and Dr. Penmann's shoes appeared next to his. They were talking in hurried voices, but their words were warbled.

Violet managed to part her lips and whisper, "Jax," just before a blast of icy wind hit her in the face.

Chapter 13

Violet

Frigid wind burned her *cheeks, and Violet threw her hands up to protect* herself against the blast. The breeze settled, and her chest heaved as she let out a few large breaths.

"What the heck was that?" she asked, slowly lowering her arms. "Jax?"

The panic that had ribboned its way through her brain spread to her extremities when towering pine trees surrounded her instead of the off-white walls of the exam room. Their rich scent filled her lungs with each inhale, and her breath puffed out in front of her with every exhale. The chill that had blasted her face hung in the air as small white flakes lazily drifted to the frozen ground.

Violet spun in a slow circle. She didn't recognize this forest or these trees. "Jax!" she yelled, then froze when the sound of her voice softly faded away, like music in a room with great acoustics. "What is this place?"

She started walking, instinct telling her to keep moving in the cold. Maybe she would find help, or shelter, at least. One step. Two. Three—

The screech of car brakes split the night, making her jump. She lifted her gaze toward the sound and flinched at the following crunch of metal. Two cars tumbled down the embankment not even fifty feet in front of her, their careening only stopped when they smashed into the line of trees.

A small silver sedan was closest to her, leaning on its side against a tree, its tires still spinning. Her feet slid over the snowy ground as she hurried to its front bumper.

"Hello?" she called, her voice hanging in the air once again as she bent down to look inside the windshield. Whatever this place may be, the people inside those cars needed help. "Hello? Can you hear m—."

The sight inside the vehicle was enough to twist her stomach, so she stared at the ground and willed her heightened hearing to work on demand, for once. At first, nothing changed. Then, the hiss of the car engines grew louder. She could hear the rotation of the tires as they began to slow their dizzying spins. An animal scurried away in the underbrush, its heart frantically thumping away, probably frightened from the crash.

But no human heartbeat.

Tears stung her eyes as she stood and looked toward the black sedan a little farther away. It was resting on its back, just as smashed as the silver car. The thought of finding the same scene made her heart hurt... how many had lost their lives tonight?

Not willing to give up, she focused her hearing on the wreckage pleading with the goddess that someone survived. Anyone. Even just one.

Then out of the dark sounded a single panicked heartbeat and Violet's feet were flying through the snow as it started to gather along the ground.

"Hello!" she cried, hoping for the person to answer.

An anguished cry met her ears before a foot smashed into the windshield, spiderweb cracks burst from the impact point and one more kick brought the foot clean through the compromised glass. The foot retracted, but the hole wasn't quite big enough for someone to fit through. Knowing it would hurt, but that she would heal, Violet raced forward to grab the window and pull the hole apart... but her hands went right through the glass as if she were not a solid mass of flesh and bone.

She stared at her hands and backed up a couple of steps. "What is happening?" she quietly said to herself, the sound—though quiet—still lingering around her.

Two hands, larger than her own, grabbed either side of the glassy hole and she flinched when the first spots of blood stained the ground. The person had the same idea as her and with a soft grunt from inside the car, the hole easily grew. Violet knew that kind of strength didn't come from a human.

Curiosity held her in place while a head of curly dark brown hair poked through the enlarged breakpoint. The boy crawled away from the wreckage, leaving bloody handprints in his wake, and Violet walked beside him. Boy wasn't the right word. He was easily bigger than she was, but his limbs were lanky, and only just starting to show signs of muscle bulking.

"Are you okay?" she asked, then immediately felt silly. Her hand had just gone through the solid mass of glass like she was the illusion here... wherever *here* was. She nibbled on her lower lip before asking, "Can you hear me?"

His body trembled, but showed no sign of hearing or seeing her. He sat back on his heels, breathing heavily. When he rolled his palms skyward, Violet realized his fingernails had been replaced with claws. She took a step toward him, sucking in a quick breath before she spoke, but the words died on her tongue when the scent of chocolate peppermint filled her lungs.

Surprise rounded her eyes. "Patrick?"

The boy's scent was slightly different. Patrick's scent always had a hint of cedar, but pine was the added touch to this boy's smell. What was it Cas had told her... every clan had a unique smell.

His head was still down and blood covered the ear closest to her, but she could tell it had a tapered tip. The trembling throughout his body grew violent and the teen threw his head back as an anguished roar tore from his throat.

Surprised by the outburst, Violet jumped back—then froze when she found herself staring at a younger Patrick. He looked exactly the same way he had the first day he'd arrived at Sentinel Clan's gate, except for the claws, pointed ears, and the fangs glimmering in the night. And one final important detail; shimmering moonstone eyes. He stared skyward, tears falling from the corners of his tormented gaze. The longer he yelled, the more the sound twisted into a mournful howl and slowly bright ruby red began to consume the brilliant moonstone.

Violet pressed a hand over her mouth as tears trailed down her cheeks.

The young Patrick's fangs shortened, his claws faded to nails, and the tapering of his ears rounded out. With the loss of his lycan abilities, a final bone wracking sob left him before he leaned forward and pressed his palms against the ground.

She reached for him, but stopped short of touching his shoulder, knowing she would pass right through him. Somehow, she was seeing the memory of that night. The night he'd kept to himself, a hellish secret, shouldered alone.

"I'm so sorry," her voice broke with emotion. "I had no idea."

"Violet?" called a familiar, deep voice to her left.

Jerking toward the sound, she found herself staring at the young man she'd given her whole heart and soul to. An older Patrick who had grown and bulked. The sides of his hair were shorter and the top a little bit longer, hanging down over one eyebrow. He stared at her through wide, hazel eyes that she adored as he breathed heavily.

Violet looked down at the younger Patrick, but he was gone. Along with the bloody handprint trail and the destroyed cars. There was no sign of it.

"Violet, what are you doing here?" Patrick asked, his voice much closer now.

She turned back to him and squeaked in surprise when he was only inches from her. "Where is here, exactly?" She'd practically breathed the words, but somehow the sound still lingered around them.

Patrick's brow twitched as he gazed over her head as if he heard the strange acoustic sound, as well. He blinked, then looked back at her. "You shouldn't be here."

"Again, where is here? I have no idea what's going on."

The screech of car brakes split the night, making her jump. Violet spun toward the sound and flinched at the following crunch of metal. Just like before, two cars tumbled down the embankment, their careening only stopped when they smashed into the line of trees.

Her brows pulled together as the memory played through and the younger Patrick kicked his way out of the vehicle.

"What is this?" she whispered to herself.

"Violet?" called Patrick, but his voice was more gravelly and it came from her other side.

Slowly, she turned her head toward the voice and found Patrick slowly, but confidently, stepping out of the trees. Although it was dark, his eyes glowed like garnet in the sunlight. When he saw her staring, one side of his mouth kicked up into a breathtaking half smirk, revealing the tip of a fang.

There was no doubt in her mind who this second... or third... Patrick was. "Alistair."

His smirk grew and he lowered his chin a little. "Hello, Gorgeous."

A panicked laugh left her as she looked between the two versions of Patrick. The younger version of them was only a few feet away leaving bloody handprints in the dusting of snow.

"Leave her alone, Alistair," growled Patrick, stepping forward until he was side by side with her. "I don't know how you managed to conjure her in this place, but I won't—"

"Let me hurt her. Yes, yes. We know." Alistair snorted. His narrowed gaze relaxed when he looked at her again, and a slow, heart-stopping smile tugged at his lips. Deep, throaty laughter sent goosebumps up her arms, just like the first time she'd heard it. "As if that would be my objective if I managed to materialize our mate."

The younger version of them bellowed his anguish, driving a spike through Violet's chest.

"Alistair!" Patrick snarled, ignoring the memory as he started toward his other half.

Violet twisted her body so her back was to the more-than-slightly demented Alistair and she held up her hands to stop Patrick. "Stop. You can't fight him. I already know we're mates."

Patrick's eyes rounded a little and his lips parted, then his typical mask slipped into place and he shook his head. "Of course you know," he huffed a laugh and ran a hand through his hair. "You're in my mind. You know everything I know."

"I'm..." Violet blinked. Her hands lowered to her sides. "Where?"

Large hands fell over her shoulders, giving a light squeeze, and Alistair's lips brushed the shell of her ear. "In our mind, Shortie, but Boy Scout here thinks I brought you here. As much as I would love to take credit for that magical occurrence, that's not in *my* bag of tricks."

Her breathing gained speed and she tried to lean her head away from him, but he followed her and his low chuckle caused another wave of goosebumps to spread across her body. Alistair lowered his mouth to her neck, just behind her ear and planted a warm, shiver inducing kiss along her cooler skin.

"Let her go," Patrick ordered, closing the distance between them. His features clamped down in rage while his hands curled into fists.

Another laugh bubbled out of Alistair before he released her. The heat of his body disappeared and a chill spread through her body. It hadn't been that cold before. While Patrick stayed near her, he didn't touch her. He wouldn't even look at her.

"Patrick." She tried to get his attention, but looking over her head was all too easy for him. "Patrick, look at me."

He shook his head as the screech of car brakes split the night. The horrible sound didn't make her jump nearly as bad this time, but the crunch of metal made her flinch. "You'll disappear soon. I'm just here to make sure Alistair doesn't try anything until then."

"I'm not going to disappear and you can't ignore me."

Anger flashed across his face and he lowered his chin, pinning her with his narrowed gaze. "You're not actually here."

"You might want to rethink that, Boy Scout." Alistair's voice called from a short distance away.

Violet turned to find him leaning his shoulder against a tree trunk.

His head cocked to the side and he grinned at her. She had to admit she liked that he always had some sort of smile for her. "While I thoroughly enjoyed that, when was the last time I was able to touch a figment or a memory?"

Realization fell over her, followed quickly by confusion nipping at its heels. "How were you able to touch me? I tried to pry the glass apart to help and my hands went right through it."

Alistair said nothing. He only continued to smile at her.

"You tried to help?" Patrick asked, his tone much softer than before.

She tilted her chin up so she could look at his face instead of his chest and smiled sadly. "Of course I did."

His face pulled together while his gaze roamed over her entire being. A small step brought them toe-to-toe and he lifted a hand slowly toward her face. The back of his warm knuckles brushed a feather-light touch across her cheek, and a rush of air left him, deflating his chest before it began to rise and fall in rapid succession.

Slowly, his hand turned, and he buried his fingers in her hair, cupping her cheek in his palm. "How is this possible?"

"So you're allowed to touch, but I'm not?"

"Shut up, Alistair," Patrick told him, but his voice held no authority or threat as he gazed in awe at her.

Violet released a short laugh, then leaned into Patrick's touch. "I don't know how this happened, but I guess I'm... in your mind?"

"You're really here?" Patrick asked. "That's not possible."

"I could tell you something only I know." Violet offered.

The hint of a smile touched one side of Patrick's mouth, but he shook his head. "How would I know if it's real or not?"

"I don't know." Violet shrugged and Patrick lowered his hand to her upper arm. "But I was sitting beside you in one of Doc's exam rooms, waiting for you to wake up." His hand followed the length of her arm and she tried to focus on what she was saying. "I told you to come back to me." Words failed her when his fingers slipped around her hand. After clearing her throat she continued explaining, "I felt this pull to touch you and when I did there was a blast of wind and then I was here."

She squeezed his hand and then brought it in front of her so she could hold it with both of hers. "We need to get out of here. You need to wake up."

Patrick gazed at her sadly.

The screech of car brakes split the night.

"He won't go with you," Alistair spoke, and she turned her head to find him only an arm's length away. "No matter how much we both want to."

Metal crunched in the near distance.

"Unfortunately," Alistair continued. "He has always been very good at keeping me on a tight leash. That leash has become more of a fine line though."

Violet stared at him, but when he didn't go on, she asked "What do you mean?"

Alistair took another step toward her. "I have had to fight for my foothold inside of our Boy Scout's mind every day. The trial was the first time I was able to break free completely. Most times, I was only able to influence what he did."

"Like when he pummeled that Bloodmoon scout," Violet remembered, and there had been other times too where he would do something a little too intensely.

A toothy grin spread across Alistair's face, and Patrick's hand slipped out of hers. When she looked up at him, he was staring out at the wreckage of cars amongst the trees—agony clearly written across his solemn face.

"The point is, since working together to find you, my little peanut, the line holding me back has greatly thinned. Boy Scout isn't convinced he can keep me away from you any more." Alistair lifted a hand and she held her breath as he traced a clawed finger along her jaw. "What it means, gorgeous, is that I have the same power now as I did that night, when he was the sole survivor of a crash that killed five others." His claws brushed across her throat. "The night I ripped his lycan abilities away from him."

The animosity poisoning his final words made Violet flinch away from him. She stumbled back, crashing into Patrick, who steadied her with his gentle hands. His misery coursed through her when their eyes met, but he turned back to the crash site without a word.

Violet followed his gaze and found the younger Patrick only a few feet from them, palms toward the sky. He threw his head back and screamed in anguish while blood-red devoured the pure moonstone in his eyes.

Chapter 14

Violet

***Violet slowly shook her** head while she watched, with tears running down her* cheeks, as the younger Patrick had his lycan abilities torn from him. She blindly reached out and found Patrick's hand before she wove her small fingers between his. "I'm so sorry," she said softly.

Alistair sighed, and slowly began to circle them as the younger Patrick faded away. "And I thought we were beginning to like each other, Violet. Yet here you are, apologizing for my birth."

Violet watched him circle around to her back, but something tickled her thoughts. He came back into view on Patrick's side. "Lycans don't have wolf spirits."

He looked at her with raised brow. "We already know that, sweetheart."

A huff of sad laughter left her. "*You're* not a wolf spirit."

Alistair stopped his circling and turned his feet toward her, curiosity illuminating his crimson eyes. "Your point, darling?"

Relief flooded Violet's being, making her laugh again. She hadn't been able to deny that she was attracted to Alistair. How could she not be when he looked exactly like Patrick? His mannerisms were similar, but always on the wrong end of the scale—too harsh, bitter, mean, more animal. But if what she was feeling was true, it lined up with what Jax had read, and it all made sense. A beautiful, horrible sense.

The screech of brakes pierced the silence.

"Patrick, why do you replay this memory over and over?" Violet asked, turning to the spot she knew the cars would appear moments later, tumbling down the embankment into the trees. The sound of grinding metal made her clench her teeth.

Beside her, Patrick stood with his shoulders slumped. His jaw pulsed a few times when the vehicles careened toward the tree-line. When they stopped, he slowly lowered his gaze to hers. "So I never forget."

Violet watched him, her thoughts whirring through her mind while Alistair started pacing.

"He tortures himself with this day-after-day, minute after minute. It's one of the ways he's been able to tether me so well. Confining me in this memory. This place in our mind. It's aggravating!"

Patrick glared at him. "Only to someone who doesn't care what happened here."

"Care?" Alistair snorted and his voice grew louder. "Of course, I care! This was the day I was born!"

"No," Violet interrupted, her quiet tone drawing both their attention. "You were born January twenty-sixth."

Both versions of Patrick blinked at her. Alistair's brows lowered while Patrick said, "That's *my* birthday, Violet."

"I know," she said. "But lycans don't have wolf spirits, Patrick. Alistair isn't some bloodlusting wolf spirit you can push away."

Violet reached out to Alistair and was a little surprised when he immediately captured her hand with his own long fingers. Her surprise was short lived when he swaggered forward to press his chest against her hand. Although her immediate response would have been to pull away, something in her told her not to. Alistair held her hand firmly over his heart, then winked at her.

A growl thundered through Patrick and Violet released an exasperated sigh. Alistair smirked in response, his ruby eyes shimmering with amusement as one of his fingers began to draw lazy circles over the back of her hand. It was quite distracting. Exactly like it was when Patrick did it.

"Jax has been reading everything he can find about lycans," Violet explained, trying to keep her thoughts on the right track. "There was one book that said something about how a lycan's soul can be torn in two."

The lazy circles stopped.

Alistair's teasing expression drained away.

Violet smiled sadly at him. "Lycan's don't have wolf spirits."

"No. They don't." Patrick confirmed and she slowly dragged her gaze away from Alistair. "He showed up after I killed them. He took most of my abilities, anything that even closely resembled the lycan parts of me. I only had basic abilities, making me more closely resemble a wolven than a lycan."

Violet swallowed the knot in her throat and she sent a silent prayer to the goddess to guide her through this next part. "I think—I think your soul was split, Patrick." She squeezed his hand. "And because both sides still reside in you, you didn't really notice."

"What are you talking about?"

"Vi," Alistair said her nickname with a pained note that pulled at her heart.

He almost sounded like he was pleading with her. His grip on her hand tightened and she turned to him. There, radiating in his crimson eyes, was an emotion she'd never seen before—fear.

She watched him closely while she spoke, "Alistair is every part of you that you hate. The deepest, darkest parts."

Alistair's eyes slowly closed and if her hand hadn't been on his chest, she wouldn't have noticed the deep breath he drew in.

"But he is also the most passionate parts of you," Violet added.

Alistair's eyes opened again and his head tilted to the side in curiosity.

"What are you talking about?" Patrick asked, disgust ringing through his voice. "There is nothing good about him."

She looked up at him and raised a brow. "Not even your lycan abilities?"

He blinked at her. "But he isn't..." He glared at Alistair. "I wouldn't..."

"You're going to tell me that the things he's done, or that he has thought about doing, wouldn't have ever crossed your mind even if it was in a much smaller way?" She watched Patrick's face closely and saw a crack in his façade. No, he couldn't tell her that and she knew it, but he wasn't going to say it. She decided to try something else. Drawing in a deep breath, Violet pulled her hand free of Patrick's and took a step away from him—toward Alistair.

"What are you doing?" Patrick asked.

Alistair shifted her hand position so he could keep holding her hand, while he wrapped his other arm around her waist, making Patrick growl.

"You're going to stand there and tell me that you haven't thought about holding me the way he is? About kissing my neck the way he did earlier?"

Frustration shattered Patrick's mask and he seethed, looking off to the side, then back at her. "Of course I want to hold you and kiss you, but I can't."

"Why?"

"Because..." Patrick thrust a hand through his hair and shifted his weight.

"Why, Patrick?"

"Because I can't!" He yelled, surprising her. "If I get too close to you or think about you at all like that, *he* pops into my head and twists it."

Alistair lowered his head and chuckled in her ear. "You should have heard the things I was saying to him the night he finally gave in and kissed you."

"I'm sure it was passionate," Violet said carefully before adding, "and dark and twisted."

Alistair clicked his tongue and returned to his full height, still holding her against his side.

"Exactly," Patrick huffed his annoyed agreement. "Dark and twisted."

"But your passion comes from him."

Patrick growled and turned his back on her, slamming his hands into his pockets.

"That's why he shows up every time you get passionate about something; whether that's me or protecting the clan!" Violet insisted, stepping out of Alistair's hold. It took her a moment to realize he'd let her go without complaint, but when she turned to look back at him he simply shrugged with a sad, resigned smile on his face. She was on the right track and he knew it. "Your lycan abilities are powerful and exciting and that's a type of passion, too."

"Violet, stop."

"No, you can't stay here, reliving this horrible memory over and over again." She tried to get in front of him, but he turned away from her again. "You can't give up on living your life. You need to wake up. *I* need you to wake up!"

The memory of a younger Patrick howled with her, emphasizing her words with a painful note.

When it ended, Patrick slowly turned toward her, his hazel eyes filled with torment. "Why?"

Violet leaned back. "*Why?*" she repeated.

"I deserve this, Violet. I killed them. It doesn't matter that I was trying to protect them, *I killed them*!"

Tears stung her eyes and she tilted her head to the side. "It was an accident, Patrick."

Moisture lined his eyes while he shook his head. His face scrunched and he took a step away from her.

"It was an accident," she repeated, more firmly this time. "Protecting people is what you do. It drives you to act, it always has."

"No."

"That's why you can't stay locked in your head." She insisted, her voice rising as the turbulent amount of emotions rose up inside her chest. "People need your protection. Sentinel clan needs you to help them against Blood Moon."

He shook his head.

"I need you to help *me*!" Violet yelled at him, her tears falling down her face now.

A sad scoff left him. "As much as I love to hear that you need me, you don't, Violet. You are incredibly strong on your own."

She nodded and thumped her fist against her thigh as those bottled up emotions began to overflow. "You're right. I don't *need* you. I am strong. Stronger than anyone realized and maybe I could find another lycan to teach me."

Confusion tugged Patrick's brows together.

"Maybe, they would give me a chance to try and explain how I transformed into a wolf for the first time ever when I was eighteen, or that I can't control the astounding number of abilities that are showing up in rapid succession, or that I can apparently enter people's minds—"

Patrick's hands flew in the air, palms facing her. "Wait, wait... what?" He looked over her from head to toe.

"Oh yeah, I'm lycan, by the way." She laughed, and it sounded a little off kilter even to her own ears. "Apparently that can happen."

He blinked at her, his lips slightly parted like he knew he needed to say something, but didn't know what.

"That's not the point." Violet waved her hands while she closed the distance between them. "The point is that you are a protector and there are hundreds of people who need your protection right now. So, you have to wake up!"

"I can't!" Patrick shouted and the sound hung in the air around them, the weight of it crushing Violet's heart. "If I wake up, so does *he*." He pointed at Alistair who was watching their conversation with a surprisingly stoic expression. "And I don't think I can stop him anymore."

A soft sob left her. "Patrick. *He* **is** *you*." She walked to Alistair who gazed at her with a sad, loving smile as she stretched out her hand to him. With a nod, he placed his hand in hers and followed her back to Patrick. "What happened here was an accident and Alistair is a part of you."

Patrick staggered back a step.

"You have to accept that," she told him softly. "Or stay here and leave everyone behind. Leave them to fight for their lives on their own." She shrugged a shoulder and shook her head. "But that's not the person who stole my heart."

"Vi," he whispered her nickname and her heart tumbled about in her chest.

She held out her other hand to him. "Haven't you tortured yourself long enough?"

He stared at her hand. "I've held onto this..." he looked around the forest, then over her shoulder at Alistair. "Onto him... alone for so long. I don't think I can anymore."

A smile burst across her face and she almost laughed. What a pair they made. Two outsiders to their kind. Two people left to carry heavy burdens alone, not realizing they had people around them to help ease that burden. She let go of Alistair's hand, closed the distance between her and Patrick, and rose up on her toes. Surprised, he caught her around the waist as she reached up and pulled his head down. "Patrick, you're not alone anymore."

He stared at her for a moment, the forest around them quiet for the first time since she'd arrived. Then he let out a breath that took away all the tension in his body. A breath he'd been holding far too long. His lips brushed hers, softly, almost hesitantly. When he started to pull away, she leaned closer and his mouth melted against hers. His arms tightened around her waist, drawing her against his body and lighting every inch of hers on fire. If they could get out of here, she promised herself that there would be many more kisses just like this one.

With that thought, she tilted her head away so she could look at him and sucked in a small breath of surprise when he gazed down at her with ruby-red eyes. She opened her mouth to speak, but the crimson gave way to hazel and then back again. The garnet held for a moment longer before slowly fading away.

A warm breeze blew through the trees drawing both of their attention. Violet settled back onto her heels as she stared at the snow collecting on the ground around them. The flakes were bigger now and falling heavier.

Patrick looked around them. "This is different."

"Different can be good," Violet told him softly, then lifted onto her toes to plant a gentle kiss on his lips. When she stepped back, she grabbed his hands. "Let's go home."

Patrick drew in a deep breath and a soft smile spread across his lips. "Home."

The snowflakes falling around them froze in midair. Violet looked at the floating flakes, then back at Patrick and squeezed his hands. Light pulsed around them, seeming to come from every flake in both the air and the ground. It grew brighter and brighter until Violet had to close her eyes, but even behind her lids, the light was incredible. When it began to fade she blinked her eyes open to find the off-white walls of the exam room surrounding her.

Jax and Dr. Penmann stood on either side of her watching with wide eyes.

"Did it work?" Violet asked, as a heavy wave of exhaustion washed over her.

Patrick jolted on the table in front of her, making the three of them jump. He sucked in a sharp breath, and his ruby eyes glittered under the bright lights. But as he slowly released the air from his lungs, the crimson tone paled until all that was left was gorgeous silvery-blue moonstone.

Chapter 15

Patrick

A trio of mirrored *expressions stared at him with wide eyes when Patrick* lowered his chin and looked around the room. His vision was blurry, so he blinked away the lingering effects of sleep while Dr. Penmann stepped around to the other side of the exam table.

The older woman's hands were a flurry of anxious movement. "How are you feeling, Patrick?"

Honestly? Strange. He felt strange.

The last thing he remembered was being on the phone with Jax and feeling his body give out. He'd been trying to escape Blood Moon.

He looked around at the familiar exam room. This had to be real because there was no way his imagination was this good. Even the dream he'd just woken from had issues with it; like the echoing voices. But... he searched the recesses of his mind and furrowed his brows.

"Alistair?" he called into his mind for his darker half.

There was no answer. No pressing weight against his skull. No stabbing through his heart. The memory of the accident rippled across his thoughts, but for the first time ever, it felt like the distant past. Sorrow accompanied the awful moment, but his guilt had softened. Had that dream actually helped him?

"Patrick?" Dr. Penmann's raspy voice pulled him out of his thoughts and he found himself staring at the woman. "How are you feeling?"

He blinked. Then opened his mouth to speak, but a cough escaped him, rattling his chest.

A cup with a straw appeared in front of him and he greedily sucked down its entire contents. Fresh, cold water ran down his throat. When was the last time he had water? He didn't know. He didn't even know how long he'd been gone.

Warm, cinnamon spiced vanilla surged through his senses, enveloping him in the scent of Christmas cookies. His gaze focused on the hand holding the cup in front of him. Small, delicate fingers were latched around the cup, which was shaking ever-so-slightly.

"Come on, Patrick," said a soft, familiar voice in his mind. Violet's gentle prodding flowed through him as if it were his own thoughts. Effortless. But concern left an imprint on each of her words. *"Answer her."*

Patrick flicked his gaze to Dr. Penmann and he nodded. "I'm good."

The doc's shoulders sank when a large, rushed breath left her. "Anything I need to know or be concerned about?"

He tilted his head to the side and his gaze wandered as he mentally checked over his body. "No," he told her with an air of amazement in his low voice—lower than usual. He sounded like Alistair, but without the growly after tone.

"No." Violet's voice fluttered through his thoughts again. *"You sound like Patrick."*

Slowly, Patrick turned his head toward his other side. The purple eyes he collided with first were full of brotherly endearment. Jax dipped his chin, then his hand clamped on Patrick's leg. "Glad to have you back."

A smirk tugged at Patrick's mouth and he immediately threw up a mental barrier, prepared to push Alistair back... but there was no sinister presence waiting in the wings to take over. Only a warm sense of comfort, reaching toward him. Patrick furrowed his brows, the smirk falling from his face.

That warmth spread through his limbs, thawing every frozen part of him, as he turned a little more to find identical amethyst eyes to Jax's. But these were the eyes that had melted his heart the first time he'd seen them, full of cunning and an inner strength that no one else noticed, three and a half years ago. Eyes that could cut his soul, but also see to the depths of his heart.

Keeping his gaze locked with hers, Patrick swung his legs over the side of the exam bed. Warmth turned to a roaring fire in his stomach and he reached for her. Violet's gaze dropped to his hand when he neared her cheek, making him check his actions. He lowered his hand and disappointment flickered across his thoughts.

"Hey," he said... and immediately felt lame. That's the best that he could come up with? Really?

Jax snorted, making Patrick grumble.

Violet tipped her head to the side, narrowing her eyes in thought while a silly grin spread across her lips. "Hey, yourself."

The tips of his ears warmed while Violet chuckled. Her laughter reignited the fire in his belly, but he planted his hands on the edge of the exam table behind him and squeezed. He couldn't let his emotions get out of control. His restraint didn't stop Violet though. She slowly closed the distance between them. Her hands trembled when they settled against his sides. Patrick almost grabbed her arms to help steady her, but she wasn't falling over—she was leaning into him. The added height Violet gained when she lifted onto her toes was not enough to close the foot long gap of height between them, but it didn't take a seer to know what she wanted.

Excruciatingly aware that her twin brother was only a couple of feet away, Patrick politely pressed a chaste kiss to her forehead. His hands had left the exam table and his arms found themselves around her waist, holding her tiny frame against him.

Patrick tensed and searched for Alistair in his mind... but once again there was no one but himself in the confines of his mind.

"*Breathe, Patrick,*" Violet's voice caressed his thoughts and he looked at the top of her head while she leaned into their embrace, pressing her cheek against his chest.

"How are you doing that?" Patrick asked, his voice much quieter than he'd meant and a little rough.

Jax reached for the cup of water, but Patrick shook his head. Jax nodded, then tightly crossed his arms and stared at Violet.

"Doing what?" Violet's voice was slightly muffled against his chest, making Patrick chuckle.

He slid his hands across her back to wrap his fingers gently around her arms so he could move her backward. "Speaking to me through the clan-link. I'm not part of the clan." A chord of fear struck him and his gaze snapped to Jax. "Alpha Draven—"

"Won't have anything to say about your return," Jax interrupted, holding up a hand to stop him. "Not that it would matter even if he did."

Patrick blinked. His brows pulled together in confusion. He looked between Jax and Violet, then at Dr. Penmann when she walked around the table into his line of sight. His gaze settled on Jax again as he thought things over. If Alpha Draven's word didn't mean anything, that must mean...

"You're the alpha," Patrick said and found himself bowing his chin respectfully to his best friend.

In the past, when he'd lowered his gaze around Alpha Draven it had always been to preserve the ruse that Patrick was subject to the older man's rule. There were so many times Patrick had to restrain himself, especially as Alistair grew stronger. At first, it had been out of respect—he'd owed so much to the man for taking him in when no one else would. Time went on and he saw how the man treated his clan... how he treated his own daughter. He had very little respect for the former alpha Draven, now.

Jax did not react the way Patrick thought he would. His friend had always been very accepting and even excited about becoming the next alpha, but what Patrick saw now was a young man with the weight of the world on his shoulders. It dragged his friends shoulders lower, and a bone-tired expression settled over his face.

"I'm the alpha," Jax confirmed, his tone flat with no hint of exuberance. He shrugged a shoulder, and a small smile lifted some of the exhaustion from his face. His purple eyes churned into molten gold as he said, "Welcome home, Beta."

A bolt of electricity zapped through Patrick's limbs. When Alpha Draven had severed his connection to the clan, it felt like a part of him had been ripped from his chest. That peace of him had remained hollow, but now his connection to a clan filled the void. A bond snapped into place, a line connecting him to every other member of the clan. He sucked in a sharp breath when hundreds of conversations flooded his thoughts. Grinding his teeth, he quickly suppressed them.

"Jax." Patrick drew in a settling breath through his nose. "I can't be your beta. The clan won't accept me. My eyes—"

"Are beautiful," Violet interrupted and then smiled wearily at him when Patrick lowered his chin to look at her. Her hands trembled against his sides as she continued, "They look like moonstone."

Worry flooded his senses when he took in her pale expression. "Are you okay?" he softly asked.

A brave, assured look passed over her face. "I'm fine."

Patrick hadn't thought anything of it before because he'd assumed she was as nervous as he was about embracing in front of Jax. But her fingers were clenched in his shirt at his sides and she hadn't tried to step away. He opened his mind, feeling for her presence. When he'd searched for her in the past it was like wading through a sea of his clanmates, and even then her energy was dull. Hard to find, even harder to grasp. Speaking to one another through their link took great effort. But now, when Patrick searched for her an immediate, all consuming, warm energy filled his mind. Their connection was immediate, and the strongest he'd ever experienced. It was easy to reach for that warmth, but when he did, exhaustion rolled over him like a tidal wave.

Startled by the strength of her weariness, Patrick slumped slightly against the exam table, making everyone in the room lurch for him.

"I'm okay," he quickly told them as he lifted one hand to ward them off. His other arm wrapped firmly around Violet's waist, offering her support. Relief and gratitude flowed through their link, making him tighten his hold a touch more. "This is just... a lot." He glanced at the doctor who was looking between him and Violet with great interest. "Think I'm good to go, Doc?"

Dr. Penmann's brows rose on her forehead. She smirked, shook her head, and shrugged. "As far as I can tell, you're better than ever. Your wounds have all healed." She moved for the exam room door and pulled it open. "I suggest taking the rest of the night and possibly the next couple of days to recover, but you'll be a better judge of that than I will, I imagine."

Jax followed the doctor. "Thanks for everything, doc. I'll keep an eye on him, and Violet, and let you know if we need anything."

They left the room, but Dr. Penmann's raspy tone was easy for him to hear as she said, "Make sure they watch over you, too, Alpha. You've all been through a lot tonight. We know next to nothing about these events, but I'm sure you're going to have a lot of questions to answer tomorrow."

Patrick tuned out their conversation and looked down at Violet who was leaning heavily against his side.

"You're really okay?"

She nodded. "Yeah, that just took a lot out of me."

"If you're too tired, I can carry you," he offered.

Violet snorted.

A smile spread across his face. "I'm serious."

Slowly, she tilted her head back. Her eyes were narrowed, but the hint of a smile betrayed her. "I'm not letting you carry me, but I'll hold onto you."

A low chuckle rumbled in his chest. "Stubborn as always."

Her smile grew in response, and her beautiful amethyst eyes sparkled with amusement.

Holding her firmly against his side, Patrick lowered his head to press another kiss to her forehead. He lingered there, allowing her warm scent of cinnamon spiced vanilla to wash over him. When he pulled back, her eyes were closed and she released a deep breath. "Let's get you home."

They made their way out of the exam room side by side. Patrick kept a firm hold around her while Violet clung to his side. He was not expecting an entourage for their walk to Alpha House, but when they stepped out of the small clinic there was a half circle of warriors with eyes only for him. Silver and bronze swirled in their eyes, and Patrick lowered his chin when he felt his own eyes begin to change in response.

Violet's head turned as she looked around, then up at him. Her arm squeezed his middle. "Don't," she insisted. "You don't have to hide anymore."

His mind raced through the events of the dream he'd had and how Alistair was missing inside his mind. Then when she'd mentioned his eyes before— "You said my eyes were moonstone."

A half smile tugged at one corner of her mouth. "Because they are."

"How do you know that?" He asked. "They haven't been described that way in years."

Violet's smile grew and the purple faded from her eyes. Shimmering opalescence filled her gaze, accented by flecks of gold, silver, and bronze. "Your eyes are moonstone, Patrick. The red is gone."

Surprised, Patrick stared at her eyes.

He'd only seen lycan with eyes like that, but even theirs paled in beauty compared to hers. But if she was lycan...

His dream came crashing back to him. She'd told him she was lycan and if that were true, then—

Could his blood red eyes really be gone? The outward expression of his guilt and an ever present reminder of what he'd done? He searched the memory of the accident, but the emotions attached to it were different than before. Guilt had weighed him down for so long, consuming the events of that night, but it was no longer the primary emotion. Sorrow branded the old memory, but guilt had finally taken a back seat.

Relief deflated his chest when Patrick huffed a laugh. New, fresh air filled his lungs and for the first time in a long time he felt like he could truly breathe.

A wide smile spread across his mouth and he let out another soft laugh as he bent over to press a kiss to Violet's lips. A surprised squeak left her, making him smile against her lips, but her mouth quickly melted against his. Her hands found their way to the sides of his face, cupping his cheeks and holding his mouth to hers. Roaring warmth spread through him, but instead of retreating, he allowed the passion to fill him. He lifted Violet off the ground, hugging her waist to hold her securely against his body.

"Ahem," someone called loudly.

Heat prickled over Patrick's face, and he broke their kiss only to press another quick one to Violet's lips, making her laugh. He kissed the tip of her nose and then her forehead, before slowly lowering her to her feet again.

Jax stood glaring at them with his arms crossed tightly over his chest while Violet settled snugly against Patrick's side.

"Sorry, Jax," Patrick chortled, feeling anything but.

His friend simply shook his head.

Patrick looked around at the warriors who were watching him and Violet with intense curiosity and some confusion. Some of their eyes had returned to a normal color while others still held on to their silver or bronze.

With a deep breath, he extended one of his hands in front of him and imagined claws replacing his nails. He remembered the light pressure in his mouth when his fangs would grow and the tingling along the tips of his ears as they tapered. He tried to recall every detail of the control he once had. And then his ears began to tingle like they once had and a light pressure filled his mouth. An odd sensation warmed his fingertips before his nails transformed into long, dark claws.

The burst of laughter that escaped him was a mix of so many emotions. Relief. Surprise. Excitement. Astonishment. Wonder. He rolled his hand over and flexed his fingers. Slowly his claws returned to nails, but he left his other lycan features. Living amongst other lycans, he always had his ears tapered and fangs elongated. He didn't know how his fellow wolven clanmates would feel about his new appearance, but as he lifted his moonstone gaze to the warriors surrounding him, he was excited to find out.

Chapter 16

Violet

***The warriors had responded** to Patrick's reveal in a variety of ways.* Some visibly relaxed while others seemed more tense than before. The ones that had worked more closely with him in the past whooped in celebration.

But there were a couple who walked away. Jax hurried after them, shooting her a quick message that he would catch up. And catch up he did when she and Patrick had made it to Alpha House's walkway. Only a few of the warriors remained, but they settled outside the house while the three of them made their way inside.

"They're okay for now, but I told them we were going to talk about this more tomorrow," Jax explained while he held the door open for Patrick and Violet.

"I think that's a smart plan," she agreed as Patrick led her to the couch. For a moment she thought he would set her down and then move to the armchair, but his hold around her waist held firm while he sat down with her. He even leaned against the arm of the couch a little, allowing her to more easily rest against him. She closed her eyes and sighed her contentment, earning a kiss to the top of her head. "A lot has happened in a short amount of time. Not everyone is going to be as receptive or welcoming of this new one."

"I'm glad I was able to make some friends with the warriors before all of this happened," Patrick stated.

His fingers drew lazy circles against her hip and Violet couldn't decide if they tickled or if it was comforting. Thankfully, she was too tired to think it through and the longer the circles continued, the more relaxing she found them to be.

An armchair groaned and Violet opened her eyes to find that Jax had claimed the spot, but was leaning forward, pressing his elbows against his knees while he watched them. "This is gonna take some getting used to."

Patrick stiffened and the lazy circles stilled. "Would you like me to move?"

Jax's eyes darted between her gaze and what she assumed was Patrick's. Finally, he sat back, relaxing into the armchair and shook his head. "No. I'm sure it's nice to be in the arms of your mate."

Patrick sucked in a breath.

Her brother held up a hand. "Just keep the kissing to a minimum around me, please."

A smile spread across her lips and she closed her eyes again. She was so tired.

"We can do that," Patrick's voice rumbled in his chest against her cheek. He tightened his hold on her momentarily. "So you told her?"

"I had to," Jax explained, his tone firm and assured. "She thought Zander was her mate. I had to let her know that he was wrong, that she had you."

"He also told me you're lycan," she mumbled, and felt rather smug about tattling on her brother.

"Okay, to be fair, I thought you already knew. It was really confusing when I realized you didn't know."

"And somehow you're lycan, too?" Patrick's question lingered in the air.

After a few quiet moments, Violet shakily pushed off Patrick's chest so she could sit beside him. She bent one leg and faced him while the other dangled off the couch. "A lot has happened since you disappeared."

Patrick nodded slowly a couple of times, then wrapped his fingers around hers. "I want to hear it all, but I need to hear about this first. I saw you in my dream, and you said you were lycan and needed help. Then I woke up and you actually are lycan." His gaze drifted over her and his shoulders lifted into a shrug. "Other than being worn out, you seem fine."

Violet blinked. She opened her mouth, but no words came out. After wetting her lips, she tried again. "That wasn't a dream, and I'm far from fine."

"What do you mean that wasn't a dream?"

Her gaze dropped to their fingers entwined in her lap. "I'm not really sure how to explain it. One second I was sitting beside you in the exam room, and the next I was standing in a forest I didn't recognize."

The armchair moaned when Jax leaned forward again and Patrick watched her intently.

"It was the night of the accident. Or at least, the memory of it," Violet offered the information quietly, not sure if he wanted Jax to know the details, but well aware he was sitting only a few feet away. "You and Alistair were both there, and I realized Jax was right."

"I was?" Jax's eyebrows shot up his forehead. "About what?"

Violet wet her lips then nibbled on the lower one for a second. "The thing you read about a lycan's soul being split when their eyes turn red." She looked between the two young men. "Alistair was Patrick, but all of the more intense and passionate parts of him. That's why you couldn't ever fully push him away. That's why when you started getting more emotional about something, he was closer than ever."

A silent moment passed between the three of them before Patrick leaned toward her to brush a stray hair behind her ear. "So how did you manage to get in my head, short stuff?"

His gentle touch over her ear and down her neck set a delightful roll of goosebumps down her arms. His hand settled on her shoulder and he splayed his fingertips into her hair, making it hard to think.

"I uh..." Her eyes fluttered shut. "Mmm... don't know."

Jax cleared his throat and Patrick's fingers stilled.

When she opened her eyes, Patrick had a sheepish—if not a little smug—smile lifting the corners of his mouth. Jax on the other hand was glaring.

Patrick's hand returned to his own lap, and Violet tried to hide her disappointment.

A quick smirk flashed across Patrick's face. She was about to ask about it, but he started talking first, "Lycan often have abilities that are linked with some sort of element. Entering someone else's mind isn't one of those skills though. That sounds more like a witch ability."

Violet groaned. "Not more witch accusations."

"I'm not calling you a witch," Patrick assured. "Just saying I've never heard of anything like that among lycan."

"Jax and I both have abilities that we shouldn't," she blurted, then directed a hand toward her twin whose eyes had rounded at her announcement. "When we found you, you were on the brink of death. Your heart..." Violet's throat clenched, cutting off her words. She swallowed the knot in her throat and continued, "Your heart stopped."

Patrick froze and Violet wondered if he was even breathing, but then he said, "I died?"

"You were dead long enough for Violet to start feeling the effects of losing her mate," Jax spoke up, taking control of the story. "I just remember thinking that it couldn't end like that. That you both deserved better. Then your heart started again."

Jax shrugged like nothing had happened and anger boiled in Violet's belly. "Oh yeah, just like that, huh?"

"Violet," Jax's warning tone did nothing to stop her.

"Nothing else happened, Jax?" Violet demanded, quirking a brow.

"Nothing of importance," Jax groused at the same time Patrick asked, "What happened?"

Annoyed, Violet turned back to Patrick to finish the story. "Jax got super intense. You started healing, but he suddenly had your injuries." The remnants of pain from watching both of them die passed through her and moisture lined her eyes. "Your heart restarted, but his stopped."

Patrick's expression locked down and he glared at Jax.

He said something, but Violet's rage was crashing through her. A dull roar filled her ears and she grabbed the throw pillow behind her and then chucked it at her twin.

The fluffy pillow smacked him in the face, interrupting whatever he'd been saying. "Hey!"

"Jerk," she growled, then spun on Patrick who had an amused smile lifting the corners of his mouth. When her finger pointed at him, his smile was replaced with wide eyes. "You, too! Don't you ever do that to me again. Either of you!"

"It's not like I meant to die," Jax grumbled.

Violet dove for another pillow. Her fingertips grazed the edge, but large hands snagged her upper arm and waist, pulling her back against a solid, warm chest.

"Easy," Patrick's low, soothing voice feathered across the shell of her ear and sent a ripple of delightful shivers down her spine. "I can feel how exhausted you are. Don't wear yourself out more."

"Hey, hey, hey," Jax protested. He waved a hand at her and Patrick and she felt him lean away from her. "None of that either."

A rumble of laughter shook Patrick's chest. "I was just telling her to calm down."

"Yeah, well..." Jax waved a hand again, like he wanted to say something disapproving, but didn't know what.

"Like I was saying," Patrick continued while Violet settled into the couch, clasping her tiny hand around Patrick's. "The abilities you're describing sound like things a witch could do. I don't have a ton of experience with them, but they did come and help out from time to time in the lycan community."

Violet jumped when Patrick suddenly twisted, and a sense of unease settled in her thoughts.

"Where are the former alpha and luna?" Patrick wondered. His hazel eyes were sad and his tone full of dread as he added, "Violet, when you were in my head you mentioned that you had shifted."

"Like she said," Jax sighed wearily, sinking into the armchair. "A lot has happened."

Patrick sat quietly and Jax didn't seem eager to share, so Violet drew in a deep breath and began the tale, "The full moon after mine and Jax's birthday came. I still didn't show any signs of a wolf or shifting so they only sent Jax to the trial. Mom found me outside, and we were talking about a deal she'd made with a witch. It ensured I would live and have a wolf, but when I shifted, she would die."

Patrick's lips parted ever so slightly, his expression pinched in grief.

"Vikter led an attack from Blood Moon that night." Violet spit the words like they were poisoned, but couldn't find the words to continue.

Thankfully, she didn't have to because Jax did. He stared unseeingly as he finished the story, "He killed her. I killed him." The lack of emotion in his voice was chilling. "Violet was in her wolf form, standing guard over Mom's body. Our father went crazy, I locked him away, became alpha, and Violet has been dealing with random abilities showing up and not knowing how to control them."

"Like what?" Patrick asked, his voice raw with emotion.

Violet tapped one of her fingers against the back of his hand. "Like hearing everyone's conversations through the clan-link. Random shifts in appearance that I can't reverse or change. Heightened hearing at random times that I can't turn on or off, but I was actually able to in your mind..."

His fingers lightly squeezed hers. "Those are all normal things that lycans go through, but we usually learn how to control it by the time we're eight."

"Eight?" Violet and Jax said together.

Patrick nodded. "A lycan's abilities are more magic based. We don't have a wolf spirit—" he stared into Violet's eyes. "We are the wolf. It's who we are." He gestured to his ears, which had remained tapered to short points since they'd left the clinic. "Ears, fangs, claws, eyes, morphing into our wolf forms. It's not something we have to work with our wolf spirit to do, it's something we do instinctually. When that control and those abilities were taken from me after the accident, it was like part of myself was missing. Only Alistair could do those things."

"Is that why you shifted like a wolven does during your trial?" Violet ran her thumb over the tip of one of his fingers and his eyes dropped to the light caress.

His head tipped side to side. "Possibly. Alistair had those abilities so I think he would have been able to let me shift like a lycan if he wanted to, but as you both learned, he wasn't the nicest parts of me."

Violet squeezed his finger and his gaze jolted to hers. "He had some of the best parts of you, too. Like this." She lifted their intertwined hands. "The passion that allows you to do things like this, was his."

"True." Patrick pulled her hand toward him and kissed her finger before placing their hands back in her lap. His attention turned toward Jax. "I do not envy what you have to go through each time you shift."

Jax shrugged a shoulder. "It gets easier. I hardly felt it last time." His eyes turned golden and his wolf growled, "I am learning how to make it painless for him."

Patrick stared and one of his brows raised. "Dalim, I'm guessing?"

Jax nodded as his eyes returned to purple. "He doesn't speak out very often, but he has the freedom to speak when he wants to."

A heavy breath filled Patrick's chest, making it expand, before he released a long steadying breath. "Alright, so Alpha Draven has lost his mind and is...?"

"In Lockup under heavy sedation. Any mention of his daughter or her name sets him off. In his lost state, he fully believes that Mom's death was her fault and he is dead set on taking Violet's life."

The surge of protectiveness that branded her thoughts surprised her and she stared at Patrick with wide eyes. Was she feeling his emotions?

"That's not going to happen," he growled while his hazel eyes glowed moonstone.

Jax's eyes returned to molten gold in response. There was a strange echo as he spoke, like both he and Dalim were saying the same thing at the same time, "No. It won't."

"Okay, cool it, boys." She patted Patrick's hand and the moonstone faded from his eyes while Jax settled down in his armchair. "I'm fine."

"And Luna..." Patrick's voice came out a whisper.

Violet's heart broke as moisture lined Patrick's eyes. Anguish that mirrored her own hung in her thoughts. Violet rolled her lips together and bit them lightly when her chin trembled. The tears for her mom came too easily, rolling quickly down her cheeks. "She's gone, Patrick," Violet wept softly. "I'm sorry."

Patrick's brow furrowed. He gently shook his head, then gathered Violet in his arms. She wrapped her arms around him and felt his body break under the weight of a sob. The armchair groaned. Violet blinked through the tears to see Jax appear over Patrick's shoulder. He laid a comforting hand on Patrick's shoulder and squeezed. Patrick buried his face against Violet's neck while he and the twins mourned the loss of their mother and Luna.

Chapter 17

Jax

It took some convincing, *but Jax and Patrick were able to wrestle Violet into* her room to sleep. Heavy circles had begun to darken around her eyes, and neither young men were going to allow her to stay awake any longer. She hadn't even bothered to change her clothes, which grossed Jax out to no end. There were lingering stains of blood and dirt from their earlier adventures that he would never climb into bed with, but their differences in hygiene had always been vast.

Patrick on the other hand hadn't hesitated when Jax told him to take a shower. He had greedily hurried to the bathroom, and steam began escaping from beneath the door a few minutes later.

Using the time it took for his friend to shower, Jax pulled the air mattress from the hall closet and set it up on the floor of his bedroom. Patrick had no desire to return to his apartment, and Jax didn't blame him, but there was no way he was allowing his best friend to sleep in the same room as his sister. Even if they were mates.

No argument was made against him, thankfully. That was a war he didn't want to wage that night.

The water shut off, and a couple of minutes later, Patrick emerged wearing a pair of sweats he'd snagged from Jax's drawers. He rubbed a towel through his hair as he walked into Jax's room. "Thanks for letting me borrow these." He tossed a ball of fabric at Jax. "The shirt doesn't fit though."

Jax caught the material in one hand, then threw it in the garbage. "That must be one of my old ones. Sorry about that." He opened his closet, pulled a shirt off a hanger, and lobbed it at Patrick. "Try that one. I know you're taller than me, but I think we're about the same size right now."

After setting his towel on the desk chair, Patrick pulled the shirt on. "This will work. I'll grab some of my stuff from my apartment tomorrow."

Jax dropped a folded blanket onto the air mattress, but didn't bother laying it out. Wolven temperatures ran hotter than humans, and lycans tended to be even warmer, so it was unlikely the blanket would even be used, but his mom would have made sure one was available just in case.

He headed toward the door while Patrick picked up the towel again and worked it through his curly hair. "You're welcome to hang out in here, or sleep, or—"

"Why did you do it?" Patrick interrupted

Jax froze in the doorway. Slowly, he turned to find Patrick staring at the towel he was holding. "Do what?"

"It's not that I'm not grateful. I am. But you could have died, Jax." Patrick dropped the towel onto his temporary bed. "Violet needs you."

"I did die," Jax stated, feeling Dalim press to the forefront of his thoughts. When he spoke again, Dalim's gravelly tone echoed his. "We knew we were going to die. It didn't matter. Our sister needed her mate, so we said our goodbyes and offered our life as sacrifice."

Patrick crossed his arms over his chest. "If this is going to work, you can't do that again. You can't give your life to bring someone back from death."

"It's not like I would try to bring a corpse back," Jax insisted while Dalim returned to the recesses of his mind. "I watched you die, Patrick. Your body was still warm."

"It doesn't matter," Patrick argued. "You knew, which means you know your limits. Don't do it again."

Jax stared at his best friend unblinkingly. "I can't make that promise. If it was Violet, or Lexie, or Mya, or you again, I wouldn't hesitate to trade my life. I know you'd do the same if you could."

Tension pulsed through Patrick's jaw, but he nodded. "Then we need to do our best to make sure those situations don't happen."

A smirk tugged at Jax's mouth. "After Blood Moon is taken care of."

Patrick's expression relaxed. He nodded. "After Blood Moon."

"Alright," Jax looked over his shoulder, then back at his friend. "I have a meeting, so I'll be back later."

Patrick's head tipped to the side. "What? You have a meeting?"

Stopping in the doorway, Jax nodded. "One of the many duties of being alpha."

"This late?"

"It was a last minute meeting."

Patrick's eyes narrowed. "Without your beta?"

Allowing his relief to show through his smile, Jax leaned against the doorframe. "I didn't want to push you into anything tonight. You just got back, and this meeting isn't going to be pleasant."

His friend looked down at himself and held his arms out. "Is casual attire accepted?"

Jax laughed. "I don't care what you wear. I'm just glad to have you back."

Patrick shrugged and headed for the door, bare feet and all. "I think I might be in a better position than either you or Violet. I feel totally fine." His head dipped to the side as he threw the towel over his shoulder. "Trying to wrap my head around a few things, but I'm good to go."

Shoving off the door, Jax started down the hall. "Let's get this meeting over with then."

After darting into the bathroom, Patrick returned without the towel and followed Jax down the stairs. "Catch me up. What's this meeting about?"

Jax grimaced. "You actually."

"Me?"

"Paul has been very outspoken about how he feels regarding your absence and my refusal to pick another beta. He's also been nosing his way into any business of mine that he thinks he can." Jax pulled a key ring out of his pocket and jammed the now familiar key into the lock. "I think he's turned some of the warriors against me as well, but I have no proof of that. I know there are people who don't approve of the way I'm doing things." He turned the knob and led the way into the room, leaving the door wide open.

"From what you've described, you were thrown into a position you weren't totally prepared for." Patrick followed him into the room, then stood in the corner. "You accepted that your role was going to be alpha, but that's not the same thing as being ready for it."

Jax rifled through a few papers on top of the desk. "Unfortunately there are a few people who don't see it that way. There are also a few who are appalled that I'm not leading the same way my father led."

"I would think that was a good thing," Patrick grumbled.

"I agree, which is one of the many reasons I chose you as my beta." Jax slid a couple of those papers into a drawer and then looked at Patrick who was leaning comfortably against the wall. "No one is going to change my mind about that."

Patrick nodded his agreement.

Relief relaxed his shoulders a fraction before he grabbed a paper he'd printed from an email. "Before Paul gets here, I need to discuss this with you." He held the paper out and Patrick stepped forward to take it.

His eyes darted across the page.

Jax stayed quiet to allow his friend to read and process the information there.

"They want to turn Sentinel territory into a war base?" Patrick asked, lifting his gaze over the paper.

A slight nod of his chin was all Jax needed to give to make Patrick lower the paper to his side. "Whisky and Mammoth want to bring their warriors here."

"It's not a bad plan, but it's not a great one either." Patrick set the paper down on the desk, then pressed his palms into the wood.

Jax sighed. He returned the paper to the pile he'd been messing with earlier, but continued staring at it as he sat down in his father's old chair. "They clearly realize that Blood Moon has focused their attacks here. I know they've both been attacked, as well, but from the emails we've been sending it sounds like we've been hit the hardest."

A growl rolled through the room and Jax turned to see Patrick pacing, his fists clenching and unclenching at his sides. "I was going to leave because I thought they would stop, but they aren't going to, are they?"

"I think this has become a lot bigger than you." Jax leaned his elbows against the desk.

"So how is Sentinel going to respond?" Patrick asked, casting a quick glance at Jax. "Where do we go from here?"

Jax's gaze drifted to the paper again. "I think we take them up on their offer."

Patrick stopped pacing.

"We can't defeat Blood Moon alone. We've lost too many people as it is. Mammoth doesn't have the best fighters, but they are willing to lay their lives on the line. Whisky though—"

"Whisky's warriors could turn the tables," Patrick nodded.

Jax smirked. It was like his friend had never left. Patrick knew exactly what he was thinking and had the same thought process. "What about the rest of the clan?"

Patrick returned to the desk, pressing his palms into the wood once again, but this time he didn't look away from Jax. "Send them away."

"Curious." Dalim puzzled in Jax's mind. *"That's not what I was expecting him to say."*

"Me either," he admitted.

He dipped his head to the side as he stared at his friend. "Explain. What do you mean 'send them away'?"

"They are sending their warriors here." Patrick lifted one of his hands and pressed his fingertips against the desk. "We don't have room to house all of them on top of the families and our other clanmates here, but if we send all who aren't able or willing to fight to Whisky territory then they will be out of harm's way. Whisky is the farthest from Stanislaus territory and as you've already stated, it seems like Blood Moon is focusing their attention here. Less casualties, more room for warriors. Better war base scenario."

Jax found himself nodding while Patrick explained. The plan had merit. "That's a lot of people to get out of here."

Patrick returned to his full height and crossed his arms. "Better they leave than get killed."

"Okay." Jax clenched his jaw. He couldn't believe he was leading their clan into war, something that most clans hadn't seen in generations. "I'll send an email to Whisky, and as soon as I get confirmation, I'll give the clan twenty-four hours to decide if they are staying to fight or heading for safety. It's not a lot of time, but I'd rather not risk added time."

"That *is* a small time frame, but hopefully the clan will respond well."

Nerves skittered though Jax. Paul would be here soon, but he needed Violet to leave in the morning and Patrick had to make a decision, too.

Dalim pressed against his mind. *"He'll understand. He may not like it, but he will understand."*

"Thanks, Dalim." Jax agreed with his wolf spirit and it needed to be done.

"Patrick, there's something else we need to win this war. Something Violet was going to leave to do before you contacted us. Her bags are packed, and I'm sending her out tomorrow morning."

His friend's dark brows pulled together. "What do you need, Jax?"

"We need the lycans."

Patrick froze. "What?" he growled, his eyes paling to moonstone.

One of Jax's cheeks puffed out as he released a heavy breath. "That's gonna take some getting used to."

"You were going to send Violet alone? To hunt down lycans?" Patrick's voice rose a little. "Are you insane?"

Calmly, Jax rose to his full height and felt Dalim's power churn the color of his eyes until they glowed molten gold. "That decision was not made lightly, Patrick.

She needed help from a fellow lycan. We know barely anything about your kind, their history, and their medicine. She has questions that none of us could answer. On top of all that, we need their powers and strength. Blood Moon has grown too strong."

"Sorry," Patrick spoke through gritted teeth as he took a step away. "I... understand. I do. I'm just struggling with all these—emotions."

"Yeah. I'd gotten used to you being very subdued." Jax quirked a brow. "You weren't when you first arrived though, remember?"

A small smirk tugged at one side of Patrick's mouth. "Yeah. I feel a lot like that right now, actually." His chest rose with a large breath and he leaned against the wall, once more. "Okay, so clearly I'm going with her."

Laughter burst out of Jax. "Clearly." He shook his head. "You'll be able to take her right to them *and* get some learning and training in on the way."

"Done," Patrick acknowledged.

"Be honest," Jax started, a sly smirk creeping across his face. "Would she have ever found them without you?"

"Did she have any idea where to start?"

"Somewhere north."

If Jax had thought his smirk was sly, it was nothing compared to the smug grin that swept across his friend's face.

"No," Patrick answered firmly. "Lycans keep their whereabouts confusing and secret for a reason. If I'd ever mentioned Willows Creek to her, even one time, her chances would have increased exponentially. But I was raised not to talk about it, and then when I was brought here, your father made it clear that I was to be as wolven as possible."

"Willows Creek, huh?" Jax tucked that bit of information away in his mind. "That's where the lycan are?"

Patrick's grin grew a little. "No. But it's a decent starting place."

"What's a decent starting place?" Paul's older voice boomed into the room before his personage made an appearance.

Jax's relaxed demeanor disappeared, his shoulders going stiff. While he saw Patrick take note of the change, his friend remained relaxed against the wall. Only his smile had disappeared.

"Bigfoot," Patrick answered, drawing the older man's attention.

"Ah, yes." Paul grumbled. "I'd heard a rumor that you returned. Although in the rumor I was privy to, you were half dead."

Patrick's chin lowered a fraction. "Clearly, those rumors were false."

The sound of Paul sucking against his teeth frayed Jax's nerves.

"Clearly." Paul swiftly turned on his heel and claimed a seat in front of Jax's desk. "So, if you weren't half dead, where have you been?"

Patrick's gaze slid to Jax and his words slipped across Jax's mind. *"What should I tell him?"*

"Tell him where you were. Give him just enough information that would allow us to say we included him."

His friend gave an almost imperceptible nod before returning his attention to Paul. "I was being held prisoner by Blood Moon. They kept me injured and poisoned so I was too weak to escape."

Guilt slammed into Jax like a battering ram. They hadn't had a chance to go over what had happened to Patrick. He'd assumed that the injuries Patrick had when they found him were new and fresh, but now he wondered how long Patrick had been that way.

"That sounds..." Paul clicked his tongue. "Awful. How did you manage to escape then?"

Sorrow flickered across Patrick's gaze, but a moment later an almost bored look swept across his face—the mask Jax had watched Patrick perfect. "There was another lycan there. He felt bad about what they were doing and found a way to help me. He died in the process."

"And yet, you appear unscathed."

"I'm a fast healer."

"Obviously." Animosity flowed from Paul's single word statement and he held Patrick's gaze a moment longer before turning on Jax. "And just like that I believe my earlier statements ring true."

Jax barely contained a resoundingly annoyed sigh. "And what statement was that? You've made so many."

"Lycans have no place in wolven communities."

Nothing could have stopped Jax's head from tipping back or the frustrated groan that left him. He was too tired to deal with this. "I disagree," he managed to sound somewhat diplomatic even if his body language said the exact opposite. "I believe we need the lycans."

Paul leaned toward the desk. "You think that having beings who are more powerful than us, and better in almost every aspect, inside our territories is a good idea?"

"Why not?" Jax asked, his tone dull. "If they are actually that much better, wouldn't we only benefit from having more of them around?"

"Because one isn't enough?" Paul shouted.

"Two," Jax corrected the older man. "Patrick and Violet."

Paul snorted. "Your sister is as much a lycan as I am a unicorn."

A snicker left Patrick and Jax stared at his friend, wide eyed. He couldn't remember the last time he heard Patrick make such a sound. But if he hadn't, Jax probably would have because the statement was ridiculous.

"Sorry." Patrick cleared his throat and righted his expression. "Don't let me interrupt."

Paul got to his feet. "That sister of yours is a time bomb," he accused. "Sooner or later she is going to explode and when she does, she's going to take this entire clan down with her."

"What exactly do you think Violet is going to do?" Patrick pushed off the wall and moved to stand at the side of the desk.

"Her abilities are elusive and dangerous. She's not learning how to control them. Sooner or later she's going to unleash them on everyone around her."

Patrick pointed at the older man. "No, see, that's where you're wrong." Silent laughter shook his shoulders. "Violet is one of the most capable people I have ever met. Even without instruction, she would've figured it all out eventually. Now that I've returned though, she'll be a force to be reckoned with in a matter of no time."

Paul's nose tilted into the air. "I see you have an inflated ego, as always."

Patrick's lips bunched together and his head shook. "I'm a good teacher. That's all I'm saying."

"I think we're done here." Paul grumbled, looking back at Jax who simply raised his brows. "Your chosen beta has returned. I've warned you against making a lycan your beta, but you have refused my advice. What happens next is on your head." With a turn on his heel, the older man stomped from the room and slammed the back door of Alpha House shut behind him.

"Well, dang." Patrick's head turned toward Jax. "I knew Paul didn't like me that much, but I thought he liked me more than that."

A disbelieving laugh left Jax. "It surprised me too. Within hours of the alpha powers moving on to me, he started hounding me about picking a different beta." He walked around the desk to lean on the front of it near Patrick. "He's been trying to insert himself everywhere he can and is always pushing me to do things the way my father did."

"We'll show 'em," Patrick promised. "You're already a better alpha than Noah was. It won't take long for the entire clan to see just how much better you are."

A sad smile tugged at Jax's mouth. "I'm glad you're home, Patrick."

"Me too." His friend's gaze took on a distant look. "We won't be gone long, Jax. I promise. I'll bring her home soon."

Jax nodded, but couldn't shake the nagging worry that had settled in his chest. He'd just gotten Patrick back. He could really use both his and Violet's help with the coming days. But the mission they were setting out on was important, too. Now, more than ever, he wished he had a mate to lean on.

Chapter 18

Cas

For the first time *in a long time, Cas had left the watchful eye of Blood Moon so* he could sleep. Unfortunately, his peaceful sleep didn't last. Around one o'clock in the morning, Ivy called. She was livid that he'd left the territory without telling her and demanded he return.

After a failed attempt to tell her that he'd be back in the morning, he found himself trudging back into the suffocating confines of Blood Moon. He snarled at a few bloody-eyed wolven who dared approach him or stare at him too long. It'd been a week since he'd had a decent night's sleep and it was wearing on him.

With a sharp jerk of the door handle, Cas threw open the door to Blood Moon's makeshift clan house. It rattled on its hinges, drawing the attention of every person in the room.

Ivy watched him with cool hatred as he dominated the space, claiming everyone's attention.

"You rang, *your highness,"* he seethed.

The white haired monster bared her teeth. It would have been more effective if she'd had fangs, but with the crazed look in her eyes it made her look unhinged.

"If you hadn't left, I wouldn't have had to call you back like a stray dog," she snapped.

Cas' laugh was humorless. "And if you had better control over your *pack* I would be able to sleep without keeping one eye open."

Her fingers blanched, gripping the arms of her makeshift throne. "We are a *clan*. I am the alpha. You obey *me."*

"You seem to be forgetting that I don't belong to you." His nose scrunched as he snarled. "This is a partnership. That partnership does not extend to my sleeping arrangements and I do not have a leash around my neck forcing me to come when you call."

A wicked gleam glistened in her ruby eyes and a devilish smile curled her lips back. "Yet here you are—answering my call."

The growl that rolled through him vibrated his entire body. "What do you want, Ivy?"

Ivy's lithe hand rose into the air. She snapped her fingers and a couple of wolven led an older man from the back room. His dark hair was graying at his temples and a weathered look hardened his brown eyes. He looked familiar, but Cas couldn't place him or remember his name.

His eyes snagged on the large table, which had been pushed to the side, when they led the man toward him. A bloody cloth had been thrown over the table, but it was clear there was a body under it. What poor soul had lost their life this time?

"He showed up a few minutes before I called you," Ivy disclosed. "Says he has information, but will only talk to you."

"I'm surprised you didn't try to beat it out of him."

"Oh, they tried," the older man spoke up and a few of the wolven around him grimaced. "I'm tougher than I look."

Cas took a couple of steps toward him, making the others shy away. "Where do I know you from?"

"Now it's my turn to be surprised. I thought you would recognize me." His nose turned upward. "Beta Paul of Sentinel Clan—or rather, the former beta since Alpha Noah Draven is no longer in power."

Warnings blasted off in Cas' mind like fireworks on the Fourth of July. He crossed his arms and narrowed his gaze. "What is the former beta of the clan we've declared war upon doing here?"

"I have information."

"So you've said." An annoyed sigh filled the space as Ivy continued. "And yet we haven't heard any of it."

"Greedy child," Paul spat in her direction. "If it weren't for me you would be blind to Sentinel's plans."

Cas' narrowed gaze thinned to slits. He quickly closed the distance between him and Paul. With Paul's attention on Ivy it was all too easy to curl his fist in the man's shirt, plant a foot behind him, and push. Surprise and fear warred for dominance in Paul's wide eyes as he gripped Cas' arm.

"Children we may be, but we hold the power here," Cas growled. "You'd do well to remember that while you walked onto enemy soil willingly, *we* decide if you leave."

"I-I have a family."

The skin on Cas' nose scrunched as he snarled. "Do you think we care?"

"We do care, Cas!" shouted Abel.

"But the rest of them don't. He needs to realize the danger he is in here and stop trying to act like he has the upper hand."

Abel scoffed. *"So you think you're doing him a favor?"*

"Go away, Abel!"

While his wolf shrank back, dark humor rippled through the Blood Moon wolven surrounding them.

"Give us the information and we'll let you know if it's worth your life." He hauled Paul back to his feet and released the man's shirt like he'd been shocked. Cas quirked a brow. "Or not."

Another rumble of dark laughter spread through the room.

Paul seemed to have the good sense to be afraid as his gaze shifted nervously. He took a few steps away from Cas and his adam's apple bobbed when he swallowed. "You lost Patrick."

Cas sucked a breath through his teeth. "Strike one—we already know that."

Tension began to build around them, but Cas didn't dare take his eyes off Paul.

Another swallow and Paul tried again, "He's alive and back with Sentinel Clan."

Cas dropped his head back on his shoulders and groaned. "Strike two! Come on, Paul." He used Abel's ability to turn his eyes silver, then stalked toward the older man as a few wolven started to circle him. "Give us something we *don't* know!"

"They are going to use him to recruit more lycan."

There it was; the token of information that could save this man's life. Cas released a heavy breath through his nose, managing to make it sound like he was annoyed. "Strike three."

The wolven throughout the room surged forward and Paul's eyes rounded.

"Unless..." Cas let the word hang in the air, pulling all the blood-lusting creatures to a halt. "... you can tell us where we can find them?"

"W-Willow Creek." Paul nearly tripped over the words in his hurry to speak. "They're going to Willow Creek."

Cas relaxed his shoulders, easing his threatening stance while the traitor spoke.

"I overheard him and Jax speaking tonight. They are leaving in the morning. If you leave now, you will intercept them. Take them by surprise."

"And why would you want us to do that? Isn't Patrick your beta?"

One side of Paul's nose scrunched with disgust. "I will never accept him as my beta and that abomination of a girl can disappear, too, for all I care."

Rage boiled low in Cas' stomach. Unfortunately, he had developed feelings for Violet—not romantic, thank goodness, although he had tried to woo her away from Patrick at first. That didn't stop him from admiring the girl. Under different circumstances, maybe they could have been friends. She was a powerhouse, but one with a loving nature. He knew that if Violet died during this war, he would regret it.

"And yet you are still blazing down this path."

"I have to see it through, Abel. For Layla."

His wolf spirit sighed. *"Layla is gone. This won't bring her back."*

"No, but at least I'll be able to sleep at night, knowing her killer is dead."

Cas looked around the room and pointed at a line of wolven nearby. "Go to Willow Creek. Wait for them. When they arrive grab them and bring them back here."

They glanced at each other nervously, but didn't move.

"What are you waiting for?" Cas increased the volume of his voice and turned his tone into more of a growl, but still they did not move.

Ivy's low chuckle sent a ripple of unease down his spine. "They won't listen to you."

Cas slowly turned to face her, framing his face into one of disinterest.

"I made them witness what happens to those who don't obey me." With another snap of her fingers, two wolven stepped up to the table and yanked the bloody cloth away.

Nothing could have stopped Cas from turning his head away from the monstrous site, but what he saw would haunt his dreams for years to come. Glassy, unseeing eyes. Wounds of every size and shape. A mouth frozen in a silent scream that rang in his ears. A mutilated body exposed atop a table for all to see.

An example had been made.

He couldn't help wondering if the person had actually been guilty of whatever Ivy accused them of, or if she just wanted to tear a person apart. It didn't really matter. No one deserved that.

Another chuckle left Ivy, but this one was laced with pride that Cas hoped would be her downfall one day. "Do as he says, but kill them instead. We don't need any more prisoners."

"That's not what we agreed to!" Cas started toward her, but multiple people got in his path.

"Plans change." Ivy's nasty grin fell from her face when she thrust her chin toward the door, dismissing the wolven he'd told to go. Once they were gone, Ivy got to her feet and started toward Paul. "Now what to do with you?"

Paul wisely took a step back, but was blocked by more wolven waiting to fulfill her every wish.

"He could help us," Cas urged.

Ivy's cold eyes landed on him. "How?"

"Send him back to Sentinel Clan. Let him feed us insider information so we can better plan our attacks."

"I can do that," Paul insisted, nodding a bit too eagerly.

Her jaw jutted to the side and Cas hoped she was actually giving the idea some thought. "Alright. First things first, return to Sentinel without them suspecting you of anything. If you can't deliver any useful information, consider your life forfeit when we bring war to your gates."

Paul gave a curt nod. "Understood."

"Escort him to the border." Ivy ordered, never taking her eyes off Paul. "And leave him with a reminder of the pain he'll endure if he fails us. Nothing visible."

Two wolven seized Paul's arms and hauled him out the door with a handful of others in their wake.

A long nailed finger rose to point at Cas' face. Ivy's voice dripped with unfulfilled promise as she said, “If you ever try to undermine me again, or order my clan around without my consent, I'll tie you to that table and fillet you myself.”

He did not break eye contact with her. To do so would give her an opening to attack then and there. Instead, he waited. When she finally turned away, he allowed himself to swallow the knot in his throat.

Chapter 19

Jax

Nerves crashed through Jax *as he headed to the clan parking lot. After his* and Patrick's discussion the night before, he'd immediately sent an email to the other clans approving the plan to turn Sentinel's base into a war base. The first of Whisky's warriors had shown up at five in the morning. A few from Mammoth were only an hour behind them. Both had stated that they were only the first wave and more would be coming. On a hunch, he'd reached out to Sierra, as well, but still hadn't heard anything from their luna.

There was no turning back now.

He rounded the hedge and started for the old red truck that was parked close to the gates. A weird sense of comfort, protectiveness, and disgust whirled through him when Patrick swung a backpack into the bed of his truck then turned to lift Violet into the air.

His sister's squeak of surprise made Jax smile.

"Put me down!" Her order rang through the parking lot, but the hostility was lost when she laughed through the words.

Instead of immediately lowering her to the ground, Patrick kissed her.

Jax froze midstep and clenched his jaw. Yeah, that was gonna take some getting used to. He reminded himself that they were allowed to kiss and that he didn't need to punch Patrick for making a move on his sister.

Dalim's laughter filled his mind. *"Just remember that when we find our mate, and Violet has to watch."*

Jax shuddered. *"I could never be so openly affectionate."*

"Says the boy who showed up late to a party because he was messing around with a girl."

"Not in front of everyone!"

"Didn't matter," Dalim snorted. *"It was obvious."*

Thinking back on that night, Jax shook his head. He never should have acted that way. His mate would have to understand that. He was the alpha. He couldn't get carried away like that.

"She'll understand," Dalim reassured him. *"For now, be happy for our sister and best friend. Because they are mates, we will be forever connected. That is a blessing from the moon goddess if I've ever heard one."*

A soft smile tugged at Jax's lips. That was a gift he could fight for.

The slam of a car door pulled him out of his thoughts, and he turned to see another three more unfamiliar faces walking toward him.

"Alpha Jaxon," called the woman. Her expression was stern and the sleek bun atop her head only intensified the look. Two men flanked her, following her every move and glance. When they were within ten feet of him, all three bowed their respects. "I apologize for not being with the first wave of warriors who arrived earlier this morning. I was on my way back from another meeting when I received the news and had to gather a few things before coming here. My name is Adeline. I'm the head of the Whisky warriors."

"Welcome, Adeline." Jax held out a hand and the three of them shook them in turn.

The two men quickly introduced themselves as Oscar and Daniel, then returned to their positions just behind their leader's shoulders.

"The apology isn't necessary. Your alpha made me aware of your situation so I wasn't expecting you until later today," Jax informed the three of them, then glanced toward Patrick and Violet. His sister sat along the side of Patrick's truck bed while Patrick was jogging toward them. "I'll inform my clan of the plans in about an hour. I wanted to be polite and wait until it wasn't so early before telling them they would be leaving their homes."

Adeline's shoulders relaxed a fraction. "That was... very thoughtful, Alpha." She sucked in a deep breath, but whatever she was about to say was interrupted by Patrick stopping beside Jax. "Hello."

"Hi," Patrick's chin dipped in greeting to the three of them.

"This is my beta—" Jax scrunched his eyebrows and turned to look at Patrick. They hadn't discussed how he wanted to be addressed.

Seeming to catch on to the confusion, Patrick thrust a welcoming hand toward them. "Beta Cowen."

"Interesting." Jax shot the thought to Patrick. *"I thought for sure you would use your first name."*

"It's easier to say." Patrick replied. *"Why did you choose to go by your full name? I thought you preferred Jax?"*

Jax mentally sighed. *"I didn't pick that. People who don't know me have been calling me Jaxon and it feels more official than Jax so I haven't corrected them."*

Patrick made a sound that almost resembled a restrained sneeze, making Jax look at him. His friend rubbed his hand over his mouth, forcing a smile off his face, but it didn't completely work. "I'm sorry," he lightly chuckled when Adeline's face twisted in confusion. "It's good to meet you all. I'm just..." His gaze turned toward Violet who happily waved from her spot on the truck. "A little distracted."

A flush rushed across Adeline's face and the two men smirked. "Congratulations," she offered.

"You're such a liar," Jax mentally laughed at Patrick. *"You were laughing at me having to go by my full name."*

Patrick's glee rippled through his thoughts. *"They don't need to know that I'm comfortable making fun of my alpha."*

Jax shook his head. *"Your emotions are weird."*

"Tell me about it," Patrick agreed.

"Patrick is heading out with my sister in hopes of finding a few more people to help us," Jax informed them. "I was heading over to say goodbye, but then I can help get you settled in."

"Your... sister?" one of the men asked, looking between Violet and Jax. "The impossible twin?"

Jax lifted his brows. "I don't think I've heard that one before, but yeah. That's her."

The same man then stared at Patrick. "And you're *Patrick* Cowen—the lycan."

Jax turned his head to find Patrick's eyes shining the color of moonstone. "I am."

Adeline took a step toward Jax. "Your beta is lycan?"

A smirk lifted one corner of his lips. "Sure is."

The three of them looked like they weren't sure what to do with that information. They shifted about, obviously uncomfortable, but none of them spoke.

Jax lifted a palm to placate them. "I'm not sure how you know about Beta Cowen, but I'm happy to answer any questions you have about the situation after we get them on their way. We don't know how quickly things with Blood Moon will escalate and they need as much time as we can give them if there is any chance of Beta Cowen convincing the lycans to help."

Adeline blinked, but Jax was impressed that she managed to keep a neutral expression as he unveiled his plan. "You are... different than your father." She glanced at Oscar who stood behind her left shoulder. When she returned her gaze to Jax, there was a hint of a smile at the corners of her mouth. "I am looking forward to working with you more."

Pride welled up in Jax's chest and he smiled broadly. "Thank you." He bowed his chin. "If you'll excuse me, I'll be right back."

The three Whisky warriors bowed low to him as he walked toward the truck with Patrick.

"Way to go, alpha," Patrick said quietly when they were a good distance away. "You're already beginning to show your metal."

"Let's hope that I can keep it up."

Patrick raised a brow then looked ahead again. "You know... my dad and I used to travel a lot together."

Surprised, Jax shot a wide-eyed look at his friend. He could count the number of times Patrick talked about his dad on one hand. From what he'd gathered, the two hadn't left on very good terms. Maybe they never had a great relationship, but Patrick didn't talk about him enough to know.

"We would go to the surrounding wolven clans to check in and establish relationships. There were a lot of alphas that I thought could have done things differently," Patrick recalled.

Violet hopped off the truck bed as they approached. She headed for the passenger door and Patrick hurried to open the door before she could. With a cheeky grin she turned away from him, heading for Jax. "Don't burn down the base while we're gone," she teased.

Shaking his head, Jax pulled her into a tight hug. "No promises."

Her laugh vibrated through him, then she let go and climbed into the truck.

"Be safe," he ordered, trying to ignore the worry that made his chest ache.

Violet's playful nature fell away. The anguish that pulsed through their twin bond mirrored his own. They'd lost enough. They couldn't lose each other, too. With a nod from her, Patrick closed her door. She rolled down the window right away, and leaned her elbows against the door.

"We'll be back soon," Patrick told him. "I'll make sure she returns home safely."

"I know," said Jax. "I trust you."

A quick smile quirked across Patrick's face. "Look, those other alpha's that I was talking about. They aren't you and you aren't your father. You're already a good alpha, Jax, and you're only going to get better."

The pride he'd felt when Adeline had approved of the difference between him and his father surged again. People believed in him. He just had to figure out how to believe in himself. "Thank you."

Patrick nodded, then hurried around to the driver's side of the truck. Jax walked up to Violet's window while Patrick climbed inside and shut his door.

"So, you really think Violet wouldn't have found them on her own?" Jax asked, making Violet scoff.

A laugh burst from Patrick. "No." His hand closed the distance between him and Violet and his fingers squeezed her knee. "Sorry, that's nothing against you. There are witches who actively protect the lycan community. They cloud the mind of anyone who manages to get close without permission and make the person get lost in the woods."

Concern flickered through Jax. "You haven't been back in years. Do you think they'll let you through?"

"Things have changed," Patrick replied. "If for no other reason, they'll see me just to cure their curiosity."

"With your red eyes gone, your clan will probably welcome you back."

Patrick's expression softened, but there was something else there—a pain that his friend usually tried to hide.

"If you ask me, I will release you from being my beta."

Surprise loosened Patrick's jaw. The rest of him froze and Jax waited for a reply.

After a quiet moment, Violet's soft voice called his attention. "Jax," she said out loud before her words flooded through his mind. *"I don't want to leave you. I don't want to live with the lycans."*

"He's been away from his family a long time, Violet. We have to give him the chance."

Tension bunched Violet's shoulders and the muscles in her neck constricted when she drew in a deep breath. Finally, she nodded. *"You're right."*

"Besides," Jax tried to replicate a happy note to his thoughts, but wasn't sure if he succeeded. *"We're family. You can't ever get rid of me."*

"I'm a Sentinel." Patrick's firm tone captured Jax's attention. His gaze locked with his best friend's and there was no denying the conviction there. "My family is here. My heart is here." Patrick smiled gently at Violet, then looked at Jax once again. "I am honored to lead with you as your right hand."

Life had been difficult lately. Loss weighed heavily on everyone. But as Jax looked between his sister and his best friend, all he felt was gratitude. He pulled a deep breath into his lungs, patted the truck, and said, "Good. Hurry back so we can get Blood Moon out of here."

"You got it." The truck roared to life when Patrick turned the key and he grinned. "Man, I missed that sound."

Both Jax and Violet chuckled.

"We'll keep you posted on our progress." Patrick promised. "Whether we have their support or not, we'll head back in a few days."

"Sounds good." Jax stepped back, giving them room to leave. "Drive safe."

His friend nodded. "Will do." Then he looked at Violet who was waving to Jax. "Let's go introduce you to Bigfoot."

The truck started to leave as Violet's eyes bugged and she spun to face Patrick. "Bigfoot is real?"

Patrick's low laughter hung in the air while they drove away.

Determination settled over Jax's shoulders. It was time to tell the clan that war was coming to Sentinel. As he neared the exit in the hedge, Paul's angry tone rumbled through the air on the other side.

"I told you, get out of my way!"

Curious, Jax stepped closer to the hedge, keeping his steps light against the gravel.

"The alpha is tending to business that doesn't concern you."

The voice belonged to one of the Whisky warrior males, but Jax hadn't learned their voices enough yet to know which. A couple more steps and he could see the shoulder of one of them. Another let him see enough to know that Adeline and her two men were blocking Paul.

"I was Alpha Draven's beta," Paul snarled.

"Which means you are not the current beta," countered the other male.

There was a heavy sigh before Paul tried again in a softer tone. "You just arrived. You don't know how things work here. I advise Alpha Jax in all things while he and his... beta... learn the ropes."

"From what I've witnessed, Alpha *Jaxon*," Adeline's tone showed she didn't approve of Paul's use of his nickname. "seems to have a good head on his shoulders."

Jax grinned.

"Then clearly you only just met him."

Jax cleared his throat. He stepped around the hedge and the Whisky warriors parted to allow him through.

Paul's face paled. He dipped his chin, but the meager movement was not enough to even pretend at being respectful. "Alpha."

Clenching his jaw, Jax turned his head toward the warriors. "Thank you."

"Of course," Adeline replied, bowing her head low.

Jax returned his narrowed gaze to Paul. "Let it be known that while Paul was my father's right hand—he is not mine. We do not see eye to eye on many things." A smug smirk quirked the corner of his lips. "Like the fact that I just sent my beta away."

He'd never seen Paul's face turn the shade of tomatoes before.

The older man clenched his jaw, then spoke with a forced calm. "You found your beta only to send him away?"

"Yes," Jax admittedly freely. "I did."

Paul huffed a humorless laugh. "The apple fell very far from the tree. You are the worst alpha I've ever—"

"Enough!" snapped Adeline. "A true Alpha works *with* others; which Alpha Jaxon has proven by joining with other clans to defeat this rising threat. A true alpha delegates tasks to those he trusts; which was also proven by sending his beta on an important errand. A true alpha listens, serves his clan, and protects them at all costs, even if that cost is his own life. I've only been here for a few minutes, and this is the first time I have met Alpha Jaxon, but I can already tell he is far better than many alphas I have met." She drew in a breath, then snorted. "This isn't the first time I've run into *you* though, Paul." Adeline closed the distance between herself and Paul, nearly coming toe-to-toe with him. "I could have said many things about your former alpha, but I held my tongue out of respect for his position and respect for myself. Do not disrespect your alpha in front of me again."

Her adamant defense of him surprised Jax, but with Dalim's help he managed to keep a calm exterior.

Paul's gaze darted between the four of them and he slowly backed away. "I see." He focused on Jax. "So, this is how you choose to rule your clan?"

Many retorts scorched Jax's tongue. The things he wanted to say to that man were astounding, but Dalim's presence filled Jax's being and forced his mouth to remain closed.

"We are better than that. Do not stoop to his level."

"He's getting more aggressive," Jax worried. *"What if he leaves?"*

"Let him," Dalim grumbled. *"There will be people who don't want to follow us. That's their decision."*

"What if he turns on us?"

Dalim sighed. *"We'll deal with that if it comes to that. For now, let's keep him away from any further planning or meetings. Give him small bits of information if he asks, but nothing that could hurt our chances against Blood Moon."*

"Solid advice." Jax complemented his wolf.

"Thank you," Dalim preened happily.

The force holding Jax's jaw shut relaxed and he stepped up to Adeline's side while he released a large breath. "I'll remind you again, Paul. I am not my father and I will do things differently than he did. I never wanted to rule. I want to lead."

Out of the corner of his eye he saw Adeline's gaze slide to him. An open expression of approval softened her sharp features and Jax couldn't help but wonder how many times she'd had to deal with his father.

Paul backed farther away and without another word, turned to leave.

With him gone, the three Whisky warriors turned to Jax.

"I gotta say, I am impressed, Alpha Jaxon," Daniel chuckled. "For such a young and new alpha, you have some fire in you."

Jax allowed an easy smile to spread across his face. "I plan to use that fire to defeat Blood Moon."

"Good." Adeline gave a sharp nod. "We would like to hear what you have planned, Alpha."

Lifting an arm, Jax directed them down the road toward the clan chefs. "And I want to discuss your thoughts, too, but first... have you had breakfast?"

The three warriors looked at each other, shook their heads, then visibly relaxed while they followed Jax down the road. He smiled broadly as the visiting warriors hungrily accepted the helpings given to them and made a mental note to always ensure people had eaten before starting a multi-clan meeting.

Chapter 20

Violet

Bigfoot was real. Well, *if you included a twenty-five foot wooden representation of a bigfoot as being real.* Patrick had promised to introduce Violet to bigfoot and he'd kept his word. She stared at the massive figure with her head tipped back and a Twizzler dangling from her mouth while Patrick stepped away to make a phone call.

He'd been on the phone for a while, but by the sounds of it, he'd been passed from person to person on the other end. A low growl rolled through the parking lot and Violet snapped her head in his direction, making the Twizzler whip her cheek. She yanked it from her mouth, taking a bite out of it as she did so.

"No, you're not listening." Patrick's agitated voice cut through the calm she'd been feeling, making her back away from the massive wooden beast. "I need to speak to my father... no, I don't... No. Just give the phone to my father and..."

Knowing Patrick wouldn't mind, Violet tried to exercise her heightened sense of hearing, but when she concentrated on her ears a tingling sensation spread along the tops. Panicking about being in public, she hastily pulled out the hairband holding her ponytail up and flattened her hair down around her shoulders. When the prickly feeling subsided, she felt along the shell of her ears to find small tapered tips.

She groaned and let her arms fall back to her sides. "Practice, my butt," she muttered under her breath.

Patrick's head jerked in her direction with an amused expression plastered on his face.

Flames licked at her cheeks and the now pointed tips of her ears. "Sorry," she softly called.

His shoulders shook with amusement that died a second later. "Hello, this is Patrick Cowen. Tell my father I'm coming home whether he likes it or not... I know how to get around the wards... He taught me himself."

Not knowing what else to do, Violet popped the last of the Twizzler into her mouth, walked to his side and slipped her fingers through his.

Patrick's hazel eyes settled on her face as he lightly squeezed her hand.

Being this close allowed Violet to hear when the female on the other end of the line started talking again, "Matthews Creek Campground. Eight o'clock. Don't be late."

"Really? You're bringing me in through The Witch's Pass?"

"You said you had someone with you."

"Yeah, but she's—"

"Eight o'clock, Patrick," she interrupted, and then hung up.

Patrick glared at his phone. "Gah, I never liked her. I can't believe she still works for him."

Violet raised her eyebrows and stared at him, unblinking. "You okay, there?"

With an aggravated groan, Patrick slipped his phone into his pocket, then ran his hand through his hair. "Yeah, I just..." He stared into the trees for a tense moment before continuing. "I've told you that they kicked me out, but I've never explained how bad it was in the end." He shook his head, letting out a heavy breath.

"But your dad brought you to Sentinel Clan. I remember. He left you the truck."

Patrick snorted. "That truck was mine to begin with. I asked an old man if I could buy it from him. I didn't know how I was going to afford it because I knew my dad wouldn't pay for it, but I saw beauty in her." He tugged Violet closer and let go of her hand to wrap his arm around her shoulders while they headed back to the truck. "The old man must have seen something in me, too, because he just handed me the keys and said if I could get her running then she was mine."

He pulled open the passenger door for her and Violet smiled when he kept his hand on her back while she climbed in. She transferred the Nerd Ropes from her seat to the dashboard, then sat down. Once she was settled, Patrick leaned his shoulder against the truck.

"It took me two years to get her started." Patrick smiled wistfully. "I was so proud." He patted the door affectionately. "But, I wasn't old enough to drive yet.

So, my step-mom came with me one time and drove it home against my father's orders." A chuckle rolled out of him before he continued, "She was so bad with the clutch, I thought she was going to break my truck all over again. Her face was beet red by the time we made it back."

Violet found herself smiling as he recalled the memory. But it was short-lived.

Sorrow feathered across her thoughts and when Patrick spoke again, his voice was quiet, "The accident was two weeks later."

She nibbled on her bottom lip while the silence stretched between them. Finally, she offered a gentle "I'm glad he let you keep the truck."

An easy smirk quirked one side of Patrick's lips. "Yeah?"

"Of course. How else would we get anywhere?" Violet jested, earning her a deep rumble of laughter.

Patrick ducked his head into the car. "Nah, you like my truck."

Violet sucked in a shallow breath when the tip of his nose brushed across hers. "Yeah, almost as much as I like you."

Moonstone flared in Patrick's eyes. "Aaaand, you like me a lot, right?"

"Patrick Cowen," she chided and his gaze dropped to her mouth. "*Like* doesn't even begin to explain my feelings for you."

A low growl of approval rumbled through Patrick's chest before his lips melded with hers. He tipped his head slightly to the side, deepening the kiss and heat coiled in her belly. Violet's fingers curled into his shirt, pulling him closer, but she must have pulled harder than she thought. He crashed against her shoulder and his hand slammed into the bench seat on her other side.

Patrick's lips broke into a smile against her mouth. Deep, breathy laughter shook his shoulders, and he softly rested his forehead against hers. "By the way, your emotions can affect your abilities." He chuckled again. "I didn't realize how strong you are."

Embarrassed giggles bubbled out of her and she pinched her eyes shut. "Sorry."

"We'll work on it." He pressed a quick kiss to her forehead before his warmth disappeared, making her open her eyes. He stood just outside the truck door while he passed a hand through his hair. "Whew, I'm starting to miss Jax."

Violet blinked a few times. "Uh... why?"

A wolfish grin tugged at his lips. "It was a lot easier to control myself knowing he was watching."

Her eyes bugged, and nervous laughter escaped her lips before she pressed a hand over her mouth. Patrick responded with a round of low, husky chuckles.

"So, um, how—ahem." Violet's thoughts were mush as she tried to remember what her question was.

Warm affection softened Patrick's gaze, and he closed the gap between them to take her hand in his. He lifted her hand in the air, then pressed a soft kiss to her knuckles. "Breathe," he gently told her.

She nodded and followed his instruction when he told her to inhale and exhale. Slowly, the heat winding in her belly loosened as she focused on the air going in and out of her lungs.

"Better?" He asked with one brow quirked.

Violet nodded again. "Thanks." After clearing her throat, she tried again. "How long will it take to reach Matthews Creek Campground?"

"About two hours. I was thinking—"

Ruby red blinked in the trees behind Patrick and Violet had just enough time to shove him out of the way before a giant copper wolf slammed into the side of the truck. The Nerd Rope box flew into the air and Nerds showered her as she scrambled backward along the bench seat to escape the massive jaws snapping at her feet.

She heard Patrick call her name, but the only sound that left her mouth in reply was a grunt as she smashed the heel of her foot into the wolf's nose. It yelped, then backed up enough for her to turn and fumble for the driver's door handle. There wasn't enough time. The beast was back, snarling through a bloody muzzle while its teeth made for her leg.

Curling her fingers into a fist, she slammed her hand down on top of the creature's muzzle. Its teeth snapped together and she pushed the same arm forward before pulling her elbow back. The force of her blow knocked the wolf's head into the back of the seat, and its body went limp. Its red eyes were closed while it dangled halfway out of the truck, muzzle still bleeding on the leather seats.

Grunts and snarls sounded outside the truck, telling her that Patrick was still fighting. Determination rolled through her, and Violet shoved against the wolf. Its unconscious form shifted a little, but ultimately didn't move far. She groaned, then turned to the driver's door. It jolted away from her, opened from the other side before a guy launched toward her. A surprised scream left her when his large hands clamped around her arms and yanked her from the truck's cabin.

"Violet!" Patrick yelled in her mind. *"Hang on!"*

A dark shadow passed over them and her attacker glanced up, his mouth going slack as a mass of black fur and claws flew over his head. Violet didn't wait for the wolf to land. She threw her fist skyward, then brought the point of her elbow down on the inside of her attacker's elbow. He hollered and released her other arm to grip his.

"Hurts doesn't it?" She growled, surprising herself with how wolf-like she sounded.

He smartly backed up a step when she started toward him, but the obsidian wolf had found his footing and now stood snarling behind the guy. Its lips curled back, baring long fangs glistening with blood and saliva.

"Stupid Guy, meet my mate, Patrick Cowen," Violet snarked as she moved around the man to stand beside the black wolf. "Patrick, meet Stupid Guy."

Wolf-Patrick lurched forward, snapping his jaws near the guy's face. Stupid Guy jumped back, hit the side of the truck, and screamed like his life was over.

"Ask how he knew we were here," Patrick's growly tone rippled through her mind.

"My thoughts exactly," Violet tipped her head to the side and winked at him before glaring at Stupid Guy. "How did you know we were here?"

"I d-don't know. I was just following orders," he whimpered.

Patrick gnashed his teeth and took a menacing step toward the guy.

"I swear!" He threw his hands into the air. "I had no idea you two were mates or that you—" he motioned toward Patrick, "—were lycan."

Violet crossed her arms. "Actually, we both are."

Light pressure filled her mouth and her nails transformed into claws. In any other situation, she would have whooped and hollered her excitement over the perfect timing, but right then she just beamed at the guy who's face had lost all color.

"How do you get sent on a mission you know nothing about?" Violet asked.

"I just joined Blood Moon a week ago. The only thing I know about you is that they want you dead and that you are supposedly a twin, but everyone knows that's impossible."

Violet snorted. "Yeah, well, impossible gets less impossible when you add me to the equation."

The guy's face contorted into confusion. "What?"

"Never mind, who gave you the order?"

"Ivy. Actually, Cas said it first, but we have to listen to Ivy."

The mention of his name sent a flood of ice through her veins. "How did they know?"

"Some guy came and told them he had information."

"What guy?" Violet yelled while Patrick released a warning growl, making the guy shrink away.

"I don't know! He was older. Had gray hair along the sides, but that's all I know, I swear!" He sputtered. "She'd just carved up one of our clanmates because she suspected they were unfaithful. She didn't even have proof! I wasn't really paying attention to anything else."

"He doesn't know anything," Patrick grumbled.

Violet clenched her jaw. She extended one of her clawed hands and lightly pressed one sharp tip under the guy's chin. "Last question: Does Cas have Lexie?"

The guy blinked. "Who?"

"Lexie!" She fumed. "Tall, gorgeous blonde human with giant blue eyes that could've be on a runway, but got tangled up with our kind!"

Blood trickled down the back of her finger and she eased the pressure against his skin when he whined. "I swear, I don't know anyone by that name, but there is a human. She matches your description, I think."

Rage boiled her blood. "You think?"

"I don't know. She's crazy. They did something to her. We aren't allowed to interact with her, but we have to make sure she doesn't escape. Cas visits her. That's all I know!"

Violet's chest heaved with each breath and red tinted her vision. They hadn't found any trace of Lexie because Blood Moon had her the whole time. Zander said he didn't have her. He lied.

Human-Patrick jumped in front of her and slammed his fist across Stupid Guy's face. He crumbled to the ground while Patrick turned to face her. His large hands rubbed her upper arms while he spoke soft, soothing words, but she didn't understand them. There was only one question still burning in her brain.

"Did you know?" she whispered.

Patrick froze. His wide, worried hazel eyes scanned her face.

Tears tumbled down her cheeks when he swallowed hard, but stayed silent.

Her claws faded away and the sharp points of her fangs shortened as a sob sank her chest. "Did you know?"

Chapter 21

Violet

Panic overwhelmed her senses *as Violet waited for Patrick to answer her. She* wanted him to deny it. She wanted to believe that he had no clue, but the reality was that Patrick was very clever and very little got past him. If they were held in separate rooms though, maybe...

"Not for sure," he whispered.

Violet pulled out of his grasp. She drew in a deep breath, but it didn't help. Her palm pressed against her chest as her breaths grew shorter. Why wasn't there enough oxygen?

"Violet, I was drugged and chained the entire time I was there," Patrick explained, closing the gap she'd created between them. "More than half the time I was unconscious, and the other times I wasn't sure if what I was seeing was real."

She held up a hand to stop him as her body trembled. Quick, short breaths made her dizzy, but even her lungs felt like they were shaking. Something was wrong.

"There was one time I saw hair that was similar to Lexie's, but I never saw a face or body and they never said her name."

"Patrick!" She tried to yell, but her voice quivered.

Her knees buckled and she fell to the ground, but the impact never came. Patrick's arms encircled her waist, pulling her tightly against his chest. "What's wrong?" His breath was warm against her ear. "You gotta tell me what you're feeling."

"I can't—" Violet's voice broke. Speaking was difficult. Breathing was harder.

"I can't stop..."

"Try to slow your breathing," Patrick instructed her as he lowered her to the ground and then knelt beside her. "I can only guess based on what I'm feeling from you, but I think your body is instinctively trying to shift due to your extreme emotions."

There were so many questions to unpack with that statement, but all she managed was a breathy, "What?"

"Breathe," he said slowly, softly rubbing her back. "In... and out... Just like before." He was quiet for a moment, then added, "That reason was a lot more fun, though."

A strangled laugh left her, making Patrick's wrinkled brow ease and a small smile inch across his face.

"When was the last time you shifted?" He asked quietly, still rubbing her back.

Violet shook her head, and then leaned into him. His arms wrapped around her, holding her tight. The warm, compressive hold soothed her shot nerves and the steady rhythm of his heart lulled her into closing her eyes. "I've only shifted once."

"When Luna was killed," Patrick said reverently.

A heavy weight pressed against Violet's chest, mirroring the emotion that flickered across her thoughts.

"The only time you've shifted," he squeezed her gently. "You were under heavy distress and your emotions were chaotic. Unlike wolven—who need to rely on their wolf spirits to help them shift—lycan are often triggered into shifting because of their emotions. That's one of the reasons we typically first turn around puberty. Fun right?"

Violet released a shaky laugh. "That sounds awful."

"It can be. Imagine looking at a smoking hot guy and suddenly turning into a wolf."

This time her laugh came out in a loud burst. "Just like that?"

A rumble of laughter bounced through Patrick's chest. "Not quite, but you would feel it; the tingling in your ears, the pressure through your mouth, you might even feel your skin kinda vibrate. If you were lucky, you'd be able to turn away and get the rush of emotions to calm down. If you weren't lucky... you better make a break for it."

"I can't imagine that happening to you."

"It didn't. I had much more control than other kids my age, but only because I had been shifting for a couple of years already."

"What?" Violet tipped her head back to look at him. "How?"

Patrick's throat bobbed as he swallowed. A distant look fell over his hazel eyes followed quickly by something dark and angry. "My sister's life was in danger. I shifted to protect her. I was nine."

Violet's eyes bugged and her mouth fell open. She didn't know which part of that was more shocking—that he had a sister or that he was only nine. She decided to focus on the first one. "You have a sister?"

A wide grin replaced the haunted expression on Patrick's face. "Rochelle. She's gonna love you."

Her building excitement quickly fizzled out, leaving her feeling weak and worn down. "You should have told me about Lexie."

"Vi, I didn't know."

"I know," she closed her eyes and drew in a deep breath before continuing. "You still could have told me it was a suspicion or even an off the wall wild guess. And how am I only just now hearing about your sister?"

He sighed and Violet pushed out of his comforting arms. Her shaking had subsided, there was no need for him to hold her together anymore. No matter how wonderful it felt to be in his arms, and that she could have stayed there for days on end... except she couldn't. They had a job to do. A mission to complete. Their clan needed them.

"I wasn't trying to keep secrets from you," Patrick followed her lead when she rose to her feet. "But I was told not to let anyone get close to me. I wasn't supposed to draw attention or let anyone suspect who or what I was. I had to keep you at arms length. And as far as Lexie goes..." His arms lifted to the sides before thumping against his legs. "I didn't even remember seeing her hair until you brought her up. You could have asked me, too."

Violet shook her head. "I didn't think to ask you."

"Vi," Patrick breathed her nickname before his large warm hands fell over her shoulders. When she didn't meet his gaze, he tipped her head back with one knuckle under her chin. Something soft and heated passed over his pleading expression as he stared into her amethyst eyes. "Ask anything you want and I will tell you, but you can't get mad at me for not saying anything until now. The rules have changed. Nothing is holding me back anymore." His fingers traced her jaw before burying into her hair and she closed her eyes briefly.

When she opened them again, Patrick's smoky grin made her stomach flip. Warmth flooded her face and ears... and then they started to tingle. "No!" She jumped out of his reach, clamping her hands over her ears. Images of her turning into a giant wolf because her mate was hot flashed through her mind. There wasn't time for her to figure out how to change back. They needed to leave!

Patrick's eyebrows shot toward the sky, then his smoky grin grew to a wide smile. Mirth lit his eyes with a spark of mischief before he bent forward, laughing.

"This is not funny!" Violet tried to sound angry, but his laughter was infectious and her harsh tone was ruined by her own chortling. "You said heightened emotions. My emotions are definitely heightened!"

Shaking his head, Patrick stumbled toward her, still chuckling, and wrapped his long arms around her. He planted a kiss to the top of her head, then softly pulled her hands away from her ears. Violet nibbled on her lower lip as his fingers tucked some hair behind her ear. A delightful shudder ran through her body when he traced the outline of her now tapered ear.

"You might be new to being a lycan." Patrick gently rubbed the tip of her ear as he spoke. "But you're not new to heightened emotions. You're not a brand new teenager trying to figure everything out. I don't think you need to worry about randomly bursting into wolf form."

"Are you sure?"

"Not completely. This is new for me, too, but based on what I've seen I don't think that'll happen."

"Good," Violet's body relaxed when she released the breath she'd been holding and she leaned against Patrick. "We don't have time for that."

Patrick's chest rumbled against her cheek while his arms tightened around her. "We'll figure it out." He ran his hand up and down her spine, then leaned back so he could look at her. "Together." His hands trailed down her arms until his fingers wove through hers. "I know this has all been a lot for you, but we're heading into the heart of lycan territory. I need you on my side."

This time when Violet drew in a deep breath, her chest was a little looser. Her shoulders relaxed and a soft smile spread across her lips. "I'm always on your side, Patrick."

His chin lowered, and he closed his eyes. A large breath deflated the tension that had built along his arms and shoulders.

Moisture built along her lower lashes, and she reached up to softly cup his cheek in her small palm, which he gently leaned into.

Patrick gathered her in his arms once more, then planted a kiss on top of her head. "Let's find the lycans and then go get Lexie."

Sniffling, she looked around. The bodies of their attackers, both unconscious and dead, were surrounding them. They'd gotten lucky so far with no one seeming to notice them, but more cars were starting to show up at the gas station across the road and people would be gathering at the restaurants nearby soon. They'd gotten lucky that the museum had odd, limited hours and the parking lot was completely empty.

Patrick's head bobbed in the direction of their attackers. "Let's hurry and take care of them then get back on the road. We're running out of time."

With a sigh, she moved to grab Stupid Guy. "You can get the wolf that's stuck in the truck."

"Wish I could make him pay for damages," Patrick grumbled as he headed around the hood of the truck. "But I don't think the insurance would go for, 'Hey, a giant wolf smashed into my truck and dented the frame. You'll cover that, right?'"

Shaking her head, Violet snickered before shoving her arms under Stupid Guy and hauling him to the back of the museum.

When they were finished, Patrick cleaned up the bloodied bench seat with a mini bottle of hydrogen peroxide and some paper towels, while Violet attempted to pick up all the Nerds that had escaped their box.

"I wanted to take you to Bigfoot Steakhouse, but we don't have time for that," Patrick said when he finished, and then stashed the cleaning items away in the glove box. "We'll grab something on the way."

Violet sighed. "Sorry about the Nerds."

He smirked. "I knew candy was going to be a big part of my life a long time ago. Every time I find a Nerd in my truck, I'll think of you."

A burst of laughter left her as she circled the truck to climb in. "Okay. Well, at least I finished the Twizzlers otherwise those would have been all over, too." Patrick closed her door after she was seated, then jogged around the hood. After he'd brought the truck roaring to life, she asked, "What's gonna happen at Matthews Creek? You said something about a Witches Pass?"

"*The* Witch's Pass," Patrick corrected her, then grimaced. "It's a not so pleasant experience that visitors must go through to prove their good intentions."

She frowned while Patrick backed out of the spot they were in and started for the road. She shifted in her seat, twisting at the hem of her shirt. "And what if they don't have good intentions?"

Patrick's jaw clenched and the muscle just below his ear pulsed. "They never make it out."

Chapter 22

Violet

***The sun had lowered** just enough to make Matthews Creek Campground eerily* dark by the time they arrived. Violet watched the dark silhouette of tree after tree pass while Patrick easily maneuvered the truck down the lane. He skipped over one site after another until he pulled into the furthest space away. When he shut the truck off, Violet reached for the door handle, but froze when she realized he wasn't doing the same.

Instead of moving to get out of the truck, Patrick stared into the trees in front of them, tightening and loosening his hands around the steering wheel.

Her fingers slipped off the handle as she turned toward him. "You okay?"

Patrick's gaze darted her direction and a flash of a smile that didn't reach his eyes spread across his face. "Always."

A crack sounded in the trees, making Violet jump, but a moment later a couple of deer wandered through the trees.

When the deer had passed, Violet turned back to Patrick whose narrowed eyes were focused on the trees around them. "What do we do now?" Violet asked, her voice sounding far too loud in the quiet forest around them.

Patrick glanced at the time and she did the same.

7:51

A deep inhale puffed Patrick's chest. "Now, we wait."

"For what?"

He shook his head, then pushed open his door. Violet followed his lead and left the truck. By the time her foot hit the ground, he was there, holding the door open for her. "I don't know what to expect or what to tell you. I've been gone for years. Things could have changed. And..." he drew in a deep breath. "I've only been through The Witch's Pass once."

Once she was clear of the truck, Patrick gently closed the door behind her. "Is it an actual pass? Like a mountain pass, but of... witches?"

"No." His hand found hers and he gave it a soft squeeze as he leaned against the side of the truck. "From my understanding at the time, there were a number of witches employed by the lycans to help protect and keep the community hidden. They lived with us, were our friends, and when the time came that their skills were needed they were happy to help. Sometimes they would strengthen the wards around the community. Other times, they acted as The Witch's Pass. I don't know all the details of it or how it works, but I know they are able to ascertain the true intentions and desires of the person they are vetting."

"And what... if they aren't pure of heart they shall not pass?" Violet asked in a mocking tone.

Patrick snorted. "Something like that."

"Sounds like quite the story," spoke a male voice through the trees.

Patrick shot away from the truck, placing himself slightly in front of Violet.

But as she looked around, there was no one in sight. Her lycan vision was incredible, allowing her to see in the dark like never before, but even that had its limits. She couldn't see through the trees surrounding them.

Patrick was drawing in a deep breath after deep breath and it took Violet a moment to realize he was smelling the air. She tried to do the same, filling her lungs with as much air as possible, but the only thing she could smell was trees and dirt... and the spiced meat someone was grilling a few sites down that made her mouth water.

"Show yourself," Patrick commanded. His hand reached back and he curled his fingers around her waist. "We are unarmed and mean you no harm."

A chorus of laughter rose from the trees. Low and high tones mixed together in the light breeze that brushed past them. Patrick's head whipped in the direction the wind had come, his eyes narrowed. When Violet turned the same way, her eyes widened at the thick blanket of fog clawing its way toward them.

"Lycan's are never truly unarmed, now are they, Patrick?" spoke a musical female voice.

"What's going on?" Violet wrapped her hand around Patrick's arm as the fog spread, creating a circle around them. "Where are they?"

"Here," a couple of voices answered followed by a round of more 'here's.

A low growl rumbled through Patrick as he pressed back against her. Violet laid her other hand on his back, ensuring him that she was still there. The fog was rising now, obscuring her view of the trees.

"Afraid we're going to take your little girlfriend?" laughed the first male who'd spoken. "So you do remember our games."

Patrick's fingers tightened at her waist. "You will not take my mate."

Just like the 'here' before, now the word 'mate' seemed to be whispered around them.

"She's a bit small isn't she?" the first male teased, but the laughing tone was gone, so were the mystical notes of the others.

Something about her being Patrick's mate had changed their game. The fog had created an opaque dome, swirling all around her and Patrick and his truck. An oily feeling slithered over her thoughts and a wave of nausea washed over Violet as she threw a mental wall up. She curled her fingers into Patrick's arm.

"Come now, *Rick*."

Patrick stiffened.

Violet closed her eyes as the smarmy presence in her mind caressed the wall like a lover might trail a hand enticingly over their significant other. The thought made her shudder.

"Don't you recognize me?"

The male voice seemed to be right in front of her now, but whoever was in her thoughts did not relent. They pressed harder, their soft, enticing prodding turning rough and angry. A quiet whimper escaped Violet when the presence slammed against her thoughts. She wasn't strong enough to hold them back. She was a fighter, but she hadn't been trained for mental assaults. There were no fists in a mental battle... or were there?

Images of her and Patrick kissing in his truck consumed her thoughts then shifted to the dead wolven they'd left behind. Her memories and thoughts were on display, and as hard as she tried, she couldn't stop them. Soon she was watching her heart break over Patrick's death, then her mother's lifeless body filled her mind. Blood on her hands. Blood everywhere. Death followed her wherever she went. She was a threat.

No. Violet told herself, shaking her head. *These were the acts of another clan. I didn't cause this.*

The memory of her sitting with Jax right after her mom had died emerged in her thoughts. *"I made the choice that killed her."*

No. Violet repeated, but the word was stronger now. *You have no right to use that against me. You don't understand.*

Her thoughts shifted again, revealing her father standing over her. *"You endangered the life of a human... You nearly killed your best friend tonight."*

Anger bubbled up inside her, making Violet's chest rise and fall with heavy breaths. *You have no right to dig through my past and bring up things you don't understand.*

Memories flashed through her mind like someone leafing through the pages of a book.

No! Violet mentally shouted and the memories flickered. *No more! My past is* mine. *You don't get to rifle through it and find things to suit your desires. We came for help.*

A disgruntled feeling settled over her. Whoever was in her head, pressed harder shooting pain across her skull. She couldn't stop herself, she let go of Patrick's arm to press the heels of her palms to her head.

Stop! She commanded, but they only pushed harder. Warmth seeped from her body, trickling out of her as they shoved their way into her mind. Her body trembled and her heart thundered in her chest, pounding in her ears. A guttural roar tore from her throat and she screamed at the intruder. *"GET OUT OF MY HEAD!"*

Their oily aura disappeared when her mental shield slammed back into place feeling stronger than ever.

Heavy breaths had Violet's chest and shoulders heaving when she opened her eyes to find five pairs of eyes staring at her like she had two heads. A guy with blonde hair was kneeling on the ground rubbing his temples, while the girl beside him clamped a hand on his shoulder.

"Vi?" Patrick's gentle voice pulled her attention and she sucked in a sharp breath when her eyes landed on him.

A purple aura surrounded him, pulsing in rhythm with the rapid beat of her heart. It outlined his body, following his arms to where his hands held her waist, then flared around her limbs as well. She held out her trembling hands to find the aura surrounding her, as well.

"Your nose," Patrick whispered.

She looked at him, then softly touched above her lip. Blood smeared the tips of her fingers when she pulled them away and pounding began to build in her ears again. Her gaze swept over the people surrounding them—witches, she realized.

"What are you?" Asked the blonde who was still kneeling on the ground.

Violet slipped her non-bloodied hand into Patrick's before stepping toward the guy, making a couple of other people back away. "I really hope witches are taught better manners than what you just did to me." She held out her bloody fingers and then gestured to her nose. "I may not know what I am or what I can do, but I know I didn't do this to myself. You pushed too far."

"Mate," snorted the male voice from before, like the word was poison on his tongue.

Violet whipped her head to the side to find a cocky young man with dark hair and an easy smile leaning against a nearby tree.

"Figures you'd be matched with a puissant half-pint."

Her brows tugged together. "Pui...sant?"

"Pyoo-is-uhnt," he slowly pronounced. "Powerful. It's a compliment."

He shoved away from the tree, then closed the distance between them, extending a hand toward her. "Name's Elias."

Violet stared at Elias. There was no way she was shaking his hand. Reacting to her emotions, the purple aura around her pulsed. A ripple of power broke away, similar to a flare breaking away from the sun, and knocked into Elias.

A low laugh rumbled out of him while he retracted his hand to rub at his chest. "Not too friendly, are you?"

Truthfully, Violet had no idea how she'd done that, but she shrugged like it had been totally intentional. "You attacked us first."

Elias glared at the blonde who'd managed to make it to his feet. "Some of us can get... a little overzealous."

"Is that what you call it?" Patrick growled, drawing Elias' attention. "When a witch steps out of line, it's simply being overzealous?"

A toothy grin spread across Elias' face. "If we are following the orders of the King, anything is possible." He tipped his head to the side and looked at her again. "Violet, allow me to be the first to welcome you to the Western Lycan Territory."

She didn't bother asking how he knew her name. He'd either heard Patrick say it or was somehow privy to what the other guy had seen in her mind. What she did wonder about though was the fog that had now settled at their feet and the trees that had changed position. Patrick's truck was still behind her, but no longer on an asphalt pad. Instead, the large tires dug into soft dirt covered by a spattering of leaves.

"I didn't realize witches could teleport people," she muttered as she looked around.

"We can't," Elias confirmed. "However, the spot *Rick* here parked his truck, is bound to this area. Witches far more powerful and ancient than us created the fold in space that allows a group of witches to bring someone from one point to another."

"So... teleporting," Violet repeated.

Patrick gently squeezed her hand and she looked up to find a slight smirk tugging at the corner of his mouth.

Elias snorted. "Leave it to a wolf to diminish something magnificent to something trivial."

Raising her brows, Violet returned her attention to the young man standing before them. "If you think teleportation is trivial, I think you're the one with the problem. Not me."

Elias opened his mouth to respond, but Patrick's snarl silenced him.

"Enough of this. You know who I am. You've looked into her mind. Let us pass."

"You were banished for good reason!" Elias thrust a finger in Patrick's direction. "You were never supposed to return. I've seen your eyes. I know how close you were to becoming a Ripper before you left, and I can't imagine it's gotten any better. I've seen you lose control. Your true nature outweighs anything we may find about your intentions."

The purple hue surrounding Violet flared when she took a step forward, planting herself between the two young men who towered over her. "Then you didn't look close enough. If you were actually looking for evidence of our intentions you would have seen answers to all of that." She threw a glare at the blonde who flinched under her scrutiny. "So what *were* you looking for?"

Elias lowered his chin, then his head, and even bent forward a little until they were eye-level. Being a witch, he didn't have the same physical benefits as a lycan or wolven, but he still stood right around six foot. "Here's the thing, little wolfling, if *we* don't like you... you don't pass."

"Then what?" Violet tipped her head to the side and lifted her chin defiantly. "You'll hold us here forever? Kill us? Send us on our way? I'd really like to know because we have things to do. Places to go. People to save."

Amusement sparked behind Elias' eyes and Violet fought the urge to smack the hint of a smile right off his face. "Please. If there was something that dire, we would know about it."

"Guess you don't know everything then do you?"

Elias' brows slammed down as anger replaced his amusement.

She wasn't done though. "Blood Moon has claimed the land of a neighboring clan. They killed the alpha and a lot of the clan mates. They've launched assault after assault on the Sentinel Clan. They killed our Luna." Violet's voice broke and she swallowed the knot that threatened to stop her from speaking. "My mom. She was the best Luna there is, and I know she tried to contact people for help. The Whisky, Sierra, and Mammoth clans are joining us to launch a war against them, but most of them are not fighters. We can't face Blood Moon alone."

Elias' lowered brows had pulled together while she was talking. He looked troubled, but still wasn't saying anything.

Violet dared a step toward him. "People are counting on us, and you are wasting our time."

A moment of tense silence passed through the area before whispers began to flit through the air.

When Elias closed the remaining distance between them, Violet felt Patrick tense behind her. "Lower your shield and open up your mind to me, little wolfling."

It took everything she had not to look at herself and the aura pulsing around her. A shield, huh? Cool. But lowering it...

"Patrick, I don't know how to do that."

His fingers lightly squeezed hers. *"Don't let them know that. Try a few deep breaths. Remember you are not alone. I'm here. I won't let them hurt you."*

Violet closed her eyes and drew in a deep breath while Patrick's words wrapped around her like a warm blanket. She wasn't alone. She would never be alone again. The tension in her shoulders eased and she let out a long breath before opening her eyes to find that the purple shielding had disappeared.

"I'm ready," she announced.

Slowly, Elias raised his hands to hover on either side of her face. When he moved like he was going to touch her, Patrick's large, clawed hand shot out over her shoulder. Heat radiated from Patrick, warming Violet's back while he clenched Elias' wrist. She imagined what he looked like—fangs out, ears tapered, and based on the shocked expressions on everyone's face... his eyes were probably glistening like moonstone.

"Hurt her and I'll kill you," Patrick growled and a shiver rippled down Violet's spine.

Elias had been the only witch to manage keeping a calm face, but one of his brows lifted at that. "Is that a threat?"

"That's a promise. You will not harm my mate."

A long, drawn out sigh left Elias, but a vein in his neck betrayed his false bravado, exposing his rapidly thumping heart beating beneath his skin. "If she doesn't resist, this will be painless."

Violet rested her hand on top of the one Patrick had clenching Elias's wrist. She tipped her head back and looked at Patrick over her shoulder. "I'll be fine." She returned her attention to Elias who watched her a bit more cautiously now. "I have nothing to hide."

Patrick's fingers unclenched Elias' wrist and the witch slowly placed his fingers along the sides of her face, near her temples. His gaze held hers intently. "Do not fight me."

"I'll try not to," she whispered.

When he closed his eyes, she reached behind her for Patrick's hand and his warm fingers encircled her hand. A sigh of relief left her, then she gasped as she was plunged into darkness.

Chapter 23

Violet

Inky blackness swirled around *Violet like a cyclone. Her breathing quickened* as it churned in a tight circle, threatening to drown her in its depths. There was no escape. No way through. There was nothing but darkness.

What had Elias done to her?

"Patrick!" Her voice echoed across the void shouting back at her until it faded into the abyss.

Without warning the cyclone died. Its power slammed into the ground all around her and eerie silence pressed against her. She stretched a hand out in front of her, then released a large breath when she could easily see her fingers wiggling. There wasn't a source of illumination as far as her eye could see, but she was grateful for the light.

Water splooshed when she began to spin in a slow circle, making her gaze drop. She lifted a foot, then set it back down. Ripples spread away from her. There was maybe half an inch of water, but her shoes were completely dry.

Where was she?

Violet lifted her gaze and scanned the area once again.

"Patrick!" she tried again, only to have her voice echo back to her.

"He can't hear you."

Violet spun around to see Elias standing a few feet away. Small ripples spread away from him, colliding with the ripples coming off her. This Elias was different. His hair was a bit disheveled, and his shoulders drooped as if he had the weight of the world on them. Gone was the cocky bravado. The corner of his mouth tipped down into a slight frown.

"What did you do to me?" Violet walked toward him until there was only a foot or so of space between them. "Where are we?"

"We're still in the forest." Elias' gaze narrowed. "You aren't reacting like I thought you would."

With a snort, Violet crossed her arms. "What were you expecting?"

He tipped his head to the side. "Most people meltdown when presented with a void of darkness."

"Yeah, well, my life isn't exactly normal, so I don't tend to meltdown when odd things happen to me." When he didn't respond, she raised her brows. "Are you going to answer my questions?"

"I did a mind dive," Elias stated bluntly.

She blinked. "Am I supposed to know what that means?"

One of the downturned corners of his mouth twitched. "No. You grew up in a wolven base. Wolven are kept in the dark about a lot of things." He gestured around them and that same corner of his mouth raised into a slight smirk. "Figuratively, of course. Not like this."

"So explain." She started pacing, keeping him in the corner of her vision. "What is it?"

"It's a rare ability. Most witches can sense someone's thoughts and intentions. Some can even read people's thoughts. Being able to enter the mind of someone else is another thing."

Violet froze. "Enter their mind?" That was what she'd done to Patrick.

"Yes." Elias's eyebrows lowered. "That's what I just said."

"Can you see memories?"

Suspicion rolled off him in waves and he dropped his head to the side. "Sometimes. If I'm really close with the person or I'm Mind Diving into a specific memory. Or if the person willingly shows me a memory while I'm here, like you're about to do."

A short laugh burst out of her. "Oh, I am, am I?"

"Yes," Elias snapped. Any trace of humor had disappeared. "Or I'll leave you here, trapped inside your mind for eternity."

Violet smirked. "I think I'd be alright."

"Show me the first time you encountered Blood Moon," Elias ordered.

The memory of that fight readily came to mind. It was the first real fight she had ever been in. She saw the red eyes of the Blood Moon scouts before anyone else had. She'd called out a warning when they attacked. Jax's arm had been broken.

He'd been furious. The terror that had seized her when her attacker had scaled her prone body like a rock wall... And Patrick... the image of him hammering his fists into her attacker's face, breaking bones in the process, sent shivers down her spine.

"Reaper," Elias breathed the word like it was a curse.

Violet snapped her gaze to him and glared. "No. Patrick is not a reaper."

Elias thrust his arm out, directing her to something over her shoulder. "That proves otherwise!"

She spun around to see her memory playing out like a movie. "No." She shook her head. "This doesn't show you everything. This was when Alistair was at his worst."

"Who is Alistair?"

A long sigh left her and the movie memory shifted to a forest she'd only ever seen through Patrick's eyes. Panic shot through her veins. This was not her memory to share. "No, no, no." She threw her hands forward and then to the side as if she were throwing the images out.

To her amazement, it worked.

"Huh." Elias clicked his tongue. "Well done. Most people don't figure that out right away."

"I didn't know I could do that. I just wanted to stop you."

A sinister smile spread across Elias' face.

He was trying to trick her. Get her to describe what it was. Get her to think about it. Is that how this memory tv thing worked? If she thought about it, would he see it?

"I'm not some weak minded imp you can trick into getting what you want," Violet grumbled.

Shrugging a shoulder, Elias walked toward her. "Then we will sit here until you're ready to show me."

"It's not my memory to share."

Elias stopped mid-stride. "What did you just say?"

"You heard me."

He blinked. Then blinked again before speaking. "There is only one way to share another's memory and be able to recall it like that."

Violet slowly nodded. "What did you call it? A Mind Dive?"

"That's not possible. You're lycan."

"With some witch abilities thrown in apparently. I'm an odd conundrum that shouldn't exist and yet here I am!" She threw her arms to the sides then let them thump against her legs when they fell. "I'm the impossible twin. The lycan born to wolven. A wolf with witch abilities. And to top it all off, I'm the average height of a human."

Elias stared at her with wide eyes.

"You want to see my memories?" Violet seethed. "Fine. I'll show you my memories." She spun on her heel and threw her palms into the air.

The darkness around them disappeared as memory after memory came forth, surrounding them like a dome of TVs. She played that first encounter with Blood Moon on repeat while she pulled more and more forward. The attack during the Clan Games. The bombing of the Clan House. The ambush during the full moon. Being kidnapped by Zander.

Tears gathered in her eyes as she reached deep inside herself and pushed the most painful moments forward. Memory after memory of missing and worrying about Lexie. Standing in front of her parent's house, not being able to tell them anything, except how sorry she was.

Aiden's funeral. She lingered on the image of her friend's body burning on the pyre then shifted to seeing Mya for the first time after his death. A shell of herself, void of life.

"Who are they?" Elias asked, his voice gentle as if he recognized the pain of these moments.

"My friends," Violet's voice broke and she swallowed the knot in her throat.

With hesitation, she tugged the memory of the full moon forward and let it play.

"Everything I did, I did for you."

She listened to her mom's voice, closing her eyes so she could soak in the sound.

"So you could live the life you deserve. With a wolf. With a mate."

Violet kept her eyes closed for a while, just listening until...

"Shall we see who's stronger, Luna?" A dark smile had spread across his face. *"Or do you want to hand over your daughter to me now?"*

"Over my dead body," Luna growled, sinking low in front of Violet.

"That can be arranged."

Violet's eyes rounded when the translucent aura wavered over Evalyn's skin. How had Violet not connected that before? There had been a glowing, translucent aura around her just a few minutes ago.

It was a short moment of reprieve amongst the sorrow. Something she would have to think about another time because Vikter was racing toward her mom.

Even with her new heightened speed, she hadn't been able to reach Evalyn in time. She hadn't been able to stop Vikter's dagger from driving into her mom's back. Then the other came crashing down from the enemy Evalyn had been pairing off against.

Violet watched with silent tears trailing down her cheeks as the concussive blast, and its subsequent aftershocks, left her. She watched her mom die in her arms and she kept the memory present until the blinding light of her first transformation burned out every other memory around them.

Silence hung heavily between her and Elias. She didn't dare look at him. Not yet. Not with her cheeks soaked in tears. Not while she fought to keep her chin from trembling and her body from collapsing under the weight of so much loss. So much anguish.

When she was sure she could call up another memory, she pulled at the one of Patrick waking up. His eyes shining as bright as glowing moonstone. Then tried to remember every good moment they'd had since. Every funny comment. Every kiss. Every instance that showed he was no longer held back by Alistair.

And finally—she tugged each memory of her and Jax talking about needing help to fight off Blood Moon.

Soon the word "help" was echoing around them.

"Jax!" she heard herself shout and watched as Jax turned his full attention on her. *"Let me do this. I'm asking you as my brother, not my alpha. Let me go and find some more help. Let me find a way to tip the odds in our favor."*

When the last memory faded away, she turned to look at Elias who was staring into the abyss like he could still see the memories playing out in front of him.

"This..." words seemed to fail him and he shook his head. Slowly, he turned his gaze on her. "Has this all happened in the last couple of months?"

Violet lowered her chin in a small nod. "It's been a rough year."

A humorless huff of laughter left him. "It's only April."

She nodded again and repeated, "It's been a rough year."

He stared at her. "I thought I was invading the thoughts of a spoiled princess. Not the mind of a warrior."

Light blossomed in her chest. It pulsed with the beat of her heart, growing brighter and brighter. She placed a hand over her heart, but it did nothing to dampen the light.

A small smile tugged at Elias's mouth. "Take us home."

The light turned into a blaze, washing out Elias' features and then his body entirely. When it was too bright to look at, Violet closed her eyes. Slowly, it began to fade and she found herself staring into Elias' face, only inches from her own.

Tear tracks glistened off his cheeks as he removed his hands from her head. He took a couple of steps back, brushing at his face as he did so, then looked at Patrick. "I'm sure I only saw a fraction of what you've been through, but for what it's worth, I'm sorry." His gaze drifted back to Violet. "You need to know that without her, you would not be welcome back here."

Warm fingers threaded through Violet's and she looked down at her and Patrick's hands intertwined before tipping her chin back to smile at him. It was a heavy smile—one full of sorrow, but also hope. With his other hand, he brushed away a tear that was rolling down her cheek, then pulled her close to lay his lips against her forehead.

When he pulled away, his voice rumbled through his chest. "I know."

Violet looked at Elias who was watching them with the same expression she'd seen in her mind. No more games. No more facade.

He nodded, then held his arm out to direct them where to go. "Let's get this party started, shall we?"

Chapter 24

Jax

Jax slumped into the *large chair behind his desk in the Alpha House office.* He dropped his head back against the cushioned headrest, closed his eyes, and let out a long breath through his nose. It had been a long day. Now, finally behind a closed door and alone, he was able to relax and breathe.

Sentinel families had made quick work out of leaving the base, and there had been a steady trickle throughout the day. The apartments and homes that were emptied were then filled by warriors streaming in from Whisky and Sierra. Mammoth Clan had finally responded after lunch. Their clan was much smaller, and more secluded, but they had agreed to send a few warriors. Thankfully, that was something he could handle tomorrow.

"Alpha, are you ready for the Evening Report?"

A long sigh deflated Jax's chest before he opened the link he had with his commanding warrior. *"Go for it, Cal."*

"All visiting warriors from the Whisky and Sierra clans have been settled into their temporary housing. We've double bunked where we could and have a few left for those arriving from Mammoth tomorrow, along with a handful of other homes that will be vacated first thing tomorrow."

"Excellent. I know this isn't really part of your job, but thank you for overseeing this."

"Of... of course, sir."

The note of shock in Cal's tone made Jax smile. Cal was among the first to welcome Jax as the new alpha, but he was still thrown off guard when Jax thanked him. Jax offered the man a little reprieve by turning the conversation to a job his commanding warrior was actually in charge of.

"How are the borders doing today?"

"All clear. We've patched up the holes that were made in our fencing during the full moon attack."

"And the rotation? Has that been evened out?" One of the first things Jax did when he became alpha was learning how the warrior and guard shifts worked. He learned that they were extremely lax at night, and immediately got to work to fix that. Now the numbers were more even, but it meant more people were working the night shift.

Hesitation filtered through Cal's next words. *"Yeees. There was some disagreement on that opinion. A few warriors fought against it, but are all working compliantly right now. I believe it is a good change. Especially with recent events and those to come."*

"Sounds good. Have a good night." Jax pushed himself out of the large chair.

"Sir?" Cal's voice lingered in his head. *"Excuse me, but... that's it?"*

Jax grabbed the long tube of paper and began to slide the rubber bands off it. *"You tell me. Was there something else you needed?"*

"No, it's just—" his commanding warrior grew silent.

Jax lowered the paper roll and concentrated on his connection with Cal. Closing his eyes, he searched for his clanmate's aura. They'd already been talking so it was easy to latch onto that chord and follow it. What he found was a ball of uncertainty and worry. Jax's heart beat a little harder in his chest. *"Cal, talk to me. What's going on?"*

"Sorry, sir. I'm still adjusting to the way you do things."

With a sigh, Jax opened his eyes and finished prying off the rubber bands from the paper. *"I'm not my father, Cal. What were you expecting me to do?"*

"I don't want to speak ill of a former alpha."

"Cal," Jax reprimanded him. *"I am your* current *alpha. What would Noah have done?"*

"He... he didn't handle it very well when people disagreed with him."

Jax snorted. That was an understatement.

"There would have been some sort of punishment for those that hadn't readily obeyed and agreed," Cal's grumbly tone rolled through Jax's mind.

Reaching for Dalim, Jax used his wolf's calming presence to make sure his next words reflected peace and understanding. *"There's no need for that. You said they were being compliant. I trust you."*

There was a long stretch of silence and Jax held the connection with his commanding warrior tight, feeling Cal's emotions shift into relief and appreciation.

"Thank you, sir." Cal finally responded, sounding more at ease. *"Good night, Alpha."*

Jax released his link with Cal and leaned into his wolf's presence. "This job is hard," he said out loud.

A wave of comfort washed over him as Dalim pressed against his thoughts. *"I know. If it's any consolation, I think you are handling it well."*

"I couldn't do this without you, Dalim."

"Thankfully, you never have to."

Jax's gaze drifted across his desk to a picture that hadn't been there last night. He'd noticed the frame earlier, but hadn't had a chance to really examine the photograph inside until now. When Jax set the paper down, it made a shhhh noise as it unrolled a little. Instead of flattening the roll out, his fingers wrapped around the edge of the frame and turned the picture to face him.

The image made his breath hitch. His thumb traced the light, plastic surrounding the picture of six teenagers. Smiles. Laughter. New love. Friendship.

Aiden's brown eyes pierced through the picture, straight to Jax's soul. He'd always held a more lighthearted presence than anyone else Jax knew, but there was a confidence in his gaze here. He'd said something that made them all bust up laughing right as the picture was taken. Jax wished he could remember what it was because the pleased expression on Aiden's face was undeniable. The only thing shining more brightly was an astounding amount of love. This was shortly after he and Mya had accepted their mate bond. His arm was stretched over her shoulders while she threw her head back in laughter. Her eyes were pinched shut, her mouth wide, and she leaned heavily into Aiden's side. Usually a curl was wrapped around one of her fingers, but in this picture, her hand rested against Aiden's chest.

Violet stood to the right of them, looking at them with amusement, and Jax realized they must have bent their knees because she was almost their same height. Patrick stood behind them, watching it all with a small smirk planted on his face. Jax was beside his best friend, but he wasn't looking at Aiden and Mya. Instead, he had been caught looking to the side... where Lexie stood beside him. Her big blue eyes were wide with mirth.

The sound of her laughter rang like a bell in Jax's memory. Goddess, he loved that sound. Not that he would ever admit it out loud. He filled his lungs with a deep breath and traced the edge of the frame with his thumb once more. This was the only picture they had of the six of them together. There would never be another like it.

Aiden was gone.

Mya was getting better, but would be forever changed by his death.

Violet was lycan.

Patrick had the full range of his emotions again.

He was alpha.

And Lexie...

He set the picture down and spread the rolled paper out, pinning each corner with a random object so it wouldn't roll again. It hung off the ends of his desk, but that was fine for now. Pressing his palms against the top of the desk, he stared at the blown up image of Stanislaus' Territory.

Blood Moon's territory—where Lexie was taken.

Jax hadn't told Violet what he knew about Lexie, yet. If Patrick knew, he hadn't said anything either. Finally, some information had paid off from countless hours of searching. Paul of all people had reported back to him, excited for the information he was relaying from another search party member. An odd reaction coming from the older man, but there was nothing Jax could do right then. He'd been forced to pull the wolven he had investigating Lexie's case because he needed them for the coming fight. All he knew was that Lexie was taken into their territory. He didn't know if she was alive or dead. If she was alive, they would need to hold her somewhere, but he didn't know where. If she was alive... what horrors had she been exposed to?

A low growl rumbled through Jax's chest and he felt Dalim's metaphorical hackles rise.

"Let's win this war..."

"And bring her home," Jax finished his wolf's sentence.

Power spread through his limbs and he knew if he looked into a mirror his eyes would be churning with molten gold. He stared at the map before him, burning it into his memory. Tomorrow he and the other clan representatives would begin their battle plans. Tomorrow war would officially be at their gates.

Chapter 25

Cas

The ambush had not *gone as planned. One of the two surviving party members* had called to tell Ivy about it a couple of hours ago, and the result had been bloody. Her fury was unhinged. She lashed out at anyone standing near her, killing three of her own pack members and severely injuring several more. Before she could turn on him, Cas had slipped from the room and gone for a long run.

With sweat dotting his brow, he carefully returned to the meeting house. His steps slowed as he approached, listening for any warning sounds, but all was quiet. He started forward again when movement to his side caught his attention.

"You know I'm under Ivy's protection. How dare you approach me like that," Cas snarled at the blood lusting wolven who'd dared sneak up on him.

The pitiful creature shrunk away, baring his teeth and glowing red eyes. "Ivy's protection means less and less every day." A quiet snicker shook the guy's shoulders. He pushed a few greasy strands of hair out of his face and stepped toward Cas again. "We'll be hunting you soon."

Abel threw his power forward and Cas felt his eyes change color. The pathetic Blood Moon member scrambled back, making a sound that could almost be classified as a hissing noise. "Try it and you'll find yourself at the goddess's feet."

The man's eyes bulged. He shook his head and his body tensed. "I'm one of Ivy's hunters."

Cas scoffed. "That explains the general lack of hygiene." He stalked forward two steps, making the man scramble away from him. "But don't mistake that title as protection from me. I'll gladly rip out your heart and feed it to the scavengers."

His skin blanched. He opened his mouth, but when only a whimper escaped, he snapped it shut. Then, with quick, jerky steps the man backed away from Cas before turning and bolting into the trees.

"Would you really rip his heart out?" Abel wondered as Cas turned back toward the meeting house.

"What do you think?"

Abel sighed. *"Once I would have said you weren't capable of such violence. Now... I wouldn't put it past you."*

"You disapprove?" Cas grumbled and fought the sudden urge to roll his eyes. *"Shocking."*

"Of course I disapprove! I believe in—blood."

Cas stopped abruptly. His face bunching in confusion. *"Blood?"*

"Look at the steps. It's fresh."

Narrowing his eyes, Cas lowered his gaze to the steps he was about to ascend. A streak of blood smeared up the steps. It was fresh, nearly still dripping down the concrete. And the stench! Cas clamped a hand over his nose and mouth. He thought humans smelled bad, but this flowery perfume smell was mixed with a rotting egg malodor.

Wait.

He knew that scent.

His stomach roiled as he smashed his shoulder against the meeting house door, throwing it open to hear Ivy's lullaby tone issue an order, "Hunter, dispatch the girl. She's no longer of any use to us."

Multiple ruby eyes turned his way when he burst into the room, but the only person he cared about was the almond-skinned man stalking to the center of the room. White blonde hair spilled over a feminine form writhing against the bloody shackles that chained her to the floor. They would have allowed her to stand, but she stayed lowered in a crouched position. She let out a savage growl and Hunter's lips curled back in a snarl as he lifted a dagger high into the air.

"Stop!" Cas darted forward, saying a silent prayer of thanks to the goddess when Hunter stayed his hand. He turned his attention to the white haired woman sprawled over the dark throne at the head of the room. "What are you doing, Ivy?"

Ivy groaned. "Why are you interrupting my entertainment?"

"Killing Lexie was never part of the deal!" Cas shouted. Rage and dread warred within him, making him sweat. His hands trembled at his sides, and he rolled his fingers into fists while a dull pounding filled his ears.

"Oh, please," Ivy rolled her head to the side, giving life to her bored tone.

Hunter eyed him, then Ivy, then Cas again and ultimately sheathed his dagger, but stayed where he was.

"I don't care about your deal," Ivy continued. "She's a waste of space and resources. The last person who watched her was found with his throat ripped out and then she tried to run away. It took us half an hour to track her down and that much longer to get her to stop trying to decapitate herself." She gestured to Lexie and Cas took in the poor excuse of a human.

Only Lexie's outward appearance could be considered human and even that was a loose description. Blood and grime covered her from head to toe and precious ruby drops fell from each cuff around her wrists, saturating the floor and filling the room with her rotting stench. The band around her throat and the ones on her ankles weren't any better. Her clothing was in tatters. She had no shoes. Two fangs had replaced each of her canine teeth. And her white blonde hair was in so many knots that he wondered if she'd just have to cut it when this was all over... if there was enough of her left to care about her hair.

Inside was a different story. Gone were the moments of clarity. Gone were the pleading words that broke Cas' heart. Gone was the life from her blue eyes. All that remained was a crimson eyed animal in human skin, but her eyes weren't like Blood Moon. The red filled her entire eye.

Pressure built in Cas' chest, warning him that he needed to take a breath. He drew in a deep breath and swallowed the bile that had risen to the back of his throat. His voice was rough when he managed to grumble, "If she's so troublesome, why bother tracking her down at all?"

Ivy flipped her hand over as if the answer was obvious. "She could have ended up in a human community." She scrunched one side of her nose. "As much as I don't care for humans, I would rather not have to deal with their government hunting us down."

Cas' mouth went dry. "We could use her."

Hunter growled his displeasure.

"Caaaas," Ivy dragged his name out and then clicked her tongue. She slowly stood from her throne before slowly sauntering toward him. "Cas. Cas. Cas. You and your plans are going to find you on the wrong side of my daggers."

"Not this one."

"Cas, no." Abel's voice was hard against his thoughts. *"I won't let you do this."*

"There is nothing you can do to stop me," Cas snapped.

"You can still come back from everything you've done. It isn't too late."

If he'd been alone, Cas might have closed his eyes and shaken his head. If he'd been alone, he might have given that some thought. But he knew what he was walking into when he started down this path. *"I burned that bridge a long time ago."*

"And why not?" Ivy asked, stopping just out of arm's reach.

Cas wet his lips and forced an icy smile to his face. "Because she is how you get Violet."

Abel raged against the confines of Cas' mind while Ivy's mouth spread into a wicked grin. "How so?"

"We've kept quiet about having taken Lexie." Cas explained, "If we announce that we have her, I guarantee that Violet will come charging in to find her."

Ivy's sea green eyes narrowed to slits. "How can you be so sure?"

"Because Violet would do anything for her human friend," announced former beta Paul as he walked into the room like he owned the place.

Ivy eyed Paul as Hunter placed his muscly form between her and Paul. "What are you doing here?"

The older man shoved his weathered hands into his pockets. "I thought I'd deliver what information I could on the Sentinels and discuss the astounding failure of an ambush on Violet and Patrick."

An enraged shriek left Ivy.

She was starting toward Paul when Cas lifted a hand to stop her. "Careful. You could end up losing your inside man."

Her snarl lightly echoed through the room. "Fine! I'm not sold on this plan of yours Cas. It seems your plans are a double edged sword. They get results, but they hurt Blood Moon in the process."

"I promise, Ivy." Cas forced his smile to shift into a grin. "The only person getting hurt in this plan is Violet." He huffed a laugh. "Which will ultimately hurt Patrick, as well."

Ivy's lips pressed together. Her gaze shifted back and forth between Cas and Paul before the latter said, "It's a viable plan."

With an agitated groan, Ivy raised her hand and snapped her fingers. A young, red eyed wolf hurried forward with a cellphone ready to take down notes. "Send a message out to Sentinel Clan. Let them know we have their precious human. Don't ask for anything in return. No placates. Plain. Blunt. Simple."

"You're basically throwing them into *Check* and saying, 'your move'," Paul observed.

Cas bit the inside of his cheek to stop himself from speaking. In the grand scheme of things—this is what he wanted. To hurt Patrick. He knew there would be casualties. He just hadn't planned on caring about those casualties.

Slowly, Ivy's mouth spread into a toothy smile. "Exactly."

Chapter 26

Violet

Growing up, Violet believed *that lycans were akin to gods. They were all* powerful, and legends were told about the special abilities some of them had. She spent many moments daydreaming about what their home might look like. Beautiful, old homes that were immaculately kept always came to mind. Their marble finishes gleaming in the sunlight atop pristine lawns. Walkways would always be joined with well-manicured shrubbery that was a paradise of colorful botany.

She wasn't expecting to find a small community of old cabin-like homes bunched closely together. There wasn't anything spectacular about the lycan's home, except that the cabins were built with the land and trees in mind. Forest surrounded them every way they turned and instead of cutting down the trees, it appeared that they built around them. A couple of the homes even had a tree growing through them.

As unexpected as all of that was, what made her even more uncomfortable was the number of eyes that followed them once they reached the edge of the community. Everyone recognized Patrick. They either called out a greeting of sorts or began whispering behind their hands. Violet tried to concentrate her hearing on what they were saying, but she couldn't pick anything out. And of course, once they were done whispering about Patrick, they would turn to her. Some people stared openly. A few even dropped their jaws. Violet was used to unwanted attention. Being one half of the only pair of twins in lycan and wolven history, on top of being short... and here she was *really* short... kind of made her a magnet for that sort of thing. But this—this was a different level of gawking, and she found herself moving closer and closer to Patrick.

His hand found hers and he tangled his long fingers through hers.

"Breathe." His soothing voice filled her mind.

After drawing a deep breath, she lightly squeezed his fingers. *"Thanks. I needed that."*

"Always." Patrick lifted her hand and placed a gentle kiss on her knuckles.

They were headed for a larger cabin-like structure, and Violet swallowed the knot that built in her throat when the front door opened.

"Violet, there's something you should know about my stepmom." Patrick's words were hurried, making the hair on Violet's neck stand on end. *"She's—"*

A tall, lithe woman full of grace hurried out of the door after a butler-looking man. Her dark chocolate hair flew over her shoulders in perfect barrel curls when she came to a sudden halt at the top of the front steps. A wistful smile tugged at her lips, and moisture lined her large gray eyes, which only grew bigger when they tore away from Patrick to land on Violet.

Violet's brows pulled together. "Mom?" she whispered, staring at the woman that could have been her mother's doppelganger.

The woman clamped a hand over her lush lips, and the tears that had gathered in her eyes tumbled down her cheeks. A moment later the woman was rushing down the steps. Her arms flew around Violet's shoulders in a crushing hug that Violet didn't know how to return. Warm vanilla wafted from the woman, but when amber accompanied the scent instead of cinnamon, tears flooded Violet's eyes.

"Oh, Violet," the woman cooed gently. "My sister's little miracle."

"Sister?" Violet jerked back and the woman released her.

Patrick sighed. "As I was trying to tell you... my step-mom is—"

"Your aunt," the woman finished.

Had Violet heard that right? The tips of her fingers went numb and the sensation spread up her arms as Violet stared at the reincarnation of her mother, unable to find words.

"I'm Jerrica," she held out her hand in a friendly gesture. "I suppose I should have introduced myself before launching at you."

"I don't..." Violet's gaze locked onto Jerrica's lithe fingers, just like her mom's. The comparison stopped there. Jerrica's nails were neatly trimmed and painted a hot pink color.

Slowly, Jerrica's hand drifted back to her side, fingers fidgeting with the material of her gray pants. "Our father fell in love with a human, but unfortunately your grandmother was killed a short time after Eva was born."

Violet nodded, though the feeling hadn't quite returned to her limbs. "Yeah, my mom mentioned my grandmother had been killed in a territorial dispute."

"One of the last." Jerrica offered a sad smile. "Anyway, my mom met him a couple of years later, and then I showed up. I know Eva and I both took after your grandfather, and while I haven't seen my sister in almost twenty years, I'm sure we still hold a lot of resemblance."

"That's an understatement."

The woman's sad smile spread a little farther. "I always was a copycat of Evalyn—the only difference was our height—and half our DNA."

Not sure what to say to that, Violet glanced at Patrick, who was watching her with his brows pinched together. She opened her mouth, but no words came out. His gaze dipped to her lips then back to her eyes and his throat bobbed as he swallowed. A wave of nerves crashed through her—not her nerves. She wasn't sure what she was feeling, but Patrick was clearly worried about how she would react.

"I understand if this is a bit much for you." Jerrica took a step toward her and Violet mirrored her moving, backing away. The smile on Jerrica's face wavered. She shot a quick look at Patrick before starting again. "You probably have a bunch of questions, especially since Patrick was commanded not to talk about his past. I'm happy to answer all of them. I just want you to know how excited I am to meet the niece I'd only read about in emails."

Niece. Aunt. Secret sibling. Stepmom.

Violet's head spun. She pressed her fingertips against her temple, closed her eyes, and drew in a deep breath. Whispers broke through the wall she'd built in her mind. The white noise filled her head like the sound of a thousand bees buzzing. Someone touched her arm and she shied away.

"I apologize for my wife's enthusiastic nature," a deep, rich voice cut through the hum of noise.

Opening her eyes, Violet found a man standing at the top of the stairs, glaring down at her.

"She can be a bit..."

"Overwhelming?" Jerrica offered, but her voice was a bit pinched as she turned to look up at the newcomer. Her fingers intertwined with each other behind her back, which was now facing Violet and Patrick.

Everyone around them bowed their heads until their chins touched their chests—everyone except Violet, Patrick, and Jerrica.

Patrick's eyes were making the same path over and over again from Violet's eyes to her body. *"You're glowing,"* he whispered into her thoughts.

Horrified, Violet dropped her gaze to her hands, which were covered in the same colorful aura she'd seen before. She rubbed at her arms, attempting to make the glow disappear, but it didn't help. If anything, it made the effect even worse by making the aura glow brighter.

She reached for Patrick, *"Help."*

Without a moment's hesitation, Patrick shot a hand forward to snag hers, and he pulled her against his chest. A pained grunt left him, but he wrapped his arms around her waist and dropped his chin atop her head. *"Breathe, Violet. I'll explain everything later, let's just get through this next part."*

A sigh of contentment, mixed with relief left Violet. She buried her face against his chest and breathed in his mint chocolate scent. *"I'll hold you to that,"* she told him and a huff of laughter from him made her head bounce lightly off his chest.

"Ahem," the man cleared his throat.

Patrick released Violet just enough so she could turn to look at the man, but kept a firm arm around her middle.

"Patrick," the man said his name as a way of greeting once he'd descended the steps.

There was a brief moment of silence before Patrick responded, "Dad,"

Violet's gaze snapped back to Patrick, then returned just as quickly to the man. Her jaw slackened while she gaped at him.

There was zero resemblance.

Where Patrick was tall with lean, corded muscles—this man was tall with bulky muscles that made his shoulders look like mini-boulders.

Dark loose curls fell in Patrick's eyes, while nearly white blonde hair had been neatly combed back on the man's head.

Patrick had a tanned olive complexion. This man was fair-skinned.

But when the man smirked at his wife, Violet caught the same twitch at the corner of his mouth that Patrick did. He descended the steps and Violet found herself staring at his eyes. There was no mistaking those hazel eyes.

Patrick tensed beside her, his fingers tightening around hers ever-so-slightly.

"Breathe." She copied him, hoping to ease his discomfort.

A low rumble of laughter rolled through her thoughts. *"Turning my words against me?"*

"Did it work?" She asked and cast a sideways glance up at him.

He lowered his chin and smiled softly at her. *"Maybe."*

"Then yes, I am."

Patrick's shoulders jerked a little as he silently laughed.

When Violet returned her attention to Jerrica and the new guy, her smile slipped. Patrick's dad was watching their exchange with apprehension. His gaze narrowed while he took the two of them in and lingered on their joined hands.

The guy sniffed, then looked his son up and down. "It's been a long time."

"Yes, it has." The bite in Patrick's voice made Violet squeeze his hand.

Mr. Cowen released an aggravated sigh.

"Easy," Violet advised her mate. *"I know you haven't seen them in a long time, and I'm sure there are things you all need to talk about, but we need their help."*

Jerrica rubbed her hands together, then shot forward, grabbing her husband's and son's arms. "We have a lot of catching up to do, don't we?" She smiled tightly at both of them. "I'm sure you're exhausted from your travels, though, so we can talk more tomorrow after breakfast."

"What?" Violet's mouth was open before she could stop it. "Can't we talk tonight? We've driven all this way, and our clan is expecting us back soon."

Gray eyes rounded as they found her. Hesitantly, Jerrica released Mr. Cowen's arm and reached for Violet, but she shied away. A flash of hurt pinched Jerrica's face, but she recovered quickly and rolled her shoulders back. "I understand there are different customs in the wolven territories, but here we like to start fresh with a new day. Beginning this conversation while emotions are running hot will not end well."

"But—"

"AAAAAAAHHHHHH!" A wild, high-pitched battle cry split the air, making Violet jump.

"Rochelle, no!" Patrick tried, but there was no time to stop the human-shaped wrecking ball from smashing against Violet's side, taking her to the ground.

Violet clutched her chest when all of the oxygen was punched out of her lungs. She pinched her eyes shut until the seizing eased and she was able to draw in a breath again.

"Oh my goodness!" squealed the wrecking ball that was now straddling Violet's waist. Rochelle leaned forward until her nose was almost touching Violet's and stared into her eyes. "You have purple eyes. That's amazing. They're gorgeous. You have to be Patrick's mate!"

Violet blinked. The girl had a mane of loose, dark curls that hung around Violet's head and bright, excited green eyes. "I'm guessing you're Patrick's sister?"

"So, you *are* his mate!" Rochelle sat back and her weight pressed Violet's hips against the ground. "I knew the only girl he'd bring home would be." She eyed Violet again and then chuckled. "You're a little... well... little, aren't you?"

A bubble of laughter burst out of Violet. "Yes. I am. And you're pretty much a giant to me, so can you get off?"

Horror washed over Rochelle, widening her eyes and tensing her body before she launched off of Violet. "Oh my goodness, I am so sorry. I didn't even think about that." Rochelle reached down and lifted Violet to her feet like she weighed nothing more than a doll. When she set Violet down, Rochelle began dusting her off.

Violet lifted her hands as the young woman swiped her hands around Violet's middle.

"You're wolven aren't you?" Rochelle asked, then snorted and chuckled to herself. "Of course, you are. He was living in a wolven territory, after all, and you're so small you couldn't be anything else." She jerked into a straight standing position and stared at Violet with round eyes. "You are okay, right? Did I crush any bones?"

Rochelle's saucer-sized eyes made Violet's already smiling lips spread into a wide grin.

"I'm okay," Violet assured her, lifting a placating palm toward the panicky girl. "Really. And I'm actually lycan—I think."

Rochelle blinked. Then blinked again. "I'm sorry, what?"

Patrick was at Violet's side a moment later. "You're okay?"

Nodding, Violet leaned against his side. "Totally fine."

"You found a lycan mate in a wolven community?" Rochelle's words seemed to echo around them and Patrick tried to shush her.

"She's lycan?" Jerrica asked above the hum of whispers that started. Soon she was standing beside Rochelle, staring at Violet. "You're lycan?"

Violet shrugged. "Amongst the other things we need to talk about, that's one of them. Any idea how that's possible?"

Jerrica's head tipped from side to side. "Only the goddess would know, but I know your mother was more lycan than wolven. Maybe there was just enough lycan in your father as well to make you." Her brow furrowed. "Is your twin..."

"No. Jax is completely wolven, but he has some extra abilities."

"Extra abil..." Jerrica cut herself off, placing a few fingers over her lips. "Hmm. Definitely something to talk to Laurel about."

"What?" Mr. Cowen snapped. "They've only just arrived and you want to take this trespasser to our most guarded prisoner?"

"Gavin!" Jerrica turned toward him as he approached. "This is your son's mate. She's not a trespasser, and Laurel will be able to answer these questions better than I can. Better than you can, too."

"No."

"Gavin," Jerrica chided, repeating his name. She sighed, then turned toward Violet once again. "He and I will discuss this matter tonight and have a more concrete answer for you tomorrow. For now, I'll have one of our warriors escort you both to your room." She waved over one of the women standing nearby.

"Room?" Violet squeaked. "As in *one*?"

A warm chuckle left Jerrica. "You *are* mates, are you not?"

"Moon fated, even," Patrick added.

Joy spread across Jerrica's face with a wide grin. She squeezed both of their shoulders in a tight hug. "Wonderful! Then you will be perfectly happy with your living arrangements."

"Living?" Violet squeaked again as Patrick's step-mom... her aunt... gently shoved her toward the female waiting to escort them.

They weren't going to *live* there! They had to get back to Jax and the Sentinels! But when her eyes drifted to Patrick, sorrow coursed through her. If his family accepted him back, there was a good chance he would want to stay.

"There seems to be a lot of one-word questions right now," Patrick chimed in, taking Violet's hand. "Maybe we should save the questions for tomorrow."

"Good plan!" Jerrica nodded, ushering them away. "Sleep well. See you in the morning." She turned and seized Mr. Cowen's arm, walking him back up the steps and disappearing into the building.

Rochelle grinned. "I'll catch you guys later. I have something I gotta do." She started to turn and walk away as she continued, "but I'll see you soon!"

Any other stragglers left, while the warrior Jerrica had assigned to them stepped onto the path and nodded her head for them to follow. The cold shoulder made it clear she was not up to chatting, but it was the two other warriors that fell into step behind them that told Violet they were not trusted there.

Chapter 27

Violet

Their cabin wasn't too *far away, but when the warrior slammed the door* shut, Violet had the distinct feeling that it was closer to a prison cell than a home. Slowly, Violet turned in a circle. It was laid out like a studio apartment. Everything was in the same room, except the bathroom, thank goodness. She stood in a small, but cozy sitting space with a loveseat that looked like it'd been stuffed with clouds, and pointedly ignored the large bed beyond. To her right was a kitchenette with a table set for two at the back of the room.

The large bed would not be ignored for long. Soon her eyes drifted back to the mass of blankets and pillows, and she swallowed hard enough that she was sure Jax would have been able to hear it back at the Sentinel base.

Patrick chuckled as he made his way around her to the loveseat. "Nervous?"

"What?" Violet asked, her eyes wide as she watched him lower their bags onto the couch cushions. "No. Me? Nervous? Why would I be nervous?"

A single brow climbed Patrick's forehead. "Well, if that didn't give it away," he laughed. "Maybe the fact that you haven't moved from the door and look like you're about to bolt at any second."

"They're expecting us to share a bed."

"And?"

"Patrick!" she squeaked.

"Violet!" he mimicked.

She probably would have laughed any other time hearing Patrick's voice go so high pitched, instead her fingers twisted around one another as she stared at him.

He watched her steadily, waiting for her to speak.

"You're really okay with this?" her voice was nearly a whisper.

His head dipped to the side as he gave her a look like he couldn't believe she'd just asked him that, then said, "Absolutely."

Flames consumed her face and licked the tips of her ears. "I guess, since we're mates we probably should live together... but... I mean..." A thread of doubt wormed through her. Her brows pinched together and she looked at the floor. "We *are* mates, right?" She started pacing before he could answer, talking as she moved from the kitchenette to the loveseat and back again. "I never felt this crazy connection moment like everyone talks about, but I have *always* felt connected to you. It feels right to say we are mates and you keep saying it and Jax said it. But... but so did Zander and... how do you know?"

Patrick made his way around the loveseat, closing the distance between them before lightly cupping her jaw with his palms. His lips warmed hers when he pressed against her and the tension through her body melted away. With a mind of their own, her hands slipped up his sides and her fingers curled into his shirt. He ended the kiss, but quickly kissed her again as if he needed just a bit more. Then, he lightly brushed his lips across the tip of her nose and then her forehead.

Warmth spread through her entire being at the gentle, yet intimate touches. A sense of calm and belonging she had been needing.

"I have no doubt, Vi," Patrick whispered, brushing a stray hair behind her ear. "Come here." His hand circled hers and he lightly tugged her over to the loveseat. She waited patiently while he moved their bags to the floor then claimed the spot beside him when he sat down.

"I've been meaning to talk to you about this, but with everything going on, I didn't think it was the right time."

Violet's stomach twisted into knots.

A soft breathy laugh left him. "Relax." He threaded his fingers through hers. "We *are* mates. And we are moon-fated."

She bunched her lips to the side, then said, "I have a feeling that means something different in wolven terms."

"Only a little."

The strand of hair he'd tucked away had come loose again and he pushed it back once more. A small shiver rolled through her when the pad of his fingers trailed the tapered point of her ears. She shook her head and then batted his hand away before covering her ears while he laughed. "Why are they so sensitive?"

"They're brand new." Patrick shrugged. "Give it time. I'm sure they won't be quite so bad in a year."

"Great."

With a gentle touch, he pulled her hands away from her head. "Moon-fated wolven have a stronger connection than other mates. They are what humans would probably classify as soul mates."

Violet nodded. "Yeah. I got that. Other mates are a match that could do really well together. Relationships range from friends that grow to love, to deep love, but it's not on the same level as a moon-fated match."

A gentle smile tilted the corners of Patrick's mouth up. "It's very similar for lycan only we don't have to wait until we're eighteen to find out."

She rubbed her chin and waited for him to continue.

"For lycans, if you are moon-fated you *can* know as early as eight years old. At that age the two kids are inseparable. They are best friends. As time goes on, their relationship grows and transforms."

"Is that what led you to the Sentinel Clan?" Violet asked, her voice sounding a little airy. "Did you know the moment you saw me?"

Patrick shook his head. "No. I wound up in Sentinel Clan because Jerrica was afraid I'd end up being a lone wolf. She had tried to convince other clans nearby to let me stay, but they all declined. So, she reached out to her half-sister and Evalyn immediately agreed. When I first arrived at the Sentinel Gates, my emotions were almost completely locked down. Everything was muted. But when I saw you, some part of that barrier broke. You were by far the most beautiful girl I'd ever seen."

Heat washed across Violet's cheeks and she looked at her knees until Patrick guided her gaze back to him with a finger under her chin.

"But, it was more than that. I knew you were special. I just didn't know why. Somehow, being around you made me feel more than I had since the accident, but that also terrified me. Alistair became more and more prevalent. Anytime you were around, it was harder to control him. At my eighteenth birthday party, Alistair threw it all at me. Everything he'd been holding back from me. All the emotions. All the power." He gave a single shake of his head. "I'd tried to tell myself you weren't my mate, but there was no denying it after that and it was terrifying. After the accident, I had planned to reject my mate if I ever happened to find her," his fingers slowly trailed her jawline. "but I could never reject you."

"But what about me?" Violet fiddled with the hem of her shirt and tried to concentrate through his touch as it trailed down her shoulder and arm. When his hand settled on hers in her lap, she continued, "I never had an epiphany moment.

All I know is that it's you and it's always been you. Lexie tried to get me to date someone else and pushed me to give Cas a chance—"

"What?" he growled, but she kept going.

"It never felt right. And watching you with other girls was like a knife to my heart."

Patrick sucked a breath through his teeth. "I can't apologize enough for that."

"I know." She leaned toward him and he met her halfway, pressing his forehead against hers.

"There is something else that's different. Something that might help. Wolven bonds snap into place when they make eye contact with their mates. They then have the option to reject it—you know all of that."

Violet nodded, making both of their heads move and a shared laugh rolled between them.

"Lycan's have to call on the goddess and verbally accept the mate bond." His hazel eyes poured into her soul, a silent pleading that she'd accept what he was saying. Violet felt his hope blossom inside her chest, mirroring her own as he continued, "Sometimes there is a ceremony, so if you want that then we can wait—"

"No." She squeezed his hand. "I don't need a ceremony. I don't want to wait." Her hands wrapped around to the back of his neck, pulling him closer as she gently spread her nails through the short hairs at the base of his skull. "I only want you."

"You have me," Patrick breathed, his lips brushed hers as he spoke. "Body and soul, I am yours."

Violet's smile spread against his mouth and she briefly kissed him. "Show me. Show me how to do this."

One corner of Patrick's mouth kicked up toward the ceiling, then was quickly followed by the other. He reached back and pulled her hands from behind his neck. "Follow me," he softly requested, then led her to a door at the back of the little cabin. It slid open with ease and he stepped out onto a small porch. A cold breeze greeted her when she followed him, sending a shiver up her spine.

Patrick's eyes were cast to the sky. "There she is," he breathed. "It's perfect."

Violet tipped her chin back to find the moon almost directly above them, its waning crescent shape smiling down. Warm fingers spread through hers, drawing her back to Earth, and she smiled at Patrick. His soft smile warmed every inch of her that had been made cold by the wind.

With their hands clasped between their bodies, Patrick returned his gaze to the moon. "Goddess of the moon and all creatures who thrive under her brilliant light, we come before thee this day..."

Energy pulsed through Violet, warming her to her core. The moon seemed to grow brighter, its beams stretching toward them, scorching her nerves until she felt like she was an extension of that moonbeam.

"... in gratitude of this moon-fated pairing, to accept thy gift." Patrick lowered his gaze until his moonstone eyes locked with hers.

The details of the world around them sharpened as her own eyes changed from purple to an opaline kaleidoscope with swirling gold, silver, and bronze.

Patrick's smile grew before his throat bobbed with a deep swallow. "I, Patrick Matteo Cowen, accept the gift of this bond to Violet Ayah Draven. She is my heart. My soul. My strength when I am weak. Through her, I am made whole."

Warmth trickled down Violet's cheeks and it took her a moment to realize she was crying. "I'm sorry," she whispered. "I promise I'm not sad."

"I know," he beamed at her.

Violet shook her head, "I don't know how to do this."

"The first and last parts are all that are required," he told her as his smile grew, revealing a set of pearly elongated canines.

Pressure built inside her mouth as her own canines grew, responding to his change. She shook her head and flashed him a toothy grin that made him chuckle. With a deep breath, Violet raised her gaze to the moon. "Goddess above, I couldn't have asked for a better match. Someone who stands beside me. Someone who encourages me. Someone who never lets me use my size, or previous lack of abilities, as an excuse. Someone who strives to protect me," she smiled at Patrick whose features had gone soft. "but also knows that I can protect him, as well."

A soft huff of laughter left Patrick as he closed his eyes and nodded.

"I, Violet Ayah Draven, accept this—"

"The," Patrick whispered the correction, meeting her gaze once more.

"*The* gift..." she amended, then waited, not wanting to mess up.

His smile spread before he began to guide her through the words. "Of this bond to...

She bobbed her head in thanks, then repeated, "Of this bond to Patrick Matteo Cowen. *My* heart and my soul." She stole his words, but she couldn't think of a better way to state her feelings and the warmth that spread through his gaze told her it was the right choice. "My other half."

Patrick quietly cleared his throat. "Through him, I am—"

"Through him," she interrupted, grinning at him. "I am made whole."

The moonbeam shining upon them brightened to rival the sun at midday. Energy surged through their joined hands and Violet tipped her head back as it shot through each of her extremities. Emotions that were not her own filled her heart and mind; wonder, awe, gratitude, acceptance, belonging, and an unfathomable amount of love. Then, like a few times before, a second heartbeat thumped in her ears. Patrick's heart beat in time with her own, two hearts beating as one.

"So, it is done." A low, womanly tone, as gentle as a mother's lullaby, brushed through Violet's mind. "In this, you are made one."

The light ebbed, and the moonbeam returned to the crescent above as Patrick's emotions faded to their companion position in her thoughts. Heavy breaths made Violet's chest rise and fall. Patrick stared at her with wide eyes, his own breaths mimicking hers.

"Wow," she breathed, but it was the only word she got out before his lips claimed hers. She sucked in a breath through her nose as her arms wrapped around his neck. His large hands held her waist, pulling her against him. When they swept around her back and his fingers splayed across her back, her knees weakened.

A husky chuckle rumbled through his chest. He lifted her off the ground and sat her on the railing so her legs fell on either side of his waist. An unromantic squeak left her when her body weight shifted backward and she tightened her arms around his neck, terrified she was going to tumble to the forest floor. She clung to him like a monkey, making Patrick's laugh deepen and he buried his face against her shoulder.

"I would never let you fall, *kitten.*"

Violet narrowed her eyes at the nickname he'd told her he wouldn't use ever again. "I am not a cat."

"No, you're not." He smirked and planted a quick kiss on her lips. "You're my fun-sized lycan mate."

She sucked in a breath as his words shot through her. "Say that again."

His smirk grew into an ear-to-ear smile. "Fun-sized lycan?"

Her palm lightly smacked his back, but she refused to let go of him, so that was the best she was going to be able to do. It only made him laugh harder. "No," she chuckled with him. "The last part."

Patrick sobered and his playful smile softened along with his gaze. He leaned into her to rest his forehead against hers. "You are my mate."

Tears gathered in Violet's eyes as the hope of years gone by flooded her. A fulfilled wish she'd begun to think would never come true. The proof of her emotions spilled down her cheeks, and Patrick lifted one hand at a time to wipe them away with the pad of his thumb.

"Under the moon," he whispered while he worked. "And beneath these stars, I promise myself to you, Violet."

They were beautiful words and she wanted to say them back to him. "Under the moon—"

"You don't need to repeat that," he interrupted her.

"I know." She softly kissed him. "But I want to. I promise myself to you, Patrick. Heart, body, and soul."

The warmth of his gaze grew to a living flame before moonstone consumed the hazel in his eyes. A low growl vibrated through him and his lips melded against hers. His hands pressed against her back, holding her to him as he tipped his head to the side and deepened the kiss. The tip of one canine grazed her lower lip, followed by his tongue.

A startled squeak left her when Patrick's hands slipped under her and lifted her off the precarious railing. Her legs turned into a vice, clenching his waist, making him grunt.

Patrick lightly tapped one of her thighs while a low chuckle rumbled through his chest. "I won't let you fall, Vi."

The heat in her face increased, but she eased her python grip a tad as he carried her through the doorway. His lips found hers again, softer this time, then began a slow trail across her cheek to her jaw. He shifted his hold on her to close the door. The lock slid into place a moment later before his hand returned to her, spreading up the length of her spine until he was cradling the back of her head. She tipped her chin toward the ceiling when his lips trailed lower, scorching her skin.

A quick, quiet knock of triplets rattled off the door and they both turned their heads to stare at it. Violet looked back at Patrick. His narrowed eyes had softened and returned to hazel. "It's Rochelle."

With a last, quick kiss, Patrick slowly lowered Violet until her feet were on the floor. She slid her fingers through his and they made their way to the door. Patrick's gaze trailed over her once before he pulled her into another quick kiss that left her breathless. There wasn't time to calm her face before he pulled the door open to reveal a widely grinning Rochelle.

One brow inched up her forehead as she said, "Having a good night, are we?"

Chapter 28

Violet

If there had ever *been a moment when Violet's face could have spontaneously* caught fire, that was it. Standing in front of Patrick's sister moments after solidifying their mate bond and teetering on the edge of something beautiful, but most definitely private.

Rochelle's green eyes practically glittered with amusement as she stared at them.

A cough of laughter escaped Patrick, then he swung an arm around Violet's shoulders and pulled her against his side. "Want to come in?"

Rochelle leaned to the side to peer into the room. "Uhhh, I'm not sure."

"We'll behave, I promise." Patrick pushed the door open a little further and gestured for her to enter. "I wouldn't want to scar my little sister."

"Younger," she corrected him, pointing a finger in his direction. "I'm not so little anymore."

Violet grinned as the teen stepped through the door and walked by them.

"You'll always be little to me, Shelly," Patrick said as he closed the door.

Rochelle turned around halfway to the loveseat and scrunched one side of her nose. "No one has called me that since you left."

Agony stabbed through Violet, sharp enough to make her gasp. She clutched a hand over her heart and stared at the floor until it passed. The pain Patrick felt over his past was obvious, and she'd felt hints of it before, but this... This was still raw and deep. Or maybe it was reopened and carved deeper by coming here. When she looked up, both Patrick and Rochelle were focused on her.

"Are you alright?" Rochelle sincerely asked, her green eyes wandering over Violet's small body.

Nodding, Violet let her hand fall away from her chest. "Yeah. I'm fine. I'm still getting used to some of the lycan bond, connection, stuff."

Rochelle's worried expression softened into sorrow. "Oh. I'm guessing Patrick didn't have a very happy reaction to my comment?"

"Please, don't tell her how painful those memories are," Patrick pleaded in Violet's thoughts. His hand found hers, hanging at her side, and he wove their fingers together.

Violet gave a light reassuring squeeze to his hand. "I know you're his sister, but I hope you can appreciate the loyalty I have to your brother. His thoughts and feelings are his own to share, not mine."

To Violet's surprise, Rochelle's face lit up and a beaming smile spread across her face. "I knew you'd be fated to a good one."

"The best one." Patrick's voice was soft in Violet's ear and she turned her head to find his face inches from hers. His lips brushed lightly across hers once before Rochelle cleared her throat.

"You said you'd behave," she scolded, and Violet turned back toward her with wide eyes as flames consumed her cheeks.

A low rumble of laughter rolled out of Patrick. "I know. And we are. We're allowed to share a kiss, Shelly."

Rochelle didn't respond right away, but her expression tightened at the nickname. "I overheard that you two are looking to return to Sentinel territory as soon as possible. Can I ask why?"

Unease rippled through the mate bond before Patrick said, "I'm not sure that's something you should hear."

"I'm sixteen, Patrick," she scoffed. "I spy on every meeting Mom and Dad have. I know there's an issue with Blood Moon that Dad doesn't want to touch. Mom keeps pushing him to, but that argument has led literally nowhere."

"You call her mom?" Violet asked without thinking, then clamped a hand over her mouth. "I'm sorry, that was rude."

Rochelle shrugged a shoulder. "It's cool. I was so little when our bio-mom died that I only have a few short memories of her. Dad married Jerrica when I was eight, so yeah, I call her mom."

"I was starting to before the accident," Patrick added softly.

A snort from Rochelle drew both of their attention again. "Sorry. Dad always calls it the *incident*. It's interesting to hear you call it an accident."

"It *was* an accident," Patrick insisted, his tone defensive.

Violet placed her free hand on his chest, offering what comfort she could. His heart pounded beneath her palm, but it steadily slowed as the silence stretched on.

Rochelle was the first to speak and her voice was barely above a whisper, "You're not a killer, Patty." She offered a small, sad smile. "I've always known that."

The silence that followed was torture. Uncertainty flickered through the emotions Violet felt from Patrick, and Rochelle looked more uncomfortable than she had when she'd seen them kiss.

"We need to get back because Blood Moon is killing our clan," Violet blurted.

A quiet groan of reluctance met her ears. Patrick gave her fingers a light squeeze. *"If you think this is a good plan, I'll follow you."*

"She's here and wants to know. I think she deserves some answers."

Rochelle's brows pulled together at the center and she crossed her arms over her chest. "What do you mean, killing your clan?"

"There's a guy named Cas that wants revenge on Patrick," Violet shifted her weight so she could lean lightly against Patrick's side. "I'm not entirely sure why, but I think he got Blood Moon involved and it's become something much bigger. Blood Moon has taken over Stanislaus' territory and wiped out the clan. We've lost countless neighbors, friends, and clanmates." She swallowed the knot that built in her throat while she spoke before quietly adding, "Including my mom."

A deep sigh left Rochelle. She closed her eyes and lightly shook her head. When she opened her eyes, they were unfocused and sad. "I'm so sorry. I don't remember much of my mom, but I remember the pain of losing her. It's stayed with me ever since."

Violet lowered her chin as the hole in her heart left there from the loss of her mom throbbed. "Thanks."

"Okay, so Blood Moon needs to be stopped." Rochelle tipped her head to the side. "That's obvious. They are breaking pretty much every law we have." She raised both shoulders nearly to her ears. "So, stop them. The Kings and Queens would approve of any action taken against them in a heartbeat."

"That's just it, Shell," Patrick's low tone rumbled through his chest against Violet's back. "Blood Moon has grown too large and strong for one clan to take down. We've teamed up with Whisky and Mammoth, but neither of those clans have very well trained warriors, and their numbers are small. We need the strength of the lycans, or the Paladins, at least."

One of Rochelle's eyebrows had tugged lower as she listened intently to Patrick, and then she looked off to the side in thought. "What does the witch have to do with this?"

"Oh," Violet's mouth was moving before she could stop it. "That's really just for me. Well, me and my twin." She waved her hand in the air casually dismissing the matter and quickly ran through a list like it was no big deal. "You know, the whole twin thing. Plus, me being a lycan born to two wolven and having some sort of witchy abilities. Jax can heal, and I know that's not normal."

"All wolven heal quickly."

"No," Patrick jumped in, offering clarification. "She means Jax can heal other people."

Rochelle's eyebrows shot toward the roof and she looked back at Violet.

Violet nodded. "I figured that while we were here, maybe I could get some answers about that, too. Jerrica suggested we talk to someone called Laurel."

Rochelle's cheek poked out, like she was pushing her tongue against it, and she looked away again. Her green eyes darted back and forth like she was doing calculations in her brain. Finally, she let out a long breath and looked at Patrick, letting her crossed arms fall to her sides. "I can't make the lycans join you. I don't have that kind of pull."

"I know," Patrick replied, his breath ruffling the hairs on top of Violet's head.

"But," Rochelle wagged a finger at him and then tapped her chin. "I might have an in with the Paladins, and I can definitely get you in to see the witch tonight."

"How?" Patrick asked, his tone sounding suspicious at the same time Violet said, "Really?"

A pleased smile crossed over Rochelle's face. "There's a guy I like that just joined the Paladins. We've kept in touch. And as far as the witch... it isn't like there's a schedule or anything. All you have to have is an approved escort."

Violet tipped her chin back to gaze up at Patrick when he chuckled.

"And let me guess, you're one of the approved escorts?"

Rochelle offered a little mock bow. "Guilty as charged."

"Sounds like a plan, but we'll need to talk about this guy," Patrick grumbled.

"Patrick," Violet chided, having had more than enough brother protection to last her a lifetime.

"Do you want a connection to the Paladins or not?" Rochelle dangled the offer like a carrot on a stick and he fell right into the trap.

"Of course."

"Then I guess you better approve of Paladin Guy," Violet teased, drawing a curious look from Rochelle.

Tilting her head to the side, a slow smile tugged at Rochelle's lips. "Paladin Guy?"

Patrick chuckled. "Violet likes to nickname people when she doesn't know their actual names. Two recent ones were Stupid Guy and Scar Face."

"And Napkin Hero," Violet added, then cringed. "Hero was the wrong word."

A surprisingly low laugh tumbled out of Rochelle. "I think you and I are going to be fast friends, Violet." She winked, then headed toward the door. "I'll send a message to my friend while you're talking to the witch, but let's get you in there first, 'kay?"

Violet blinked multiple times, then hurried to follow after Rochelle. "Lead the way."

"Do we need to be concerned about warriors tailing us or word of our visit getting back to Jerrica or Dad?" Patrick asked after easily catching up to the two girls.

Rochelle froze with her hand on the doorknob, then turned around with a wicked little smirk quirking the corner of her lips. "Would that change anything?"

Violet hesitated, not sure how she should answer that, but Patrick had no such reservations, "Nope."

With a small snort, Rochelle tugged the door open. "I didn't think so. Follow me."

Not even ten steps away from the building, the female warrior from before stepped out from behind a nearby tree. "What do you think you're doing, Rochelle?"

Patrick's sister nonchalantly shrugged, but there was a ribbon of tension through her shoulders as she continued walking, this time toward the warrior. "I'm just visiting with my brother, Kenzie."

The female warrior's eyes narrowed. "Then why are they now following you away from their designated housing?"

"I never said we were visiting inside the house." Rochelle laughed, but the sound was tight and lacking any humor.

"Rochelle." Kenzie's tone was full of apprehension and warning.

"Kenzie," she mimicked, closing the distance between them.

The warrior's brows slammed down and her body stiffened. "Don't disobey your dad, Rochelle, not again."

"Again?" Patrick asked, his voice sounding much too pleased for the moment.

Violet elbowed him in the side, but it only made him snicker.

Rochelle lunged for the warrior who startled and tried to jump out of the way, but she wasn't quick enough. Surprise widened Violet's eyes as Rochelle seized Kenzie's arm. They grappled to gain control, each gaining the upper hand for a brief moment until the other would switch things up. Patrick's arm moved in front of Violet and she looked down at it stretched across her waist only to find that she'd taken a step forward.

"You have to let her handle this," he said gently.

"But we can help," Violet argued, grabbing his arm to push it down.

Patrick turned toward her and encircled her waist with both of his arms. "If we're seen fighting with any of the lycan clan, we will be labeled as threats and traitors."

Warning bells went off in Violet's mind. She stopped pushing against him and tipped her chin back to find his golden-flecked hazel eyes staring down at her. Something in his gaze made her reach for their bond and she easily found it, like it'd been waiting for her to grab onto. Patrick's aura in her mind was steady and firm... and sad.

"What are you not telling me?" she asked through their link.

A deep sigh brushed across her thoughts before Patrick's sad tone filled her mind. *"I've seen what happens to wolven and lycan alike when they are labeled that way. We wouldn't make it out of here alive."*

"Rochelle," Kenzie choked, drawing Violet's attention again. The warrior was leaning back against Rochelle, frantically clawing at Rochelle's arm, which was locked around Kenzie's throat.

"You never could get out of my headlocks, could you?" Rochelle tsked. "I thought you would've learned how to do that by now."

Rage flashed across Kenzie's face and she swept her leg back like she was trying to get around Rochelle to knock her off balance. Instead, Rochelle moved her body into the step so Kenzie's leg went between hers instead. The warrior threw her arm back to wrap around one of Rochelle's legs, but the teen drove her knee up into Kenzie's ribs. She gasped for air and held her ribs, until the two young women tumbled backward.

Violet flinched when the two of them slammed against the ground. They landed with a hard thud, and then Rochelle's legs were grappled around Kenzie's waist, locking her in place.

"When you wake up," Rochelle grunted when Kenzie struggled, then continued. "You're probably going to have a headache. Just remember one thing: I took you down *alone*." Her green eyes lifted to Patrick, then shifted over to Violet. "I acted of my own free will. They had nothing to do with this."

"You're... going to..." Kenzie gasped for air. "Regret... this."

A sad, little smirk tilted one corner of Rochelle's lips up. "Maybe, but I doubt it." She positioned her head a little closer to Kenzie's tapered ear and added, "They shouldn't have sent my brother away."

Violet pressed a hand against her chest as she stared at Patrick's sister. Anger, sorrow, regret, pain, passion, determination, pride... all the emotions she could feel from Patrick seemed to be mirrored in his sister's gaze. So much damage had been done. So much pain had been caused. Patrick hadn't been the only one affected. Whether Mr. Cowen knew what he had done or not was irrelevant because his children—brother and sister—would not be stopped, and something told Violet that they wouldn't be kept separated anymore, either.

Kenzie's eyes fluttered shut, and her arms went limp, falling to the ground on either side of her. Rochelle slowly released her hold on the warrior before gently pushing Kenzie off her and then rolling her to the side.

When she was back on her feet, Rochelle turned to stare at Patrick with a fire burning from within. "Let's get you to the witch."

Patrick relaxed his hold on Violet, then stepped toward his sister. "Shell, you've done enough. We can find our way, just point us in the right direc—"

"I meant what I said, Patty," Rochelle interrupted. Moisture lined her eyes. Her jaw clenched and she lifted her chin. After a deep breath through her nose, she said, "They shouldn't have sent you away. And they shouldn't be refusing to help now. It's wrong. There are a lot of things that are messed up and backward. I was too young to do anything about it back then, but I've spent the last three years training and getting stronger. I've learned everything I could on lycan, wolven, and clan law. Studied every book on strategy that I could get my hands on." Moonstone swirled into her eyes, devouring the green as she added, "I can do this. And no one is going to stop me."

A heavy, deep breath lifted Rochelle's chest before it then fell again followed by three more large breaths.

Patrick released Violet and closed the distance between him and his sister in three long strides. His arms swooped around her shoulders, gathering her smaller frame in a tight hug. Violet's brows pulled together when Rochelle froze and didn't immediately hug him back, but slowly her body relaxed into his embrace. She swung her arms around his middle and pinched her eyes shut.

"I'm sorry," Patrick said and the anguish filtering through his voice matched the emotion pounding through Violet's chest. "I didn't mean to make you grow up so fast."

Rochelle shook her head against his shoulder, then pushed away from him. Green had returned to her eyes when she opened them again before wiping her hands across her wet cheeks. "Don't apologize. This wasn't your fault. You said it was an accident."

"It was, and I'll explain that at some point, but I was still the cause of this."

"No," Rochelle argued. "Dad was the cause of this. *He* sent you away. *He* didn't give you a chance. *He* gave up on you!" Her fingers curled into fists. "*He* was wrong."

Patrick's head bobbed up and down slowly. "Maybe, but if he hadn't, I might not have ever met Violet."

The rage that had tightened Rochelle's expression faded away, softening her gaze when it slid to Violet.

"It's not always black and white." Patrick sighed. "Even though it would be easier that way."

"I... think I understand." She rubbed one of her palms over her other arm and looked uncomfortable as she turned away from them. "Let's get you to Laurel."

Violet stepped forward and slid her hand into Patrick's, offering a small squeeze when he looked at her.

In turn, he offered a small smile, one that didn't reach his eyes, before they followed Rochelle down the path.

Chapter 29

Violet

It took a few *minutes to weave through the trees to their destination, but when* they passed another warrior, and he didn't try to stop them, Violet's gratitude toward the teenage spitfire that was Patrick's sister increased tenfold. Rochelle stopped a little further down the path and pointed at a post sticking up about ten feet ahead.

"That marks the barrier the witch made." She turned and looked at Violet as she lowered her arm. "When you pass through it, it should feel similar to the barrier when wolven have their trials."

"Why is it here?" Violet asked.

One corner of Rochelle's mouth quirked toward the sky. "To keep people out. I have to go first, and we need to be touching. If you try to go in first, or without me, it will feel like you walked into a brick wall instead."

The imagery made Violet flinch. "Ouch."

The other side of Rochelle's mouth lifted to form a full smile, but it was short lived. "Are you sure you want to do this? Laurel is the most powerful witch alive. She's deadly and dangerous and is here because she broke the laws of nature."

Knots twisted in Violet's stomach and she pressed a hand over her belly. "Jerrica said she was the one I needed to talk to. I need answers."

Rochelle's cheek poked out. Her eyes narrowed for a moment before she gave a decisive nod and thrust her hand toward Violet's "Then follow me."

Without hesitation, Violet seized Rochelle's hand and they all walked toward the barrier together.

Rochelle paused right in front of the post marker, took a deep breath, and then stepped through, pulling Violet along with her.

Violet knew the moment she touched the barrier. An ice cold presence washed over her skin, starting at her hand and traveling over her body as she made her way through the magical barrier. It prickled any exposed skin and made goosebumps raise along her arms and legs. The little hairs along the back of her neck stood on end and for a brief moment, her lungs felt constricted. Then the cold was replaced by warmth that slowly spread through her veins which then extended to the tips of her fingers and toes. The inky feeling eased into a gentle caress.

"Welcome, daughter of Luna Evalyn Draven," whispered a chorus of voices in Violet's ear.

Grinding her teeth against their chatter, Violet closed her eyes. She drew in a deep breath and tried to focus on the feel of Rochelle's hand in hers, grounding her to this moment, and the sound of the second heartbeat that mimicked her own. With each breath, the rhythm of Patrick's heart drowned out the voices more and more.

"Laurel," Rochelle called, making Violet open her eyes to find that they were now standing only a few feet in front of the hut. "I've brought someone to meet you."

"I know," the voices whispered, but a low female tone rose up amongst them. The door of the hut flew open to reveal a woman with long, white blonde hair and nails that rivaled Violet's lycan claws. Her dark eyes swirled like a black hole, consuming all of the color that had once been there. When she tilted her head to the side, a shiver ran up Violet's spine. "I knew the moment she stepped onto this territory."

Violet swallowed the knot in her throat and tightened her hold on both Rochelle's and Patrick's hands.

"But there are supposed to be two of you," the witch lifted her hand, flipping her palm over to reveal a star tattoo on the inside of her wrist while she pointed oddly at Violet. "Where is the other?"

"Other?" Violet managed without too much trouble.

A knowing smile passed across the woman's face. "Your brother. Or shall I call him your twin, my little miracle?"

Ice water splashed down Violet's body at the sound of her mom's nickname for her. She almost missed Patrick stepping forward.

"Quit playing games, witch!" he snarled.

Laurel clicked her tongue disapprovingly. "Oh, little prince, must you be so rude? This is the only entertainment I've had in years." When Patrick didn't back down, she sighed and rolled her other palm over so both faced the sky, revealing matching star tattoos. "I am bound to the lycans. I am not to harm them in any way, nor can I leave their territory. The black tattoos glowed silver like the moon above them and the swirling vortex vanished from her eyes to reveal pale irises. "Satisfied?"

Rochelle gave a curt nod.

"Good." The tattoos returned to black and then Laurel crossed her arms over her chest. "What do you want?"

Violet eyed Rochelle, then Patrick, then their hands. What was she supposed to say?

The witch snorted. "You can let go of each other. My barrier spell won't harm you now that you've passed through and I know who you are."

Violet's right hand was instantly cold when Rochelle pulled her hand away, but Patrick's grip tightened. A clear signal that he wasn't letting her go. Narrowing her gaze, Violet tried to gain control of her wild thoughts. "How do you know who I am?"

"It's not every day a set of wolven twins survives."

"That's not an answer."

"Isn't it? Although perhaps not the one you were looking for. If I were anyone else, you would have accepted the answer and moved on. Why the directed annoyance at me?"

"Because I was told to talk to you!" Violet snapped, annoyance flickering through her. "That you were the only one that could answer my questions."

"Then ask!" Laurel snapped back. "Knowing who you are is simple. You are the second twin born to Noah and Evalyn Draven. You should not have survived and therefore would be considered a miracle to some. Others know better and would call you an *abomination*."

Violet flinched at the harsh word.

"But they would be wrong." Laurel's voice softened. "Because the moon goddess herself had plans for you, and nothing was going to stop her."

Confusion pulled Violet's brows together. "What do you mean?"

The witch stared at her for a long moment before asking, "Do you know what your mother did?"

Shaking her head, Violet shifted her weight. "She was trying to tell me the night she died, but she never got the chance."

"Because you shifted."

"Because she was stabbed in the back by a wolven who betrayed us, and then again in the heart from the one she was fighting off."

Laurel's pale eyes darted over Violet's face and her hardened features softened. "Evalyn was killed?"

When Violet didn't answer, the witch stepped down off her porch and slowly closed the distance between them. Patrick moved forward half a step and Laurel stopped a few feet away from them. A large breath filled her lungs before she spoke again. "I performed the spell that would have saved your life in exchange for your mothers. It wasn't necessary. I tried to tell her that. She wouldn't listen."

"Would have? Not necessary?" Violet shook her head. "What are you talking about?"

"Evalyn was thrilled to find out she was pregnant. Everyone was thrilled. Myself included. She and I used to be friends, and I was so happy for her. I was in hiding when his father," she tossed her head in Patrick's direction, "paid a visit to your clan. I would have been able to tell her. Maybe if I'd gotten to her first this wouldn't have happened. But we'll never know." Laurel shook her head. "You should come inside. We have much to discuss."

"No." Violet practically whispered the word, but Laurel stopped about halfway through her turn. "I mean. I can't. We can't. We have to get back."

Laurel squared her shoulders with them once again. "And why is that, little miracle?"

"Quit calling me that."

A small, half smile tipped one corner of the witch's mouth skyward.

"Our clan is in danger."

"Violet," Patrick hissed a warning.

"What kind of danger?" Laurel questioned, ignoring Patrick.

Something inside of Violet pressed her to keep talking. A yearning to tell this woman everything. A promise that she could be trusted. "Blood Moon," her mouth formed the words before she could stop them. "Heard of them?"

Color drained from the woman's face. "What about them?"

"They slaughtered Stanislaus and took control of their territory. They are waging a war against Sentinel, but there is concern that we aren't strong enough to fight them alone. Whisky and Mammoth are going to aid us, but it might not be enough." Violet clamped a hand over her mouth.

"Violet." Patrick stared at her, his expression pinched in exasperation.

Why was she saying all these things?

Laurel laughed. "Don't worry, lover boy. She's only saying all of this because of our connection. She knows beyond a shadow of a doubt that she can trust me."

Warmth blossomed in Violet's chest, and she lowered her hand to rest over her heart.

The silvery light from the moon gleamed through the trees, drawing all of their attention.

When the light faded, Violet looked at Laurel and sucked in a small breath of air. A circlet of moonlight rested upon her brow and her hair had taken on a silverish-blue moonlit glow.

"My body acts as a vessel for Luna whenever she deems fit to grace our plane of existence. There is always one witch called to such glory. When I die, another will replace me. We are the daughters of the moon, beacons of light, and gifted with magic beyond any other. We speak directly to Luna herself, but only when called upon." Laurel's eyes reflected the same silverish-blue as her hair as she spoke, but soon black ink began to consume the mystical hue. "I've only tampered with the darkness of blood magic once and it cost me greatly."

Laurel closed her eyes and the circlet evaporated from her brow while her hair returned to its normal tone. When she opened her eyes again, she smiled sadly. "That was for your mother—for you."

"Why?" Violet breathed.

"When Patrick's father heard two hearts beating within your mothers womb, he told her by saying, *I'm sorry.* He left after that without an explanation. Evalyn became desperate. She was terrified she'd lost the baby, but that terror was nothing compared to the horror that filled her when she found out about you."

"Our doctor says there is only one wolf spirit given to every wolven pregnancy and that it goes to the stronger of the two."

Laurel nodded her head. "Yes."

"So I should have died."

"Traditionally, yes, but your mother was closer to three-quarters lycan and so is your father." Laurel tipped her head back to stare at the night sky. "Luna saw something in your little baby heart and mind that she needed here on this Earth. She knew you could be the key to right a wrong done to so many."

Patrick's fingers tightened around hers. "What do you mean?" he asked, his voice tight with emotion.

Laurel's chin lowered and she gazed softly at him. "You know exactly what I mean, Patrick. You've experienced it firsthand."

A rush of air left him.

"Lycan are presented with gifts. Often they resemble one of the elements. Many don't realize that spirit is one of the elements. It's a rare one, and it's been a long time since a lycan was born with a gift linked to that element. You had enough lycan blood in you, that Luna was able to tweak your DNA ever so slightly to make you a lycan. You were bestowed with spirit as your element and the ability to save those with red eyes who have been wronged."

Violet's chest was rising and falling in rapid succession. "But... when I did it for Patrick, I was exhausted. There must be thousands of wolven who need help."

"Your mate will make you stronger. You are stronger together."

"But that isn't all, Violet." Laurel held up a hand, as if she were concerned Violet would leave now that she had some answers. "I was in hiding when your mother found me. I'm still not sure how she did it other than through sheer determination to save the life of her child. She demanded that I perform a spell that broke the natural law. I could have refused her; she might have killed me, but as I said before... we were friends once. So I performed the spell, imbuing you with magic that would save your life in exchange for your mother's. I then turned myself in to the lycan council and have been here ever since."

Chapter 30

Violet

***"You imbued me with** magic?" Violet stared at Laurel with wide eyes.*

"Yes," the witch admitted. "But a spell like that couldn't be contained to just you. It affected your brother as well. Was he born with any special gifts?"

Violet looked at Patrick who slowly closed his eyes and shook his head as he huffed a laugh. "Aren't we just the perfect band of misfits?"

A small laugh left Violet before she relented, "He can heal people. Patrick's heart stopped and Jax healed him."

"Patrick's heart did what?" Rochelle's high-pitched voice made Violet jump. She'd nearly forgotten the teenager was with them, standing with her arms crossed tightly over her chest. "You died?" she yelled.

"Only for a couple of seconds."

"Patrick!" Rochelle shouted, going behind Violet and seizing her brother's arm before pulling him away.

Violet turned to go after them, but Laurel held out a hand to stop her. "Leave them be. They've been through a lot and Rochelle is close to exploding. She needs a minute with her brother."

"What is Patrick's gift?" Violet asked, without thinking. "I mean. What element does he connect with?"

Laurel smiled. "That's not really my secret to share."

"How do we make each other stronger?"

"Well," Laurel brushed a hair out of her face. "Mates do that for each other anyway. They feed off one another's strengths."

Violet shook her head. "I know, but—"

"Your mate will have to tell you the rest." Laurel interrupted.

"Then I guess I only have one more question for you."

Laurel's head dipped to the side. "What might that be?"

"What am I?"

With a deep breath, Laurel stepped forward and planted her hands on Violet's shoulders. "You are a daughter of the moon. A lycan born to two wolven. A miracle. A redeemer. A warrior."

Shaking her head, Violet tried again, "Am I a witch?"

The smile playing at Laurel's lips deepened. "Of course."

Her bluntness made Violet flinch.

"Only witches can ***mind-hop***, my dear." Her hands fell away from Violet's shoulders. "That gift is one you received from me. I'm sure it will come in handy when you're piecing the souls of the wronged back together." She flicked a finger into the air. "Just remember you can't be hurt while in their minds. As long as you remember that, you'll be safe. As long as you know how to get out—you'll be safe."

Panic rose in Violet's chest and her skin felt itchy. "But I don't know how to do that. With Patrick, it just sort of happened. I knew when it was time to leave."

"Ground yourself. Make sure you have an anchor back to this world. Patrick can be that for you. If he's not there, it will be a lot harder. You need to have someone who can guide you back if you get lost. You're lycan. Anyone who cares about you and can speak to you through your link would suffice. If you don't have that, you must find ways to remember where you are in reality. The smell of the room. The feel of the ground beneath you. The sounds that surround you. Hold something in your hands. Anything to pull you out when you get lost."

"When? Don't you mean if?"

Laurel's chin lowered. "No, child. I mean *when*. Every witch born with these abilities gets lost from time to time." Her head tipped back and she froze.

It took only a second for Violet to follow her gaze and realize the witch was staring at the moon above them.

"Which you are out of," Laurel's voice was airy and when she lowered her chin, moonlight shimmered in her eyes. The circlet of moonlight was back, brighter than before. "My little miracle, you have been blessed with a gift to rectify what I could not. I am bound by the law that was created to punish those who took a life. It did not account for the ones who did so without savagery. I've waited a long time for someone like you to come along. The bloodline that emerges from you and Patrick will be blessed. The gift to piece souls back together will rise once in every generation, forevermore. Go. Urge the Lycan King to side with you. He will say no, but his defiance will spur others into action. Then leave. Lexie needs you."

Goosebumps scattered across Violet's skin. "Lexie? How do you... how do I..."

Laurel's eyes fluttered, then shut. Her body crumpled and Violet barely had enough time to lurch forward and catch the woman before she collapsed on the ground.

"Laurel?" Violet softly called her name, but there was no response. Cradling the woman against her chest, Violet lightly shook her and tried a little louder. "Laurel!"

"What happened?" Patrick asked, jogging to her side with Rochelle right behind him.

Shaking her head, Violet turned toward him and tried to shift Laurel's dead weight. "I'm not sure." When Patrick held out his arms to take Laurel, Violet gladly relented. She shifted the unconscious woman into Patrick's arms as she spoke, "She was saying all this stuff with the moonlight swirling around her and it was kind of creepy, but kind of amazing at the same time. Then she passed out." Patrick hoisted Laurel off the ground and headed toward her house, but Violet grabbed his arm. "She mentioned Lexie."

Patrick's dark brows pulled together. "What about her?"

Laurel groaned, then rolled her head off Patrick's shoulder. "That she needs help." She slapped at Patrick's chest with the energy of a sloth. "As handsome as you are, you're too young for me. Put me down."

Her feet thudded against the ground as if Patrick had dropped her, but she latched onto his upper arm to steady herself when she wobbled on her feet.

"Are you okay?" Violet stepped toward her and offered her arm for balance. "What was that?"

Laurel snorted as she took Violet's arm and headed toward her house. "I thought a lycan raised amongst wolven would recognize dual possession."

Confusion lifted Violet's brow. "Dual possession?"

"I told you, I am a conduit. A vessel for the moon goddess, Luna, herself. She felt I wasn't being forward enough with you so she took over. Usually she is a bit more gentle!" Her voice rose with each word and she glared at the moon above.

Violet blinked at her as they made their way through Laurel's front door and warmth wafted over her. "Did you just chide the goddess of the moon?"

"Meh." Laurel waved a dismissive hand, then pushed away from Violet to make her way into the small kitchen. "Our relationship is closer to that of two sisters than a goddess and her accolade."

Warmth surrounded Violet as she looked around the tiny home. Not just the temperature, but the colors and decorations. Everything was earthy and welcoming, from the deep umber brown of the leather couch to the forest green of the walls. Plants stretched out from every corner of the room while some dangled from the ceiling. Candles flickered atop every surface, laughing at the lights above them that remained unused. Violet imagined spending her time here, peaceful and quiet.

Glass smacked against stone, making Violet jump. She spun around to find Laurel leaning over her kitchen counter, resting her elbows on the hard surface, her now empty glass settled in front of her.

"What are you still doing here?" Laurel grumbled. "You got your answers. Luna told you to go. So go."

Violet blinked. "That's what you're used to, isn't it? People coming for answers and then leaving without so much of a thank you."

A loud snort filled the air. "Well, are you going to thank me?"

"No."

"Figures." Laurel flipped the faucet on again and snatched her cup, shoving it under the stream of water.

"I'm going to ask you to come with us."

The glass slipped from Laurel's hand, landing with a crack in the sink that made Violet flinch. She hoped the glass wasn't broken, but Laurel didn't seem to care. Instead, the woman continued to stare at her, not blinking.

Violet felt Patrick's presence before his deep voice cascaded over her. "They have a witch with them. Blood Moon. They have a Blood Witch. We could use your help."

Laurel's eyes grew moist and she looked down into her sink. "I know. She's my twin."

"What?" Violet and Patrick said at the same time.

Amusement kicked up one side of Laurel's lips, but it was clear the humor didn't settle very deep. When she lifted her gaze, it was dull and sad. "Wolven often call twins a curse because only one survives. Witches call it a blessing of balance, but it may as well be a curse all the same. One is born with extraordinary powers of good... while the other will forever be drawn to the dark arts. Blood Magic." A deep sigh left Laurel. "I tried to help her. Your mom did, too." Her gaze flickered to Violet. "It wasn't enough. She grew obsessed and was eventually consumed by it. I..." Her throat bobbed when she swallowed. "When I broke the laws of nature, I shattered something inside of myself, as well. I don't know if I'm strong enough to face her anymore."

Violet didn't know what to say. Her jaw fell open, but no words came out. What do you say to a woman who lost everything because of you and your mother?

"Besides, I'm bound to the Lycan territory. They would never let me leave."

"A spell you performed yourself," Rochelle stated from behind Violet, and she turned her head to find the teen leaning against the door frame as she spoke. "I know the stories. You had to do it, because no other witch was powerful enough to do it." Rochelle shrugged. "So undo it."

"It's not that simple. There are rules."

Rochelle snorted. "Rules that are meant to be broken in times like this."

"Not this time," Laurel grumbled.

With another snort, Rochelle shoved away from the doorframe and left. Patrick released a heavy sigh, kissed the top of Violet's head, then hurried after his sister.

Hesitantly, Violet started after them. "If you change your mind," she called back to Laurel, resting her hand on the doorknob and looking at the disheveled witch. "You know where to find us."

She had started to close the door, when a soft, broken version of Laurel's voice reached her. "You're just like her, you know? Your mother. She was fierce and determined also. Don't ever lose that, little miracle."

Not knowing how to respond, Violet finished closing the door and turned toward Patrick and Rochelle who were arguing a few feet down the path.

"I want to come with you guys."

"Shelly, you're not ready."

"How would you know if I'm ready or not?" Rochelle growled. "You haven't been here in three years!"

Patrick flinched back a step and Rochelle's eyes widened with regret.

"I'm sorry. I didn't mean it like that," she sputtered over her words, then rubbed her arms. "I know that wasn't your choice."

Without hesitation, Patrick swept his arms around his sister and pulled her into a tight hug. "This is going to be dangerous. I don't want to see you get hurt."

"Patrick," Violet softly chided as she stepped up to the pair of siblings. "How many times am I going to have to tell you that's not your decision to make?" She rested a hand on one of Rochelle's shoulders and waited until the younger teen looked at her before continuing. "The difference here is that you're his little sister, and you're right, he has been gone for three years. Which gives him even more reason to not want you in harm's way. He doesn't know how good you are in a fight."

"I'm really good," Rochelle insisted.

Patrick smirked. "I'm sure you are, but this isn't a practice ring we're going into."

She lifted her chin defiantly. "Every warrior must step out of the practice ring and into the warzone at some point."

A huff of laughter escaped Patrick. "Not at sixteen."

Rochelle looked at Violet for help, but she only shrugged. "I never listen to him so I'm probably not the best one to turn to."

Amusement sparked behind Rochelle's eyes. "That means you're exactly who I should turn to."

Patrick grumbled and shook his head.

"Laurel said we were out of time. We can't wait until morning. We need to speak to the Lycan king, now."

Patrick and Rochelle looked at each other.

"You haven't told her yet, have you?" Rochelle shifted her weight to one side, kicking her hip out.

Patrick rubbed the back of his neck and shrugged. "We've been a little busy."

"Busy sucking face."

"Rochelle!" Patrick scolded. "That is not what I meant."

"Guys!" Violet raised her voice a little over theirs, regaining their attention. "What is going on?"

Patrick's hand returned to his neck and he gave her a sheepish look. "The Lycan King reigning over the western territories is my dad."

Violet blinked. And blinked again. She bunched her lips together and began to nod as she attempted to shove down the panic and anger rising within her. "Okay. Well, when I saw everyone bow to him I figured he had a high rank. I figured it was beta or something though since you never thought it was a good idea to tell me your dad is a *KING*?" She started pacing and Patrick watched her as he stood frozen in place. "First your step-mom is my aunt, a secret sibling of my mom, then you have a sister, and now *KING*?" Violet's fingers were going numb and she realized she had her hands tightly clenched into fists so she shook them out and kept going. "Patrick, that makes you a prince. That makes you the next in line to take over the western territories! I can't take you away from that, but—"

"Stop." Patrick jumped toward her and wrapped his hands gently, but firmly around her shoulders. He lowered his head, making them closer to eye level as he spoke, "Listen to me, Vi. My place is with *you*. Not this territory that turned its back on me. I'm not next in line for anything, that title was stripped from me when I was banished, and I have no desire to get it back. I've heard that the person they picked is really promising, so I'm not worried, either." He shot a quick look at Rochelle, who nodded, before returning his gaze to Violet. "We are Sentinels, and our clan needs us."

After drawing in a few deep breaths, Violet nodded. "Okay. But, you have to promise me, no more secrets."

Large hands stretched across her back, nearly encircling Violet as Patrick wrapped her in a giant hug. "No more. I promise." He groaned. "Except, I think I figured out why Cas is after me."

"He believes you killed his mate."

"Yeah, but..."

"It had to have been in the accident." She snuggled her face against his warm chest. "I know."

A soft laugh left him, lightly bouncing her head. "You're incredible."

"I know," she teased, and then smiled as it rewarded her with another head-bouncing laugh. "Okay." She tipped her head back, lifted onto her toes, and planted a small kiss on Patrick's lips. When she pulled away, Patrick was smiling softly at her. "Let's go stir up some trouble with your dad."

Chapter 31

Violet

Slipping through the witch's *barrier from inside felt nothing like when they* arrived. In fact, it felt like nothing at all. There was no spark of magic. No tug as they left nor a shove to get them out faster. It was as if the magic had vanished. Violet looked over her shoulder for the twentieth time since they left Laurel's house.

Warm fingers slipped into her hand and she curled her hand around Patrick's out of reflex.

"She made her choice, Vi," he reminded her softly.

Returning her gaze to the path in front of them, Violet nodded. "I know."

Patrick gave her hand a light squeeze and they fell into tense silence as a long, log building came into view.

Rochelle had rushed off ahead, threatening to beat down every council member's door until they answered. She would bring them to the meeting house, where Patrick and Violet would be waiting.

There, at the heart of the lycan territory, Patrick and Violet would wait for the king and his councilors to arrive. There, in the middle of the night, they would find out if they had any brothers in arms. There, in that wooden building, they would finally know how deep the lycan's loyalty to Patrick ran.

Patrick let go of her hand and lengthened his stride to get to the door of the meeting house first. He turned the knob and held it open for her, giving her a lopsided grin, which she returned as she passed through the doorway. She looked around, waiting for her eyes to adjust while Patrick closed the door, and let out a low whistle when the room came into view.

"Daaaang," she chuckled. "Lycan eyesight is amazing."

A low rumble of laughter met her ears before Patrick's lips pressed lightly against her neck, his arms circling her waist from behind. "You're amazing."

"You're being cheesy again," she teased, but leaned back against his chest instead of pulling away because she kind of loved when he was corny. It was so rare before, but it was a pretty prominent part of his personality.

"You like it," he mumbled into her hair.

A burst of laughter left her. "I was just thinking that." Her eyes rounded. "Wait." She turned in his arms to stare at him. "Did you read my mind?"

That rumbling low tone was back, making her stomach flutter as Patrick's chest shook with mirth. "No. I didn't hear or read anything. I just know you."

"Oh, okay." She looked around the room again and sighed. "Do you know where the lightswitch is?"

Patrick took a couple of steps to the left, reached back, and without looking, flipped a switch.

The lights clicked on and Violet blinked away the harsh change in lighting. "How did you—"

"I helped build this place when I was ten." He looked around, his features softening. "I remember it being a lot bigger."

"That's because you were a lot smaller."

A ghost of a smile lifted the corners of his mouth. "True." His eyes caught on a chair rack in the far corner. "We should put out some chairs. Nine should be enough."

Between the two of them, the chairs were set up in a neat circle a couple of minutes later. Violet rubbed her cold hands together and eyed their work. "Shouldn't be long now. Right?" When Patrick didn't answer, she turned around to find his back to her. "Patrick, what's wrong?"

"The last time I was in this building, I was standing right there." He pointed to the head of the room, the farthest point from where they were. "This was where they decided to send me away."

"Against our say," came an older voice from behind her, making her jump.

She spun around and backed away several steps as four older men stepped into the meeting house. Patrick was at her side a second later, looking over the faces of the men who'd joined them.

"Haven't attended a territory meeting since," sniffed one of them as he settled against the wall near the door, and then tipped his fedora at her.

"It's good to see you again, Prince Cowen," spoke the first man again as he shoved his hands into the pockets of his knee-length, black trench coat.

Violet's eyes bugged and her lips pinched together.

"Please, just Patrick. I haven't gone by that title in years, and it's no longer mine."

The older man simply nodded, and Violet had the feeling he was going to use Patrick's old title whether he liked it or not. "We were against it, I hope you remember that."

"Not all of you," Patrick responded quickly, bitterness slipping through his tone. He let out a long breath, and when he spoke again, the harshness was gone. "I appreciate what you tried to do for me—how some of you spoke up against him."

"If I'd known..." said the man who'd come in last. He'd kept his salt and pepper-covered head down, chin low against his chest. "If I'd known it could be controlled, even reversed... I'm sorry. I've lived with the regret from my decision since the day you left, and felt it driven deeper each time I saw your sister." He lifted his gaze finally to reveal moisture-lined brown eyes. "She drove that stake home again tonight, reminding me of the pain I helped cause her."

Patrick made his way to the salt-and-pepper-haired man, and without slowing down, clasped his large hands on the man' shoulders. The older man stared at him with wide eyes, fear trickling through his features. "What's done is done, Martin." Patrick patted one of the man's shoulders. "And I'm sorry you had to face Rochelle's wrath. She can be a spitfire."

All five of them chuckled, and Violet found herself smiling.

The last of the four slapped a hand against Patrick's back. "It's good to have you home, Patrick."

"It's good to see you again, Henry." Patrick turned and gave the youngest of the four a hearty hug, each smacking their hand against the other's back.

"So, this is how it's going to be?" an angry, deep, rich voice cut through the joyous reunion, but instead of jumping apart and falling in line as Violet expected them to, the four older men slowly turned toward Mr. Cowen. *KING* Cowen! As if hearing her reminder, the four men lowered their heads in respect. "Turning my councilmen against me?"

Rochelle and Jerrica stood behind him. Jerrica looked a little uneasy, meanwhile, Rochelle appeared as if she was about to launch herself onto her father's back and pummel some good sense into him.

Trench Coat Man raised a placating hand in the air. "No one is turning anyone against you."

Fedora smirked. "Not any more than we already were, anyway."

"Arthur!" hissed Henry.

The door burst open to reveal a disheveled-looking young man, close to her and Patrick's age, as he shoved the ends of his shirt into the waist of his jeans. "Sorry!" he exclaimed as the doors swung shut again. "I got here as fast as I could. What did I miss?" His easy smile faltered, and his blue eyes bugged when they landed on Patrick. "Prince Cowen!"

"Just Patrick. I've heard the title has moved on to very capable hands."

"Ah, ahem, hopefully. I mean, I'll do my best."

Patrick's head tipped to the side. "You?"

"Me. I'm Bartholomew. You can call me Barry, though."

Patrick narrowed his eyes and turned toward his father who was smirking in the corner nearest the doors.

"Since you were calling a council meeting I thought *all* of its members should be present," Mr. Cowen said.

"Just as long as everyone gets a vote this time." Patrick's tone was even, but there was a dig in his words. A reminder that his father had made a mistake.

When Mr. Cowen's smirk faltered it, was clear he got the message.

Violet cleared her throat and wove her arm around Patrick's. "Since we are all here, why don—"

"Yes," Mr. Cowen grumbled. "Please, tell us why you deigned to interrupt our nights with this uncalled-for meeting."

"I'll ask that you all allow my mate to speak without interrupting," Patrick raised his voice, drowning out the last couple of words from his father and the slight whispers that had started between Fedora... erm, Arthur... and Henry. "We're sure you'll have questions, but this will be easier if we can explain the whole story to you in one go. I've set out chairs for everyone." He stepped back and gestured to the circle of chairs they'd placed, then looked back at Barry. "I wasn't aware you were coming, but you're welcome to grab a chair and join us."

Barry nodded and headed off to the chair rack in the corner while the rest filed into the chair circle to claim their seats.

Violet tugged her chair closer to Patrick's, and he ran a hand comfortingly across her back.

"You can do this."

His voice was a velvety caress against the nervous determination fluttering about in her mind and twisting her stomach. The steady brush of his hand was a solid reminder that he was there. That he would always be there. Even before, when he was keeping his distance, he had always been there for her. Yeah, there were times she got into trouble, but that was because he was doing his best to respect her wants. From the moment she had met him three years ago, Patrick had been a constant in her life. Her gaze connected with his, and a slow smile spread across his face. He was her mate, and she loved him.

Patrick's eyes glazed over a little as he stared back at her. His smile slipped a fraction, only to be replaced by a goofy, lopsided grin that chased away her nerves and made her let out a soft laugh. Quickly, she leaned toward him and left a feather-light kiss on his cheek before making her way to her feet.

"As you all know, the Sentinel Clan has been home to Patrick for the last three years. In that time frame, he has helped keep us safe, trained some of our greatest warriors, and earned the title of Beta."

There were a few confused looks as people cast their eyes around the small group.

She opened her mouth to start again, but Barry had returned with his chair. He unfolded the plastic seat in the air before sliding it into position beside Mr. Cowen, and the screech of the legs against the wooden floor made them all flinch. "Sorry. Sorry," he muttered as he clamored into his seat.

"For those of you who are not aware of recent events..." Violet swallowed the knot in her throat as her eyes landed on the spitting image of her mother.

Jerrica offered a small, reassuring smile, one that mirrored Evalyn's and made Violet's heart ache.

"Blood Moon has taken control of Stanislaus's territory," Violet said with a sure, firm voice and continued even when a couple of people started whispering to one another. "They wiped out most of the clan members in doing so. They have grown in strength and size and now have a strategist on their side, leading them in a revenge plot against Patrick... and the Sentinel Clan. They've killed so many. Our clan-mates, our warriors, our friends..." The knot in her throat was back and it pinched the last word off. She forced it down with a hard swallow and added, "My mother, the Luna of Sentinel Clan."

Heavy silence fell over the room. Tears fell from Jerrica's gray eyes, and she quickly wiped them away.

"We are facing a war that we're not sure we can win, even with the help of the Whisky and Mammoth clans. We've come to ask for the lycans help. Will you join us in driving Blood Moon back? In protecting our fellow wolven and keeping the peace amongst clans?"

No one moved.

In fact, Violet wasn't even sure if anyone was breathing.

"I'll join you," Rochelle launched to her feet, casting accusatory glares around the circle.

Barry eyed her like she'd gone mad. "You're not old enough to be part of a war, Rochelle, sit down."

"I can kick your butt in the ring, Barry. Need a reminder?"

Barry turned his head away, making Rochelle smirk.

She rolled her shoulders back and stood a little taller. "I've trained day in and day out for years. I'm ready and I can help."

"Absolutely not," Mr. Cowen waved a dismissive hand. "You're sixteen. You're not joining a war front."

"Need I remind you that many of us were fighting at her age?" Arthur tipped his head to the side while he swung his fedora in a circle off the top of his hand. "I've seen her fight. I think she could handle it."

"Handle it or not, she is my daughter, not yours. I don't want her in a war," Mr. Cowen snapped.

"Then who else, Dad?" Rochelle griped, throwing her arms out to the side. She shifted her weight to one side and crossed her arms. "You sure as heck aren't going to risk your precious neck. You're not going to let mom. And I'd be willing to bet that when they leave, you won't offer the chance to help to the rest of the territory either, will you?"

"Sit down, Rochelle," the king told her, casting a quick glance to her empty chair waiting beside Jerrica.

"No. You decided everything after Patrick's accident, and that's not how it's supposed to be. You have counselors for a reason! You don't get to stop me from helping my brother this time!"

"I said *sit down.*"

His voice didn't change. Not the volume anyway. Nor the tone. But there was a weight behind his words that pressed against Violet. Rochelle's butt slammed into her chair, and she stared at her dad with wide, disbelieving eyes.

Jerrica's arm went around Rochelle's shoulders while she glared at her husband. "You promised," she said softly. A whisper of something that had just been broken.

A low growl rumbled through the room, and everyone except Violet and Patrick lowered their gazes. Mr. Cowen pushed to his feet, nearly knocking over his chair as he thrust his hand through his hair and rubbed the back of his neck.

"This is not something that can be decided in one night." The king turned on both of them and pointed a finger in their direction. "You come here, demanding answers, and seeking help without offering anything in return. You expect us to have an answer for you in the same night that we've learned of the devastation raining down on our wolven companions."

"Don't try to pretend like you didn't know about any of this," Patrick snapped, getting to his feet. "You're the *king!* It's your job to know what's going on in your western territory."

Violet rested a hand on his arm and added, in a much calmer voice, "My mother was also trying to get a reply from you before she was killed." Swallowing the accusations she wanted to sling at him, she lowered her chin instead. "She never received a reply."

Mr. Cowen stared at her for a long moment, then straightened his posture and rolled his shoulders back. "Regardless, this is not something that can be decided in one night."

"Why not?" Henry asked, scratching his chin. "Each of us is easily three of them. Even us older folks. We have the numbers."

"Our numbers are dwindling," corrected Mr. Cowen. "And it doesn't help that lycans keep finding mates in wolven." His eyes flicked to Patrick and Violet.

She lifted her chin defiantly. "I am not wolven."

Mr. Cowen snorted. "Do you even know what you are?"

"It's time." Patrick's voice filled her thoughts calmly and a smirk began to spread across her face.

Violet called on her abilities and felt them readily flood her being. A warm caress brushed against her chest, enveloping her heart. Pressure built in her mouth, making her stretch her jaw, while the tips of her ears tingled. She fisted and then flexed her hands at her sides before raising one of them to watch as magic lengthened and sharpened her nails.

"Mystic, if you're in there, help me. Guide me to the magic that was gifted to me. Let the spirit within me be seen externally."

"I will always be with you, my little miracle." A deep lullaby tone eased her nerves. One that mimicked her mother's when she was a child being sung to sleep. *"Show them who you are."*

With a deep breath, Violet closed her eyes and tipped her head back, spreading her fingers and turning her palms forward. Audible gasps flew around the room before the whispering began. When she opened her eyes again, she knew they would be opalescent, swirling with golds, silvers, and coppers. "I am a lycan born to two wolven. The spirit of my mother resides in me and strengthens my elemental gift—a blessing of Spirit bestowed upon me by the moon goddess Luna, herself. The magics that have coursed through this earth long before you sounded your first cries, pulse through my veins, imbued into my blood by the most powerful witch of this generation." She spread her fingers through Patrick's, and the purple-blue aura glowing around her form flared, filling the room with light like that of the sun. She rapidly blinked her eyes against the brilliant light, then looked at Patrick who was grinning from ear to ear as he too was now surrounded by the same aura. "Our children, and our children's children, will be blessed with our unique talents. To right a wrong made long ago. To mend the souls wrongfully torn in two."

Mr. Cowen's eyes had rounded to the size of saucers while Jerrica pressed a hand over her heart. To her left, Rochelle had a deeply satisfied, smug smirk pulling at her lips. And Barry...looked like he was about to pass out.

Slowly, the blinding light faded until it was just Patrick and Violet standing in the center of the circle, holding hands and staring down the King of the Western territories.

Shaking his head, Mr. Cowen managed to make his way to his feet. He ran a hand through his hair, a habit that would have made Violet smile affectionately if she weren't so angry with him. A long breath filled his chest, puffing it out before it fell again. "You can never leave."

"Excuse me?" Violet growled.

"You're too valuable." Mr. Cowen began to circle them, claiming the spotlight once again. "When word gets out about the things you can do, and it *will* get out, you will be hunted for the remainder of your days. Your children's children, and their children, and their children... You've cursed your entire bloodline to a life of confinement."

"No!" Rochelle shouted, but when she went to stand up Jerrica pulled her back down.

Calm rage settled through Violet. "We are not staying. You can't keep us here."

"Watch me." Mr. Cowen snarled as he squared his shoulders off with hers. "You may have all of these abilities that no one has seen before, but you are still a tiny child. A girl pretending to play warrior. By keeping you here, you will be safe and protected."

That calm rage burned Violet's core and when he reached for her, Violet thrust an open palm against his chest. A blast of light burst from the impact, tendrils of blue, purple, and green. A kaleidoscope of colors that knocked Mr. Cowen back into his seat, nearly toppling it over. Violet lowered her arm and clutched it to her side to hide the evidence of her trembling. The room spun a little, and she squeezed Patrick's hand.

As if it were the most natural thing for him to do after she'd just blasted his father into a chair, he slid his fingers from hers, trailing them up her arm so they remained in contact. His hand slipped around the back of her head, spreading his fingers through her hair, and then tipped her head ever slightly toward him. One, beautiful, lingering kiss to the top of her head spread warmth and strength in ripples throughout her entire body. Breathing became easier. Her trembling stopped. Keeping her eyes open didn't feel like quite the chore anymore.

"You will never feel weak again, short stuff," Patrick promised her.

"So, that's it then." Mr. Cowen laughed disbelievingly. "You'll leave, fight, and die in this war you've started. All for the sake of pride."

"Pride?" Violet asked, tipping her head to the side. "No. I will leave and fight in this war to protect those I love. To offer a second chance to those who were never given one. And I don't do this alone." She dared a step toward him, then another when she saw him swallow. "I am a Sentinel. We rise to defend our clan. To protect those we love. We are a clan of warriors. They have spent their entire lives protecting me. It's time I return the favor."

Anger pulsed through a vein on Mr. Cowen's forehead as he turned his attention to his son. "And you? You'll abandon your clan for this... abomination."

A low, rumbling growl filled the room and Patrick's voice was full of gravelly restraint. "That is my mate you are talking about. Do not insult her again."

Mr. Cowen held Patrick's gaze, assessing the threat that his son had become, but remained silent.

Patrick looked around at his family, then settled back on his father. "You once asked me what I would do for our territory. You banished me, but I left without a fight because *you* said it was best. I believed I was helping my people. Now, you should be asking what wouldn't I do for her."

Violet felt the heat of his gaze on her, so she looked up at her mate who was beaming down at her with the intensity of a blazing fire.

His hand lightly squeezed hers. "She is everything to me." He turned back to his dad. "When you turned away, she stepped forward. When others were afraid, she was fearless. When I thought she would be my undoing, she repaired my soul."

"We won't let you strong-arm us again, Cowen," Arthur spoke up after a long stretch of silence. "You picked us to help you make decisions like this. Let us help. Let the lycans show that we aren't hiding anymore. That we are still here. That we still mean something."

"Enough. We will discuss this in private." Mr. Cowen growled, glaring at Arthur before returning his narrowed gaze to Patrick. "You have a chance to come back, son. If you leave, that offer will not be available again."

Pain lanced through Violet's chest, and she clutched Patrick's hand. Three light taps of his fingers against her hand made her realize that the pain was her own. She was hurting for him, but Patrick's emotions were... happy.

"I know." He lifted their combined hands and pressed a soft kiss to her knuckles. "Let's go home."

"What?" Jerrica launched to her feet while the two of them headed toward the door. "Now? It's the middle of the night. You haven't even been here a day, yet. You haven't slept!"

"We told you we didn't have a lot of time," Patrick reminded her, turning back toward her.

Violet smiled sadly at Jerrica. "After meeting with Laurel, and speaking with the moon goddess, we realized we had less time than we thought." Her gaze lingered on Jerrica's gray eyes, and for a moment, allowed herself to imagine it was her mom standing in front of her. "I wish there was more time. I have so many questions, but—"

Warm, slender arms were around her shoulders a moment later. Patrick's hand disappeared from her grasp when she readily hugged Jerrica back and breathed in her familiar, yet foreign scent.

"I promise this is not the last time we will see each other," Jerrica said softly in her ear. "We can visit. Patrick can give you my number. Email. Anything."

Moisture gathered in Violet's eyes, and she pinched them shut to keep the tears from falling. "Thank you."

"I'm coming with you," Rochelle exclaimed as Jerrica and Violet pulled away from each other. She stopped right beside Patrick, looking up at him expectantly.

"No, you are not!" Mr. Cowen demanded.

Patrick winked at Violet, then turned to his little sister. "I can't encourage you to go against Dad. A lot of people are going to die. This isn't a game."

Anger flashed across Rochelle's face. "I'm not—"

Her words were cut off when Patrick pulled her into a tight hug. Violet was close enough that she could tell Patrick was whispering something, but it was so low and fast that it was impossible to catch it. When he released Rochelle, she still looked angry, but resigned.

"I love you, Shelly. I can't put you in harm's way."

Rochelle crossed her arms, but didn't respond.

Patrick looked at the remaining council members. "You know what we are headed into. We could use your help. If you decide to come, our gates will always be open for you." He offered his hand to Violet, and she readily took it. "Let's go save our clan."

Chapter 32

Jax

***Rubbing the sleep from** his eyes, Jax rolled out of bed. His heart was still* pounding and a thin sheen of sweat glistened across his brow. How many more times was he going to wake up from the same nightmare? Wasn't knowing Lexie was in danger bad enough? Why did he have to dream about it? Hear her calling his name over and over again, crying in agony. No matter what he did, he couldn't reach her.

With a shake of his head, he turned to stare at the clock.

4:39 AM

His groan rolled through the room, ending in an annoyed growl.

"We need more sleep," Dalim complained.

"I know," Jax answered out loud, too tired to speak telepathically with his wolf spirit. "These nightmares..."

"I know." Dalim sighed. *"Do you think it's a sign from the moon goddess?"*

"A sign? What do you mean?" Jax asked as he pressed his bare feet against the floor and snatched a pair of joggers from the drawer.

"We know where she is, Jax. It's been eating us both up, not being able to do anything about it." Dalim paused for a moment, then hesitantly added, *"Maybe, it isn't us who saves her."*

"What do you mean by that, brother?" Jax tugged a black, long-sleeved shirt over his head.

Dalim paced in his mind, back and forth, back and forth until Jax was about to snap at him. *"I think it's time to tell Violet. Maybe this is the goddess' way of telling us that we are not meant to save her, but that doesn't mean that someone else can't. We know they are in the Blood Moon's territory. Patrick and Violet could stop on their way back and infiltrate–"*

"Absolutely not," Jax interrupted and slammed his sock drawer closed, flinching at how loud it rang in his ears. "I'm not sending them on a suicide mission. Patrick barely made it out of there alive." He snorted. "Actually, he didn't. Patrick died trying to get out of there. I'm not sending him back in."

"Then send Violet."

"What?" Jax snarled internally, finally awake enough to speak using their link.

"Think about it, Jax. They want her. They've wanted her this entire time, but now that Patrick has escaped, who do you think they'll be after in an attempt to get him back?"

"How do you know that's still their plan?"

"I don't." Dalim answered, gravely. *"But if we don't do something soon, I'm afraid it will be too late for Lexie."*

Pain lanced through Jax at the thought of losing his sister's best friend, nearly bringing him to his knees. His hand shot out to brace himself against the bed until he sat down. That's all it was... he tried to convince himself... to ignore the growing connection he'd felt to Lexie for years. It didn't matter what that girl was, she could hold her own and commanded beings multiple times stronger and deadlier than her like she was a luna. Goddess, how he admired her.

He'd never admit it out loud, of course. He'd never hear the end of it from Lexie.

"We'll never hear anything from her again if we don't do something," Dalim added glumly.

Jax dropped his head into his hands, bracing his elbows on his legs. *"Violet would never forgive me if she found out that Lexie died and I didn't tell her where she was."*

Comforting warmth pressed against his thoughts as Dalim said, *"If we lose Lexie without telling Violet anything, we could lose them both."*

Another minute passed before Jax nodded. "Wanna help a guy out? It's gonna take quite a bit of power to reach her so far away."

"Not as much as you think," Dalim cooed. *"It seems we may be just in time. I can feel her stronger than I could last night."*

"What?" Jax stretched his abilities, searching for his sister amongst the many minds of his clan. All he had to do was find the two dimmest lines and grab the one that mirrored his own. Dalim lended his abilities as well and the search quickened.

There, in the darkest corner of the clan-link, were Patrick and Violet. "Got'em. And yeah, they are a lot closer than last night."

Drawing in a deep breath, Jax mentally tugged on his twin's link, he pictured it was like tugging on her braid as a kid. *"Hey, sis. Can you hear me?"*

"Loud and clear, braid-puller," she responded instantly.

"How did you–"

"Long story, but I think I can kind of read minds. Also, you were practically shoving that image at me when you opened the link."

Dalim and Jax snickered together.

"We thought you'd be asleep for a few more hours, so we were going to wait to tell you, but we're on our way back. Only a few hours to go."

"Not to throw a wrench in our joyous reunion, but–" His throat tightened around his words. Could he really send her into a life threatening situation?

Dalim urged him to continue. *"She can handle herself, brother. Let her do this."*

"Let me do what, Dalim?" Violet asked, sounding instantly awake and rearing to go.

"We know where Lexie is," Dalim announced, taking over the conversation. *"Not her exact location, but she's with Blood Moon."*

Violet was quiet for a moment, then softly replied. *"I know."*

"You know?" Jax griped. *"How do you know? And when were you going to tell me?"*

"Jax, this isn't the time," she chided, and he grumbled his reluctant agreement. *"What do you want me to do?"*

Jax stared at the mirror over his dresser and froze. His purple eyes, an exact mirror of his sisters. If this went wrong, it was possible he would never see her again.

"Being the alpha really sucks sometimes," he admitted to her. *"I don't want to tell you to do this. But, I think it's Lexie's only hope."*

"Patrick is dropping me off on the edge of their territory," Violet blurted in a rush, and he could almost see her clamping her hands over her mouth.

"What?"

"You're right. The moon goddess told me herself that Lexie needed me. I can't wait until we get back to base to leave and hope she is still alive. I could already be too late, but I have to try."

"I guess... I don't have to order you to rescue her."

Violet chuckled. *"Come on, Jax. We're twins. We're usually on the same page, and we'll always have each other's backs."*

"Always," he agreed. *"I don't have to tell you to be careful."*

"Then why are you telling me?" She said with a smile in her voice even though her tone was ribboned with worry. *"Patrick will be home in a few hours. I'll keep you posted when I can."*

The link between them faded away, and Jax's eyes refocused on his reflection. His heart was thundering in his chest, and his palms had gone clammy. This was what fear felt like. A very real terror that was threatening to take over his entire system. The knowledge that this fight was only just beginning gripped his throat and caged his chest, making it hard to breathe. He'd already lost so many... he couldn't lose Violet, too. He couldn't do this alone.

"You're not alone," Dalim assured him. *"She is strong and resourceful and smart. She'll be okay. Plus, she has her lycan abilities now."*

Jax nodded. "Yeah. Okay." He shook his head then shot off the bed and grabbed his sneakers. "I need to run."

An hour and a half later, Jax slowed to a walk as Alpha House came into view. He'd run along the base fence line, waving to warriors as he went. It wasn't long into his run when people started reaching out to him via the clan-link.

"I don't mean to interrupt your run, but..."

"Sorry to disturb your run, but..."

"Hey, since you're awake..."

The one that had really gotten to him was former beta Paul, *"We need to talk before any of the other meetings you have today."*

The order made Dalim snarl and Jax's pace had drastically increased. Talking to his father's beta was the last thing he wanted to do.

The first thing on his list was a war council meeting with the other clans. Everyone had finally arrived, and it was time to begin the true planning and preparations.

Jax pushed through the back door of Alpha House and then froze, because former beta Paul was leaning against the kitchen counter, staring at him expectantly. Thankful for the control his wolf spirit gave him, Jax maintained an even expression as he opened the door even further and directed Paul toward it. "We do not have a meeting scheduled and I don't appreciate the drop in on my personal time."

"We need to talk."

"Paul, you are not my beta," Jax said bluntly, leveling the older man with a steely gaze. "You were my father's. You've made it clear that you don't agree with my methods, and I feel that I've been equally as blunt in taking your advice."

"And where is your beta when you need him?" Paul grumbled. "He should be here, by your side, preparing for this war."

Jax sighed. "I have already told you that Patrick is off on another errand that I needed him to run. He is performing his beta duties, whether you think he is or not."

"What errand? Where is he?"

"Where my beta is and what he is doing is none of your concern." Jax crossed his arms over his chest.

The older man's mouth bunched as he clenched his jaw. Clearly, that wasn't the answer he wanted. "And what about Lexie?"

Jax's eyes narrowed and warning bells sounded in his mind. "What about her?"

"You've known where she was for a while now and yet you have no plans to rescue her?"

"Easy. Something's fishy here. He wants something." Dalim warned, his metaphorical hackles rising.

Lifting his chin a fraction, Jax grabbed the edge of the door and swung it shut. If he'd looked away even for a second, he would have missed the slight widening of Paul's eyes and the deep swallow that made his throat bob. With deliberate steps, Jax moved toward the former beta, purposefully driving his heels against the floor to increase the sound. "What do you want?"

Paul pushed off the counter and backed toward the front door, mirroring Jax's steps. "I only want to be helpful." His words were flat, rehearsed and lacking emotion.

"Maybe you did at one point," Jax growled. "I don't believe you anymore."

"Ja—Alpha Jax," Paul remedied as he stumbled into the side of the couch. "I assure you. Attaining information is the first step in knowing how best to help the clan."

Jax's feet stopped. "Which clan?"

Paul blinked and the color drained from his face.

"Checkmate," Dalim snarled.

"We've suspected we had a mole in our clan for a while," Jax's tone relaxed into an eerie calm that made Paul's fingers twitch at his sides. "I've been narrowing it down, but you know who was at the top of my list the entire time?"

With a defiant raising of the chin, Paul stayed silent.

"You," Jax offered the answer then tilted his head to the side as a small smile curled his lips. "After all—you're the one who came to me with Lexie's location, insistent that you had heard it from one of the patrols I'd sent out. Were you hoping we would split our power and invade Blood Moon to save the life of a human? Is that what they were hoping for? A moment when we were weak to make our annihilation easier on them?"

A vein bulged in Paul's forehead, but still he remained silent.

"After everything you did for my father and this clan... you destroy that legacy by feeding information to Blood Moon."

"The only person destroying that legacy is you," Paul spat, finally breaking the vow of silence he'd chosen. "Everything he worked to build. Everything he stood for. Where is it? Because all I see is an ungrateful child attempting to do a true alpha's job."

Dalim pushed forward at the same time Jax called for him. Power surged through Jax, exuding off him in waves and barreling into Paul who yelped in surprise before doubling forward. He hurriedly backed toward the front door, but before he could reach it, Jax threw his power outward. He'd never tried to use his entire alpha aura before. He tried not to use it. That was how his father had ruled, fear and force. Jax wanted to lead by example and earn the trust and loyalty of his clan, but this... This was a show of power. A show that Jax did indeed have the strength and abilities he needed to run this clan. A final drive home, that he was the true alpha of the Sentinel Clan.

Paul's knees clanked against the floor barely before his palms. An excessive whine passed through his lips, but Jax didn't back off until the older man's fingers curled against the wood, nails dragging against the hard surface.

"I've tried to be understanding," Jax informed the man he'd once thought of as a mentor while he lightly pulled back the reins of his power. Being a former beta, Paul could withstand a lot more than most wolven, so Jax kept his hold firm as he messaged the Sentinel warriors to tell them he needed four of them right away. "I've tried to give you time to adjust. My tolerance has an end and my patience has worn thin. All of that would have given me reason enough to do this. If I was my father, it would have happened a lot sooner. Maybe it should have. Maybe I could have stopped you from crossing the line of treason."

A gasp for air behind him made Jax turn to see one of the female warriors from Whisky. Adeline stood a couple of steps inside the back door, struggling to breathe. Jax quickly relaxed his aura and she collapsed to her hands and knees. Her eyes were wide with fear, but Jax had to push that out of his mind as he closed the distance between himself and Paul who had started to sneak toward the front door. Snatching the back of Paul's shirt, he hauled the older man off the floor. "You chose to betray your clan."

With a savage snarl, Paul's fist slammed into Jax's jaw. The surprise attack made the young alpha stagger a step, releasing Paul in the process.

Instead of backing down like he should have, Paul pressed forward, challenging Jax even more. "Don't do this," he warned Paul as he took a step toward the older man and drove his fist into Paul's stomach.

As if he hadn't heard Jax, Paul delivered a quick five-punch strike that Jax managed to block four of. The last glanced off his ribs, making his nose scrunch as the bones cried out.

"Paul, I order you to stand down."

Paul didn't listen.

Jax feigned to the left, snatched Paul's wrist, then stepped behind the older man and twisted as he yanked back.

Something snapped. Another thing popped. Paul howled in pain and Jax released him.

"I don't want to kill you, Paul," Jax told him, softening his tone. "But if you insist on fighting me, your life is forfeit." He shook his head, brows pulling together as he stared into Paul's glaring face. "You know that."

If Paul continued to fight, Jax would be forced to. It would turn into a battle to the death, a bloodbath for power. And Paul would lose. Only another alpha would be able to challenge Jax at this point, and his power was still growing.

The front door flew open, nearly being thrown off its hinges as two warriors dressed in black athletic wear stormed into the room. Two more came through the back door, and a large wolf growled from the other side of each door, signaling their presence, as well.

"I told you guys I only needed four of you," Jax chided lightly, snuffing out his alpha aura while the warriors surrounded Paul.

"We figured the more the merrier, Alpha," one of them nodded respectfully to Jax while another gave a lopsided grin.

Jax shook his head and overwhelming pride for his warriors surged through him. They wouldn't have come with extra help if they didn't respect and care for him. There were moments he doubted if he was doing things right, and then there were times like this. He still had a relationship with his clanmates along with their respect and loyalty. They came to him, over-prepared, to ensure his safety.

Once they had their hands on Paul, they looked to Jax for more instruction. "What do we do with him?"

"He is a traitor," Jax told them bluntly. "We have found the mole in our ranks. He will be banished, but for now, take him to Lockup."

"Alpha Jaxon," called the Whisky warrior, Adeline, as she used the counter for leverage and made her way back to her feet. She shortened the distance between them, stopping only a couple of feet away. "You're going to let this traitor live?"

Jax lifted his chin. "I'm not an executioner."

"I understand that, and have a lot of respect for the mercy you showed, but this is a matter of life or death for your clan. Not just you."

Jax rolled this information over in his mind for a moment before speaking again, "He will go to Lockup until Blood Moon is defeated and our clans are safe once again. When that time comes, he will be banished and handed over to the Lycan council for them to deal with."

The remaining color in Paul's face drained. Traitors weren't treated well amongst the lycans, and it was well known. Some were put to death. The others were stripped of their wolven strength and ability to shift by the moon goddess, through the hands of her witch conduit. From there, some lived out their lives as outcasts in whatever clan would take them while others attempted to integrate themselves into human society. Most spent their lives in servitude to the lycans where they could be closely watched.

Seemingly satisfied with that plan, the warriors began to haul the former beta away.

Once the Sentinel warriors and the traitor were gone, Jax turned to Adeline. "I'm sorry you had to witness that."

Adeline's hands disappeared behind her back as she rolled her posture into place. "There is no need to apologize, Alpha Jaxon. I heard what was happening and I understand why you did it." Her chin lowered a little while she continued, "I must say though—I have never felt power like yours before."

"If I can avoid it, you'll never experience that again," Jax assured her, then moved to the kitchen to grab a glass of water.

Adeline remained silent while he drained his glass.

Once he'd set the glass in the sink, he pressed his palms against the counter and asked, "Now, what brought you here so early?"

A small smile lifted the corners of Adeline's mouth, softening the stern expression that she usually carried. "Oscar, Daniel, and I were wondering if you would like to eat breakfast with us before the meeting. They admired your approach to having a full stomach before such important events."

Jax's lips slipped into a wide grin and a soft laugh left him. "Glad to hear it. Let's get some breakfast."

Chapter 33

Violet

Darkness continued to dominate *the sky when Violet and Patrick arrived at* Blood Moon's border. With lycan eyesight being what it was, Patrick could still safely see even after he'd killed the lights a few miles back to help disguise their approach. Violet loved that truck, but she silently cursed the loud rumble that rolled from the engine, alerting every living thing in the trees surrounding them. Not that it mattered. She was about to willingly enter the enemy's territory and hope they didn't kill her on sight.

Patrick's large hand encircled hers, and she turned her head to look at him. "If you're not sure, then we don't have to do this."

"*We* aren't doing anything," she reminded him, squeezing his fingers lightly. "You promised. I'm doing this alone and you're returning to help Jax."

"You don't know what you're walking into."

"You've told me plenty," she argued. Ever since ending her conversation with Jax, they'd gone over every detail Patrick could remember. A lot of it made her stomach sour, and she fought against the need for revenge. Revenge wouldn't solve anything. "I'm not doing this lightly. I know what I heard from the moon goddess. Lexie is in trouble and she needs me."

Silence fell between them. A deep canyon of fear filled to the brim with worry beat against their bond and Patrick's heartbeat thundered in her ears. "I won't be there to help you," he finally answered in a quiet, breathy tone that laid out everything he was feeling.

Violet tightened her hold on his hand, then released him to unbuckle and slide across the bench seat so she was pressed up against him. After quickly buckling, she leaned her head against his shoulder and held his hand in both of hers. "I can do this," she told him, her voice near a whisper. Then a small smirk lifted one corner of her mouth. "I'm a crazy strong lycan with an even stronger mate, and our completed bond strengthens us even further."

"Yeah, that's how it's supposed to be, but we haven't tested that theory out yet."

Fighting off the fear that had been attempting to wiggle its way into her thoughts, Violet briefly buried her face against his arm. "No better time like the present," she mumbled against his sleeve, then lifted her head to stare at the side of his face. "Patrick, I need you to understand why I'm doing this."

"I do," he answered without hesitation. "That's why we're here. I do understand."

She sighed. "Good. Now, I need you to trust me."

Patrick turned the steering wheel and she felt the tires slip off the paved road. He released her hand to maneuver the truck into Park before he turned to face her. "Trusting you has never been a problem."

"No." Violet shook her head. "I need you to trust that I can do this."

His chin lowered and his chest rose with a large breath. "I know you can do this, Vi." When he lifted his gaze to meet hers, his eyes glowed with moonstone. "I'm terrified for what you're going to have to face. I don't want you to go through that alone."

Panic reared its ugly head in her chest, and she imagined herself beating it back down into the box it'd come out of and then sitting on the lid. "I won't be," she flinched when her voice came out much too cheerful.

Patrick grimaced, then let out a soft laugh. "Yeah, you'll be surrounded by Blood Moon wolven."

"No," she corrected him. "I'll have Lexie."

"If you can find her."

Releasing a large sigh, Violet brought one hand to his cheek and rested her palm there. His eyes closed while he turned into her touch. She could hear him draw in a deep breath, but he didn't move again. "I *will* find her, Patrick. She and I are both going to survive this. We will survive the coming fight, and you and I will live a long life together."

His eyes shot open and he stared at her, his moonstone eyes glimmering brighter than before. "I love you."

Violet blinked rapidly a couple of times. They'd said as much already, but not those exact words. Her heart galloped away without her and butterflies took flight in her stomach as a soft smile stretched across her face. "I love you too."

Patrick's lips brushed lightly against hers, and she responded in kind, closing her eyes and leaning into the kiss. His fingers trailed up her arm, then buried themselves in her hair before trailing down her jaw. He leaned back when his fingers found her chin. "You can do this, Vi."

A band of tension she hadn't known she'd been carrying, broke at those words. She'd been telling herself that all along, but hadn't realized she needed to hear it from someone else. With a nod, she quickly kissed him once more, then scooted her way back across the bench seat toward the door.

"We're close to where you and Jax found me," Patrick informed her. "Just start walking. I'm sure they'll find you soon."

She nodded again, not trusting her voice, as she opened the door and slid off the seat. Her shoes crunched the dirt beneath her when she landed and she stared into the dark forest before her. The leaves came into crispy clear focus as her lycan abilities took over. Nothing but trees and other shrubbery. Not even an animal. Which meant either they were scared away by her and the loud truck, or Blood Moon wasn't far away.

"Vi."

Turning around to offer one more farewell to Patrick, she froze as she stared at him. They'd said goodbye too many times lately. A fierce determination coursed through her, and a deep ringing filled her ears. She would make sure this was the last time.

One side of Patrick's mouth kicked up in a smirk and she wondered if he could feel her shift in emotions. "Go save our friend."

A fast, sure smile lit Violet's face. With a soft laugh, she shook her head. "I'm gonna kick some butt, too."

Patrick's smirk grew to reveal his elongated lycan canines. It was one of the features he chose to keep now that he had control again. That and the tapered ears. Warmth pooled in her stomach as she stared at her mate. She didn't mind those added features, at all.

"Definitely," Patrick growled softly, then jerked his chin toward the trees. "Go. I'll rally the troops, and we'll be back."

"May the moon goddess light your path," Violet offered a farewell she'd only heard twice in her life. It was said when someone was going away, especially on a difficult journey. It was used a lot more often before the clans became more civilized when there were still territorial wars. This felt like an appropriate time to use it.

Patrick bowed his head. "And yours, my miracle mate."

There had never been a time when Violet enjoyed being called a miracle... until then. Being Patrick's mate was a miracle, and one she was delighted to have.

With a last smile, just for him, Violet closed the truck door as softly as she could, then headed toward the tree line. She turned to offer a final little wave as she slipped under their cover and into enemy territory.

"Alright, Violet," she spoke quietly to herself as the eerie trees stretched out around her. It was as if the entire forest was trying to scare her away. Like even the foliage knew dark things had happened here. "Let's go rescue my human." She giggled at herself for calling Lexie *her* human, but it was a nervous-sounding giggle that she quickly quelled by clearing her throat.

Time passed as she continued making her way through the forest, hoping she was walking in a straight line and not in circles. The more time passed, the less anxious she felt and the more bored she became. She hadn't seen a single animal, nor a blood moon member. Honestly, she wasn't sure if that was a good thing or a bad thing. It was likely she'd have to fight when they eventually found her, but to not have been discovered yet... True, territories were pretty large and her chances of crossing someone increased the closer she got to their base. But this felt too easy.

SNAP.

Violet jerked her head to the right.

Deep in the forest, a shadow moved along the trees, just barely beyond what she could make out between her lycan abilities and the trees surrounding her.

Her left ear twitched as a low rolling note rippled through the air.

Ah. She tipped her head back a little bit and wet her lips. This made more sense. They were keeping a very cautious distance around her. She had expected to meet them head-on, but being so focused on that thought had allowed them to surround her.

She thought about calling out to them, but found her jaw locked shut and her feet moving her forward once again.

After a while the red-eyed wolven surrounding her inched closer, and by the time she could distinguish the outline of a building in the distance and the stench of stale blood in the air, they were nearly by her side. They made no move to touch her, but made it clear they were not friendly. If she looked at one of the wolves, they would snarl savagely and raise their hackles. A few wolven in their human forms had joined as she'd gotten closer to the base, and they simply glared and nodded for her to keep moving.

The message was clear.

As long as she kept walking toward the base, she wouldn't be harmed.

But, try to leave and they would all stop her—and probably kill her.

Lucky for her, she had no intention of leaving.

Yet.

She rounded the first building and froze. Dried blood covered the ground, staining the earth with a reddish-brown hue where it had once been lush underbrush. Bile rose in her throat when her eyes snagged on a body, and the hint of many more, before she averted her gaze. Doing so only helped the problem so much, though. The rancor of blood was bad enough, but adding the smell of rotting flesh made her stomach curl. She started to double over, thinking she was going to throw up, but thankfully her body didn't go that far. One of the people tailing her shoved the heel of his hand against her back and she stumbled forward a step.

"Move!" he barked.

Violet cast her eyes around, purposefully blocking out the ground and what lay across it or stacked against the sides of the buildings. "I'm here for Lexie."

The wolven snorted, his ruby eyes glowing menacingly. "You're here to see Ivy." He shoved her with both hands toward the biggest building in the base. "Move."

Assuming she was being herded toward the meeting house, Violet walked with her head held high. *Show no fear*, she told herself, and a soft comfort washed over her.

"Do not fear, young one. You are not alone."

"Mystic?" Violet asked, awed that her mother's wolf was talking to her. *"You're there?"*

"I'm in the shadows, but I'm always here when you need me to be. Your abilities make it so that I'm not needed very often."

"I'm sorry," Violet said and felt the guilt of that realization wash through her.

"Don't be. It's a nice release from the constant need your mother had for me. Now, I get to mostly sit back and watch you flourish, but right now is not the time to rest. I am here when you are ready."

Relief flooded Violet as she started up the steps of the meeting house. *"I'm glad you're with me, Mystic."*

Violet reached out and opened the meeting house door as if she'd done it a thousand times. She didn't bother calling out to introduce herself, and there was no way she was going to let one of the wolven trailing do it first. The door lightly smacked against the wall behind it as her shoes clomped over the flooring, tracking mud with each step. Her gaze snagged on the broken chains dangling from the ceiling. Shards of wood lay at the foot of the wall behind them between another set of broken manacles that hung limply along the floor. This was where they had held Patrick.

Rage shot through Violet's veins, steadying her shaking hands as she came to a stop at the head of the room and waited.

A strange ripple effect happened when the people in the room noticed her presence. A couple of wolven along the walls had turned their heads to see them as soon as they had entered the room before turning back like that was what they did every time someone entered the room. There was only a momentary lapse before their crimson eyes were back on her, wide and alarmed. From there, the rest of the wall-lined wolven turned to stare at her. Then a pair of bright green eyes met hers.

Cas stared, his eyes slightly widened while his jaw slackened, making his lips part.

"No! That's not what I want! I want suffering, not a quick extermination, and—why has everyone suddenly stopped breathing?" A woman with long white dreadlocks shouted as she turned away from another woman who could have been her shadow. For every light feature the shouting woman had, her shadow was dark.

Black hair. Black nails with blackened fingertips that stretched toward her palms. Black lips. And something that rested on the exposed flesh of her chest that Violet was sure she didn't want to get close enough to distinguish.

"Ivy," Cas started, taking a step kind of halfway between the direction of the white-haired woman and Violet. His gaze darted to Violet's, then back to the woman when she turned on him. No words came out when he opened his mouth to speak.

Suddenly, Ivy spun around, her long dreadlocks flying into the air with the force of the movement. Her eyes locked with Violet's and she grinned a nasty, satisfied sneer. "Why hello there."

Her lullaby tone scathed down Violet's flesh, sickeningly sweet and deceptive.

"Look at this little sheep my wolves have brought back to me," Ivy cooed as she made her way across the room to Violet. She patted Violet on the head condescendingly, making a few people chuckle, then swooped down and gathered Violet's hands in her own. "Hello, Violet. Or should I call you by one of your other titles? The impossible twin? The miracle child? The lycan born to two wolven? I'm sure there are more, but those are the ones I'm used to. Take your pick."

Violet fought to keep her face impassive and her shoulders relaxed. Something told her she could not let this woman see how she was truly feeling. "Violet is fine."

Ivy pouted. "But it's not as fun. What about..." She released one of Violet's hands to tap her chin and Violet allowed her arm to swing back down to her side. "Little Lycan? Ooooh, I like the ring of that. How *are* you so small for a lycan?"

Offering the slightest, bored shrug, Violet answered, "It probably has something to do with the fact that I didn't have any abilities until my eighteenth birthday."

"Hm." Ivy's lips mushed to the side. "You're a ray of sunshine, aren't you? Cas, I thought you said she'd be more fun."

Violet slowly blinked and lazily moved her gaze to Cas', who had made his way across the room as well to stand just behind Ivy's shoulder.

"I don't remember saying that."

"Maybe not, but you did say she was special. All I see is a girl who looks more human than anything else."

"Do not underestimate her," Cas warned, his tone hardening. "I've seen her fight."

Violet bit the inside of her cheek to stop herself from screaming at him.

Ivy's head dipped to the side and one of her thicker dreads fell off her shoulder. "What do you want, Little Lycan? What could make you so completely stupid as to put yourself at my mercy?"

There was a warning in Cas' eye. The slightest shake of his head.

If he knew her at all, he knew that whatever he was warning her against was not going to stall her plan.

"I'm here for Lexie," she announced boldly.

No one moved, or breathed, for a moment.

Ivy simply blinked at her request and then burst out laughing. Her hands clutched her stomach as she doubled over with mirth and a nervous, uncertain, fearful rumble of laughter rose throughout the room. "And you what? You think I'm just going to hand her over to you and let you leave?"

"No," Violet answered honestly. "I never expected you to let me leave."

With a final chuckle, Ivy gave three slow claps. "Clever, but that also means you wandered into *my* territory knowing you were going to be captured and possibly killed." Her hand snaked out and she seized Violet by the throat.

"Ivy!" Cas shouted, jerking forward, but he did nothing more than that.

Violet wasn't being held or restrained and she'd seen the twitch of Ivy's muscles before the woman had lashed out. She could have blocked Ivy, but if Violet played this right, she could also lead Ivy to believe that Violet wasn't much of a threat, at all. So, she remained motionless like she would have before her lycan abilities had come to light. She was calm, even as Ivy tightened her hold around her delicate throat.

"Now why would someone as prized as you, do something as stupid as that?" Ivy shook her as she said *stupid*, emphasizing her point.

The lack of reaction from Violet seemed to irritate Ivy, so Violet widened her eyes ever so slightly and forced her breathing to heave a little, a show of fear that she oddly wasn't feeling at that moment. "She's my best friend. I couldn't let her be here alone."

Cas snorted. "Your love for others has become your downfall."

Violet glared at him. "And your lack of it has led to your destruction."

Ivy howled with laughter, throwing her head back and making her dreads bounce from the sudden movement. Her fingers fell away from Violet's neck and she clapped again. "Oh, I should keep you around just to annoy Cas. That was the most fun I've had in days."

Lifting her hand, Violet rubbed her throat. "Where's Lexie?"

Dark glee passed over Ivy's face, twisting her plump lips into a nasty sneer. "You want your friend? Fine." She motioned for two of the wolven standing along the wall to come closer. "They'll take you to her."

"No," Cas snapped and moved to step between the wolven and Violet, but Ivy lifted a hand to stop him... and he listened. He froze in place, though his hands clenched at his sides.

"She wants to see her friend, Cas," Ivy told him blissfully. "We shouldn't stand in the way of their reunion."

Cas' gaze followed her as the wolven led Violet out of the meeting house. Wolven in both their wolf and human forms lined the steps and path, snapping their jaws and throwing insults her way until one of the two wolven shooed them away like a bunch of animals.

"Is that normal?" Violet couldn't stop herself from asking as one of the more rabid wolves ran off.

"More normal than we would like," one of the wolven answered in a deep voice. She stared at his profile and had the strangest feeling of recognition. Thick, dark eyebrows remained low over his light brown eyes as he continued, "They still listen to orders, mostly, but they aren't much better than animals at that point."

"Do they ever improve?" she found herself asking while they headed toward one of the farthest small cabins.

"No," snapped the other. "Once they start deteriorating, it's only a matter of time before we have to kill them."

Horror washed over Violet. "How much longer do they have?"

A dark chortle passed between them both before the familiar one answered, "We're hoping they'll last one more fight. They're nasty to deal with head-to-head."

Letting that information sink in, Violet took in the rest of the guy's features. His height felt off... and his age. She felt like he should have been about her age, but he was probably five to eight years older. His dark hair was too short, too. She remembered it being longer and tucked behind his ears. "Oh my goddess... you're Talon's brother."

Both males stopped and slowly turned to look at her. Hatred oozed from the toasted almond skin of the one she'd called out. There was no doubt in her mind. Hunter Break, the older brother to the previous future alpha of Stanislaus, was standing right in front of her.

"You are, aren't you?"

"We abandoned our old lives when we joined Blood Moon's cause," answered the other one. "We either choose new names or have no name."

Violet stared into those familiar light brown eyes until they swirled with crimson.

"Hunter is dead," he growled.

Tears gathered in Violet's eyes and she lifted her chin defiantly. "So is your brother."

A spark of pain softened Hunter's eyes. He snarled and seized her shoulder to keep her moving. "I don't have a brother."

They fell silent as they finished their trek to the small cabin. When this was all over, would she be able to help them? She looked at Hunter. Would he let her? Would any of them? What about the ones that were more animal than person? Was it better for her to start with them? Or help the ones like Hunter?

"We've recently renovated this cabin," Hunter told her. "It's small, but this now accommodates two people instead of one."

"Really?" Violet asked. "Lexie's in there?"

She pulled in a deep breath through her nose, scenting the air. The stench of blood was overpowering, making it hard to smell anything else, but a thin ribbon of perfume ran through the other smells. Violet's brows pulled together. Lexie's typical perfume smell—the smell of most humans—was strong and nauseating. This was weak... old... and decayed? It was the only word she could think of.

Instead of a copious amount of flowers, there were wilted moldy flowers with a hint of old egg.

Neither wolven had answered so she tried again. "Is Lexie *alive* in there?"

"Hah!" Laughed the other wolven. "Oh, she's definitely alive."

Violet smirked. Lexie had probably been up to her usual tricks of annoying everyone around her into submission. It wouldn't surprise Violet.

"I'm positive she will be thrilled to see you," Hunter said as they made their way toward the side of the building.

"Wait," Violet paused and pointed to the front door. "Isn't that the door?"

The wolven looked at each other briefly and then eyed her warily. "We just told you there were renovations done. That door doesn't work anymore. We have to use the back door."

Violet blinked at them, then slowly followed. "O-kay." She blinked at a thick ring attached to an odd metal strip in the log cabin frame, but ignored it and followed after the two men.

Hunter hurried up the three steps to unlock the back door while she and the second wolven came up behind him.

"You ready?" He asked.

Violet nodded, but realized too late that he wasn't looking at her. He was looking at the wolven who'd placed himself directly behind her.

The door flew open at the same time she was shoved through it. She skidded on her hands and knees then a metallic clang rang in her ears. When she turned to glare at the two men, she could only see one of them on the other side of a barred door.

"What?" Her mouth fell open as she looked around the room. She was in a tiny 3x5 foot cell. The only door was backed against the door she'd been shoved through and there was a metal wall on the other side. A small visiting area spanned the rest of the room, but she couldn't see much beyond the metal wall. "This is not what Ivy told you to do," Violet snarled at Hunter who was laughing at her from the doorway.

"Actually, this is exactly what she told us to do." He leaned back a little and said, "Pull it back, Jeremy!"

A deep metallic groan vibrated her bones and Violet spun to see the metal wall be dragged away.

Tears sprang to her eyes, and she backed away a step at what was on the other side.

Curled in the far corner was a mass of white blonde hair, ratted and covered in all manner of grime and blood. Beneath that was a frail form, dirty, bruised, and scarred.

"Lexie?" Violet sobbed.

Clawed fingers stretched out from beneath the hair and Violet jerked back a step. Slowly, the mass uncurled, but stayed close to the floor, snarling up at Violet with blood red consuming the entirety of her eyes.

"Oh," Violet breathed. "What have they done to you?"

Lexie launched herself off the floor, bearing a set of wolven canines as she charged Violet.

"Lexie, no!" Violet dodged her best friend and watched in horror as Lexie bounced off the metal bars, not having bothered to stop herself.

Dirty, white blonde hair flew about her head as Lexie spun on Violet again. An ear-splitting screech-howl made Violet flinch.

"Lexie, stop!" Violet tried, but the creature before her charged again.

There was no training behind these moves. They were blind animal charges. Easy to dodge and deflect, but the fact that this beast had her friend's face made Violet's retaliation sloppy. Claws dragged across Violet's waist, making her seethe through her teeth before she managed to get behind Lexie and wrap her in a headlock.

"It's me, Violet. My brother is a smelly dog, remember?"

Lexie's struggle slowed, encouraging Violet to continue.

"That's it. The smelly dog is Jax. You like to fig... I mean, you like to banter with him."

Lexie stopped fighting.

Violet slightly relaxed the headlock she had her best friend in while she continued, "And you're friends with Patrick and Mya. You thrive in a world you were nev—AH!" Violet screamed when Lexie ducked her chin and sank her teeth into Violet's arm.

The wolven who'd locked her in laughed maniacally. "For the record, *she's* been very helpful in taking care of those wolven we were talking about. Keeps her nice and full, too."

Ringing filled her ears. Had she heard that right? They'd been feeding Lexie with... Violet's stomach revolted, but now was not the time to give in to such weakness. Lexie clamped her jaw down and Violet screamed again. She would have sworn she could feel her friend's canines against her bone. Trembling in pain, Violet tightened the arm Lexie was biting, pinning the rabid girl against Violet's chest. She thrashed in Violet's hold, but refused to release her arm. Tempting fate, Violet slammed her free hand against Lexie's forehead and then closed her eyes. She tried to imagine herself in her friend's mind. She called on all the good memories she had of the two of them together, but every time she felt like she was getting close, Lexie would thrash and break her concentration or Violet felt like she'd hit a stone wall.

"If this power was supposed to help anyone—it was you, Lexie." Violet told her. "But you've got to let me in!"

"What are you doing?" Hunter asked, rattling the barred door.

"Goddess above," Violet prayed as Lexie snarled like a feral animal. "Please, lend me your power!"

She could see the purple hue even from behind her closed eyes, and Lexie began to settle against her.

"Hey!" Hunter called and a distant clamor of keys met Violet's ears. "Stop that. Whatever you're doing!"

Violet lowered to her knees, taking Lexie with her and the feral girl leaned heavily against her. "Let me in, Lexie," Violet begged as she stretched her mental abilities outward. She met the stone wall again, but instead of slamming against it, she lifted a hand and gently rested it there. "Please."

The last thing she heard was the gate flying open, followed by a loud thud, before the familiar pulling sensation dragged her into Lexie's mind.

Chapter 34

Cas

Cas stared at the *door after Hunter and Jeremy had led Violet away. His wolf* screamed at him to go after them, beating against the mental prison Cas had built, and threatened to never let him live it down if he didn't. It was an old threat, one that Abel had said many times before, and one that Cas knew he would see through. He'd done a good job of it so far... and there was a good chance Lexie would kill Violet. Or Violet would have to defend herself, which could kill Lexie.

Ivy chuckled to herself and walked lazily around Cas, pointing a finger at him. "If she wasn't the main part of this revenge plot for you, I could almost see her as a member of my clan. Although, it would be difficult to get her to turn. She seems like the kind of person who has her head screwed a little too tightly."

"Her head is exactly as it should be," Cas muttered before he could stop himself.

Pain lit up his back sending shockwaves through his body while he stumbled forward a couple of steps. He turned and looked at Ivy with wide eyes.

Her hands were curled into tight fists at her sides, and while he was grateful she hadn't poisoned him, there was a look of murder in her eyes that made him hunker down a little lower. "Don't tell me you have feelings for that little lycan."

"All I meant was that she is a good person," Cas defended, then dared to stand straight and stretch his back. She must have hit the perfect spot to make it hurt that badly. "I can recognize that in someone, you know."

"Yes. I remember," Ivy accused, her nose scrunching as her eyes narrowed.

The tension in Cas' face drained and he shook his head. "No. This is not the same thing."

"Really?" Ivy asked, her brows lifting as she rounded her eyes in mock innocence. "Because I seem to remember you saying similar things to me about my little sister."

Guilt punched Cas in the gut almost as hard as Ivy had hit him. "That was different. I was trying to convince you to let her go. She wasn't one of you, and I wanted to spend my life with her!"

"And how did that turn out?" Ivy yelled. Her knuckles blanched at her sides while her chest heaved with each breath she took. "I let her have a night out, and she never returned."

The cold assessment made Cas' stomach plummet, but not nearly as much as the moisture lining her eyes did. She angrily wiped the tears away and growled. Anger and fear—that's how she led. Showing any other emotion, showing weakness, was a death sentence. Looking around, it was obvious that there was a ripple of unease that rolled through the wolven lining the walls.

Clearing his throat, he dared a step toward her. "Ivy, that wasn't your fault."

Hatred flashed in her sea-green eyes. "Of course, it wasn't! *You* convinced me to let her go and *Patrick* took her life! *You* told me not to kill him. *You* told me we would get revenge. I've been following *your* lead and look where it's gotten me!"

"To the top of the Blood Moon clan?" Cas yelled, casting an arm at the men and women lining the walls. "The leader of the most feared clan? No longer a pack, but a *clan*." He snorted. "Yeah, it's turned out horribly for you."

Ivy jabbed a finger at her own chest and took a step toward him. "I could have gotten here on my own, and then I would have done things my way and had Patrick's head already!"

"You haven't done things your way?" Cas glared at her. "It was not my decision to attack the clans. It was not my decision to raise one. It was not my idea to torture people or use them as lab rats to test poisons! You chained Patrick up and tortured him!"

"Don't pretend that you didn't enjoy that!" Ivy accused. "You said I couldn't kill him so I didn't, but I had to do something! He killed my sister!"

"Layla was my mate!" Cas' voice echoed through the meeting house, but the snap of Ivy's palm connecting with his cheek rang louder.

Breathing heavily, Ivy closed the distance between them. "Don't ever say her name again. The next time you defy me, I don't care what you once were or what you've done for my clan, I will end you." With her crimson eyes gleaming in the dimly lit room, she thrust her chin toward the door. "Get out."

Cas slowly backed away from her and practically walked sideways out the door, never taking his eyes off of the white-haired harpy.

The brisk morning air was a welcome sting against his heated cheek. Unwanted memories flooded his mind as he hurried down the steps and out to the edges of the base.

Layla had been less than a year away from turning eighteen when they'd met. Being fed up with her older sister dominating her life, Layla had snuck out to go to a local party she'd learned about. Cas' birthday celebration. When his gaze fell on her, it was like a truck had hit him. There was no denying that she was his mate, but she was standoffish and careful about not giving too much away about herself or her life. It took months of secret meetings for her to finally reveal that she lived with the Blood Moon pack, and that her older sister was one of the leaders.

"Stop it," Cas hissed at Abel who he could practically see crossing his arms in defiance. *"I don't need to relive these!"*

Instead of answering, another memory flashed before him. Layla had decided to run away, for good, and she wasn't going to tell her sister.

"No," Cas had told her as he wrapped his arms around her shoulders. "She'll never stop hunting you if you do that. Let me meet with her—"

"No!" Layla's beautiful sea-green eyes bugged. "She'll kill you as soon as she sees you."

He smiled. "Worried about me?"

A warm flush passed over Layla's cheeks and she shrugged one shoulder. "Maybe a little."

"What if you introduce me to her?"

Layla shuffled her feet. "I don't know."

Cas tipped his head to the side. "Come on. I can be very convincing."

"Abel!" Cas screamed into the recesses of his mind. *"Enough!"*

"Yes, Cas. It is enough," Abel agreed, pressing firmly against Cas' mental barricade. *"As soon as your revenge plot is over, Ivy will turn on us. Layla wanted to run away with you. Seeing you killed, and at her sister's hand, would have hurt her more than anything. You still have a chance to change this."*

"And do what?" Cas growled, his feet stomping to a halt outside of one of the smaller cabins. "There's nothing left for me. My family is gone. Layla was all I had. I've been chasing this plan for three and a half years. How can I abandon it now?"

"You can. We can. We have to. There are people who need our help."

"No one needs us."

A scream pierced the air, making Cas jump. His eyes rounded on the cabin he stood in front of as the scent of fresh blood filled his lungs, spiced with cedar and rain. "Violet."

"Go!" Abel shouted, but Cas' feet were already moving.

He hadn't realized where he was going in the onslaught of old memories, but he was grateful for whatever led him there. Running around the right side of the building, he skidded to a stop at the sight of Hunter with his head thrown back in hideous laughter. His eyes were pinched shut as if what he had just witnessed was the funniest thing he'd seen in a long time.

Another scream stabbed at Cas' heart and he prayed to the moon goddess that he wasn't too late.

"What are you doing?" Hunter hollered, his hands seizing the barred door and rattling it, unaware of Cas sneaking up behind him.

"Goddess above," Violet's fervent prayer reached Cas' ears and relief chased away his fear even as a feral snarl followed her words. "Please, lend me your power!"

Cas froze when a light purple aura blossomed around Violet and spread down Lexie's body as well. The wolfish girl began to settle, cradled in the warm, calming glow.

"Hey!" Hunter called and wrenched a set of keys from his pocket. "Stop that. Whatever you're doing!"

While Hunter struggled to get the right key in the lock, Violet lowered to her knees and took Lexie with her. "Let me in, Lexie," Violet pleaded and the broken sound ripped at Cas' heart. "Please."

The gate flew open. Hunter had found the right key. He made it one step before Cas' hands seized his shoulders. Abel had used Cas' surprise to press forward and take control. And for the first time in a very long time, Cas sat back and watched his wolf work. Abel may have been trapped on the bench for years, but he still remembered how to fight. It only took a couple of well-placed hits before Hunter dropped to the floor in an unconscious heap.

Abel drew in a few heavy breaths while he struggled to remain in control.

"Violet," Cas heard himself say as his body stepped over Hunter and through the gate. He lowered to his knees in the muck and grime of the cell and Cas pressed forward in his mind, getting ready to steal back control, but when his hand raised toward the purple aura surrounding the two girls, Cas halted his efforts. A tingling sensation passed over his palm when his hand moved closer, and then a loud snap made his ears ring. The pleasant tingling sensation had turned into a well-charged shock.

"What have you done?" Abel asked, but even though Violet's eyes were open, it didn't appear that she had heard him. Neither had Lexie.

A kaleidoscope of opalescent golds, silvers, and coppers churned in Violet's eyes filling every part of them. The purple aura around her pulsed lightly with a rhythm that resembled a heartbeat. Both young women breathed steadily and deeply, but seemingly okay, except for the blood pooling beneath Violet's left arm where Lexie's sharp teeth continued to puncture.

Another kaleidoscope formed, but this one wasn't made up of colors. This one was formed by emotion and centered in Cas' heart. Guilt, worry, shame, anger, protection, and more whirled inside him, bundling his stomach into knots. He did this. Lexie would never be the same because of him. She'd never live a normal life, if she was able to live at all. Violet's mother had been murdered due to a revenge plot he had started. He knew they had both lost friends and clanmates. He had caused so much pain.

"Yes. We have," Abel agreed with him. *"Isn't it enough?"*

"Dude!"

Cas jerked his head to the side, breaking Abel's control, as Jeremy appeared in the doorway. He looked down at Hunter, then blinked at the odd scene in the cell before turning his gaze on Cas. "What's going on?"

"I'll take it from here, Abel." Cas growled at his wolf.

"Can I trust you?" Abel asked, unwilling to relinquish what little control he still had.

"You don't have a choice," Cas snarled, then got to his feet and stalked toward Jeremy. "Hunter was ill-prepared to face off with the two of them."

Jeremy's throat bobbed while he stumbled down one of the steps, his gaze darting between the girls and the incoming threat of Cas. "But what are they doing?"

Shrugging, Cas stomped down the steps after the retreating male. "I don't know."

"Should we tell Ivy?"

Cas' hand shot out like a viper, grabbing Jeremy's throat. He pulled the Blood Moon member closer and snarled in his face. "Ivy has done enough to them. I wanted revenge. I didn't want to start a war."

"I-I—" Jeremy struggled to speak, his eyes bulging in their sockets while he clawed at Cas' hand. "Nee-d... air."

"I'm sorry, does the lack of oxygen to your brain make it hard to think?" Cas asked in an eerily calm tone. He jerked the male, making Jeremy sputter. "I should have listened a long time ago. Layla would be appalled by what I've done. I can't change that, but maybe..." he sighed and briefly closed his eyes. "Maybe I can help the right side win before I die."

A vein raised in Jeremy's forehead and his face took on an odd hue.

Cas let out a huff of humorless laughter, "Too bad you won't live to see it."

Realization dawned on Jeremy, making him go as stiff as stone before Cas wrapped his hands around the guy's head and twisted. He closed his eyes at the snap of bone, then immediately pulled his hands back, letting Jeremy's body fall to the earth.

"Is this real? Or are you just angry?" Abel asked.

Cas sighed while he bent down to grab Jeremy under the arms. *"What are you talking about?"*

"Are we switching sides?"

"That would be awkward," Cas grumbled, hauling the body up the stairs. *"Here I am trying to help the good guys and you're suddenly on board to demolish them?"*

"Caaaas," Abel grumbled back.

A soft rumble of laughter lifted both corners of Cas' mouth when he set the body down inside the visiting area of the small cabin. "Yeah, Abel," he said out loud. "We're done playing revenge."

*"***We** *were never playing revenge.* **You** *were."*

"True," Cas agreed, then kicked Hunter's leg out of the way so he could close the back door and lock it.

"What about Patrick?"

Cas looked at Violet. Three more thick drops of blood fell off her arm while he stared at her. "I don't know," he answered honestly, pressing his back against the wall and letting himself slide down until he was sitting. "But I can't hurt Violet or Lexie anymore."

His wolf voiced his approval and the mental prison he'd built for his wolf spirit started to crumble. For the first time in a long time, he felt like he could breathe again. Tipping his head back, he rested it against the wall and stared at the ceiling. Hopefully, wherever Layla was, she would approve of this new path he was heading down. "I'm sorry it took me so long," he whispered.

"Better late than never," Abel said softly. *"She would be sad to see what's become of her sister, but I know she would have been proud of you for ending this."*

Cas hoped so, too. "Start thinking of escape ideas, Abel," he told his wolf, then looked at the two young women blanketed in purple light. "As soon as they wake up, we're getting out of here."

Chapter 35

Jax

Jax's shoes crunched on *the sandy dirt beneath him as he circled the makeshift* war table he'd set up in the center of the training ruins. He crossed his arms over his chest, and his brow was pulled tight in concentration. A large map showcasing what used to be Stanislaus's territory sat on top of two six-foot folding tables. Someone had taken the liberty of marking where the tunnels were, along with the buildings that had once been there, but this was an older map and no one knew how accurate it was.

Warriors from all three clans had gathered around the table with their representative clan leaders standing beside the table. That is... they were supposed to be. Mammoth's representative, Xavier, had a nasty scowl on his weathered face as he watched Jax circle the table, round and round. They'd been waiting for nearly twenty minutes now because Adeline had not arrived.

"We should start," grumbled Xavier.

"No," Jax quickly replied, coming to a halt at the edge of the joined tables. "I will not begin this war council without all three clans being represented." He uncrossed his arms to press his palms against the table. "By issuing this declaration of war, we are breaking clan law. You've all been made aware of this," he addressed the crowd, then turned back to Xavier, "but I need both you and Adeline to lead your respective clans."

One of Xavier's bushy, graying brows raised. "You're not going to lead all of us?"

Shaking his head, Jax returned to his full height. "No. I don't want to take over your clans, and I don't need to prove that I can. We need to work together. Your clans respect your decisions and are loyal to you just as my clan is loyal to me—" A chorus of whoops and hollers sounded around the circle, making one corner of Jax's mouth kick up in a smirk. "That is enough."

Xavier's mustache, equally bushy to his brows, swished back and forth before he nodded. "Well said, young alpha."

"With that being said," Jax drew in a deep breath before turning to Oscar and Daniel who were fidgeting uncomfortably at the head of their antsy clanmates. "Where is Adeline?"

Silence fell over the group while everyone waited for the men to reply. Oscar's gaze flicked to Daniel. Daniel nodded and Oscar sighed. He cleared his throat and then said, "We aren't sure, Alpha Jaxon."

"You aren't sure?" Jax squared his shoulders with the two men and crossed his arms over his chest once again. "What do you mean you're not sure?"

Oscar glanced at Daniel again, who nodded once more. "None of us have had contact with her since she left breakfast. She gave us orders not to disturb her."

"So, it's normal for her not to show up for meetings?" Jax hadn't gotten that impression from the female warrior, but then again he'd only just met her. What did he know?

Oscar's eyes bugged.

"No," Daniel answered firmly. "This is not normal, sir. I haven't been able to reach her, and even when she asks to not be disturbed, she answers my call." He looked over his shoulder at a few of his clanmates before returning his gaze to Jax. "I am now officially requesting permission to search for her."

Jax held Daniel's gaze while he threw open the links in his mind connecting him to the Sentinel Warriors. *"Does anyone have eyes on the Whisky Clan representative?"*

Rapid reports streamed back to him through each link, while Daniel—and the rest of the wolven present—waited for Jax's response. Unfortunately, all of the warriors delivered the same message; no one knew where she was.

"Has anyone seen her since breakfast?" Jax tried again.

Daniel took a step toward him, calling his name and Jax held up a hand as the new reports came in. Many warriors had seen her at breakfast with Oscar, Daniel, and him. Only a few had seen her leave. Jax's stomach twisted into knots. Why would she need to step away? Had he misjudged her? Was there a second mole within the clan boundaries? His gaze shot to the Whisky warriors, all waiting for him to respond to Daniel's request. Eager to find their leader... but were they too eager? Had he let another enemy in through their front gate with open, welcoming arms?

Jax's chest rose and fell deeply once. Twice. Three times before he opened his mouth to address them.

"Alpha, Teresa here."

Jax snapped his mouth shut, praying to the goddess that Teresa had good news. *"Go ahead."*

"I saw Adeline running along the fence after breakfast. I can head back to that spot and track her if you would like me to."

"Do it," Jax ordered, his eyes narrowing as he thought things through. *"Take a couple of warriors with you as backup."*

"Yes, sir," Teresa acknowledged.

Jax returned his undivided attention to Daniel. "Request denied."

A collective breath sucked the oxygen out of the circle the clans had created. Daniel's brows lowered and his eyes narrowed, but he didn't argue.

Turning his head so he could look around the gathered wolven, he lifted his voice to make sure everyone could hear him. "Before you all start thinking whatever you're thinking, let me set the record straight—We threw a traitor into Lockup this morning. A mole who's been feeding information to the Blood Moon clan." Whispers hissed through the group, but no one spoke up so Jax continued. "This person was once the most loyal in the clan. He was my dad's beta. That, along with everything else we've had to go through in these last couple of months has affected my ability to trust." He threw his hands out to the sides. "I met most of you yesterday. I don't know you, and you don't know me either, or what kind of alpha I'm working toward being." Jax spun in a slow circle so he could look at each person there. "So, let me show you."

Making another swift turn, Jax practically stomped into Daniel's personal space, but other than his shoulders tensing and lowering his gaze, the warrior held his position. "Will you allow me to explain my reasons?"

"You are the alpha, not me."

Jax sighed. "I don't believe an alpha should rule with a *my way or the highway* attitude. An alpha should listen to the members of their clan and peers. I know I'll have to make decisions people don't like, that's part of the job, but it is not how I want to lead."

Daniel slowly lifted his gaze to meet Jax's again.

"I didn't deny your request lightly," Jax explained. "We need to discuss the upcoming fight, and we're running out of time. It would be a waste of time and resources to send the Whisky warriors when mine have already picked up Adeline's trail. In the meantime, I need her second in command to take her place." Jax lifted his brows. "That's you, right?"

Daniel nodded and the tension in his shoulders began to ease. "Yes, sir."

"Then let's get this meeting started." Jax tossed his head in the direction of the table.

The Whisky warrior took a step toward the map, and Jax clapped a hand onto his shoulder in a friendly gesture. "We'll find her."

Daniel met his gaze, "Thank you."

Xavier nodded to both of them and the three leaders stared at the map together.

"We have a hard fight ahead of us." Jax let his voice ring with authority as he spoke. "We are outnumbered, but the longer we wait the bigger and stronger Blood Moon grows. To add to the difficulty, I am requesting that you do everything in your power not to kill the red-eyed wolven you come up against in this fight."

"Are you serious?" Daniel asked while a quiet uproar sounded around them.

Jax waited, hoping the crowd would get it out of their system, but as he waited they grew louder. One quiet figure caught his eye and he turned to stare wide-eyed at Mya. He'd asked her to come, but he wasn't sure she would.

"Quiet!" She suddenly yelled, shocking everyone into silence.

Jax grinned. "Thank you, Mya."

"Why is she even here?" someone yelled.

"You're asking us to fight with one hand tied behind our backs!" called another.

Jax shook his head. "I know this is war! I know people are going to die. I'm not asking you to risk your life anymore than you already are. *If* there is a fight you can end by knocking the person unconscious, please try."

"Why?" someone called.

"To give them a second chance at life," Patrick's deep voice resonated through the crowd as it parted for him. He smirked at Jax, and nodded to Xavier and Daniel. "For those who don't know me; I'm Patrick Cowen; Beta of the Sentinel Clan." He locked eyes with Jax, drew in a deep breath and said, "and son of the Western Territories Lycan King." A few scattered whispers sounded, but Patrick kept going. "I know Alpha Jaxon's plan sounds ridiculous, but we have found a way to reverse the effects of the red eyes and restrictive bands that have been magicked so wolven can't break them."

"That's not possible! Once a red-eye, always a red-eye!"

"It is possible," Patrick assured the crowd. "And I'm the living proof of that persons' abilities." His hazel eyes swirled to moonstone. "The Sentinel Clan Warriors can bare witness that I used to have red-eyes."

Every Sentinel warrior present began nodding their heads and mumbling that they had seen it.

"Where is this person?" called out a Whisky clanmate at the same time a female from Mammoth shouted, "Prove it!"

"No!" Mya's panic riddled voice cut through the squaller, quieting the voices once again. Her smaller frame shoved around two Whisky warriors who had moved forward and blocked her. She stomped a few feet into the center of the circle. "If we proved this gift to you the person who did it would be in grave danger."

Patrick held up his hands. "They will happily announce themselves after Blood Moon is taken care of. For their safety, we are keeping their identity a secret until then."

Xavier's deep, disbelieving voice rumbled over Jax's head, "This is the truth? A person has the ability to reverse the red eyes?"

Patrick nodded. "They helped me, and we've learned it's a new gift from the moon goddess to right a wrong made a long time ago. This person is eager to help whoever they can."

Murmurs of approval and understanding softened the disbelief that had been there moments before.

Clearing his throat, Jax tapped the map covered table. "Now, back to infiltration matters... We don't want this fight to happen here, which means we need to surprise them, and it needs to happen soon."

"Tonight," Patrick amended and Jax jerked his head in the direction of his beta as a collective shock went through group. "It has to happen tonight."

Jax blinked at him. "Patrick, I don't think we will be ready in time to attack tonight."

"Violet is there," his best friend replied. "My mate willingly walked into their territory to rescue one of our own, and they allowed her to. They want her for something. Having been on the receiving end of their hospitality, I will not leave her there any longer than I have to."

"Patrick," Jax hissed, before slipping into mental communication. *"I don't want to leave her there either, but tonight?"*

The tap of knuckles pulled both of their gazes back to the table. Daniel cleared his throat and then loudly said, "Whisky Clan will follow you into battle tonight.

We have everyone here. There's no point waiting."

Xavier was quick to jump forward, jutting his chin forward and puffing his chest out. "Mammoth, too! What we have is what we're getting. Let's end this tonight!"

An uproar of approval shattered the air.

"Okay." Jax looked around the circle and grinned. "Blood Moon won't know what hit them."

Chapter 36

Violet

Entering the mind of *another person was strange. True, Violet had only done* it twice now, but she wasn't sure she would ever get used to it. From icy wind to trudging through a dark sludge; the experiences were completely different, giving her no reference point to go off of.

Violet pressed her way through the inky blackness with her hand outstretched. There had to be something else here. Oily gunk slipped through her fingers, and a disgusted shiver rolled down her spine.

Come on. She thought to herself. She didn't dare open her mouth for fear of swallowing the dark, slick, blob stuff.

Finally, her fingers felt cool, dry air and her body pressed through the last of the inky air a moment before a high-pitched scream pierced her skull, making her flinch.

Violet turned in a circle, trying to figure out where the sound had come from. She didn't see anyone. Just a lot of trees and a couple of buildings in the distance. Had she actually heard it? Had it come from Lexie's mind or whatever was happening around her physical form? It was hard to tell.

What if someone takes me away from Lexie before I'm done here? Violet nibbled on her lip, and she thought through that circumstance. *I need to hurry.*

Without another reference point to go off of, Violet headed toward the buildings in the distance. A pale form took shape a few steps in, slowing her quickened pace. She stepped quickly toward the figure until she could see around the underbrush, then jerked back and threw her hand over her mouth. Half of the guys throat was gone. Even from where she now stood, she could still see his unseeing gaze staring up into the trees.

"What did this?"

Violet jumped when the same ear-splitting scream as before tore through the quiet forest, but this time her feet carried her toward it, gaining speed as she ran. More bodies filled her line of sight. Crimson ran along the forest floor, and she didn't dare look down to see what the puddles she was sprinting through were made of.

"Lexie!" Violet called for her friend, more desperate than ever to find her. "Lexie, where are you!"

Just like it had in Patrick's mind, her voice echoed.

Silence was her answer. That was until a growl lower than anything she had heard before rumbled through the earth, rattling her bones. Goosebumps fled across her body. A large shadow passed through the trees. Violet instinctively followed it, never letting whatever it was get behind her. Then, crimson eyes the size of her fists glowed in the dark. The beast was done circling her. One step. Then another. With the third, the light from nearby buildings illuminated the dark gray fur of the largest timber wolf she'd ever seen.

"Lexie?" Violet hesitantly asked, withdrawing a step as the creature kept stalking toward her. "Is that you?"

The beast spread its jaw and released a saliva-filled snarl, pinning its ears to its head. It dragged a clawed paw through the ground, then bunched up its back like it was getting ready to lunge at her.

How the heck was she supposed to fight this thing? It was even bigger than the lycan wolves she'd seen.

Hunkering low, Violet curled her hands into fists. "I don't want to hurt you, but if that's what it takes to save you, then expect a good beating."

Icy fingers circled her wrist and she barely had time to look at the hand gripping her before she was pulled into a large, prickly bush.

"Ow!" Violet yanked a thorn from her arm.

"What are you thinking, trying to take on that creature?" Lexie hissed at her.

Violet froze, thorn still between her fingers, with her mouth hanging open while she stared at her best friend. Her porcelain skin was dirty, and her white-blonde hair was streaked with all manner of things that Violet did not want the names of. However, there was no mistaking Lexie's face and beautiful, big, blue eyes. Her arms were around her friend's shoulders before she could say another word.

After a strained pause, Lexie awkwardly patted her back. "Kind of a weird time for a hug, but okay. Hi, to you, too."

"Wait," Violet leaned back, holding her friend at arm's length. "You seem totally normal."

"Thanks?" Lexie scrunched her face and then shook her head. "What are you on? Did Jax elbow you in the face again?"

Violet laughed. "No, but..." Her smile faded as she thought about everything she needed to catch Lexie up on. She swallowed the words down and they landed like a rock in her stomach. "Lexie, where are we?"

"What are you talking about?" Lexie scoffed, knocking Violet's hands off her shoulder. "That thing is part of Blood Moon, remember?"

Not knowing how to answer, Violet stayed quiet.

It worked. Lexie snorted and began to fill the silence. "They took over everything. They annihilated the clans. We have to hide or they'll kill us, too."

"Lex," Violet breathed the nickname Jax had given the human girl as she realized how far gone her friend was. "When was the last time you saw me?"

Another snort. "Come on, Violet."

"I need you to answer me," Violet insisted over the ferocious growl that made her ears ring. "What were we doing?"

"I don..." Lexie shook her head, shifting her seat in the dirt so her back leaned against the trunk of a tree. "It was..."

While she struggled to find the words, Violet looked over her friend. There wasn't a single thorn prick along her skin, yet Violet was bleeding from a bunch of small punctures along her arms. Particularly her left one... Violet looked closer at the line of tiny holes, then looked at Lexie's mouth. The dark stains on her chin and down her throat were dried. Dark and red. Even in Lexie's mind, Violet retained an impression of Lexie's bite.

"Lexie," Violet said her name with a bit more hesitation this time and leaned back.

"I don't know, okay?" Lexie fisted her hair and rocked back and forth. "I can't remember. Why can't I remember?"

The earth rumbling growl was back, making both girls freeze.

"It's here," Lexie whispered, her large blue eyes rounding even further. She curled into the smallest ball she could. "There's no escaping it this time. It's too close."

Violet shook her head. "No. It's not real. None of this is real. Lexie, we're in your mind. I think you're having some kind of nightmare." She pointed toward the source of the growling. "That thing isn't real."

"But..." her friend followed the line of Violet's arm, her gaze snagging on the puncture wounds.

Blood had welled in each hole and spilled down Violet's arm.

All emotion drained from Lexie's face and her chin slowly lowered. "I remember."

Knots coiled in Violet's stomach. She lowered her arm, shifting it until it was behind her body, hidden from Lexie's view. "Remember what?"

"Biting you," Lexie answered with a growly tone.

Warning bells sounded in Violet's mind and she rolled onto her toes so she was in a crouched position.

Lexie followed after her. The soft, confused look had been replaced by hard, harsh lines and an icy gaze. She pressed her hands into the earth and stalked after Violet on her knees. "I remember it all. Shopping with you. Waking up chained to the floor. My blood boiling in my veins. Screaming." Her eyes shut momentarily. "Screaming until my throat was raw. Screaming more."

Violet backed out of the thorn bush, ignoring the pull on her skin and through her ponytail.

"The agony of my bones snapping over and *over* and ***over***," Lexie continued, rising from the bush.

The beast was nowhere to be seen, but Violet didn't dare take her eyes off her friend to check.

"The taste of flesh and fur. The *hunt.*" Lexie's teeth snapped together.

Tension filled Violet's body as scarlet consumed her friend's blue eyes.

"Taking the life from one after another."

Violet's heel snagged and she stumbled. Her butt hit the forest floor first, then she threw her feet over her head to roll backward, away from Lexie. She landed in a crouched position and stared as Lexie bent down and ran a hand along the corpse Violet had tripped over.

"They let me loose once, did you know?" Lexie asked, her tone eerily sweet and calm. When she lifted her hand from the body, her fingers came away coated in bright red. "I killed so many of them, but they had a hard time catching me afterward, so they locked me up."

"Lexie, this isn't you." Violet breathed heavily and thanked the moon goddess that her accusation had stopped Lexie from licking the blood off her fingers. "Whatever they did to you, it's not who you are."

Lexie snorted. "Don't you remember? You told me that a human couldn't become a wolven. You were wrong!"

"NO!" Violet shouted back. "I was right! I warned you that in history their minds were never the same. They always had to be put to death because they went crazy."

Silence fell between them.

"Is that what you're here to do?" Lexie finally asked. "You're going to end me?"

Shaking her head, Violet rose to her full height. "I think I can help you."

"With what? You're not much better than I was as a human!"

"A lot has changed since you were kidnapped."

The crimson drained from Lexie's eyes as a large shadow stretched out behind her. It grew until it formed the shape of the giant timber wolf Violet had seen before.

"I'm sorry," her blue-eyed friend sobbed, moisture welling in her eyes as she clasped her hands around her head. "Something's not right. *I'm* not right. Whatever they did... It made me evil."

The ground rumbled beneath Violet's feet as the shadow behind Lexie took form. Grey fur stretched across the large body of the wolf and it's ruby eyes stared at Violet like she was its next meal.

Drawing in a deep breath, Violet stepped toward Lexie. "You're not evil."

The blonde-haired girl nodded violently. "Yes. I am. I've killed so many people. I've eat..." she gagged on the word, then tried again. "I've eaten them."

"That is not your fault. Blood Moon fed them to you to keep you satisfied and lower the number of insane wolven they had on hand. Your only other option was to starve, and the creature they created inside you would never let that happen."

"It's a demon," Lexie cried. Her body trembled, and Violet lurched forward when she looked like she was about to collapse.

Wrapping her hands around her friend's arms, Violet lightly shook her. "Not a demon." She tried to smile, but worried it might have come across as a grimace instead. "It just needs a little training."

She'd been so focused on her friend, that Violet hadn't noticed the wolf slip away until the hot knife of sharp canines snapped down onto her arm. Lexie screamed and smacked at the giant creature's muzzle, but it didn't change anything.

It's not real. Violet reminded herself as the wolf's teeth ground against the bones in her arm. *It can't hurt me if I know it's not real.*

But it is a lot harder to believe something isn't real when you can feel it, and oh boy could she feel it. White hot pain shot through her body, blinding Violet momentarily. Lexie's pale face came into view first, then her frantic pleading reached Violet's ears.

"Please, stop! She's my best friend! Please!"

A roar from deep in Violet's chest bubbled out of her, and she drew her free arm back, curled her fingers into a tight fist, then slammed it into the side of the creature's head.

The giant wolf yelped and jumped back... but so did Lexie. She cradled her jaw then looked at Violet with wide, shocked eyes.

Well, crap. Violet thought as she looked back and forth between the wolf who was shaking it's head and her friend who stumbled over her next words.

"I-is- that *thing* me?"

Sighing, Violet gave one sharp nod. "Looks like it, unfortunately."

Moisture gathered in Lexie's eyes. "How?"

"Long story short. I have special abilities because I'm actually lycan, but my mom had a witch put a spell on me while she was still pregnant with me, so I have some witch abilities too. That spell is broken now..." Violet tilted her head back and forth. "Kind of. And now—"

The wolf righted itself and turned to face her again, ears pinned against it's skull as it curled its lips back and snarled.

"—uh," Violet stuttered, then rushed to finish her thought while the wolf prepared to lunge. "I can enter someone else's mind and can heal broken ones!" The wolf launched at her and she threw herself to the side, rolling along the ground before popping back to her feet. "Any questions?"

Lexie blinked at her. "Only about a thousand!"

"Good. I can answer them after we get out of here," Violet promised, then groaned when she realized what she needed to do. "I'm sorry about this."

When the wolf snapped its jaws at her arm again, Violet threw her fist into the air and then drove her elbow down on top of the wolf's muzzle.

Bone snapped and Lexie screamed. She clamped her hands over her nose while the wolf whimpered and pawed at it's face.

"Anything I do to this thing is going to hurt you." Violet gently pulled Lexie's hands away from her face.

There wasn't any blood and it didn't look like her friend's nose was broken.

"Then again, maybe not."

"What?" Lexie whined. "That hurt!"

"I know, but you're not bleeding. And I felt it's muzzle snap against my elbow. Your nose is as cute as ever!"

"Violet!"

"I'm still new to this okay!" Violet yelled back. "This is so different from when I helped Patrick. I don't know what to do."

Lexie watched Violet with wide eyes. "Wait, how did you help Patrick?"

Shrugging, Violet squared off with the wolf when it recovered and began stalking around her in a tight circle. "Well, he's lycan."

"What?" Lexie shrieked, but Violet kept going.

"I remembered that lycans don't have wolf spirits so it didn't make sense that Alistair was there." The wolf zig-zagged toward her and she slammed her open palm into it's head as she dodged to the side, shoving it away from her. "I helped him realize that they were one in the same and that his soul had been split."

The wolf circled back and launched into the air, it's front paws aiming for her shoulders. Violet snagged it's large paws as she rolled backward and threw her feet up, kicking the creature over her where it landed in a heap at the base of a tree.

A sharp cry left Lexie, but it didn't sound nearly as bad as her nose had. She still clutched her side, but waved Violet off when she reached her. "Is that what's happening to me? Is my soul split?"

Violet shook her head. "No. You're not lycan. You're human."

"So... what?" Lexie cried. "I'm cursed?"

Realization softened Violet's brow and a smile stretched across her face. "Lexie, that's it!" She seized her friend's head and kissed her cheek. "You're a genius!"

Lexie blinked and smacked her hands away. "Why?"

"You're not cursed. You're infected."

"That doesn't sound any better."

"Lexie, you're a werewolf!"

A ferocious growl tore through Violet's happy banter, and she turned to stare into the face of the giant timber wolf that had somehow snuck up behind her. Why hadn't she heard it padding closer or noticed the snap of a twig or rustle of leaves? Oh right. This wasn't real. Violet circled the wolf's muzzle with her hands and held it closed. The creature thrashed it's head in an attempt to free itself, but Violet snagged the scruff along its neck.

"This is a blood curse and Jax can heal that," Violet thought out loud, then pressed a giddy kiss to the wolf's head, making it thrash again. "You, are my department." She looked over her shoulder to find Lexie nervously ringing her hands. "Lexie, you've always wanted to be wolven. I know this isn't exactly what you wanted, but you have two choices here. You can see it as a curse that will torment you for the rest of your life, or you can embrace it and we can go running through the forest together. Your life will never be the same, but you'll never be alone. Jax, Patrick, Mya... we will all be with you every step of the way. We'll figure this out along the way. It's up to you."

Hesitantly, Lexie stepped toward Violet and the furious beast. "So this is what I look like as a wolf?"

Violet shook her head. "I don't think so. They wouldn't have been able to keep you in such a small space if that was the case. I think this is what your fear has turned it into."

Lexie's hands shook when she reached toward the wolf. She jerked back and stared at Violet with wide eyes. "I'm scared."

"I know," Violet softly said. Calming warmth spread through her chest and she thought about extending it out to her fingertips. It spread, seeping into the creature until it closed it's horrendous, fist-sized ruby eyes and released a contented moan. With the wolf settled, Violet held out a hand for Lexie. Lexie took it, and the harsh lines and dark circles around her eyes softened. "You can do this."

A large breath lifted Lexie's chest before she stretched out her arm and spread her fingers through the wolf's matted, wiry gray fur. She stroked along the beast's neck and a couple of inches down it's back before repeating the gesture. With each stroke the fur softened, the tangles loosened and the wiry hair turned luscious.

"That's better," Lexie breathed, her shoulders completely relaxed. When her gaze collided with Violet's again, she smiled. "Okay. I'm ready."

"Great!" Violet said, a little too loudly and the wolf startled.

It's eyes flew open and it gave a sharp bark before shifting it's weight to stand behind Lexie, who chuckled.

"Sorry," Violet muttered. She nibbled her lip then held her hand out for Lexie again. "I'm not sure if we have to be holding hands, but I did with Patrick when everything was all over so I'm repeating that just in case."

"Ha, okay." Lexie slapped her hand into Violet's.

With a nod, Violet closed her eyes and tried to focus on the room her physical form was in... and hoped no one had moved her. A small cabin with a cell inside. Hunter was there and he'd been messing with keys. Her fingers tightened around Lexie's.

"Violet?" her friend asked, her tone wobbling with a note of concern.

Bowing her head, Violet thought about how hard the floor was beneath her knees, the wretched stench of an unwashed body and a horrendous mix of bodily substances, the weight of Lexie in her arms, and the sting of her canines digging into her flesh.

The light behind her eyes intensified, bright and warm before fading once more. The exhaustion settled over Violet before the liquid fire in her arm reached her nerves. Lexie jerked, yanking her head away from Violet's arm and thrashing out of her hold. Trembling, Violet clamped her other hand over the bleeding wound as Lexie scrambled as far away from her as she could. Curled in the farthest corner, one knee pressed against her chest, Lexie stared with rounded eyes.

"Are you okay?" Violet softly asked.

Lexie shook her head, then froze. Her brows pinched together, and she slowly nodded. "Yeah," she croaked. "I think so." She stretched toward Violet, staying low to the ground until she was kneeling in front of her, their knees almost touching. Lexie reached for Violet's arm, but before her fingers could even feather a touch across Violet's exposed skin, someone cleared their throat and both girls snapped their attention to the visiting area.

Cas lounged against the wall with one leg stretched out while the other was bent so he could rest his arm on it. His disheveled rich brown hair made it look like he'd just woken up as he gave a two-fingered salute and said, "Welcome back." His green eyes dropped to Violet's arm. "We should bandage that before you bleed out."

Chapter 37

Jax

***Jax leaned over the** table and placed both palms against the table's sun-warmed* surface. His purple gaze scanned the maps while the other two clan representatives debated about the best way to infiltrate Blood Moon. Another hand appeared in his vision, pointing at one of the tunnels.

Patrick's voice rumbled low, cutting through the chatter. "Stanislaus's territory was once home to a breeder clan." He tapped his finger against the other three tunnels as he continued, "These tunnels were used to quickly cut off any possible runaway. Once that practice was abolished, they turned these tunnels into added safety measures. They all lead somewhere within the main part of the base."

"Are they easy to access?" asked Xavier, his mustache twitching with each word.

"Yes and no," Jax grumbled, returning to his full height so he could cross his arms over his chest. With a heavy sigh, he looked at Patrick. "We were there when Blood Moon invaded. These tunnels weren't enough to save everyone, but a good portion of the clan did make it out alive because Blood Moon didn't know about them. Once they realized where people were disappearing to, it made things a lot harder."

Patrick nodded. "And now they guard these tunnels with poisoned daggers." His hand lowered to his side, holding it as if the memory of his death was hurting him.

The flash of blood and the stench of poison darted across Jax's memory. He drew in a deep breath and drew in the fresh scent of cedar and pine. No blood had tainted the air. His friend was alive.

"Some of you don't know, but I was being held by Blood Moon until a couple of days ago. When I escaped, I made my way through this tunnel." He pointed to the map and dragged his finger along the tunnel line until it reached one of the buildings. "It empties right into a small office that's connected to their meeting house."

"How did you make it out by yourself?" Daniel asked, turning his head toward Patrick.

Jax opened his mouth to intercept the question, but Patrick beat him to it.

"I didn't," he answered bluntly.

One of Daniel's brows shot toward the sky.

"I was chained, beaten, drugged, and poisoned," Patrick explained, his voice was hollow, like he was trying to keep emotion out of the facts. "I knew I was going to die there, but..." he paused to clear his throat. "A fellow lycan, someone that I knew from my old home territory, cut my chains enough for me to be able to break them. He lessened the dosages I was given and then killed the remaining wolven left to watch me. He showed me the tunnel, and it cost him his life."

"What do we do about the poison?" Daniel asked, looking around at his clanmates. "Is there an antidote?"

Jax shrugged. "Yes, but—"

"Leave the poison to me," whispered a chorus of voices in Jax's ears, silencing his words.

A shiver rolled up Jax's spine, and his eyes churned to liquid gold as the smell of sulfur permeated the air.

"Witchcraft!" someone shouted as dark clouds rolled over them.

Lightning struck, loud and bright, leaving deep thundering growls in its wake that shook the ground beneath Jax's feet. Another bolt lit the sky, blinding Jax enough to make him turn his head away from the light. Static electricity hummed through the air, making the tiny hairs on his arm stand on end. The light dissipated, and Jax blinked his eyes open to see a woman standing in the center of a blackened strike on the ground. Her head was tilted back, making her long, silvery-blue hair brush her hips. Her palms were turned toward the sky, exposing old scars in the shapes of stars glistening against her otherwise flawless pale skin. When she lowered her chin, a halo of moonlight glistened off her brow, and her eyes reflected the same silvery-blue as her hair.

As the strange moonlight effect faded from her hair, eyes, and brow, so did the clouds above. When it was done, a very normal-looking, middle-aged woman with white-blonde hair and pale eyes stood before him.

"Laurel," Patrick softly said her name and left Jax's side to greet the woman. "How are you here?"

She looked up at the sky, then down at the scorched earth beneath her feet, and gave Patrick a quizzical look. "Is it that hard to decipher?"

Daniel snorted.

"I was talking about your bonds," Patrick grumbled.

Laurel turned her hands over so her palms faced the sky once again. Patrick grabbed one of her arms, studying it closely while she spoke. "I'm the only witch strong enough to cast the spell. Did you think I wouldn't make sure I could break it if I ever needed to?"

Daniel snorted again.

"Have a problem with me, wolfy?" Laurel asked, then tipped her head to the side and looked around Patrick's shoulder to stare at the Whisky warrior.

"Not just you," he answered blandly. "Witches in general. You're too powerful for your own good."

Laurel's lips bunched together and she nodded. "I agree."

A surprised gasp rippled through the crowd.

"Most of us witches do not adequately control and learn how to harness our abilities."

"And you?" Daniel snarked, crossing his arms over his chest.

A secretive smile passed over Laurel's face. "In case you missed it, I'm the only witch strong enough to cast the spell that bound me to the lycans. That means, I'm the strongest witch in the world. I am the moon goddess's chosen vessel on this earth."

"A little prideful of that, are you?"

Laurel's smile disappeared. "No. This kind of power has come at a great cost."

Clearing his throat, Jax stepped between the two and extended a hand to the witch. "Greetings, I'm Alpha Jaxon."

A wide, brilliant grin tugged at her lips again, but she did not accept his hand. "I know. I would recognize the touch of my magic anywhere."

Jax blinked.

"Besides, you have the same eyes as your sister."

Releasing a breath, he lowered his hand to his side again. "What did you mean about the poison?"

Sighing, Laurel swept across the ground to the map-covered tables. "I will cast a spell that will make your skin as strong as stone. No claw or tooth will penetrate it. No dagger will slice it. No poison will seep into your flesh. But, it is a concentration spell. If my focus is broken, so will the spell be."

"And if we don't want your help?" Daniel growled.

"We want her help," Patrick remarked at the same time Laurel said, "You want my help."

Daniel slammed his hands against the table. "Why?"

"Because Blood Moon has a witch on their side," Patrick answered first, making Laurel slowly close her mouth as she stared. "She's nasty and performs blood magic. The poison the Sentinel clan has faced in the past is nothing compared to what Ivy, the Blood Moon leader, has developed."

Growling softly, Daniel pulled his hands off the table to clench them at his sides. "Fine, but only because I don't want to see my clanmates killed by something they can't even fight against."

Laurel's pale eyes were sad when she said, "I'm sorry for what she did to you."

"Who?"

She tipped her head to the side. "The witch that made you hate us all."

Daniel's jaw clenched, but he remained silent.

"Can't you just do the thing you just did to get us into their base?" Xavier asked, waving his hand toward the black scorch mark.

"Oh, honey." Laurel shook her head, then patted the large man's arm. "No, dear. I'm powerful, but even I'm not strong enough to transport an entire army."

"Alpha, we've had a breach at Lockup!" Tucker's firm voice shouted into Jax's mind, making him flinch.

"We found her!" Teresa cried a moment later. *"Alpha, she's hurt bad. I already reached out to the doc, but I don't think she's going to be able to help."*

"Daniel, we've found Adeline," Jax softly said, interrupting whatever conversation had continued.

Every Whisky warrior turned their attention to him, and Daniel asked, "Where?"

Jax held up a hand while he closed his eyes and reached out to his two clanmates. *"Tucker, explain. Do you need backup?"* He redirected his thoughts to Teresa. *"Where are you?"*

"The ridge, by the trial ring," Teresa answered first.

"No," Tucker replied, his voice angry, but steady. *"It happened quickly. We lost Nathan, but everyone else is healing. I'm pretty sure they used magic. Everything reeks of it."*

Jax's eyes flew open, and he started walking as he shot off orders. "I need a small group of warriors to escort Laurel to Lockup." The witch bristled, but relaxed when he explained, "Welcome to Sentinel base where everything is chaos and attacks happen at random. There was a breach in our holding compound, and my head guard believes magic was used. I need you to check it out. Can you do that?"

With a sharp nod, Laurel said, "Of course, Alpha Jaxon." She sharply turned on her heel and pointed to five warriors. "You're coming with me." The five men and women, a mix of clan warriors, looked at each other and then looked at their respective leaders who all nodded. Mya jumped into the lead, wringing her hands together as she directed the small group toward Lockup.

"We will continue this meeting as soon as we return," Jax announced then pointed to Daniel, Oscar, Patrick, and two Mammoth clan members. "You five will follow me. Xavier, please stay here as possible backup for either group. If help is needed, I'll have your clanmates send you a message."

Xavier tapped his knuckles on the table. "On your order, Alpha."

"Take your wolf forms and get ready to run," Jax told his group, his voice dipping lower as his body prepared to shift and Dalim pressed forward in his mind. "We have some ground to cover and Adeline doesn't have much time."

Daniel's gaze snapped to his, but he said nothing, even as his bones cracked.

Power surged through Jax's veins and Dalim dulled the pain when his skeletal structure snapped and shifted, reconfiguring until he stood on all fours. A full body shake rolled down his spine, and his ears flopped against the top of his head. Lucious fur covered him while he pawed the ground, waiting for the others to finish shifting. The only person who was done before him was Patrick. His transformation was made easier through his lycan abilities, and although he would've stood a couple of inches taller than Jax, he lowered his giant black head in respect.

"Where to?" Patrick's voice filled Jax's mind, and he turned his head to stare into his friend's moonstone eyes. The bright contrast against his black fur was astounding.

"The trial ring," Jax told him as the last of their group finished shifting.

Without the ability to telepathically communicate with all of them, Jax had to rely on other methods. He gave a sharp bark to lead them into a run and the six of them lurched forward. Patrick stayed close to his right while a tawny brown wolf flanked Jax's left—Daniel let out a huff of air and nodded his head when Jax looked in his direction. The other three finished out an arrow formation behind them as they flew across the ground, much like an arrow soaring from its bow. Urgency hurried their paws, and a strong wind met their backs, pushing them onward.

All of them were huffing and puffing when they reached the trial area a few minutes later. The sickeningly sweet, acrid stench of poisoned blood charged the air, ribboned with sulfur that made Jax scrunch his muzzle in distaste. One of the gray wolves behind him sneezed while another growled their displeasure. They all froze when they came upon Adeline, wheezing for air, her head propped in Teresa's lap. One of her hands clenched a stab wound in her side, but her fingers were slick with blood that pooled on the dirt beneath her, soaking the ground with precious fluid.

"Alpha," Dr. Penmann's raspy voice called, making his ears swivel in her direction as she stood from her crouched position beside Adeline. She bowed her head when Jax met her gaze, then said, "I'm sorry. There's nothing I can do."

Daniel snarled his outrage, his ears pinned against his head and his lips curled back away from his teeth. Jax snapped his teeth at him for doing so to the poor doctor who simply blinked in Daniel's direction. The tawny wolf immediately backed off, but quickly made his way behind Jax to Adeline's side where he laid down and whimpered as he nudged her bloody hand.

"I'm sorry," Adeline breathed the words, then sucked in a sharp breath through her teeth when Daniel nosed her hand again. "There isn't anything the doctor can do. The poison is almost at my heart already."

Slowly, Jax padded to her other side, his forehead bunching as he took in her haggard appearance. She had defended him only minutes after meeting him. She'd been the first outside of his own clan to express hope and acceptance of his different tactics. And this was the thanks she got.

Adeline lifted her free hand and it trembled in the air while she pointed to something behind Jax. "They surprised me. Said they were waiting for Paul."

Anger lashed through Jax, making his hackles rise along his spine as he followed the direction of her hand and saw three bodies, barely discernible through the tall weeds. Their smell met him on the breeze and his lips curled back away from his teeth.

Her pained whimper made his anger disappear, and he stared down at the wound in her side.

"Think we can do it again?" Dalim asked even as Jax stretched his neck out to press his head against Adeline's stomach.

"We have to try," Jax told him. Warmth pooled in his chest, and he lowered himself to the ground so he could more easily touch her. *"Hold on Adeline,"* Jax said to himself as he closed his eyes and thought about her wound healing.

He focused on the skin knitting back together and the poison evaporating from her body. A loud groan left him, and he flinched against the pain that lanced through his side. Fresh blood spiced the air.

"Jax, no!" Dr. Penmann shouted. Something thudded on the ground beside him, and then chilled fingers pressed against his side, making him groan again. "You have to stop! She's too far gone, and you need your strength."

There was no stopping. He could fix this. He could heal her. He wouldn't let another person die. Exhaustion settled deep in his bones and Jax felt his body slumping, but he forced himself to focus on the sound of Adeline's heart—the beat was no longer running rampant like a frightened horse, but was slow and steady.

Warmth spread along his other side before a wet nose jabbed him in the shoulder. *"Keep going,"* Patrick's voice swarmed his thoughts. *"I'll keep your strength up."*

"Jax, that's enough!" Dr. Penmann shouted at him. *"You almost killed yourself last time."*

"That won't happen again," he assured her.

"How do you know that? How could you possibly know that?"

The exhaustion he'd been feeling slithered off him, like tar that couldn't stick to its target. His mind cleared, and if he could have smiled, he would've. *"Because Patrick is here."*

Dr. Penmann swore under her breath, and he couldn't stop himself from huffing a laugh.

A small hand rested on his muzzle, and Jax's eyes shot open to see Adeline watching him as the color returned to her face. "Alpha Jaxon, your head is very heavy," she groaned. "Please, get off of me so I can interrogate you on how I'm still alive."

Chapter 38

Violet

Violet launched herself off *the floor to grab Lexie's shoulders. Her forearm* burned as she tugged against her friend just before Lexie slammed into the bars of the cell.

"You!" Lexie shrieked.

"Morning, Lexie," Cas answered calmly. "Nice to see you have your beautiful blue eyes again."

Lexie jabbed a finger through the bars. "Don't talk about how beautiful my eyes are, you traitor!"

Cas sucked some air through his teeth and looked off to the side. "You know, ordinarily I would let you keep ranting and raving, but if you don't quiet down you're going to make someone come in here, and I don't think you want that to happen."

"Why not?"

"Because they don't know you're you again," Violet answered, keeping her voice soft and soothing even as she felt her energy waning.

"You will never feel weak again." Patrick's words flooded back to her.

Closing her eyes, she drew in a deep breath of chocolate mint, and as the memory of his scent filled her lungs, so did a renewed energy—charging her like she'd just woken up from the best sleep of her life. When she opened her eyes again, Cas had leaned forward to stare at her closer.

"What was that?" He asked.

"What was what?" Violet countered, releasing Lexie's shoulders so she could pace the length of the bars.

Cas' eyes narrowed. "Your arm is practically healed, the dark circles under your eyes are gone, and you look like you're ready to run a marathon. What just happened?"

"How much of all that did you see?" Violet asked, gesturing to the pool of blood where she and Lexie had been just moments before. "And where is Hunter?"

With a sigh, Cas gestured to the back door with his chin. "I came in right after Hunter unlocked the gate to stop you from doing whatever you were doing."

Violet turned her head to find the barred door open with Hunter lying halfway inside, breathing heavily. Only a couple of feet closer to Cas was Jeremy... he was not breathing.

"He's fine. He didn't see me so I just knocked him out. I'm betting he's just catching up on a lot of missed sleep at this point." Cas pushed off the floor and stretched his arms above his head, nearly skimming the ceiling with his fingertips. "Sleep doesn't come easy around here, what with always having to watch your back and keep one eye open. Jeremy on the other hand; he came, saw me, saw you—" Cas gave Violet a pointed look. "He would have told Ivy everything. Although, now that I think about it, Hunter will probably remember what you were doing." He took three long strides and seized one of Hunter's feet.

"No!" Violet yelled and snatched Hunter's arm.

Instead of pulling back, Cas dropped Hunter's foot and folded his arms over his chest. "I thought you would want to get out of here without Ivy knowing. You really want to leave behind a witness?"

Violet shook her head. "He won't."

"He will," Cas promised. "She has become their alpha. They are a clan now and have the same mind connection that other clans do. Some of the wolven don't remember we have that now or forget to use it. I'm lucky Jeremy was one of those. Hunter is not. I know he's communicated with Ivy."

"I'll make sure he won't," Violet snapped, still holding Hunter's arm out of fear that Cas would snatch him away. "I knew his younger brother. I won't let you kill him."

Cas stared at her, then looked at Lexie and back again. "What did you do?"

"I don't know what you're talking about."

She jumped when Cas slammed his hand against the bars. "The last time I saw Lexie, which was yesterday, by the way, she was practically frothing at the mouth over the body parts someone had dropped into her cell. She had no humanity left, and now she's standing like a human, talking like a human, and other than needing a bath, she looks human, too. So, I'll ask again, what did you do?"

"You'll just tell Ivy." Violet lowered Hunter's arm and stepped through the barred door to block his body with her own. "I'm not telling you anything."

Cas' arms flew in the air as a frustrated groan left him. "I just told you I killed Jeremy to make sure no one told Ivy anything!"

"It wouldn't be the first time you lied, Caspian!" Violet shouted.

Her accusation hung in the air long after she'd stopped talking. Heavy breaths made Cas' chest rise and fall while she stood in front of him, waiting.

Lexie released a low whistle.

"I'm not lying," Cas answered. His shoulders were so rigid you could have balanced a teapot on them. "I'm not helping Ivy anymore."

"Oh?" Lexie's scratchy voice was a reminder that she'd screamed long enough to damage her vocal cords and it made Violet grimace. "And when did that change?"

Cas' gaze slipped from Lexie to Violet without him moving his head. "When I heard you scream."

Violet lowered her chin and ran her thumb over the freshly healed skin along her left forearm, wiping away blood from bright pink scars.

"I know you have no reason to trust me, but I am trying to help now."

Grinding her teeth, Violet returned her gaze to his. "With any luck, I freed her mind. I'm very new to this ability so only time will tell." She pressed her lips together and then sucked a quick breath through them. "I'd do the same for you, but your type of crazy isn't supernatural."

"I'm not crazy."

"No, just vengeful."

"Patrick was the only person who was supposed to get hurt," Cas defended.

"By killing his mate," Violet seethed. "That makes two people. Not one."

"Fine, but no one else."

"And how'd that turn out, Cas?"

Cas shook his head. He planted his hands on his hips and began to pace while Lexie tentatively stepped over Hunter's sleeping form to stand beside Violet. Two rounds later, Cas stopped with his back facing them.

"The first time I ever saw you, Violet, was at the diner. You had just bought a new laptop."

Not wanting to show her surprise, Violet shrugged. "I've had to replace a lot of laptops."

"And phones," Lexie added, and Violet lightly elbowed her friend.

After clearing her throat, Violet lied, "I don't remember seeing you at a diner."

She knew exactly what time he was talking about. Cas would have been the wolven Patrick had noticed, the guy in the black hoodie sitting across the diner, watching them with his hood up to conceal his face.

"It doesn't matter." Cas waved a dismissive hand. "I had been trying to learn about Patrick and his new clan, to find out if he'd found his mate yet. Lycans can do that before they're eighteen."

"I know," grumbled Violet, even though she hadn't known that before last night.

Lexie lightly smacked Violet's arm. "Seriously?"

Violet shot her friend a look. "I told you, there's a lot I need to catch you up on."

"I had every intention of kidnapping you in that alleyway," Cas announced as he turned to face them again.

Surprise dropped Violet's jaw. "That was you?"

"Can I hit him?" Lexie growled, and Violet gave her a wide-eyed look. "It would hurt more, now."

An amused smirk lifted one corner of Cas' mouth. "If it would make you feel better."

"It might take a few hits," Lexie pounded her fist against her open palm, but when she lifted her foot to move toward Cas, Violet stretched out her hand.

"What do you want, Cas?" Violet asked.

The silence stretched long enough that Violet started to think he wasn't going to answer.

Then, he drew in a deep breath, flexed his hands at his sides, and said, "I think it's time I start honoring my mate's memory." There was no teasing glint in his green eyes. No hint of deception or malice. He held Violet's gaze when he added, "I want to help you stop Blood Moon."

Lexie snorted.

A disbelieving chuckle fell from Violet's lips. "And how do you plan to do that?"

Cas tipped his head to the side and crossed his arms again. "First, I help you two escape, but that would be better to do tonight after dark. That means I need to leave because even though Ivy and I aren't seeing eye to eye, she'll still expect me to be there for her meeting later today. If I don't show up, she will send people to find me. Once the meeting is over I can return with food so you have energy to run. Ivy keeps wolven spread throughout the forest at all times so there's no chance of getting out without being seen, but if we can make it to the border, we should be okay."

"You do know you'll be thrown into Lockup as soon as we enter Sentinel base, right?" Violet asked, mimicking his stance and crossing her arms, as well.

"I know."

Lexie clapped her hands, making both Cas and Violet startle. "Sounds like we have a plan. I can't wait to have a shower."

Cas' nose scrunched. "You need it."

"Watch it," Lexie snarled. "This is your fault, remember?"

A pained grimace passed over Cas' face and he nodded. "I won't forget." His gaze dropped to Hunter. "What about him?"

Violet turned and looked down at the still-sleeping Hunter. "Easy. I'm going to do the same thing I did to Lexie."

"That'll work?" Cas asked. "He's wolven. Not human."

"And Patrick is lycan, but I did it to him," Violet countered, glaring as she turned to look at him again. Her sneer faded when she added, "But I haven't mind-hopped two people so close together before."

Lexie's hand squeezed Violet's shoulder. "I'm back now. I'll protect you."

Offering her friend a soft smile, Violet said, "Thanks, but I'm actually more worried about being too drained to run."

"Then we'll carry you." Cas shrugged. "We're leaving tonight, whether you're tired or not."

Chapter 39

Patrick

***Patrick shifted his weight** back and forth on his paws while he waited to* see if Jax could heal Adeline. When fresh blood sent a wave of copper up his nostrils, Patrick padded to Jax's side. He lowered himself to the ground as Jax's massive wolf form began to slip to the side and pressed his nose against his friend's shoulder. *"Keep going,"* he instructed Jax, drawing on his lycan magic. *"I'll keep your strength up."*

There was a small part of him that hoped he had enough reserves of magic left. He'd felt the pull of it against his mate bond just minutes ago. What if his well of magic was near empty? Drawing in a deep breath, he closed his eyes and focused on his magic. There had to be more. And he was going to find it.

Inky exhaustion stretched over him, exuding from Jax, but it didn't touch him. He felt it wash past like seafoam brushing along a boulder. It kinda tickled, but it was harmless otherwise. He knew that with time and use and repetition, his power would grow, but it'd been years. It felt like a miracle he had any magic left at all, let alone remembered how to use it.

"Alpha Jaxon, your head is very heavy," Adeline groaned. "Please, get off of me so I can interrogate you on how I'm still alive."

Patrick blinked his eyes open while Jax rose to his paws and backed away. He sat on his haunches, and Adeline climbed to her feet before dusting herself off. Her hands came away from her pants smeared with blood and she sighed as she looked at them before curling her fingers into fists that she then planted on her hips. She reminded Patrick of an irritated mother, and when she spoke, he felt that same energy coming from her.

"What in the goddess's name did you do?"

Uncertainty ran through Patrick as he pressed back into a sitting position beside Jax. His friend was in wolf form, he couldn't answer her, and even if he was in human form, what would he say? Patrick looked at Jax and found his friend staring back at him.

"I need you to shift back for me," Jax told him.

With a sharp nod, Patrick imagined he was pulling a giant corded rope around himself. He thought of fingers in place of pads and tanned skin where luscious black fur was. But when it came to his ears, he imagined them tapered and kept his canines a little longer. A pleased smile tugged at the corners of his mouth as his muzzle smoothed out. Heavens he had missed his magic.

"Adeline," he snagged her attention as he adjusted the hem of his shirt.

She stared at him with saucer-sized eyes and then cleared her throat. "I'm sorry. I don't think I've ever witnessed a lycan transform before."

Patrick waved a dismissive hand. "It's fine. I'll speak for Jax right now."

Her gaze turned hard again and she pressed her lips together before responding. "Good. What did he do? How am I not dead?"

Patrick shrugged. "To put it simply, he healed you."

Adeline's dirt and blood-covered forehead creased. "Wolven don't have those kinds of abilities."

"Traditionally, no we do not," Dr. Penmann's raspy voice rang clear, and Patrick looked to his side to see she was examining Jax who tried to nose her away, to no avail.

"What does that mean?" Adeline asked while Daniel's tawny head rested on her shoulder. One of her hands lifted to pat him while she waited.

Sighing, Patrick shoved his hands into his pockets. "We have a witch here that will be able to answer that better than I can. Something about stronger lycan blood ties and being imbued with magic. Basically, Jax has an extra ability, and from what I understand, it will probably carry through his bloodline." He looked at Jax who blinked. "It could be the start of a whole new future for wolven."

Jax curled his lip back away from his teeth and then sneezed to show his dislike of the topic. A sharp yelp suddenly escaped him and he snapped his teeth together before standing and pressing his large body into the doc.

"If you would stop hurting yourself, I wouldn't have to do this," Dr. Penmann grumbled and grabbed Jax's scruff like he was a puppy.

Shaking his head, Patrick returned his attention to Adeline who was watching the tawny wolf.

Tears lined Adeline's eyes when she looked at Patrick again. "Daniel tells me that you know someone who can reverse the effects of the red-eyed wolven. Is this true? Can he do that?"

"No," Patrick answered swiftly.

Adeline closed her eyes and the tears fell down her cheeks. She nodded softly, as if reminding herself that that was normal.

"Jax does not have that ability, but we know who does."

Her gasp wrenched his heart from his chest and her eyes flew open. Tethered hope shone brightly in her gaze.

Patrick softened his stance, relaxing his shoulders. "Who is it?"

A sad smile lifted one corner of her mouth. "My mate."

"Do you know where he is?" Patrick asked.

She nodded. "We have a couple of our clanmates under guard. We didn't know what to do with them, but we couldn't just let them go." More tears glistened against her skin as they fell. "It's been five years."

"Once this fight is over, we'll bring him back for you."

The sob that claimed her usually firm frame, shook the atmosphere around them, charging the air with hope and apprehension. Patrick understood not wanting to hope for something in case it didn't come true. He wanted to assure her they could help, that Violet could bring Adeline's mate back... but he held his tongue while Daniel's tawny wolf form pressed his head against her shoulder.

"Patrick, we have a problem," Jax groaned through the clan-link.

Patrick turned to look at the young alpha as he stood and padded closer to him.

"Paul is gone," Jax said. *"And he took my dad."*

Chapter 40

Cas

Leaving Violet and Lexie *alone with Hunter was a bad idea. Cas clenched his* hands into fists at his side while he slowly trudged back to the meeting house. He told them he would be back. He promised, but he couldn't shake the feeling that something was about to go horribly wrong. A snarl ripped from his throat when one of the more lost wolven tried to approach him, and the beast scurried away with it's tail between it's legs.

"What?!" Ivy's normally lullaby tone shrieked and even from outside, Cas flinched against the sound.

After quickly taking the steps, Cas slammed his hand into the door, making it thud against the wall behind it. Only a couple of eyes turned to him as he entered the room, everyone else was focused on the chaos unfolding before them.

Former Beta Paul of the Sentinel Clan laid cowering on the floor of the meeting house. It took a second longer for Cas to realize he wasn't cowering, but actually curled into a fetal position while he clutched his stomach. Standing over him was Ivy, poisoned dagger in hand, her chest heaving with each breath.

Ivy pointed the dagger at Paul. "You were supposed to wait for us to come get you. You said you had information that would help us overrun the Sentinel base, and you come here with nothing?"

"Not nothing." Paul coughed and the wet sound made Cas scrunch his nose. "I brought you Alpha Draven."

Cas' eyes bugged. He took in the person standing beside Paul. Unkempt hair. Bloodshot, unseeing eyes with heavy bags under them. Drooping shoulders. This was not the alpha Cas remembered.

A snort from Ivy told him that she didn't believe it either. "This guy? An alpha?"

"Former," Paul groaned. "He lost his title when his wife was killed. Now, give me the antidote!"

Ivy crouched down, the dagger dangling from her hand between her knees. "For what? He's useless to me. Look at him."

"He's a good fighter."

"If we can get him to fight for us."

"You can," Paul insisted. "Say one name and he loses all control."

One of Ivy's slim eyebrows arched toward the ceiling. "Go on."

"Give me the antidote," Paul snapped.

Sighing, Ivy rose to her full height and then beckoned to one of the wolven against the far wall. Moments later that same wolven drove a syringe into Paul's chest, making him gasp in pain. Then came a second breath, a more relaxed one.

"Thank you," he breathed.

"It wasn't free, old man," Ivy growled. "Tell me the name!"

Paul smirked. "The one person who started all of this. The one who was killing his wife all along. The one he blames everything on."

Cas fought to keep his face neutral as dread filled him. *Don't say it*, he silently commanded. *Don't say it.*

"His daughter."

Chapter 41

Jax

Jax stood with his *arms crossed over his chest while Xavier paced the length of* the map-covered tables. Thankfully, the damage to Lockup had been minimal, but Jax felt the loss of his clanmate tearing at his heart. He rubbed his chest with the heel of his hand while Adeline repeated the plan they'd decided on so that everyone was on the same page.

"Why are we attacking tonight?" someone asked. "We could use more time to prepare."

A few murmurs of agreement sounded.

"We just witnessed the strength of their witch," Xavier added, narrowing his gaze at Laurel who stuck her tongue out at the older warrior. Xavier's mustache twitched, and he shook his head, turning away, but not before Jax saw the hint of a smile beneath his bushy facial hair. "We don't have time to wait."

"We also have two people trapped inside Blood Moon," Patrick reminded them, sounding annoyed. He stood at the head of the table, arms tightly crossed over his chest, glaring at anyone who might dare question that statement.

It had been a hard day, and night was approaching much faster than they wanted. "There is another problem, too. With the escape from Lockup, we don't know what sort of information Paul is going to give to Blood Moon or what they want with my father. Both of them are former warriors and very well trained fighters." Jax let out a long breath. "I hope none of you have to go up against them tonight."

"And if we do?"

Jax met the eyes of a squirrely looking warrior from Whisky who sank his head into his shoulders. "Pray you have backup."

Adeline cleared her throat and leaned forward in her chair that Doc had positioned at the table. "So, what is the plan? Is everyone going, or are we leaving some behind?"

"We don't have the numbers to leave anyone behind," grumbled Xavier.

Patrick nodded. "He's right."

Jax looked around at their group. These people they had designated to lead small groups into battle. He feared it wouldn't be enough.

"And the attack?" Adeline asked, looking over the map at some of the markings they had already made. "You believe splitting up is the best option?"

"Do you have a better one?" Jax asked earnestly, trying to keep his voice light, but the slight flinch in her shoulders told him he hadn't succeeded. "If this plan works, it should be the most effective." He lifted his gaze to meet each clan representative and their second in commands' eyes. "If any of us fail, we all fail."

People shifted back and forth between their feet, whispering to one another. Some had eyes so wide, it was shocking their eyeballs didn't fall from their sockets. Others looked like they were about to throw up. A few looked like they'd expected that outcome.

"Look," Jax sighed, then planted one hand on the table and swung his legs up. Once he was standing on the map-covered surface, he slowly turned, making sure he could see everyone's eyes. "This is not a light skirmish your clans threw together. This is not the Clan Games where we strengthened our skills. This may not be what you signed on for, and if that's the case, no one will fault you for leaving right now." He held his hand out, palm facing the sky, toward the gates. "Go. Now."

A few warriors glanced at each other bashfully, but no one took a step to leave.

Lowering his hand back to his side, Jax leaned into Dalim's power, relishing in the surety of his wolf spirit. His voice rang with warmth, promise, and strength when he continued. "We are heading into the fight of our lives. These are not wolven who will hesitate to kill you." He shook his head. "No. They *want* to kill you. These wolven are no longer your friends and family. They are creatures of blood and lust and whose only drive is to win this fight and come out on top. But we are more unified than they are. We are three clans working as one!"

A few "Yeahs!" flew into the air.

"We can count the number of times that's happened throughout history on one hand! We defeat the odds every single day, and we will do it again!"

More voices joined the first.

"We are Sentinels. We are Whisky warriors. We are Mammoths! We fight as one! Protectors of our clans and defenders of those who can not defend themselves!" Jax threw a fist into the air, and the entirety of the group joined him. Even Laurel, the witch, who also threw a wink his way. "We will divide and conquer and meet in the middle, and when this is all over, our clans will be better off for it. I hope to see you all in the end, but if I don't, know that I will carry each and every one of you with me for as long as I live. If you die tonight, you will not be forgotten."

The fists had lowered, but pride and honor shone brightly in their gold, silver, and bronze colored eyes.

"May the goddess guide and protect you tonight," Jax finished and was met with the farewell being spoken back to him.

He looked at the horizon, watching the sun in its descent. They would all be heading out in a few minutes to get into position. Each group had warriors from the three clans so that communication would be easily distributed. Jax had tried to turn down the head position, but he was the only alpha there. He knew the territory better than they did. He knew Blood Moon better than they did. At eighteen years old, Jax had turned into the general of a small army. That was something he never thought he would say.

The crowd began to disperse, and Jax stepped off the table. His feet created small dust clouds in the dirt as he landed, and he watched the crowd grow smaller and smaller.

Soon, he would see his sister again and yell at her for being so fearless.

Soon, he would bicker with Lexie again and shout at her for scaring them all.

Soon, everything would be made right again.

Patrick was by his side a moment later, and he looked at his beta whose moonstone eyes reflected the fading rays of sunlight. "Let's bring them home."

Only a couple of hours later, Jax said goodbye to his best friend as Patrick led his own squad to the southern border of Blood Moon's territory. Men and women waited for Jax to give the order to move out and begin their assault. He opened his mind and reached for the members of his clan. Holding on to so many minds stretched out across the area was difficult. Pressure built between his brows and spread across his forehead.

"Is everyone in position?" He asked, and the reports began to trickle in immediately. Some were so quiet he could hardly hear them at all. *"Tucker, is Laurel ready?"*

The head of Lockup had insisted that he come along. He needed to fight and be helpful. Mya had Lockup covered, and fresh sedatives had been given to those occupants who needed it.

"Gearing up right now, Jax—Alpha," the slightly younger wolven quickly added.

Jax shook his head. *"Tucker, don't be weird."*

"Sorry, still not used to the job title. It wasn't that long ago that I thought of punching you in the face multiple times a day."

A wry smile passed over Jax's face. The feeling had been mutual. *"And now?"*

The nervous laugh that passed through his mind said it all. *"I'll pass,"* Tucker said. *"Laurel says to brace yourselves."*

"For what?" Jax asked, then relayed the message to his group before a wave of sulfur assaulted their noses.

A few wolven tried to cover their faces when they sneezed or coughed. Thankfully, Jax wasn't quite as affected and simply scrunched his nose. *"Did she have to announce to everyone that we are here?"*

"She says the spell will follow each of us like a shield and that Blood Moon shouldn't smell it until we are right on top of them."

"Good to know." Jax looked around at his group.

A light shimmer reflected along any exposed skin they had, the only proof that Laurel was indeed shielding them from the poison coming their way. Some of the wolven were still rubbing their eyes or noses, trying to deal with the sulfur smell as best as they could, but most of the warriors had a twitchy appearance about them. Each a trigger waiting to be pulled.

"Final check – everyone ready?" He asked the same question to his own squad, and they all nodded while the same answers came through his mind.

He called on Dalim who flooded his body with power to protect him against the pain while his body broke itself to rearrange into a giant timber wolf. When he was done, he stood on paws the size of dinner plates and shook out his fur covered body. A few of the people he commanded had also shifted and he waited until they watched him with wolf eyes before throwing his muzzle toward the forest and sending one final message to his clan.

"Let's end this."

Chapter 42

Violet

Violet paced the length *of the little cabin over and over and over while Lexie* had settled in a corner. Her friend's glassy eyes were unseeing while she lightly rocked back and forth.

With a last look at the still unconscious Hunter, Violet knelt down in front of Lexie and placed a hand on her knee. "Lexie, are you okay?"

In a flash of movement, Lexie had grabbed Violet's wrist and twisted, but Violet yanked her arm away before her friend could do any real damage.

"Lexie!"

Wide blue eyes stared, then blinked once... twice... before she focused on Violet. Moisture lined her eyes, and a sob left her chest. "It's all coming back. The things I did... the people they fed to m..." she gagged, rolled to the side, and heaved. A small dribble of saliva fell from her mouth, but nothing else emerged, which Violet was grateful for. The last thing they needed was a puddle of unimaginable stench while they waited for Cas to return. She rubbed Lexie's back while her friend's stomach attempted to revolt over and over.

"When was the last time you ate?" Violet softly asked, continuing her soothing strokes down Lexie's spine.

Lexie shook her head, then wiped the back of her hand across her mouth. "I don't know. Everything is mixed up."

"I'm sorry," Violet whispered. "I'm sorry we didn't find you sooner. I'm sorry you had to go through this and that you have to live with it."

Lexie's body trembled as she sank onto her hip. She swatted Violet's hand away before leaning against the wall. "Just get me home and we'll call it even."

"Oh, um..." Violet nibbled on her lip. "Lexie, I'm not sure you'll be able to go—"

"Ugh," a deep, throaty groan filled the small cabin, snatching both of the young women's attention, and they stared as Hunter dragged his arms and legs under himself. "What happened?" His hand lifted to rub the back of his head. He sat back on his heels, then looked around the room and froze when his gaze landed on them.

Time seemed to stand still as the three of them stared at one another.

Everyone moved at once. Hunter lunged toward them, his eyes blazing crimson, while Lexie released a startled scream. She threw herself to the side, crashing to the floor a few feet away. Violet gritted her teeth and charged to intercept Hunter who threw a punch as she neared.

"Stop!" she ordered after deflecting a handful of attacks. "Oof!" pain lit up her side when she missed a punch to the side.

"We're on the same side!" He snarled, throwing a hook toward her head.

Violet looked at him like he'd lost it. "If we're on the same side, then why are you attacking me?"

"I don't care about you! I'm trying to get to that thing. We have to get it back in it's cage!"

Violet ducked under his arm and delivered a jab to his stomach that had him doubling over. "She's not dangerous. She doesn't need a cage."

"Not dangerous?" Spittle flew from his mouth when he spun around to square off with her. "You should have seen what it did to the people we pit up against it!"

"Why don't we starve and torture you and see what you do?" Violet argued, leaning back to avoid his next attack. "Whatever she did was because of you! Besides, if she was so dangerous, then how am I still alive?"

Hunter's fist froze in midair, his expression quizzical, but Violet wasn't going to wait for him to snap out of it. She darted into his space and clamped her hands on either side of his head.

"What the—" He pulled at her hands, then dragged his fingernails down her arms, making Violet clench her teeth. His ruby eyes blazed as he pushed her backward. "Get off me!"

Shaking her head, Violet used all of her strength to hold onto him. She scrunched her brow in concentration, throwing her magic out blindly to try and find her way into his mind.

"You're as crazy as *that thing* is. Get off!" Hunter ordered, but when she didn't comply, he thrust a leg between hers, hooked his toes behind her foot, and pulled at the same time he shoved her shoulders. "Aah!"

A deep grunt left Violet when her back hit the ground, followed shortly by Hunter's large body landing on top of her. The air was punched out of her lungs, and her eyes rounded while she clenched his hair, struggling for air.

Hunter's head shook back and forth as he maneuvered his legs so he was straddling her waist, but Violet tightened her grip even more.

Come on! She screamed at herself, searching desperately for the magic to dive into his mind. If she didn't, it was likely he would kill her.

Hunter's long arms circled around hers, and she worried for a moment that he'd drive his elbows into hers to break her hold. That wasn't what she should have been worried about. His crazed eyes blazed like luminescent blood when his fingers wrapped around her throat and squeezed. Violet opened her mouth, desperate to get even a trickle of oxygen into her lungs, but Hunter's hold was too firm.

Bending her knees, Violet bucked her hips to throw him off balance, but he rose with her, pressing harder on her neck in the process.

"Violet!" Lexie's scream echoed in Violet's mind as she closed her eyes and a cold breeze dragged her under.

The pain across her neck vanished. A certain weightlessness filled her body, but she had the distinct feeling she was falling. Her arms floated away from her and Violet's eyes shot open. Dark water surrounded her as she sank lower and lower.

Her lungs begged for air and she propelled her arms and legs to drive her to the surface. The moment her head broke through, cold wind blasted her in the face. She sucked in a breath of air, but it did nothing to relieve the pressure building in her lungs. Blinking the water from her eyes, she saw a shore not too far off and swam as quickly as she could to it before dragging her water logged body onto the rocky shore.

A breathless cough left her, casting some water from her lungs.

"Where am I?" she groaned, hauling herself to her feet.

A forest towered over her beyond the rocky shore, and she forced her heavy legs to move.

"Leave me alone, Trent!" ordered a young woman's voice.

Violet's head turned in that same direction, and the forest came to meet her. Her breathing quickened as she warped to a stop, her arms outstretched to the side.

"What the heck was that?" she muttered to herself, turning in a quick circle. There was no beach in site, though she had just been precariously balancing on the rocks there, and only the smallest bits of waves crashing against the shore met her ears.

"This is never going to be the same is it?" Violet grumbled to herself and trudged after the young woman she'd seen moments before.

"Come on, Sandy!" laughed the young man who jogged behind her. "You've been teasing me for months. You really think I'd let that go?"

"I haven't been *teasing* you at all! I don't even like you!"

Trent caught up to Sandy and seized her upper arm so tightly, Violet could see her skin and muscle bulge around his grip. "That's not nice."

"Let go of me," Sandy snarled and tried to shake his hand off.

He tugged her so hard she fell against his body. "Don't you want me to show—"

"Who are you?"

Violet nearly jumped out of her skin when an ashen skinned Hunter breathed the question in her ear. His eyes glowed bright red in the dimmer light beneath the forest canopy, and Violet swallowed the knot in her throat as she retreated a couple of steps away from him.

"I'm a friend," Violet lifted her hands in a peaceful gesture.

"A friend doesn't barge into someone's thoughts and memories."

"They do if they're trying to help."

Hunter's head tipped backward as a loud howl of laughter left him.

"Hunter, no!" Sandy's terrified cry killed Hunter's humor, but when Violet tried to look to see what was happening, the ashen skinned man followed her gaze, blocking her from seeing anything.

His lips curled up on one side. "How are you expecting to help me? I rule this mind. Not you."

Violet's shoulders relaxed a fraction, but the ache in her lungs grew and she rubbed the center of her chest. "You're Hunter's wolf spirit."

His chin lowered. "The name's Hearne."

"That's very nice for you." Violet gave him a quick double thumbs up then continued to rub her sternum. "Hearne, I'm running out of time, and I need to speak to Hunter."

"Not gonna happen."

"Hearne!" she snapped, but all that did was make one of his eyebrows raise. "You will let him speak to me, right now."

Hearne turned his head, looking over his shoulder as the scene played on repeat behind him.

"I haven't been *teasing* you at all!" Sandy growled. "I don't even like you!"

Trent caught up to her and seized her upper arm. "That's not nice."

Huffing a laugh, Hearne's arms crossed over his chest. His ruby eyes fell on Violet once again and her shoulders slumped, knowing what he was going to say before he said it. "Not gonna happen. Hunter's a little busy at the moment."

"Then we'll just have to interrupt him, won't we?" Violet snarked and stumbled forward a step.

"Hunter, no!" Sandy's shrill cry echoed through the forest and Violet was suddenly looking up at the tiny break of blue sky through the treetops.

The back of her head throbbed and one of her legs stung. "What the heck?" she groaned and rolled onto her knees to find Hearne staring down at her.

"I told you it wasn't going to happen. Why did you continue?"

Violet struggled to her feet, her head whooshing from the movement. Or was that from the scream of her lungs? How long had she been without oxygen? "I'm here to help," she repeated, her voice sounding wheezy.

A humorless laugh left Hearne. "I just took you down without you even noticing I had moved."

"Yeah," Violet agreed, leaning her shoulder against a nearby tree. "I'm usually better at fighting."

"Too bad I won't get to witness that. It's been a while since someone gave me a fair fight."

"I bet your brother would have."

Hearne blinked. "My brother?"

Violet nodded. "Talon. I met him before he was killed. He seemed like a good guy." She struggled for breath, tipping her head back against the tree trunk. "My mate told me he talked about you. How he wanted to help you."

Pain flashed across Hearne's eyes, but he shook his head. "You're lying! You're just trying to distract me to get to him!"

Snorting, Violet rolled her head to the side and glared at him. "Does it look like I have time to play games?"

Hearne's lips curled away from his teeth. "No. And neither do I."

Violet's eyes bugged when he lunged for her. She let her legs give out, dropping to her butt against the hard forest floor. A cry of pain split the air when Hearne's fist collided with the tree trunk instead of her soft body. He gripped his hand with his other and stomped his foot a couple of times. An impressive string of foul language flew from his mouth, giving Violet time to enact her next move.

Using her low vantage point, she rolled across the ground and scissor-kicked his legs, making his knees buckle. Leaves burst into the air when he landed with a hard thud and a loud grunt. She tried to clamor up his prone body, but he managed to get a leg under her and kicked her ribs. She coughed. At least she thought she did. No sound came out, but her body did the motion.

Hearne was back on his feet. His leg swung back, then drove forward against the side of her stomach. The force of his kick was so strong it lifted her hands and knees a couple of inches away from the dirt before she slammed back down.

"I told you." Hearne growled, crouching over her fetal form while she pulled her knees up closer to her chest. "I'm the master here. Hunter bends to my will, too ashamed of what he's done."

"I've always thought you talked too much," said a similar voice, but this one was warm and level.

Violet's lungs screamed for air, but she couldn't ease their pain. Instead, she let her head drop to the ground and halfway watched as Hunter and Hearne exchanged blows. She blinked. It was a struggle to lift her lids again. Hearne's ashen form had disappeared. One of Hunter's knees crashed into the dirt beside her head.

"Hey, can you hear me? Miss?" Gentle hands rolled her onto her back.

"Hi," Violet breathed the word, wondering if he could hear her at all. "I'm here to help."

Hunter chuckled. "No offense, but you look like the one who needs help right now." A blood-stained hand came into her line of sight. "Let's get you on your feet."

Every limb of hers felt like it had a thirty pound weight strapped to it, but with Hunter's help, she managed to get into a standing position.

"What's going on?" Hunter asked, his eyes free of any red, but little dots of blood splattered his face.

"I think..." Violet clutched her chest. "... you're killing me."

"Nooo, that was Hearne. And he's gone." Hunter's head tipped side to side. "Well, for now at least. I can't ever seem to get rid of him long enough to actually gain any control back." His eyes focused on hers. "Purple eyes..." One of his fingers extended toward her. "I've heard of you. You're that impossible twin, aren't you?"

Violet nodded.

"Talon used to talk about wanting to meet you and your brother!" He grinned and pushed his bloodied fingers through his hair. "Oh, wow, wait till I tell him I met you. And in my mind of all places."

Sorrow dragged Violet's shoulders down and moisture filled her eyes. He didn't know.

"Wait." Hunter's excitement died. "How *are* you in my mind? What's going on, for real?"

"Really," Violet cried, tears sliding down her cheeks. "I think you're killing me, but I'm here to bring you back. I'm here to give you leverage over Hearne. To..." a violent fit of coughs wracked her lungs, and she wheezed deeply, drawing in little air. Her fingers found her throat, and she could almost feel his hands around her neck.

"Then do it," he ordered, taking her hands. "Help me regain control, and I'll stop hurting you. Right?"

Violet nodded, could it really be that simple. Was he already good to go?

"What do we do?"

"Focus," she croaked, closing her eyes. "Feel my skin beneath your hands and imagine them on my throat."

"That's not a very pleasant thought," he grumbled.

"Focus on the wooden floor beneath your knees," Violet directed, grateful that he could understand her through her strained voice. She imagined the hard flooring pressing against the back of her head and along her spine.

"VIOLET!" Lexie's terrified scream rang in her ears, piercing the serene quiet of the forest.

Agony lanced across her throat, and Violet threw her eyes open to see Hunter leaning over her. His nose scrunched in a snarl as he bore his teeth. She released his head and curled her tiny fingers into fists, beating them against the inside of his elbows, but her arms felt like led and she knew her hits were nothing more than pebbles pinging off a brick wall.

Then Hunter's eyes fluttered shut. His shoulders relaxed first, then his hands. Violet struggled for the thinnest breath of oxygen before Hunter scurried off of her, his hands lurching away from her throat like he'd been shocked.

Violet rolled to the side, coughing and wheezing, drawing in as much air as she could. Her head throbbed along with her lungs, which sang with relief inside her chest.

"Holy goddess," large, warm hands gently wrapped around her shoulders. "Can you breathe?"

"Get away from her!" Lexie shrieked and the hands disappeared. Dirty bare feet came into view before Lexie dropped to her knees and pulled Violet's face up. "Violet, talk to me. Patrick will never forgive me if you're not okay." Her eyes rounded. "Neither will Jax, so you have to be okay!"

Grabbing her friend's wrist, Violet held her other free hand out and rasped,

"I'm okay."

"Oh my gosh. Your voice."

Violet shook her head and repeated, "I'm okay." Slowly, she made her way to her feet with Lexie's help before the two girls turned to look at the man standing a few feet away from them.

Hunter's hands dangled helplessly at his sides as he stared at her with ruby red eyes. "I'm sorry," he shook his head. "I promise I'm usually much nicer to meet." He rolled his shoulders and head, then sighed. "Thank you. I can't tell you how great it is to be in control again."

Confusion muddled Violet's thoughts. He spoke like Hunter. Not Hearne, but... "Your eyes..."

Hunter blinked. Then a heavy sigh left him. "Red?"

Violet nodded and took a step toward him, which made one of his brows raise. "I don't understand. I brought you back."

Hunter's gaze narrowed with thought and the crimson color faded away to leave behind the familiar light brown. "What do you mean?"

"Hi," Lexie piped in. "I don't know if you remember me at all, but I was a crazy wolf not too long ago and now I'm sane." She flinched. "Well... not entirely."

A soft smile lifted the corner of Violet's mouth and she found her friend's hand before giving it a light squeeze. "I can only heal the mind and soul, Lexie. The rest we'll work through together."

"Heal the mind?" Hunter repeated.

"I'm sorry," Violet shook her head, then held out a hand to the man. "I'm Violet Draven. Impossible twin to Alpha Jaxon Draven."

"Alpha?" Lexie squeaked. "Who put that puppy in charge?"

Hunter's brows shot toward the roof, and Violet looked at her friend with wide eyes.

"What?" Lexie squeaked again.

"We tend to show more respect for our leaders," Hunter reprimanded, shoving his hands into his pockets.

"Pfft," she laughed and waved a dismissive hand. "I've never been respectful to Jax. Besides, I'm huma..." Her large blue eyes darted to Violet. "I'm not human."

Violet drew in a shaky breath and took a step toward Lexie, but her friend backed up and held out a hand. "Lexie—"

"No. I knew that already... I mean... It's obvious... I just hadn't said it out loud yet. I need a minute." Lexie tightened her arms around her waist and walked away, leaving Hunter and Violet to stare after her.

"Is she okay?" Hunter whispered.

Violet shook her head. "No. But hopefully she will be." She lifted her purple gaze to Hunter. "Look, we don't have a lot of time so here's the short story of everything. Your eyes turned red, you lost control and joined up with Blood Moon. Blood Moon has been attacking and killing a lot of wolven and is led by someone who is after revenge. They..." Violet swallowed the knot in her throat and the groove between Hunter's eyebrows deepened. "They slaughtered Stanislaus."

A sharp breath left Hunter, and he stumbled back a step.

"That's where we are right now. We are in Stanislaus' territory, locked up by Blood Moon. We need to get out of here, but before I trust you with anything—" she held out a hand to him. "I need to know you're not going to turn on us."

Anger flashed across Hunter's gaze, sharpening his facial features.

"You're only the third person I've attempted to help, but you're also the only one who came back with their eyes still being red." She looked at Lexie. "Actually, I don't know if her eyes are still red or not. She's kind of a unique case."

"I'm not going to turn on you," Hunter growled, his voice thick with emotion. "I'm in control. Hearne is cowering in the background whimpering about the awful things he did."

"Then why are your eyes still red?" Violet pleaded, dropping her hand to her side. "My ability is to repair the soul and right the wrong that was done."

The sharp planes of Hunter's face eased. "That's the problem." One of his shoulders raised in a half shrug. "I killed someone who didn't have red eyes. I did it knowingly. I don't regret what I did. If the situation were the same, I'd do it again."

"What?" Violet breathed the word, not sure she was hearing him right or if her brain was still addled from too little oxygen. Probably both. "Why?"

"Do you know what happened to Lizzy?" he asked.

Violet shook her head. "Who's Lizzy?"

"Her full name was Lissandra. She preferred Lizzy. Trent always called her Sandy."

"Leave me alone, Trent!"

"Come on, Sandy!"

The words repeated through her thoughts, and Violet closed her eyes, willing them to leave her mind. If she was going to retain pieces of everyone's memories, she was going to go insane. "No," Violet answered, opening her eyes again to look at him. "I don't."

Sighing, Hunter shifted his weight between his feet. "Lizzy wasn't the first girl Trent had set his hands on. He was bad news, but he was careful so his eyes never changed red. Girls from a range of ages had horrific stories to tell. I loved Lizzy. She would catch herself flirting with me and then pull back. Somehow she always knew we weren't mates, even before we turned eighteen, but it still hurt when I passed my trials and came to that realization myself. It didn't change how I felt though." A harsh huff of air whooshed between his lips. "Trent learned that Lizzy was going to leave to travel from clan to clan in an attempt to find her mate. He decided he couldn't let her leave without leaving his mark on her first. I made sure that didn't happen." Hunter's eyes blazed crimson. "I made sure it would never happen again."

Violet stared at him for a long quiet moment, then whispered, "You're a protector."

Hunter snorted. "I killed someone, princess."

"Yes, but—"

"No," Hunter growled. "I *killed* someone. I have no regrets doing it. I deserve these." He gestured to his ruby eyes before they faded to light brown again. "But I appreciate having my sanity back."

Violet nodded, a weird sort of understanding falling over her. "Hunter, about Talon..."

His face pinched in pain and he turned away. "Knowing my little brother, he did everything he could to help everyone else before Blood Moon took him out."

"That's basically how my mate described it to me," Violet confirmed.

"He was always a better person than me."

Violet stood awkwardly, bumping her fist against her leg while her friend stared blankly in the farthest corner and Hunter quietly worked through the things he'd just learned. She brought her hand to her throat and rubbed the tender area. Her voice was nearly back to normal already, but she had one heck of a sore throat!

"Lizzy hadn't left yet when I lost control. I was with her when that happened," Hunter's voice sounded distant and thoughtful. "Do you think she got away before... all of this?"

Slowly, Violet moved so she could look him in the eye. "I don't know," she answered honestly once he returned her gaze. "But I can help you find out after we get out of here."

Chapter 43

Violet

Violet closed the distance *between her and Lexie in a few long strides, then* softly wrapped her hands around Lexie's arms. "It's time to go."

"Go?" Lexie asked, her voice sounding a bit dreamy like she didn't fully believe what Violet was saying. "Really?"

Nodding, Violet heaved her friend off the floor so she could stand. "Really." She looked down at Lexie's feet and sighed. "I'd offer you my shoes, but you know my shoes are too small for you."

Lexie shook her head. "It won't matter. I'd walk over hot coals to get out of this place."

"Easy," Hunter warned as he came up beside the two young women. "You might rethink that once you start walking." His gaze collided with Violet's. "What's the plan, impossible-one?"

Violet snorted at the nickname, but it pulled a small smile out of Lexie, so she let it slide. "We need to get out of here without being seen, if possible. Patrick told me it wouldn't be long, but I don't know exactly what that means. I understand their reluctance to tell me things since they don't want to risk their plan being found out, but it would be nice to know a little bit more!"

"Then let's get out of here," Hunter growled. "You can meet up with them and scold your mate all you want once we are safe."

Lexie nodded. "I'm with this dude." She thrust her thumb his way. "Let's go."

Drawing in a deep breath, Violet headed for the door. Her hand hesitated on the knob, remembering what Cas had said. He'd promised he would be back.

That he would help. But the light had faded from the window and based on his record... Violet pulled the door open and stared out at a dark forest. Relief and disappointment passed through her. Not that she wanted a fight, but did they always leave this cabin so unguarded?

Distant noises met her ears. "What's that sound?"

When she turned to look at Hunter and Lexie, they were both looking at each other like they thought she was crazy.

"You guys don't hear anything?"

They both shook their heads.

"Are you sure you're ready?" Hunter asked. "I know I was cutting off your air supply for a while."

Violet narrowed her eyes. "I'm not hearing things." She threw her head back and groaned. "Well, I am, but they are real! I'm lycan. My abilities are astounding even to me!"

Hunter's gaze tracked down her body and back again. "You? A lycan?"

"Shut up," she snarked, then slipped a stray hair behind her ear and turned toward the sounds she'd heard. She focused on the closest sounds then snagged on to the next one, clawing her way through each until she was finding the farthest out. Snarls and yips. The clang of something metal. A yelp of pain. Someone shouting about holding rank.

Panic weighed heavily on her chest, making it hard to breathe. *"Jax, are you attacking right now?"*

"YES!" His loud growl resonated in her mind. *"Where are you?"*

"Escaping!" Violet semi-laughed her response.

"Good! Make your way sou—" His voice cut off and his presence disappeared, then reappeared a moment later. *"South!"* He growled. *"Patrick is that direction."*

Violet hurried down the steps with Hunter and Lexie trailing after her, but then froze. *"Wait. Where are you?"*

"Hopefully, by the tunnel that leads to the meeting house. Find Patrick!" He ordered, then hastily added. *"And be safe!"*

Violet looked at her old friend and her new... friend... ish... and waved at them to follow. She took a step, then stopped and sheepishly asked, "Which way is South?"

It was Hunter's turn to snort. "It's a good thing I'm starting to remember my time here because I can actually answer that question." He turned and headed the opposite direction, leaving the two young women to trail after him.

"Wait!" Violet hissed as they caught up. "You remember? Even though you were completely taken over?"

He shook his head as they slipped into the trees. "Bits and pieces are coming back. I bet I'll remember everything eventually. Why?" He looked at Lexie. "Don't you?"

Lexie turned her head away, and her jaw clenched. "My situation is different."

"I'll say," Hunter agreed, then returned his attention to the path in front of them. "What are we heading toward?"

Warmth swelled in Violet's chest. "My mate."

Chapter 44

Jax

The whoosh from a *narrowly missed punch to the face brushed across Jax's* muzzle. They had successfully found the tunnel leading to the meeting house, but someone must have sent word about their sneak attack because ten people had been standing guard and more arrived when they heard the fighting. With his attacker's arm extended Jax opened his mouth wide, turned his head, and chomped down on the exposed flesh.

An agonized scream ripped through the air as bone cracked between Jax's teeth. Tangy copper blood filled his mouth, and he jerked away from the guy who fell to his knees, cradling his mangled arm. He would heal soon.

He released a little yip to get the attention of one of his nearby Sentinel Warriors, then tipped his nose toward the guy. *"Knock him out, then have someone wait for his arm to heal before they bind him,"* Jax ordered.

The warrior gave a sharp, "Yes, alpha!" and followed through on the order.

Trusting his clan mate to handle that, Jax turned and bolted to help a female Whisky warrior who was being herded backward into a tree trunk by two Blood Moon women. He shoved off the ground with his powerful back legs, launching his body into the air, and a startled scream escaped the woman his giant form crashed down on. A flash of metal caught Jax's eye, but he was too late to dodge the knife. Yelping, Jax scrambled away, pinning his ears to the top of his head.

With only one attacker to worry about now, the Whiskey female returned to the offensive and drove the Blood Moon wolf away.

The woman Jax had tackled jumped to her feet, smiling wickedly and brandishing her bloodied knife. "Say goodbye, wolfie."

After a moment, the stabbing pain began to ease, and he knew he was healing. Jax blinked his large molten gold eyes, then curled his lips back away from his teeth and stalked toward her.

"Wha—?" The female backed away, looking back and forth between her knife and him. "You should be dead! This was coated in Ivy's concentrated wolfsbane!"

Jax sneezed his disgust as the Whisky warrior he had helped came to walk beside him.

"You have two choices," the Whisky warrior said, her voice dipping low. "Drop the knife and surrender, or fight and forfeit your life."

The Blood Moon woman's eyes bugged while they darted between Jax's giant wolf form and the female beside him. "I-I..." Her hands shook when she held them out, knife still clutched in her fingers. "I don't want to die."

"Then drop the knife!" snapped the Whisky warrior.

Moonlight flicked off the blade as it fell from the female's hand.

"Turn around," ordered the Whisky warrior.

The female complied. His gaze narrowed while the Whisky warrior stepped up to restrain the female. A tiny click sounded, making Jax's ears twitch. He was moving before she had fully turned around, wielding a switch blade aimed for the warrior's stomach. Terror filled her gaze the moment before Jax's long maw clamped around her head and neck.

Silence rang in his ears. How many had he already killed tonight? Ten? Fifteen? More? They had hoped to save more than they killed, but at this rate... Jax was beginning to wonder if they would even save fifty.

"Don't let the death count distract you," Dalim reminded him, and the soothing presence of his wolf spirit washed over him. *"This is war. People die. But if you get distracted, we could die, and our clan needs us."*

The Whisky warrior patted her chest while she drew in deep breaths. "You saved my life. I didn't see the second knife at all. Thank you."

"And that's another thing. We may not be able to save as many Blood Moon members as we had hoped, but we are saving other lives in the process."

Jax released a long sigh then nodded his head in acknowledgment.

Her eyes glanced at his side. "Want me to take a look at that?"

Knowing it was mostly healed already, he would have normally said no, but the way her hands shook and she shifted her weight between her feet told him that she needed to be helpful. Slowly, he offered his side to her, and her frigid fingers spread his thick, blood crusted fur.

"Wow. You heal fast."

Jax lightly snorted.

"Oh right, you're an alpha," she chuckled, then took a couple of respectful steps back, wiping her red stained hands on her pants. "I guess that witch's spell is working. It doesn't look like any poison is in your system."

"I guess it's a good thing I don't need a poisoned knife to kill you then." The familiar voice made Jax's hackles rise, and he spun around to see Paul standing at the tunnel entrance, clutching the throat of a Mammoth warrior. He threw the man to the side, discarding him like a dirty towel where the man sank to the forest floor and did not move again. "I've waited a long time for this moment, Jax."

A throaty snarl-bark left Jax as he hunkered low, pinning his ears to his skull.

"That's *Alpha Jaxon* to you, pal!" snapped the whisky female.

Paul's head tipped back and he let out a howl of laughter. "Him? He is no alpha. But his father—"

One of Jax's ears twitched, but he kept them pinned.

"—now there was a man who everybody respected. No one dared stand up against him." Paul pointed at Jax. "And then you and your abomination of a sister came along. I've watched my alpha deteriorate for eighteen years! Mourning for someone who hadn't even died yet. *Violet* destroyed his life and he couldn't do anything to stop it." Paul shook his head. "As his beta, it's my job to protect him. Starting with taking out the threat."

The hulking form that emerged from the tunnel was one Jax would recognize anywhere. His jaw loosened, and fear pummeled against his chest as his father unleashed a roar of fury that rang in Jax's ears. Noah Draven's mountainous form lunged for the nearest wolf, not seeming to care what clan the creature belonged to. A loud yelp left the beast when Noah seized it by the scruff and threw it to the ground. Three more wolven in both wolf and human forms launched themselves at the deranged former alpha.

A much closer crack of bone sounded, and Jax spun his attention back to his former mentor just in time to witness Paul's form settle into a wolf. The familiar gray and black fur, marbled with a touch of red, made him hesitate to attack. This man had taught him much of what he knew... but Paul's maw spread wide and spittle flew from his mouth as he snarled. This was not the mentor Jax remembered.

Paul lunged, and Jax barely dodged to the side. Paul's teeth snapped loudly in Jax's ears, making him jump away. Using the extra space he'd made, Jax looked over to see his father pummeling his fists against one of the Mammoth warriors while two others tried to fend him off.

Sensing he'd run out of time, Jax turned his giant head to look at Paul. With lips pulled back to reveal his teeth and gums, Paul's tongue flicked in and out of his mouth. He circled Jax, timing his next attack... while Jax realized something that made his heart hurt. This was no sparring match. Paul was aiming to kill him. When had he caused so much damage to his clan that his former mentor now wanted to end his life?

Hunkering low, Jax resigned himself to the fight. He kept his paws planted when Paul started toward him at a dead run. He waited until it was too late for Paul to change course before shifting his weight. Paul's large form barreled past Jax with an irritated yip, followed closely by a second one that was higher pitched and signaled pain when Jax turned his head and chomped down the older wolf's back leg.

Even with the now bleeding leg, Paul spun in a quick circle and smashed his back end against Jax, throwing him off balance. Paul's glistening teeth descended on Jax's head, but Jax tipped his jaw up and clamped his teeth on the lower part of Paul's muzzle. Gnashing their teeth against one another's heads only ended in them both stepping away pawing at their faces.

Jax blinked his eyes rapidly, trying to clear the blood from his left side. His eye burned! He blinked some more, but his vision was a little blurry.

A sharp, angry howl made Jax pin his ears to his head. Hard, thundering paws rattled the leaves on the ground around him, and Jax turned—dropping low to defend himself.

But the attack never came.

Slowly rising to his full height, Jax stared at Noah Draven who'd captured Paul around the neck with his long arms.

"You will not harm my son," Noah growled, and the low timbre vibrated through Jax's spine. His father's strange ombre blue eyes held his gaze, even while Paul writhed in Noah's hold. Noah's jaw clenched and he spoke through gritted teeth. "You will never do anything to harm Sentinel Clan again."

The muscles in Noah's arm bulged, tightening around Paul's thick neck. A snap sounded, ringing in Jax's ears as he stared wide-eyed at his father. Paul's eyes glazed over. His body fell limp in Noah's arms, and the older man slowly lowered the brown wolf to the forest floor.

"Dad." Jax tried, taking a cautious step toward his father. *"Can you hear me?"*

Noah sighed. "Of course I can hear you, Jaxon. I'm still a Sentinel."

"Are you okay?" Jax asked, padding his way to his dad's side while the rest of the

fights around them came to an end one by one.

"My mate is gone." Noah turned his weathered face toward him. "My daughter was the reason she was dying. My son killed her murderer, so I can't even get revenge. And I just killed my best friend. No. I am not okay."

Jax's chest deflated when he sighed. What was he supposed to say to that?

"Jax," his dad started, then paused as if to think through what he was about to say. "I need you to release me from the clan."

Snapping his gaze to his father's face, Jax stared wide-eyed at Noah. *"What? No."*

"I will kill your sister," Noah said bluntly and Jax flinched. "You've seen what happens when I hear her name. I was only able to snap out of it because *you* were in danger. If I stay in Sentinel Clan and see her every day... I will kill her... and I can't keep wasting clan resources by staying in Lockup. I'm going. The only question is will you let me go, or will I have to break the clan bond myself?"

Jax shook his head. He couldn't imagine his dad, the former alpha of the clan, no longer being there. *"Where will you go?"*

"I don't know." His dad's shoulders dragged low, but when his strange ombre blue eyes met Jax's purple ones, there was a warmth there Jax hadn't seen in years. "I may have been out of my mind and heavily sedated, but not so much that I haven't seen the change in you and the members of Sentinel Clan that passed by my cell. You don't need me. You're already a better alpha than I ever was."

Emotion knotted Jax's throat. He resisted the urge to pad after his dad when he turned and started walking away. The wolven in his path quickly got out of the way, fleeing like puppies with tails between their legs.

And that was when Jax's paws moved, propelled by another worrying thought that crossed his mind. He hurried forward, placing himself directly in Noah's path. *"I can't release you until I'm sure you won't harm some other person named* Violet.*"*

Noah's jaw clenched and his eyes flared muted gold, but he remained still. Fists clenched at his sides. "I have to go," he growled. "I'll find someone to help me. Someone to teach me how to control this rage. I was able to stop. I'm not rampaging now. I don't think I'll harm anyone else."

Jax held his father's gaze for another moment, then relaxed his stance and said, *"I, Alpha Jaxon, release you, Noah Draven, from your duties and your bonds to the Sentinel Clan."*

A breathy grunt left Noah and he clutched his chest where his heart was. If the bond between them was like a thick rope, all but one strand had snapped, leaving them connected as father and son. Nothing more.

After another moment, Noah nodded, then brushed past Jax, patting his shoulder as he left.

Jax's chest swelled when he drew in a deep breath, then he started toward the tunnel. No looking back. His father had made his choice.

"Jax."

His ears swiveled on top of his head and he turned to see Noah gazing at him proudly. "Show these Blood Wolves what a true alpha is."

Warmth welled up inside Jax. His muzzle lowered in a deep, respectful nod while the surviving members of his squad began to surround him. Jax inspected one of them who had blood trailing down his side, but the warrior insisted he was good to go. One by one they disappeared into the tunnel, heading toward the center of Blood Moon's base. A Sentinel Warrior stayed behind with Jax while he shifted back to his human form. Once he'd tugged on the black joggers waiting for him, Jax couldn't stop himself from looking back where his father had been.

Only darkness remained.

Noah Draven was gone.

He may not have been the best father, but in the end, Jax knew Noah was doing what he thought was best for his children.

"Alpha," a warrior close to Jax's age softly called his attention. "They're waiting for you."

Jax looked from his warrior to the group standing just inside the tunnel. Battered, beaten, bloody, but ready to take on the next fight as long as he was ready to lead them. With a last deep breath, he slipped the shirt offered to him over his head and started the trek through the tunnel.

Chapter 45

Patrick

It was hard to *tell where the older blood and the fresh blood ended on Patrick's* hands as he lowered the small body of a female Sentinel warrior to the ground. Worry and anger twisted together inside his gut while he closed her unseeing eyes. Inky black tendrils had spread across her skin in seconds. There hadn't been time to give her an antidote, but even if she'd had one on her person, Patrick wondered if it would've been enough to stop the spread of the poison.

One minute they were fine to keep going after getting stabbed in the arm or leg—the next, they were dropping like flies. Poisoned, black-veined flies.

The witch had said her spell would last as long as she kept her concentration. The poison wouldn't touch them. Something must have happened to their witch.

Their group had gone from being aggressively offensive to debilitatingly defensive. The need for switched tactics was too much for some. And yet, not enough for others.

People had been healing. Someone had even taken a blade to the stomach a few minutes ago and was currently fighting off someone twice their size a few yards away... or had that stabbing happened an hour ago? Time was running together.

The last Blood Moon member fell and three people pounced on him, securing him in the spelled cuffs so he could be dealt with later. A collective sigh deflated the tension in their group once the cuffs were placed, and Patrick lifted his gaze to the rest of his squad. Their numbers were dwindling. Most were leaning on one another to keep each other standing. Blood, dirt, and grime covered each of them nearly from head to toe. They were nearly finished... but Patrick's lycan-enhanced hearing told him that more Blood Moon wolven were coming.

He looked around the small group gathering around him and his twisted gut knotted even further. Without the witch's protection, they wouldn't survive another wave.

Patrick turned away from his people to stare into the darkened forest.

Where was Violet?

Both she and Jax had told him she was headed his way, but he thought they would have found each other by now.

Closing his eyes, Patrick felt for his mate. It took a moment of searching, but there in the distance was the familiar scent of Christmas cookies. He tugged on the link that connected them and knew when she did the same. The line drew taut. She was right there beside him. If he stretched out his hand, he'd touch her... but not really. There was only air in front of him. He breathed in her scent.

"Where are you? Are you okay?" He asked, nearly desperate to hear her voice.

"I'm fine," she grunted, and then her presence disappeared before pulling their line tight again. *"Heavens, they are everywhere!"*

Her annoyed growl drew a small smile across Patrick's lips. *"Any trouble?"*

"No. Well... yes, but not from Blood Moon. They are just an annoyance. Lexie though..."

Dread dragged Patrick's shoulders down.

"She's hard to keep control of."

"Be careful of the poison."

"Don't worry. I have it on pretty good authority that only the wolven on the outskirts have poisoned weapons. The closer you get to their base, the less there will be. Actually—" Her voice cut off on a solid grunt, then returned. *"At this rate, there won't be anyone for you to fight by the time you get here."*

An amused chuckle rumbled through him, along with a solid ribbon of relief. *"Good. I don't think my group can handle much more."*

"They won't need to handle anything more if I have anything to do about it." Violet snarled, her voice turning more animalistic, and a roar tore through their connection.

Patrick released his grasp on their link and opened his eyes. Her roar hadn't just been in his head. It thrummed through the trees, and a few of his people staggered backward.

He lifted a hand. "Hold. It's just my mate."

"That was Violet?" asked a male Sentinel warrior, his voice vibrating with awe.

Patrick's small smile spread into a proud smirk. "She's doing her best to make our path ahead clear." He turned to look at the dwindling group. "Our task is to bring her and Lexie home, but we have to reach them first. I know you're tired. I know you're hurt. I know we have all lost people tonight." He rested a hand on the nearest warrior's shoulder. "But we are not done. If we stop now, we could lose them." Patrick shook his head. "We could lose everything. Blood Moon will regroup and destroy us all. Find it in yourselves to keep going. Dig deep and hold on to the reason you are here." He turned his attention in the direction that the thundering Blood Moon steps were coming from. "Hold on to it tightly because the next wave is nearly here."

The squad spread out, heaving heavily, but looking more fierce than they had before. Resolve clenched their jaws, and determination tightened their stance. A few rolled their shoulders while tipping their heads side to side. When the first Blood Moon member emerged into their line of sight, there was no hesitation. The entire squad fell upon them.

More red-eyed wolven streamed into their area, spreading the group out until they were fighting one on one... and then two on one. And still, more came.

Patrick drove his fist into his first opponent's jaw, dropping him to the forest floor. A second swiped at him and he ducked under the dagger he was sure was poisoned. The male drew his elbow back, then thrust the blade forward to stab Patrick's stomach. Instead of hitting home, Patrick spun to the side and the blade nicked his shirt. With his armed attacker's reach fully extended, Patrick lifted his arm before slamming the point of his elbow down into the fleshy side of his attacker's elbow.

A howl of surprise and pain left the guy, and his weapon fell from his hand to sink into the soft dirt below. Footsteps from behind made Patrick spin to see a third join their fight, but exhaustion had settled into Patrick's limbs, and he was too slow to avoid her attack. She slid over the ground, grabbing the discarded weapon as she did so, then sliced it across Patrick's thigh.

He snarled in pain while her sliding came to a stop two feet away. Tilting his body to the side, he delivered a hard kick to the back of her head and she crumpled into the underbrush, the now bloodied weapon falling from her grasp.

Clutching his thigh with one hand, Patrick only halfway blocked the jabs that followed from his second attacker. With an annoyed grunt, Patrick stepped into the guy's space, planting his foot behind the Blood Moon member's foot, and threw his arm in a wide sweeping motion. The guy's heel caught on Patrick's foot, making it impossible to stop himself from falling backward. Which he did. Hard. The thud that sounded from his body crashing to the ground had Patrick positive his second attacker had gotten the wind knocked out of him, but it didn't matter.

Patrick needed to end the fight. He brought his knee up and stomped down... His second attacker would not be getting up for a second round... ever.

Seething through his teeth, Patrick lowered his gaze to his thigh. Blood had seeped through the slice in his pant leg, but as he stretched the hole to see better a small amount of comfort passed over him. No black veins had begun to spread.

"Patrick!" screamed one of his squad members and he spun just in time to lift his crossed arms in the air as another weapon pressed down on him.

The guy was huge and his strength rivaled Patrick's. A sense of familiarity passed over him. This guy was a lycan. Patrick had wondered how many lycans had joined Blood Moon. This would make five in total so far. Too bad Patrick had been fighting off and on for hours now, and this guy looked like he'd just stepped out of his house to go for a run. Patrick's arms began to tremble against the lycan's, and the male smirked, pressing harder.

"We have to help Patrick!" shouted one of the females on his team.

"Focus on your own fight," ordered a male. "Patrick can handle himself."

"But if we lose him—" her words cut off in a pained scream.

"Miranda!" yelled the male.

Patrick shoved back against his lycan counterpart, driving the man back a step—then another—then another. "You think you have me because I'm tired, don't you?" he quietly said to his attacker.

The man smirked. "All I have to do is wait. You'll tire out before I will."

"That's the thing," Patrick grunted when the man pressed his arms down harder. "I don't have time to wait."

Confusion clouded the man's gaze and Patrick threw himself forward, slamming his forehead into the man's face. He stumbled back in surprise and pain, clutching his nose, the blade forgotten. Patrick threw a long combo of punches against his opponent's exposed torso, then switched tactics when the man managed to pull his hands away from his face to protect his cracking and breaking ribs. Pulling his elbow back and high, Patrick hurled it into the man's face, doubling down on his broken nose.

The moment of chaos between ribs and nose was enough time for Patrick to spin around and snatch the dagger from the ground. One fell swoop of the sharpened blade and the man's eyes went wide.

"Is this a concentrated dose?" Patrick growled, wielding the weapon close the man's face.

Blinking tears from his eyes, the man shook his head. His voice was pinched as he said, "There wasn't enough time to lace all of the weapons with that much poison concentrate."

"Good, then you have time."

"Time?"

"To choose," Patrick explained through heavy breaths. "I have an antidote. Let me cuff you and it's yours."

"What will happen once I'm cuffed?"

"You'll be taken into custody and, once this is over, your soul will be mended."

Ruby-red faded from the lycan's eyes to reveal dark blue eyes. "Mended?"

Patrick blinked, then made his eyes change. The reflection of his moonstone wolf eyes glimmered back at him in the lycan's eyes. "I am Patrick Cowen, once a soul-torn and red-eyed lycan, like you. I know someone who can help you be made whole again too, brother."

The man blinked a few times before holding his upturned wrists out to Patrick. "If there is even a chance I can go home to my mate and kids, I'll take it."

Without wasting another second, Patrick slapped the cuffs on the lycan who then obediently sat in the dirt while Patrick administered the antidote. Patting the man on the shoulder, Patrick returned to his full height and headed toward the next fight.

"I'd help if I could," called the lycan and Patrick turned his head to look at him. "But it's better this way. I don't trust my other half to stay away."

Patrick nodded his understanding then said, "Lycan's don't have wolf spirits. He is the worst parts of you, but also the most vibrant ones. Hold on to the love you have for your mate. It will make it easier."

Without another word from either of them, Patrick ran toward one of his male squad members and threw himself onto the attacker.

Patrick's ears rang with the sound of another group of Blood Moon, and his heart sank. How much more could they take?

That familiar lycan presence wafted over him again, and he looked at the cuffed lycan. Equal parts apprehension and hope filled his gaze as he stared off into the distance.

Patrick returned his attention to his current fight and helped the squad member defeat his opponent.

A giant wolf blurred past Patrick, and he spun on his heel to see the massive beast hurl itself into the oncoming wave of Blood Moon members, followed by three more that towered over their smaller wolven friends.

Two bright green, excited eyes that Patrick would recognize anywhere shone brilliantly against a marbled black and white coat as another wolf trotted up to him.

"I thought I told you to stay home," Patrick scolded even as he threw his arms around his sister's giant fluffy neck. He held on through the sensation of her shifting back into human form, and soon her small arms were crushing his ribs.

"If there's one thing I learned from my big brother, it's that sometimes you have to do what your heart tells you." Rochelle gave a final squeeze, then released him. "That and Dad is wrong. Often."

Patrick snorted and ruffled her mane of loose, dark curls. He looked around as bulky hero types surged through the area, allowing his squad time to stand down and breathe. "You found the Paladins."

Rochelle beamed at him. "I found the Paladins."

"You didn't feel like simply sending them a message, like I asked?" Patrick lifted a brow.

She snorted.

A male about Patrick's same height sauntered up to Rochelle's side and planted a kiss against the side of her head, making both of Patrick's brows shoot toward the sky as a fierce heat of protection rolled through him.

"I wanted to find my friend," Rochelle answered innocently as the guy bounded off into the fight.

"Friend, huh?" Patrick growled.

The back of Rochelle's hand connected with his arm, making it sting. "Knowing I could twist your final request, and sneak off to find them, was the only thing that kept me from following you guys immediately." Her green eyes flicked about and the corners of her mouth pulled down. "Where's Violet?"

Drawing in a deep breath, Patrick turned in the direction of his mate. "We're trying to catch up to her."

Chapter 46

Violet

Violet stared in horror *as her best friend rushed the nearest Blood Moon* wolf. No longer a defenseless human, Lexie pummeled her fists against the enemy and tore her short nails across his face. The red-eyed man howled in outrage and swung his arms at her.

"Lexie!" Violet shrieked and moved to disengage with her own crimson-eyed opponent, but the female cut her off by twisting her body into a solid roundhouse kick. Jumping backward, Violet arched her back and threw her arms into the air, narrowly missing the foot that brushed across the front of her shirt.

She needed to finish this fight before going to Lexie. Thankfully, Lexie wasn't human anymore, and her attacker's arms had swung through empty air when Lexie dropped to the ground to avoid his swipe. Unfortunately, her lowered position put her at a disadvantage for his following kick. She fell to her side on the ground and curled in on herself as the man drove kick after kick against her.

"Here little wolfy," taunted the female facing off with Violet, drawing her full attention yet again. "Don't worry. We'll make sure your pet gets put to good use."

Violet's nose scrunched with her snarl. "She's not a pet. And I'm not as little as I look."

The female scoffed.

Violet's magic surged through her spreading through her chest. She threw one hand out toward Lexie. "Mystic, help Lexie!"

A white-hot flash erupted from her chest, burning from the top of her head to the tips of her toes. Her chest was pulled forward as the wispy she-wolf leapt from within her. Translucent fur made of light blues, purples, and greens waved in a nonexistent breeze as her paws hovered across the ground, zipping toward Lexie.

"What the—!" screamed the female as she flailed backward to get out of the way.

The shrill wail that left the man a moment later was followed by a blinding slash of light.

Satisfied that Lexie would be safe with Mystic to protect her, Violet hunkered down, shifting her weight back and forth between her feet and mimicking her opponent. "Here wolfy, wolfy."

Saucer-sized brown eyes returned to her and the Blood Moon female backed away from her. "What are you?"

A burst of laughter left Violet. "The answer to that is too complicated to get into right now." She shrugged a shoulder. "I'd love to chat about it later though."

The female shook her head. "Pass." With that she spun on her toes and bolted.

"Lame," Violet grumbled, but quickly shrugged off the lost fight and hurried toward Lexie who was still cowering on the ground. "You okay?"

Lexie groaned as she slowly uncurled her body. "I think he broke something."

"Sounded like it," Hunter muttered as he came to meet them, having finished with his own fight. "I'd be careful taking hits. We don't know what you can handle yet."

Lexie nodded and accepted the helping hand he offered. Once on her feet, the trio looked toward Mystic who was slowly padding toward them. The large male Blood Moon member was unconscious in the underbrush a few feet away.

"Will he wake up?" Violet asked the spirit wolf.

A soothing voice filled her mind, but Mystic didn't mouth the words. *"If he wakes, he will never be the same."* Mystic's muzzle scrunched as she growled. *"I tore his spirit apart."*

"Uh..." Hunter eyed Mystic, then Violet, and back again. "What's going on?"

"Oh just one of my many new abilities," Violet sighed. "Mystic, this is Lexie and Hunter. Guys, this is my mom's wolf spirit."

Lexie's eyes bugged while Hunter stared unblinking at the translucent wolf.

"Violet... you're mom's?" Lexie softly asked.

Nodding, Violet held out a hand for Mystic, who came and rubbed her head against Violet's palm. "It's a long story, but I'll explain everything that I can later."

"There are more coming," Hunter muttered, still staring warily at Mystic. "We need to get moving."

Mystic's ears swiveled atop her head at the same time Violet turned toward the sound coming through the nearby bushes. "They're already here."

The three of them hunkered low while Mystic silently snarled, stalking toward the bush.

A head of brown hair appeared, and Cas' voice filled the small clearing. "There you are!" he hissed, and finished climbing out of the bush. "I've been looking everywhere for you, hoping that no one had caught you first. I told you I'd be back. Why didn't you wait?"

"Why didn't we wa— ARGH!" Lexie lashed out with her fingers in the shape of claws, ready to tear his eyes out. "Why would we wait for the person who's done this to all of us?"

"Lexie, shh!" Violet grabbed hold of one of her friend's arms, hauling her to a stop before she could actually claw out Cas' eyes. "We don't want to draw attention."

Cas' brows were furrowed as he stared at Lexie, then his eyes slowly slid off her to Hunter, who had stayed in the same spot, but his hands were curled tightly into fists. "You have a problem with me too, do you?"

"I think everyone in this forest has a problem with you," Hunter grumbled. "The only reason I haven't attacked you yet is because Violet stopped Lexie from doing so."

Lexie thrashed against Violet's hold, but she stayed quieter. "Not if I can wiggle free."

"Stop, both of you," Violet chided and yanked on Lexie's arm. "Cas promised to help us escape. If he's found us there are only two outcomes left."

Cas almost looked bored when his gaze shifted back to her. "And what might those be?"

Violet softened her hold on Lexie, who then seized the moment to tug her arm away. Her friend crossed her freed arm tightly over her body. Violet growled low in her throat and stepped into Cas' space. "Either you're helping us—or we are about to get ambushed."

His jaw flexed and she tipped her head to the side, listening to the thundering footsteps coming their way.

"Based on that sound, I'm guessing the latter."

Surprise rounded Cas' eyes. "What? No, I wasn't followed."

"Violet!" Patrick's deep voice called to her from the distance and Violet spun around, her heart bursting with hope.

Light filled Patrick's eyes as he appeared through the trees, then shadowed a moment later. "Cas, don't!"

Lexie shrieked and reached for her, but froze with her arms extended as the flat of a cold blade pressed against Violet's throat.

"Not another step, Patrick!" Cas yelled.

Violet sucked in a sharp breath before Cas' rough fingers dug into her shoulder, yanking her back against his chest. His arm snaked across her body, holding her tightly while he backed up a few feet, forcing her to follow.

Patrick froze. His eyes lowered to her neck and his chin lowered. Brilliant, gleaming moonstone consumed his eyes while his features turned to stone. He took another step—measured and heavy. "Let her go."

"I could end this, right now." Cas' voice was like a booming thunderclap in Violet's ears, but there was an underlying shaky note. "Kill her and make you suffer the way I've suffered."

Lexie's arms had fallen to her sides and her fingers were clenched into white-knuckled fists. "You said you were helping us."

The blade rolled against Violet's throat and she could feel the whisper of a sting as the sharpened blade brushed against her delicate skin. But even as death teased her, Violet felt a warm sense of calm. Her shoulders eased as she quietly said, "This isn't what Layla would have wanted."

"Shh," Cas hissed, his lips brushing the back of her ear.

Confusion sparked in Patrick's eyes before they rounded ever so slightly. "Layla was your mate?"

"Don't say her name," Cas ordered.

Violet opened her link with Patrick. *"Keep going. He needs to hear this."*

With an almost indecipherable nod, Patrick shifted into a more relaxed stance. "Layla told me about you that night. Really, she told anyone who would listen. She'd met a guy that she was sure was her mate—"

"Stop." The tremble in Cas' command made it almost sound like pleading.

Giant wolves appeared behind Patrick, and Rochelle carefully stalked to his side, looking between the three of them as she judged the situation.

Even with more people surrounding them, Patrick continued as if they were the only three people there. "She was going to run away with him in the morning and never look back. Layla said that many times. She was excited."

The pressure from the blade against Violet's throat eased.

Patrick's moonstone eyes faded back to golden-flecked hazel and his brows pulled together as he continued, "Layla said she was celebrating and drank, a lot. To protect her and her friends, I decided to drive them home, but it was snowing."

"Stop. No more." Cas' arm tightened around Violet, but the dagger didn't come any closer.

Patrick's gaze flicked to hers.

"Keep going," she insisted through their link and offered him a soft smile.

The giant wolves lowered their heads and began to stalk toward her sides. Violet didn't dare move her head, just in case the knife slipped, but she flared her hands at her sides. One of the wolves' ears twitched and its head lifted. The other wolves halted their progression shortly after, but none of them retreated—leaving a clear warning.

"Cas," Patrick's voice was soft, but it claimed the attention of everyone around them. "I was trying to help. I didn't know I was going too fast."

Violet flinched, remembering the screech of car brakes that split the quiet night. She closed her eyes as the crunch of metal filled her thoughts. Two cars tumbled down a snow embankment in her memories, smashing into a line of trees.

"I'm sorry for the pain I caused you, Cas."

Cas shuddered against Violet's back and his arm loosened around her shoulders.

Relief tilted the corners of Violet's mouth toward the sky as she gazed at Patrick. They would be okay.

The moonlight glinted off something white in the trees behind Patrick, and Violet sucked in a sharp breath to shout a warning as Cas lifted his blade-wielding arm. It flew from his hand before she could get out the first word.

Patrick tackled Rochelle who exclaimed loudly when they landed with a thud on the ground, but he was already getting to his feet when Ivy stepped into the shining light of the clearing. Her eyes were as wide as saucers as she stomped toward Cas.

"You almost hit me!" She shouted, brandishing a black-tipped finger at her own chest.

Snorting, Cas' hand shoved against Violet's shoulder and she took a few steadying steps to the side. "I'm sorry I missed," he grumbled.

Ivy's wide eyes narrowed to slits and she spoke through gritted teeth, "What did you just say?"

Cas' head shook back and forth. "Layla would be disappointed in both of us."

"How dare you."

"You know this isn't what she wanted," he reminded her while Violet slowly began to sneak around them.

Lexie's frigid, tight grip latched around Violet's, and she turned to look into her friend's terrified gaze. "Ivy," she whispered.

Ivy snorted, clearly not having heard Lexie or caring who else was around. Her hand raised and she waved it dismissively. "She would have come around."

Pushing against her friend, Violet forced Lexie to move toward the giant wolves, away from the crazy Blood Moon leader.

"No, she wouldn't have. I think somewhere, deep down, you know that, Ivy." Cas argued and kept going even when Ivy's white dreadlocks flew from side to side as she violently shook her head. "She wouldn't want to see you like this, and she wouldn't want me to be helping you."

"You don't know what she would have wanted!" Ivy shrieked.

Cas nodded, one hand disappearing behind his back. "We talked for hours about the things she wanted. She believed everyone deserves a second chance." His hand returned to his side, clutching another knife. "She would have wanted me to stop this, but I'm offering you one more chance in her honor."

A maniacal laugh erupted from Ivy, and her head tilted back, bathing her perfect porcelain skin in moonlight. Her lithe fingers flexed, then circled the hilt of the two knives sheathed at her sides. Black, tar-like goo dripped from their tips as she brandished them toward Cas. "I'm gonna kill you. And then I'm gonna go after your new lover and her boyfriend."

Cas' mouth opened, but whatever he was about to say was lost as one of Ivy's arms jerked in Violet's direction, releasing the knife from her black-tipped fingers.

Chapter 47

Violet

A startled scream fled *from Violet's lips, and she curled her body as best as* she could around Lexie. Her friend had endured enough. If she could save her from any more pain, she would. But the pain never came. After two shaky breaths, Violet lifted her head.

Cas stood a few feet in front of her, arms slightly outstretched to the sides.

A gurgly cough left him before he staggered backward.

"Cas," Violet breathed his name, then hurried forward to brace her palms against his back as Patrick rushed to her side followed closely by Hunter and Rochelle.

Ivy's deranged laugh rang through the hushed silence.

The small hilt of the crazy woman's knife protruded from Cas' chest, rising and falling with each of his labored breaths.

"Guess this is goodbye, Caspian," Ivy purred, twirling her remaining knife in her hand.

But as Cas continued to struggle for air, Ivy's pleased expression faded.

"Why aren't you dead already?" she snapped.

A wet laugh left Cas' lips and then he coughed. Black marbled blood dribbled over his bottom lip. "I guess I have a little luck left after all." He sputtered over his next word, through another hacking sound, then tried again. "I've been taking antitoxin every day since you started developing your potent poison. Looks like it was a good plan." With some effort, he returned to his full height and waved his hands at Violet, who released him and stepped back to Lexie's side. "Goddess bless me as I put an end to this evil reign."

Ivy sneered. "You can try." She dipped low, spreading her arms out, then released a battle cry that rang through the trees as she charged Cas.

Out of the corner of Violet's eye, she saw Hunter move to intercept and help Cas, but Ivy's rally had called to the nearby Blood Moon members. They poured through the trees behind her, following her lead.

Cas met Ivy halfway, their bodies slamming together as he tackled her. They went down to the ground, but Violet's line of sight was cut off when a red-eyed wolf jumped toward her.

A large hand snaked out, seizing the wolf by the throat before Patrick drove the beast spine first into the dirt.

Lexie squeaked beside Violet and dodged a hook from a male with crimson eyes. Using her enhanced speed, Violet darted under his arm and pummeled her tiny fists against his exposed ribs. Bone cracked beneath her knuckles. The man curled in on himself, howling in pain, and quickly retreated.

"Mystic!" Violet called for her mother's wolf spirit which had begun to fade away. Her translucent fur flared a little brighter and her ears perked. "Stay with Lexie."

With a single nod, the little she-wolf plastered herself beside the once-human girl as she raced off to jump onto the back of a female Blood Moon member.

Violet allowed a small smile to lift the corner of her mouth as she watched her friend. Lexie had a lot to learn when it came to fighting, but at least she understood she had a better chance against someone her own size.

The desire to protect and watch over her friend was strong, but with two red-eyed males bearing down on her, there was no time. Violet dropped into a defensive stance and readied herself, recalling all the training Patrick had driven into her mind about being the smaller opponent.

One charged her and she threw herself at his feet. The contact hurt her ribs, but he lost his balance and found himself with a face full of dirt while she bounced back to her toes, narrowly missing a punch from the second guy. She was smaller and faster. Ducking under his attacks was easy, but he'd been trained well to protect himself. He kept her in his sights and did well protecting his ribs.

When the first guy managed to push himself off the ground and onto his knees, Violet spun in a fast circle, whipping her leg through the air to deliver a kick to his head... but he caught her foot. If she hadn't worked so much on this exact hold, she would have been panicking. Instead, she nearly laughed and threw herself into the direction he twisted, using his momentum against him. Her free foot came with the rest of her body, smashing into the side of his face, and they both fell to the ground.

Violet's breath was knocked from her lungs, and she struggled for air. Her fingers clawed at the dirt while someone called her name in the distance. Meaty hands curled into her shirt, hauling her off the ground. A large, refreshing breath loosened her chest as the second guy pulled his elbow back, preparing one of his fists for a punch.

Her nails lengthened into lycan claws, and before he could punch, she drew them down his face.

Crashing into the forest floor again, Violet stared at her bloodied claws while the man howled in pain, staggering away from her.

She was about to push to her feet when the flora beneath her fingers began to shrivel. The forest was dying all around her, turning ashy brown and black.

"Violet!" Cas cried her name, but she couldn't find him in the sea of wolven and lycan. "Run!"

Panic shot through her veins, making her limbs struggle to comply while she made her way to her feet.

"Patrick, get her out of here," Cas ordered.

Large, strong hands wrapped around her upper arm, and Violet looked up to see Hunter dragging her away from the chaos. She turned her head to find Patrick seizing Lexie a few feet away with Mystic on their heels.

"What's going on?" Violet asked, turning back to Hunter.

"Blood Moon has been working with a—"

A vine of black and red light shot past them, narrowly missing, but sulfur singed Violet's nose hairs, and she coughed against the rancid smell.

"Hmm, my aim is off," cooed a black-haired witch as she entered the field. Violet swallowed the knot in her throat that built when she noticed the woman was hovering about an inch off the ground. "It's been a while since I had so many lovely things to play with." She turned both her palms toward the earth and pressed them downward. The ground beneath their feet began to shake, and more plants around them died.

"What are you doing?" Violet cried. "You're killing the forest!"

The woman's eyes latched onto her and Violet felt the color drain from her face. Black, soulless orbs blinked at her from the witch's gaze. "Shall I play with something else then?"

She shot her palm to the side toward a lycan in gray wolf form, and it yelped before writhing in pain. Its gray hairs turned silver and its frame shrank, growing emaciated.

"NO!" Violet cried, yanking against Hunter's hold, but while he did have to take a step from the force of her strength, he did not let her go.

The wolf's head tipped back in a silent howl of pain, its blue eyes turning white.

A blinding silvery-white light blasted against the blood witch's chest, cutting her concentration, and she landed hard on the ground.

"That's enough!" Laurel ordered, her voice booming with the strength of the goddess behind her. A circlet of moonlight crowned her brow, and plants slowly blossomed around her feet.

The wolf the blood witch had been torturing trembled as it climbed to it's paws, having been dropped like a wet rag when the magic had stopped.

"Why hello, sister," the blood witch smiled menacingly while she squared her shoulders with Laurel's slightly hunched form. "I'm surprised to see you still standing."

It was then that Violet noticed an arrow bolt protruding from the friendly witch's side.

"Don't lie," Laurel gripped. "You would have known if I'd died."

The blood witch shrugged her shoulders. "Maybe."

Laurel's body wavered, and she spread her feet to brace herself. "More wolven are coming. Your twin will be here soon."

Violet blinked, realizing Laurel was speaking to her, even though she hadn't taken her eyes off the blood witch.

"Leave. This fight is between my sister and I." Laurel rolled her shoulders back, then lifted her chin. "And it's long overdue."

Unhinged laughter curled the blood witch's shoulders inward. "You think you have the strength to beat me? Look at yourself! You're hardly standing as it is!"

Hunter pulled against Violet's arm, drawing her backward as they made distance between themselves and the two most powerful witches in the world.

Laurel's chest expanded when she drew in a deep breath. Her hands met in front of her chest, the fingertips of one hand facing up while the other facing down. With another breath, she pushed them in their respective directions until her arms were fully extended, then swept them around to create a large circle. Her palms began to glow and grew brighter and brighter by the time they met in the middle again facing the opposite way they had been.

That same glowing light shone brilliantly around her head and when she blinked, her eyes also resembled the color of the moon. "Oh, sister. I've always had the power to stop you. Just not the heart."

The blood witch's face no longer held a note of hilarity. Instead, fuming rage twisted her features until they were as ugly as the bone protruding from her chest. An outraged cry left her, and she thrust her clawed hands at Laurel.

"By my hand, I pray, Goddess put an end to our terror," Laurel's words were soft, but they rang through the forest, drowning her sister's wails. The heels of her palms stayed together when she pressed them toward her sister, bowing her head.

Blinding light consumed the forest.

Violet backed into Hunter, who tightened his hold on her arm, and blinked against the light. It continued to grow brighter until she was forced to turn her face into Hunter's body. Heat blossomed across her body, singeing her skin like she'd been in the sun just a little too long.

The heat faded, and the kiss of a cool evening in the forest eased the sting in her skin. Hesitantly, Violet pulled back from Hunter.

The light was gone.

So were the witches.

Everything was quiet.

Someone groaned in the distance, followed by a grunt of another. Most people had been knocked to the forest floor in the blast, taking the fight out of everyone. Some slowly made their way to their feet looking stunned. A girl with blood-red eyes looked around their group and slowly started backing away before she turned and bolted into the dark.

From the corner of her eye, Violet barely noticed Patrick raise his arm and give a hand signal that made two wolven chase after the girl.

It took Violet a half second longer to realize that no one had remained in their wolf forms. Shoving away from Hunter, Violet raced to where she'd last seen the wolf that had been tortured. Huddled in a tiny ball, was a little old lady shuddering in the cold.

"Oh, no," Violet cried, lowering herself to kneel beside the woman. "I'm so sorry."

The woman shook her head, and her voice trembled. "Don't apologize. This is not your fault."

A large Paladin male walked over, and then knelt beside the lady. He sighed after helping her into a sitting position. "Chirsten, maybe there's a way to reverse this."

Chirsten shook her head, and a few strands of hair fell from her head. "No. I don't want to spend whatever time I have left searching for something that might not even be there." She looked at her age-spotted hands and a sad laugh escaped her. "I had seven beautiful children with the love of my life before he died. I'm about to have my fifth grandbaby. I helped defeat a great evil." She shook her head. "No. I've lived a good life, even if it was cut short. It was better me, than you, Nathanial. Your time is just beginning." With a shaky hand, she lightly patted the young man's cheek. "Just take me home."

Nathanial lifted his watery gaze to Violet. "On your leave."

Violet jerked back in surprise. "My...?"

Nathanial blinked, waiting for her order.

"Of course," Violet shook her head, confused why he'd turned to her. "Go. Take her home."

Without hesitating, Nathanial lifted the frail old woman into his arms.

"Chirsten," Violet called before they disappeared into the forest. "I..." She clenched her jaw, then tried again. "I hope you spend your last days surrounded by your family."

If she hadn't witnessed it, Violet wouldn't have believed that this woman had just been tortured and had her life drained from her body.

Chirsten held her head high while a beautiful smile stretched across her face. Her eyes shone like the brightest stars in the heavens when she bowed her head. "May the goddess bless you, Violet – the miracle twin."

With a final bow, Nathanial turned away to follow Chirsten's final wish.

A warm hand landed softly on Violet's shoulder, and she lifted her chin to find Patrick's golden-flecked hazel eyes gazing lovingly down at her. "Hey, small fry."

The short huff of laughter that escaped her was surprising. She lifted onto her toes at the same time Patrick bent low, and their lips melted against each other's. He kissed her fiercely, then added two softer kisses before pressing his lips against her cheek, temple, and forehead.

"You're okay?" He asked, holding her at arm's length.

She smiled sadly and nodded. "Yeah. I'm okay. You?"

His shoulders relaxed, lowering a couple of inches as he released a large breath that fluttered across her face. "I am now."

"Lexie!" called a familiar voice.

A blur of movement jetted past them, flying straight toward Lexie who froze with her eyes wide. The impact pushed her back a few feet, but somehow she managed to stay standing against Jax's hug attack. His arms swooped around her waist and he lifted her off her feet.

"What are you doing?" Lexie shrieked and smacked his shoulders. "Put me down! I'm perfectly capable of walking on my—"

Violet's eyes bugged, and she gasped when Jax's mouth met Lexie's. Slowly Lexie's eyes fluttered closed, and her arms encircled his shoulders. They embraced each other like they were the very air they needed to breathe.

Violet had no idea how she felt about this development. Did she want to whoop with excitement or vomit in disgust?

Her face had scrunched in revulsion by the time her twin brother and her best friend pulled away from each other.

Jax's arms remained around Lexie's waist as he threw his head back and laughed. "Of course it's you!"

Rage bunched Lexie's face and she punched his shoulder. "Jerk!"

"Ow!" He flinched, his brows pulling together.

"What took you so long?"

"What are you talking about? I had a mate to wait for."

"Turns out I'm your mate! Is that the only reason you're kissing me?" Lexie shrieked, pushing against Jax's hold, but he wouldn't relent.

"No," he snapped, and Lexie froze. "That's the reason I finally *get* to kiss you."

Lexie's bunched face softened. Liquid gold swirled into Jax's eyes as he brushed the tip of his nose against Lexie's, and Violet sucked in a deep breath when molten gold bled into Lexie's eyes, consuming every part until she had two glowing orbs for eyes. That was when Lexie practically melted in Jax's arms, pressing her mouth against his.

Lifting her foot, Violet wrenched her shoe off and chucked it at Jax's back. It was a solid hit, but it only made him laugh. "Are you kidding me? You're grossing me out!"

A bubbly little giggle that she'd never heard come from Lexie before, made Violet pause... and then smile. Definitely gross... but they deserved to be happy and this meant she would have them in her life forever.

"Alpha," a warrior from another clan walked toward them, his face drawn tight. His gaze snagged on Violet, and then he bowed his head respectfully to them both. "I need you to follow me. Someone is asking for both of you—to see you—before they die."

Chapter 48

Violet

They followed the warrior *to the edges of the small clearing and into the trees.* A mound of white dreadlocks peaking from the underbrush made Violet startle, but it was clear from the vacant expression on Ivy's black-veined face that she'd met the end she'd forced on so many others.

Patrick's warm hands lightly squeezed Violet's shoulders before directing her away from their foe's body. There was someone waiting for them. Someone who was still alive.

A small cluster of wolven waited a few yards beyond the trees, surrounding a supine figure lying in a pool of blackened blood.

Violet sucked in a sharp breath as Cas' face came into view. A wet cough shook his shoulders, and his face pinched. One of his hands pressed against his side, but blood had managed to find a way between his fingers. Another wolven had removed his shirt and was pressing it against the wound on Cas' chest... it was nearly soaked through.

"Why did you do it?" Violet asked, her voice nearly a whisper as she sank to her knees beside him. "Why take the hit? You wanted to hurt Patrick. You could have let her kill me."

One of Cas' eyes fluttered open into a tiny slit before he closed it again. "Layla never would have forgiven me."

She shook her head. "She didn't even know me."

"No, but she was a good person. If I hadn't gotten to know you, maybe I could've let you die. Maybe I could have killed you." A splatter of blood coated his mouth when he coughed again. His brows pulled together as he opened his eyes. "But you're a good person, too. They need you. Wolven..." His gaze drifted over her shoulder. "... and lycan."

Violet followed his gaze just in time to see Patrick offer a solemn nod.

Leaves crunched beneath Jax's feet as he joined Violet at Cas' side. With a huff, he shook his head, then lowered to his knees. His fingers curled and flexed over and over, and Violet could practically hear the war going on inside his head. Jax could probably heal him. But should he?

"Patrick," Cas groaned. His eyes squeezed shut and the evidence of pain etched across his face in deep lines. When he settled again, his eyes remained closed, but he said, "I'm not ready to forgive you, but I'll try to—in the next life."

A loud annoyed growl rolled out of Jax, making Violet jump. "Screw that," snapped Jax. His palms crashed against Cas' chest, making the male cry out in pain.

"Jax!" Violet exclaimed, latching onto her twin's arm as light emitted from beneath his hands. "You can't! The last time you did this you almost died!"

Patrick moved from behind her and planted himself behind Jax. As he laid a hand on Jax's shoulder, she opened her mouth to thank her mate, but he'd closed his eyes.

"He'll be fine, short stuff." His warm tone flooded her thoughts. *"You'll always have my strength to aid you, but I can also offer it to others when needed."*

Making a mental note to kick both of their butts at a later time, Violet turned her attention back to Cas. Color had returned to his face, and blood had stopped oozing between his fingers.

Jax groaned and blood blossomed along his side.

"What is he doing?" Lexie asked, her voice frantic as she appeared on Cas' other side. "Violet, make him stop. Whatever he's doing it's hurting him."

"And you better let him hear about it later," Violet assured her friend. "But this is Jax's gift. He takes the pain. He takes the injury. He heals them."

"But—"

Violet reached across Cas' body and grabbed Lexie's hand. "Look." She gestured to Cas, who looked like he was sleeping, then to Jax, who sat back on his heels and let out a heavy breath.

"You can learn to forgive him in *this* life, jerk." Jax's gaze lifted until he was looking at Lexie, and a sudden warmth filled his eyes, tugging his lips into a smile. "Yeah, I'm definitely the reason your ankle wasn't broken."

A few blinks later, and it was Lexie's turn to groan. Her shoulders dropped, and she threw her head back, tilting her face toward the sky. "Really?" she exclaimed loudly. "As if he didn't have a big enough head as it is? You had to give him healing powers?"

Jax's hearty laugh rang through the trees. Violet stared with wide eyes when he launched over Cas' body like he hadn't just brought the guy back from the brink of death. His arms flew around Lexie, who squealed when he spun her in a circle. "You like my big head."

With eyes narrowed to slits, Lexie pushed Jax's chest. "Hmm... You're lucky I do."

Jax planted a quick peck on her cheek, and she slapped his shoulder before crossing her arms. But, Violet knew her friend and saw the hint of a pleased smile spreading across Lexie's face.

Shaking her head, Violet turned to a nearby warrior who was eying the lot of them like they'd gone mad. "Ignore them, they just realized they are mates. I'm still coming to terms with that, but oh well."

"You know you like it," Lexie teased.

"Yes... ma'am?" The warrior made a face.

Violet laughed. "Ew, yeah, that doesn't feel right. Just Violet."

The warrior shook his head. "You deserve a title."

"Then we'll have to think of one, won't we?" she sighed and gestured to Cas. "Does anyone have any spelled cuffs?"

Three warriors lifted the cuffs they already had ready to go.

Violet nodded. "Secure him. We'll be taking him back to Sentinel's Lockup."

While the warriors bound and dragged Cas away, Violet turned in a small circle. The forest was littered with carnage from their fight. A fight they won. Blood Moon no longer had a leader, and the remaining members were scattered. It would take time to clean up Stanislaus' territory, and even more time for a clan to return there, but hope was shining brightly once again.

A faded, translucent wolf caught Violet's eye. Mystic sat patiently beside a distant tree and dipped her muzzle respectfully. Violet broke away from the group, but Patrick seized the tips of her fingers. She looked up into soft hazel eyes and smiled.

"Come with me," she whispered.

"Always," Patrick answered without hesitation.

The two of them made their way to where Mystic waited, and Violet held out her hand to the little she-wolf. "Thank you for watching over Lexie and I. I guess you've always protected me, haven't you?"

Mystic bowed her head. *"And I always will."*

"You don't have to stay," Violet told her, but her voice cracked while moisture filled her eyes. "I'll be okay if you want to find my mom, wherever she is."

A sneeze shook Mystic's head. *"I am bound to you. To go where you go. To help when you need me."* Her soothing, feminine voice was an echo of Violet's mom's, and it brought comfort and grief to Violet's heart. *"I'm happy to watch over our little miracle for Evalyn until the day we are all reunited."*

The sob that sank Violet's chest also brought her to her knees in front of the colorful wolf. "I'm so grateful to have part of my mom with me."

Warmth poured over her when the wolf pressed her paw against Violet's leg. It spread through her body and soothed her aching heart. Closing her eyes, Violet relished in the comfort of such a simple touch. When she opened her eyes again, Mystic was gone.

"Where—?" She looked around, but there was no sign of the spirit wolf.

Patrick's large hand came into view and when she placed her palm in his, he helped her back to her feet. "She sort of... melted back into you."

Violet lifted one of her brows. "Melted?"

Shrugging both shoulders, Patrick added, "Blended? Sank? I don't know how to describe what I just saw. You closed your eyes, and she sort of just walked into you."

An amused huff left Violet, and she wiped the tears from her face. "What a group we make." She looked back at Jax and Lexie who were back to bickering. "A set of twins; one wolven and one lycan with witch abilities. A human turned wolf. And a soul saved lycan."

"Soul saved," Patrick mulled that over, wrapping his arms around her shoulders from behind. "That could work."

Violet leaned into him, but her eyes snagged on another figure. One that stood alone, separated from the rest of the people there. His shoulders were sagged and his head lowered. "Hunter."

She'd said his name softly, but he lifted his head, and sorrowful eyes clashed against hers. Almost moving as one, Jax, Lexie, Patrick, and Violet joined Hunter. He turned his head and looked through a small gap in the trees where one of the Stanislaus homes could be seen.

"I don't know what to do now," he admitted. "My clan is gone. My brother is dead. I have no family. No friends. No where to go."

"Come with us," Patrick answered before Violet could even get her mouth open.

Hunter shook his head. "Thanks, but no. I don't belong in Sentinel." He dragged his gaze off the home and settled it on Patrick as his eyes swirled crimson. "No one wants a former Blood Moon wolf in their midst."

Patrick smirked. "You're talking to the lycan who lived with them for years with a set of ruby eyes of my own."

"Yeah, but yours changed back. I saw them earlier." He looked at Violet. "I'm guessing you helped him, too?"

Violet wove her fingers through Patrick's. "He was the guinea pig. I didn't even know I could help someone that way when I landed in his mind."

Hunter released a low whistle. "I'd love to hear that story sometime."

"Maybe," Violet nodded. "But most of it isn't my story to tell."

"You know," Jax's voice interrupted and they all looked at him. "Stanislaus needs a new alpha."

Hunter's eyes bugged. "No. No way. I'm not alpha material."

"Except you are," Patrick countered. "Talon told us about you. It was brief, but he believed in you. He wanted to find a way to help you."

Tension pulsed in Hunter's jaw, but he stayed silent.

"Honor his memory by doing the same for others."

A deep line appeared between Hunter's dark, thick brows. His head tipped slightly to the side. "How?"

Patrick opened his mouth, but Violet beat him to it. She clamped her hand around his arm in excitement as she spoke first. "A clan for those who have, or are recovering from, a torn soul. A clan for people like you who long for a clan, no matter if they have red eyes or not."

Mulling it over, Hunter's light brown eyes darted back and forth as he stared into the distance. "A place to rest and recover. A safe place. A haven."

"Exactly," Violet breathed the word as her chest filled with warmth. "We could build a facility to hold those waiting to be helped, and Patrick and I could come every week."

Hunter's gaze snapped to hers, then up and over her head. "You would do that?"

"Of course," she exclaimed at the same time Patrick said, "Absolutely."

Hunter's throat bobbed when he swallowed.

"Would you do it?" Jax asked, entering the conversation again. "Would you be willing to lead a clan like that? It wouldn't be easy."

Resolve settled Hunter's shoulders and he rolled them back as he gave a sharp nod. "Yes. But Stanislaus doesn't fit. We would need a new clan name, and the lycans would have to approve this change."

"You need two lycans present for a change to occur," Patrick smirked, and his gaze drifted to Violet. She smiled at him as he continued, "We are already here."

"You've got a lot more than that!" Shouted a familiar voice as Rochelle led a company of Paladins in both human and giant wolf form. She stopped a few feet away, crossing her arms over her chest as a similar smirk lifted one corner of her mouth, mirroring her brother's. "I think between the lot of us, we can convince the lycan council of anything."

Hunter's eyes trailed over everyone present, and Violet felt the emotions rolling off him in waves. Gratitude and awe lit his face when he nodded. "Blood Haven. Let's call it Blood Haven. A place for all to be welcome, to heal, and live in peace. A name that shows the past, but promises the future."

A brilliant smile stretched across Violet's face. "It sounds perfect."

Chapter 49

Patrick

A week later, Patrick *stood in front of the newly constructed Clan House inside* the Sentinel base and watched as family after family checked in before heading back to their homes. Wolven and lycan from across California had been arriving all week to help rebuild the damage done to both Sentinel and Blood Haven, and construction was moving quickly.

With an alpha, beta, the miracle twin, and nearly fifty Paladins all standing before the lycan council just two days before, the name change and plan for Blood Haven had quickly been approved. Hunter was Blood Haven's alpha, but under watch for a year. The council wasn't fully convinced Violet had helped him, and being ashamed of letting Blood Moon gain as much power as they had, they wanted to make sure it wasn't a ploy.

Drawing in a large breath of fresh air, Patrick closed his eyes and listened to the familiar sounds of the clan he loved. This place. These people. This was his home. They'd taken him in when no one else would. They'd accepted him when they'd learned of his tainted past. They'd welcomed him home with open arms just the same when he'd returned healed.

A light tone of laughter, the most beautiful sound he'd ever heard, made his tapered left ear twitch. He opened his eyes, knowing they were glowing moonstone with the love he had for his mate, who was giggling over something Lexie had just done. The once-human girl was beet red and arguing while Violet held her stomach from laughing too hard.

Lexie hadn't returned home yet. She didn't know how to face her parents, but one day, with Jax, Violet, and himself at her side, they would all help her through that reunion.

"It's beautiful," said a warm voice that would forever sound too grown up to Patrick's ears.

He turned to find his little sister beside him, but she wasn't so little anymore. With her weight on one leg, and her arms crossed over her chest, she stared out at the crowd of families with awe.

"It's a mess," he admitted, but a smile tugged at his mouth.

Rochelle grinned. "It's a beautiful mess." After a small shake of her head, she turned her hazel green eyes on him. "So, what now, big brother?"

That smile stretched across his face. "Now, I fulfill my role as Jax's beta and enjoy life with the mate I'd only dreamed of."

"Sounds perfect," Rochelle said blissfully.

"What about you?" Patrick asked.

"I don't know," she admitted, shrugging one shoulder. "I'm not going home. I don't agree with Dad. A lot of lycans don't."

Patrick squared his shoulders with her and gave his best scolding face. "You're not an adult yet, Shelly."

Rolling her eyes, Rochelle chuckled. "No, but I could live here with you."

The male Paladin that Patrick had seen kiss her during the battle with Blood Moon passed by. He gave a flirtatious nod and waved. Pink flushed across Rochelle's cheeks, and she waved back.

"Or I could join the Paladins for a while."

"Oh no you don't," Patrick growled and planted himself between the male and his sister. "You're not running off to join the Paladins until I say you're ready, and not because some guy is shooting googly eyes at you."

A hearty laugh rolled out of his sister, and the tension in Patrick's shoulders eased. “You don’t get to make choices for me, Patty. The Paladins accept anyone who passes their trials as long as they are sixteen." She pointed at herself. "Which I am.”

Patrick's shoulders slumped, and a low growl rumbled through his chest. "You sound like Violet."

"Good," Rochelle gave a sharp nod, grinning from ear to ear. "You need someone to knock some sense into you every once in a while." She sighed lightly. "I want to help the Paladins make sure Blood Moon is gone for good, but—" she held up a hand when Patrick opened his mouth. He snapped it closed and let her finish. "—I will stay and train with you until you think I'm ready."

Relief and a healthy dose of happiness spread through Patrick's chest. He wrapped an arm around her shoulders and kissed the top of his sister's head. "I like this plan."

She laughed. "Of course you do."

"Mya!" Jax's voice rang out over the crowd.

Patrick said goodbye to Rochelle before joining his best friend and alpha on the hill.

"Are you heading to Lockup?" Jax asked Mya who nodded emphatically.

"Yup," she said, twirling a coil of brown hair around one of her fingers. "It's time to start getting everything ready for dinner, and I'm going to go over next week's rotations with Tucker."

Lexie and Violet joined them and Lexie added, "I think it's amazing that you took control of Lockup like you did, Mya. From everything I've learned, it sounds like you're doing an amazing job."

A soft smile lit Mya's face. "Thanks, Lexie."

"How's Cas?" Violet asked, drawing a light glare from Jax.

He'd been reluctant to heal Cas, and even more reluctant to keep him here. Patrick didn't want Cas there either, but agreed with Violet that this was the best place for him—for now.

"Um." Mya's fingers fiddled with her hair a little faster. "He's only said thanks once or twice. He won't look at me, but he's been sleeping a lot, and has really only eaten about one meal a day." Her hands settled. "He ate breakfast this morning. I'm hoping he'll eat dinner, too."

"Sounds good," Jax snapped. Lexie elbowed him in the side, and he bent away from her, rubbing his ribs. "Ow. Sorry," he grumbled. "It does sound good, Mya. You're doing great."

Mya looked like she was trying not to laugh as she eyed Jax and Lexie. "Thanks." She gave a little wave as she headed away. "See you later!"

Lexie seized Jax's elbow and hauled him off. "You need to be nice."

"You're the one who elbowed me!" Jax argued.

Chuckling, Patrick wrapped his arms around his mate's tiny shoulders. "They're an odd couple."

A burst of laughter left Violet. "That doesn't even begin to cover what they are, but they're happy. Jax is less stressed, and Lexie is picking up Luna duties like she was made for them."

"I know," Patrick said softly, pressing a lingering kiss against her temple. "The clan is in good hands. It's still weird though."

"Totally weird," Violet laughed again and turned in his arms till they were facing each other. "Speaking of good hands. Ours are needed elsewhere. We promised Hunter we would be there every week."

Patrick shook his head while entwining his fingers against the small of her back. "I called him. He doesn't need us today."

"We should still go," she insisted, even while lifting onto her toes and tilting her chin up.

That's all it took for Patrick to lower his head and claim her lips. Warmth swelled in his belly as he held her close against his body. He'd never get used to how perfectly she fit with him. He was content to stay there for the rest of the day, but Violet eventually pushed softly against his chest, making him grumble.

"There are other things we can help with," she giggled, then pressed another quick kiss against his lips. "And it would show our dedication to showing up every week."

"Fine," he agreed. "But you have to sit in the middle. It's a decent drive and I want you as close to me as possible."

Violet smiled. "I was hoping you'd say that." She slipped her hand into his and Patrick held on tight as they walked down the road to his truck.

Chapter 50

Cas

***The sterile white walls** of the cell gave Cas a headache. He closed his eyes and* lightly bounced the back of his head off the wall. Jax could heal. He hadn't seen that coming. Now he had to live with the things he'd done and figure out how on Earth he was supposed to forgive the man who'd killed his mate.

Yeah, being locked up was understandable. Even with the simmering anger he still felt toward Patrick, the revenge had bled out of him. Maybe it was the poison. Maybe it was the choice to save Violet. Maybe it was the choice to save Patrick—even if it had only been to stop Violet from feeling the same agony he faced.

Cas knew Layla would be proud of him. He knew she would've been happy he'd changed. He knew she would've been pleased that he switched sides and fought for good. It didn't heal the hole in his heart from losing her, but it was a start.

The click of a lock sounded down the hallway and Cas sighed.

Mya.

She was relentless. Always showing up with a smile on her face with a platter full of food. Not that he had seen her smile, but he could hear it in her cheery voice. He usually pretended he was asleep when she came by, but the last few times, he'd just flat-out ignored her.

Guilt twisted in his gut.

Yeah... that was rude, but he wasn't ready to talk to anyone.

Layla would have laughed in his face for saying that and then would have goaded him with something along the lines of, *"So, you're choosing to wallow in your own misery? That's really smart."*

Really smart. Cas groaned. That was him. So very, very—

"Evening!" Mya's cheery voice filled his ears like the sweet scent of a cherry blossom tree. Which coincidentally she also smelled like.

He wanted to be angry with her. He wanted to be annoyed. He wanted to tell her to go away.

But her scent was soothing. It eased his tense muscles as he drew in a deep breath through his nose.

"I was so happy to see that you finished your breakfast this morning, and I was hoping, maybe, you would be up for eating dinner, too."

He grunted a response, but kept his eyes closed.

The whisper of a sigh met his ears, and the disappointed note hurt his heart. What did it matter if he ate or not?

"Maybe..." her voice wavered with nerves. "Maybe you'd eat with me?"

That almost made him open his eyes. As it was, his chest froze and he held his next breath.

"I've eaten alone... in my room... upstairs ever since my mate died."

Familiar pain twisted his gut. He knew that solitary well. It plagued him for months after Layla's death.

"I miss eating with people and thought maybe you did, too."

"Why do you care?"

Cas internally flinched after the harsh tone flew from his mouth. He hadn't meant it to be so rude, but there it was. Out in the open. He couldn't take it back.

The shifting of cloth sounded in his ears, and the light clatter of a plate on the floor beside him. Warmth bled into the front of his legs before the softest touch he'd ever felt brushed across his hand.

"Everyone deserves a second chance," Mya whispered.

Cas' eyes shot open and his green gaze crashed against her wide, gorgeous emerald eyes. A spark, just a flicker, ignited in his chest before a thin link between them fell into place. His lips parted as he looked over the explosion of chestnut curls draping over her warm tawny skin. The longer he stared the more pink her cheeks became, emphasizing an adorable line of freckles dotting her cheekbones.

"Sorry," he muttered. "I didn't mean to..."

"Be rude?" Mya asked, but her voice was soft.

The ache in his heart eased as her previous words repeated in his ears, matched with Layla's. His shoulders lightened, and he could almost feel the warmth of

Layla's smile. Could this be a gift? His second chance?

"Yeah," he answered.

Mya released a long, slow breath, then settled back into a crisscross seated position on the floor in front of him. "So, are you going to eat with me?" She nodded to the platter at his side. "Or should I go back to my room... and try again tomorrow?"

Her determination almost tugged a smile out of him. Instead, he looked down at the platter beside him to find a heaping serving of mashed potatoes, a large dinner roll, and some sort of marinated meat that made his mouth water. A loud rumble rolled through his stomach, betraying him.

The resulting, breathy chuckle that left Mya was worth it, though.

"I guess, I don't have a choice now," he grumbled, hiding his pleasure.

Mya's head shook, scattering her hair in every direction. "Not really." She reached up and tied her mass of hair back with the tie around her wrist then pulled her own plate into her lap.

There was a much smaller helping on her plate, and Cas decided immediately that he was going to dump some of his food onto her plate... but in a few minutes. She was forcing him to eat, taking care of everyone else... while it looked like she'd been starving. Who was taking care of her?

They sat in silence, eating their food, while occasionally catching each other's eye.

Mya finished her food, and Cas was about to shove some of his potatoes onto her plate, when she said, "Are we going to talk about what happened?"

A pit formed in Cas' stomach, and he lowered his plate onto his crossed legs. She could want to talk about any number of things... "What do you mean?"

Her lips bunched to the side before she blurted, "Do you believe in Second Chance Mates?"

Cas blinked. Honestly... "I didn't."

Hope sparked in Mya's eyes. "What about now?"

"It's kind of hard to deny it at this point."

The tiniest smile tugged at the corners of Mya's mouth. "So I'm not crazy?"

A huff of laughter lifted a little more of the weight off his shoulders. "No, Mya. You're not crazy. I know how rare it is, but..." He drew in a long deep breath and mentally reached for the bond he thought he would never have again. The link was so fragile. So thin. But, he held it delicately in his thoughts and gently pulled. *"There is no denying this."*

Mya gasped and dropped her plate to clamp her hands over her mouth. The plate clattered to the ground between them.

"But Mya..." he released the link and shook his head. He shifted his plate to one hand, righted hers, and started pushing some of his potatoes onto her plate. "I've spent the last few years lost in revenge. I developed a revenge plot against your closest friends that triggered your mate's death." Lifting his gaze, Cas stared into her moisture-lined eyes. "Why would you want to be my mate? You could just end it here."

Her lower lip disappeared between her teeth. She lowered her gaze to her refilled plate and slowly lifted it back into her lap. "I'm not saying I'm okay with everything you've done. This... this is going to take time. And work." She laughed lightly as she dragged her fork through the mashed potatoes. "A lot of work. But we were given this second chance for a reason, right?"

The glimmer of hope in his chest blossomed and the heavy grief of loss was eased a little more. "I'm willing to try if you are."

A ghost of a smile touched her lips, and she scooped a bite of potatoes into her mouth.

The corner of Cas' mouth tugged into a pleased smirk.

"Okay," Mya said as she prepped another bite of potato. Her emerald green eyes claimed his when she looked at him again. "Let's try."

Epilogue

Violet

Cheers erupted around the *hundred-yard AstroTurf field as the Sentinel and* Blood Haven teams entered the pitch. Stadium lights lit the area, illuminating the players as they moved into position. A brilliant full moon lit the winter sky, giving a perfect light source for the return of the Clan Games. As soon as the teams were ready, the giant lights would be turned off and the game would begin.

Violet's breath turned white in the cold January air as she excitedly watched the teams set up. It was the first Clan Game since they'd been canceled due to Blood Moon nearly a year ago, and energy pulsed through the crowd. The bleachers were packed, and people had brought chairs out for those who didn't have a stadium seat. Even the visiting team had almost filled their bleachers with spectators.

Hunter hadn't been sure if he wanted to set up a team for Blood Haven quite yet, but after talking to the teenagers in his clan—and their parents—he decided to give it a go. They'd had just enough people interested to form a team with two subs. Sentinel and Blood Haven had grown very close, and it felt fitting to have them be the first teams to square off. Violet knew it was going to be a good, fair game.

Patrick's towering form leaned toward her. "It feels weird sitting in the bleachers."

"Tell me about it," Jax agreed, as he climbed into the open spot in front of them and held out a fresh package of M&M cookies, which Violet greedily snatched away. "Lexie told me to give these to you."

A happy smile spread across Violet's face as she tore into the package and shoved a cookie into her mouth. Amusement fluttered through her mate bond, making her look up to see Patrick lovingly watching her. "What?" she asked through a full mouth. "They're cookies!"

He shook his head then pressed a quick kiss to the top of her head. "I'm glad Hunter was able to get a team together."

"And that there were enough interested kids," Jax added.

Blood Haven's numbers had grown slowly at first, but lately new people were showing up every week. There was a high turn around since some people decided to move on after they'd been healed, but Hunter was okay with that. They needed a safe place for a while, and Blood Haven was able to give them that. Some stayed though, like Adeline and her mate. Two of their four kids were playing for the Blood Haven team tonight.

"You guys realize that most of those *kids* are close to our age?" Violet reminded them and both young men stared at her like she had three heads.

"Nah." Jax waved a dismissive hand. "After what we've been through, we had to have gained ten years, at least."

Violet snorted. "I think Lexie would have punched you for that."

A sharp laugh left Patrick. "Probably."

The flat look adorning her twin's face said that he was not so amused.

Violet cleared her throat as the stadium lights flashed to signal they would be turning off in five minutes. "Speaking of my best friend, how is she?"

They'd had a fun surprise when the first full moon came around after the final fight. Lexie couldn't control when she turned like the rest of them, and they'd begun to wonder if Violet had completely cured her. Unfortunately, that was not the case. Lexie had spent the three days surrounding the full moon as a wolf for almost a year. There was no stopping it. There was nothing to take away the pain of her bones breaking and shifting. And there was no communicating with her—except for Jax.

Thankfully, she maintained her humanity and usually stayed around the clan during those three days, but sometimes the two of them would disappear and leave the clan to Violet and Patrick.

"She's good," Jax smirked, then turned his attention back to the pitch when the Sentinel captain signaled they were ready. "The shifting sucks, and she's always exhausted afterward, but it's easier than it used to be. I'm going to meet up with her after the game."

"Sounds good," Patrick answered. His fingers slipped into Violet's hand as he continued, making her smile. "How long will you be out?"

Jax shrugged. "At earliest, tomorrow night. Probably the next morning, though."

Lifting Patrick's hand over her head, Violet rested his arm across her shoulders so she could snuggle against his side. "Take all the time you need," she told her brother, then smiled at Patrick. "We can handle things here."

The grin on Patrick's lips spread across his face.

"I know you can," Jax assured them.

"Did I miss anything?" Rochelle's breathless voice sounded on Violet's other side, and she turned to see Patrick's younger sister staring wildly out at the stadium. "Has it started?"

Violet chuckled. "Not yet. You're just in time." She held out the cookie package and Rochelle thanked her with a smile as she took a cookie.

A loud scoff made Violet turn to stare at Jax who was watching the exchange with wide, disbelieving eyes. "When did you start sharing?"

"She likes me," Rochelle teased, then snapped a large chunk of cookie off with her teeth. "And I haven't had dinner yet."

"Why not?" Patrick asked, his voice teetering on the edge of scolding.

Rochelle's eyes rolled. "I just got back. The Paladins called a bunch of their pledges to help find a breeder clan, but we didn't find them."

The cookie Violet had pulled from the crinkly packaging froze halfway to her mouth. "Breeder clan? I thought those were all abolished after the Breeder Act was terminated."

"Not all of them."

Unease coiled in Violet's belly. "That's what you were helping with?"

With a nod, Rochelle said, "Yeah. We've been hearing rumors about this one clan that's really bad, and we've been looking for a long time, but haven't found them. Supposedly they're just above Blood Haven's territory, but no one knows exactly where."

"Stanislaus was one of the first to end the use of breeders. I can't believe no one knew about this clan." Violet leaned against Patrick's side, absorbing his warmth and comfort. "Hopefully you'll find them soon. No one should have to live in those conditions."

"I think Blood Haven would be a good location for a lot of the refugees when this is over. Do you think Hunter would agree to that?" Rochelle's gaze paused on each of them, but Violet didn't need to look at her brother or mate to know they were all thinking the same thing.

"Absolutely," Jax answered at the same time Patrick said, "Of course."

Violet laughed and took another cookie bite. "I think Hunter would be thrilled to know Blood Haven's reputation is spreading and people know it's a safe place."

Tension melted from Rochelle's frame, making her shoulders sag. "Oh good. One problem solved."

Tipping her chin back, Violet looked at Patrick. "Mya sent me a message earlier today. She said they had a new wave of Blood Wolves arrive, and was wondering when we would be coming next."

A line appeared between Patrick's brows. "We've gone to Blood Haven every two weeks for almost a year."

"Apparently a couple of these wolves are particularly violent, and they are wondering if we can come sooner," she explained. "They've had to lock down a section of the new holding wing."

Patrick's chest deflated as he let out a long breath. "Jax, do we have any meetings when you get back?"

Shaking his head, Jax turned away from the field to look at them all. "No. You're good to go as soon as I return."

"Great!" Violet smiled and pulled her phone from her leggings pocket. "I'll let her know." She handed the cookie package to Rochelle so she could text her friend. "Oh, Rochelle, I can talk to Hunter about the breeder clan while I'm there. He might know something."

"That'd be great," the seventeen-year-old answered, opening and sifting through the cookie package. Finally she snagged a cookie and held it in front of herself triumphantly.

Laughing to herself, Violet pressed the power button on her phone, and the screen blazed to life, in perfect condition. After she'd broken two more phones, Patrick had bought the best case he could find. He'd surprised her with a purple Otter-box case, so it would protect the phone and match her eyes at the same time. She'd had the same phone for almost seven months, which felt like a miracle.

Her thumbs flew across the protected screen. *Hey Mya! Patrick and I will be there in two days when Jax gets back with Lexie. Does that work for you guys?*

Three dots at the bottom left of the phone started bouncing. Paused. Then bounced again before Mya's response came through. *Sounds good. Let us know when you'll get here. Cas and I will be waiting for you.*

Will do. See you in a couple days! Violet sent back, then pocketed her phone as Blood Haven's captain signaled that they were ready.

The stadium lights blinked out.

Violet let her eyes lull closed while Patrick's hand trailed her shoulder, up her neck, and into the loose ends of her ponytail. His fingers combed through her hair while the refs gave another thirty seconds for the player's eyes to adjust to the dark.

The whistle blew, and Violet's eyes flew open as the crowd erupted into cheers and the players took off to find their opponent's flag.

Sighing contently against Patrick's side, she looked up at the stars shining above them. Usually it was harder to see the stars with a full moon, but that night they shone brighter than ever.

Patrick pressed a kiss to her forehead, then trailed a line of kisses to her ear. "Under the moon," he whispered, his breath tickling the shell of her ear. "And beneath these stars, I promise myself to you."

Warmth spread through Violet's chest. The night of their lycan vows felt like a lifetime ago, but Patrick often repeated those exact words to her. Each time it felt like that promise was being spoken for the first time. The promise of love. The promise of safety. The promise of a lifetime of happiness.

The End

NOTE FROM THE AUTHOR

Thank you for reading *Stars & Promise*! Please consider leaving an honest review on Amazon and/or Goodreads!

Acknowledgments

Being an author has been a lifelong dream, but for many years I believed it to be impossible. Now, closing out my first trilogy there is a feeling of excitement with a hint of sorrow. I've been with these characters for so long, it's sad to say goodbye! But there are other characters who have stories that need to be told and other worlds to explore! Unfortunately, the space on the page does not stretch far enough for me to adequately thank every person I need to, but I'll try.

I will always thank my Heavenly Father first and foremost. Without Him—my stories would fall short. Without Him—the worlds in my head would be flat.

Richard – you are the light and love of my life. Thank you for your encouraging words when my inner critic won't be nice. Thank you for following me to book signings and always being there to lend a helping hand. Out of all the love stories in the world, ours is my favorite.

My kids – LW, ZABs, and KidO – I love you to the moon and back. You have all shown extreme thoughtfulness during this books making. Thank you for trying so hard to give me extra time and being excited for every step along the way! You will forever be my favorite little fan club.

Some of the best advice I've ever received is from my big brother, Tony. Thank you for telling me to trust my own voice, for teaching me, for suffering through my comma allergy, for bear hugs, and coffee smells.

Oh, Mom. You are stronger than you know. Never forget you are a warrior, both in this life and in the eyes of God. Words are not strong enough to express my love and appreciation of you. Thank you for your exuberant excitement that you readily share with the world! Never stop asking me for the next chapter.

Forever and always will my action scenes be dedicated to you, Dad. Thank you for sharing your love of Shoto-kan with me and instilling a love for martial arts and self defense in my heart.

To the Happy Heart Club – I wish we weren't stretched across the country, but I carry you all in my heart. Thank you for your notes, encouragement, and artistic abilities. Each of you have helped make these books come to life!

To my Betas – Some of you weren't able to read it this time around, but each of you helped in one way or another. An extra special thanks to Debby B., Tony N., Heather F., Juli M., Kimberly F., Angel C., Melanie S., and Peaches - You're amazing!!!

A huge shoutout to Irlen Institute for helping me and my family. Thank you for opening the doors of possibility and helping me realize a love for reading and storytelling.

And finally, thank YOU! My reader. Thank you for falling in love with Violet and Patrick and following them to this epic end. Thank you for spreading your love of these books with those around you. Thank you for being a member of my clan.

About the Author

Crystal Frost currently lives in Utah, guarded by the glorious snow-capped mountains with her husband, three rambunctious kids, and Merlin the Poodle. She loves geeking out over Harry Potter and Zelda, plus many more geeky fandoms, and enjoys shapeshifting through cosplay from time to time.

As a dyslexic author she had a lot to overcome before her books finally made an appearance in the world. She is thrilled to be beating the odds and living her dream writing stories. She's a sucker for action-packed fiction, complex characters, and breathtaking slow-burn romances and strives to incorporate those into her own writing and leave imprints on her reader's hearts.

Learn more about Crystal at frostcrystal.com

www.ingramcontent.com/pod-product-compliance
Lightning Source LLC
Chambersburg PA
CBHW030547310726
48979CB00010B/2071/J

* 9 7 8 1 9 5 7 0 5 1 0 7 9 *